The Best New
Irish Short Stories
of 2005

The Best New Irish Short Stories of 2005

EDITED BY DAVID MARCUS

CARROLL & GRAF PUBLISHERS

NEW YORK

THE BEST NEW IRISH SHORT STORIES OF 2005

Carroll & Graf Publishers
An Imprint of Avalon Publishing Group Inc.
245 West 17th Street
11th Floor
New York, NY 10011

AVALON
publishing group incorporated

Library of Congress Cataloging-in-Publication Data is available.

ISBN-13: 978-0-78671-636-4
ISBN-10: 0-7867-1636-3

Printed in the United States of America
Distributed by Publishers Group West

Contents

Introduction

Not long ago, when I was preparing this collection of new Irish short stories, I happened to be travelling in the London Underground and trying to pass the time by scrutinising the ads above the windows facing my seat. One of them, trumpeting the name of a well-known London newspaper, went something like this: 'Increase the enjoyment of your journey by reading London's sharpest writers.' It made me wish I could suggest to the travellers: Whether you are relaxing or seeking something good to read, increase the enjoyment of *your* journey by reading Ireland's best, sharpest, and most magical contemporary short-story writers.

I recalled that such was my very own life's journey, my ticket constantly being stamped by some of the world's greatest short-story masters, Irish, British and American. Sean O'Faolain, one of Ireland's greatest, said in his book *The Short Story* that 'the Americans and the Irish do seem to write better stories', a claim later bolstered by the opinion of the important American critic Richard Ford that the short story was Ireland's national art form. V. S. Pritchett, regarded as one of England's most outstanding critics and story writers, stated that 'the short story is, above all, the *memorable* form of imaginative writing', adding that it was the form in which Irish writers excelled and that their best work 'stood beside the masters in Italy, France, Russia and the United States'.

The previously unpublished stories in this Carroll & Graf collection were specially written by many of Ireland's best and best-known exponents, who clearly follow Saul Bellow's advice that 'A story should be interesting, as interesting as possible – inexplicably absorbing. There can be no other justification of any piece of fiction.' Where, however, they more often differ intriguingly from their best-known predecessors is in choosing plots and characters that aren't inked in green.

Today's world has found new frontiers, as indeed has today's short story. But just as the former have to be protected, the latter has to battle against readership's decline.

In the beginning was the creator; in the end, without growing support, only the commentator may remain.

David Marcus

Another Country

MOLLY McCLOSKEY

I'm a paper conservator. I arrest decay. I rescue old and often beautiful material objects, instead of churning out new junk. When I tell people what I do, they get a look in their eyes that says they like me better than they did a moment ago. I'm one of the good guys, they think, I'm part of the solution. People take comfort in the fact that they live in a world where work like mine exists. They think it says something hopeful about what awaits them.

My studio is on the sixth floor of a disused mill on Grand Canal Quay. My window overlooks the old gasworks, the canal basin, Misery Hill, and the periwinkle neon of the Ocean Bar. On wet winter evenings, just before twilight when the rain has stopped, the sky is capable of so much. It starts subtly, an agreeable light but one you could easily ignore. Another minute and you look again, because you can almost sense it, over your shoulder, the colours deepening, insistently, as if provoked by your indifference. The indistinct layer above the rooftops becomes a clear blue window. Above that, a dense band of lavender declares itself. Higher still, the washed-out pink intensifies, forming what looks like a dome of deep rose nothingness. And for a few moments, for miles around, faces are upturned in wonder and eyes are peering out of office windows and a whisper is traversing the city, like in a film when something miraculous is passing overhead.

I live in Blackrock, on the other side of the city. If I set out to, I can skirt the electronic headlines on my way to work. They're on the M50 and as you enter the Port Tunnel, on the Naas Road and the M1, the top of O'Connell Street and in a dozen other places, hoisted above our heads, like surtitles for an unsavoury opera. The latest information on crimes, criminals-at-large, and the missing.

CAUCASIAN MALE SLIM BUILD, APPROX 40, GREEN GORTEX ANORAK, WANTED RE: 3 DEC ARMED ROBBERY HAROLD'S CROSS P.O.

ANYONE IN VICINITY OF ORMOND QUAY BETWEEN 2–5 A.M. SATURDAY 1 NOV, PLEASE CONTACT GARDAI. YOU MAY HAVE VITAL INFO

FIVE-YEAR-OLD GIRL WEARING BLUE COAT, ANSWERS TO SOPHIE, DISAPPEARED FROM HER GREYSTONES NEIGHBOURHOOD BETWEEN 3–4 P.M. THURS 21 JULY

It's an idea we got from LA. But some ideas don't travel well. Grisliness plays differently under grey skies. Some people say you get desensitised, but I've found the opposite is true. Still, I try not to avoid them. When I do, I always wonder was I the one who could've helped.

Her daughter calls me Mr Banana.

Isabella is five and totes a threadbare penguin everywhere. Her socks are always halfway off her feet and she wears natty flowered tops, sleeveless, like the ones women wore in the sixties

'Why am I Mr Banana?' I ask. I'm sitting in Veronica's kitchen, waiting for Veronica to get ready. We're taking Isabella to the pier in Dun Laoghaire. She loves it there. She loves walking way out on top of the sea like that. Already, she knows the thrill of conquering nature.

' 'Cause . . .,' she says, swinging her penguin around by its feet, '. . . you're a nincompoop.'

'And what's that got to do with bananas?'

She thinks, pursing her lips and staring me down like she's a spell-casting witch in a cartoon. Clearly stuck for an answer. And then she shrieks and dashes off, dive-bombing five feet later into the sofa and assuming the bent-knee headstand position, so that she is now looking at me upside-down.

'Bravo!' I give her a round of applause.

She rights herself and climbs down off the sofa, stuffing the penguin up underneath her shirt because it's easier to carry that way and will leave her hands free for whatever is next on their agenda. She approaches me stealthily, squintingly, and I figure I'm in for something like a penguin-bopping. But her demeanour undergoes a sudden transformation.

'Aah,' she says softly, and strokes the top of my head like I'm a house pet. 'Aah, that's a nice banana.'

'Isabella . . .'

She looks at me.

'I would like to be five years old again,' I say. 'Just for an hour.'

Isabella stops stroking my head. She stands straight up, her eyes flash and she executes a 360-degree turn, giving birth to the penguin on the way, then shazams me and says, 'You! Are. Five.'

She knows about the five-year-old who disappeared from Greystones. She sees her face in photocopied fliers taped crookedly to poles, she sees it in the newspapers and on TV. Isabella, in fact, is obsessed with this girl. She says a prayer for her at night and sometimes thinks she sees her on the street. She tugs on Veronica's hand and her eyes go big. Isabella wants nothing more than to be the one who finds Sophie.

'Is that good?' Veronica asks me. 'Is that healthy? Is it morbid? I don't know.'

I don't know either. 'I think it's the first stirrings of empathy,' I say.

Isabella's theory, admirably romantic, is that Sophie has simply forgotten who she is and wandered off. As if Sophie has Alzheimer's. Isabella knows more about Alzheimer's than she does about paedophilia. Recently, there was a media campaign which explained why the elderly sometimes went missing and what we should do to find them. On TV, someone from the Mountain Rescue Association – they are often called on in such cases – explained that people with Alzheimer's 'tend to insert themselves into briars, dikes, and drains, going into the foetal position and staying there'.

Isabella has applied this MO to five-year-old Sophie. She peers into abandoned lengths of piping and drags Veronica into the small wastelands of brambled concrete that checkerboard their neighbourhood. As though she and Sophie are playing hide'n'seek. Veronica is terrified that one day Isabella will find something, which may or may not be Sophie.

In the beginning I was a bit of a romantic. I tried to imagine how the damage had been done. Sometimes it's obvious – humidity, ultraviolet light, the nocturnal labours of certain small animals; the way people pull a book off a shelf, their index finger hooking the top of the spine, tearing it eventually. Other times, it isn't so clear. A hole in the middle of a page, or a tear in an unusual place, where stress doesn't often fall. When was it torn? How? I'd picture someone packing books into a crate, by gaslight; maybe they were his and he was going away and didn't want to go, or maybe the owner of the books had died. The man dropped one, or he opened one that caught his eye and the pages stuck together – they'd never been cut, the book was never read – and without meaning to, he tore the page. He sat down then, crumpling. He'd been brave up to then, he hadn't wept, and this small rift in the physical world, this reminder, was the thing that broke him.

I don't do that any more. Gradually, something clinical kicked in and now I seldom notice what's in front of me, the content: what was news-worthy in 1885 or letters home from Australia, turn of the last century. I look instead for the extent of the damage, and it is only on certain evenings, when the light is right and the brevity of its perfection a sad reminder, that the work assumes its old magic.

Veronica wonders if the job colours my worldview. Like everyone now, she's an amateur psychologist.

'You mean do I look at people's spines and gauge the damage?'

'Kind of,' she says. 'Or do you see people like a plastic surgeon might? You know, thinking how to cut and paste them.'

'Don't be silly,' I say. 'I leave my work at the office.'

'What about, I don't know, holding onto things for longer than you should?'

'That metaphor is so pat, I'm cringing.'

We're having lunch in Stephen's Green, on the grass in front of the duck pond. Veronica chews her sandwich and stares straight ahead of her, and then I do the same.

'So,' I say finally, 'I'm still seeing that guy. The one I mentioned.'

'You're not exactly *seeing* him,' she says.

'Semantics,' I say. 'Old-world semantics.'

'Well,' she says, 'e-mail's a start. So what's he like?'

'His name is Steve. He lives in the Bay Area. He's an ex-military man.'

'Lovely,' she says.

Two ducks with green heads glide by. They scan the banks as though for snipers.

'No, no, no,' I say. 'He never killed anyone. He was in the band.'

'The band?'

'And now he's got the pension. I'm a little confused as to how he avoided military service through all those wars, but there you go.'

'So what does he do now?' she says.

'He's studying to be a psychiatric nurse.'

'Oh?' She reconsiders. 'So he's got compassion.'

'Yeah. And it's handy, if I ever go mad.'

She rolls her eyes at me, then begins to divest her sandwich of raw onions, making little piles in the grass, like she's playing ring toss.

'I read this thing about immortality the other day,' she says, 'or not immortality, but long, long, longevity. And it said that one of the downsides of our ability to keep getting older and older and not dying is that we won't want to have sex with each other. All the old people.'

'I thought old people didn't want to have sex anyway.'

'I don't know,' she says, taking a bite of her sandwich. 'I haven't been old yet.'

She looks sad when she says it, and I have the urge to do something corny and affectionate, like bop her over the head with a soft toy. But there, in front of the duck pond, all I have is a half-eaten chicken tikka wrap from Insomnia.

'You know,' I say, 'a hundred years ago, I would've married you. No, fifty. No. Thirty.'

'Why?'

'Because that was the way it was. You got on with someone, you married them. Then you lived these monosyllabic lives, milking and churning and threshing and digging and reproducing. In some ways it was better. Now, we're paralysed by options. We have exceeded the human capacity for analysing alternatives.'

'You couldn't live a monosyllabic life if you tried,' she says.

I look at her. 'You're right,' I say, 'and I'd only be trying to fuck the stable hand.'

'Ooh,' she says, and shivers excitedly. 'Not the stable hand!'

She pulls a bit off her roll and throws it to a duck already making a beeline for us.

'He knew what I was thinking,' she says. 'That duck.' And then, 'Companionship in old age is very important. I worry about you. You're not very good at forming relationships.'

'I'm hardly on the verge of old age. Anyway, what about the trumpeter-cum-nurse.'

'What about him?' she says.

We chew the stubs of our sandwiches and watch the duck, who's swishing its derrière as it heads off to read somebody else's mind.

'It's just to pass the time,' I say, sounding, even to myself, defeated.

She rolls her wax paper into a ball and puts it into the brown bag our sandwiches came in.

'You're holding on to that sadness like an identity, you know. *I am the guy who got left. I am the guy who doesn't do relationship.* Everybody gets left,' she says. 'You're stuck. Stop glorifying it.'

Her tone surprises me. She is not a practitioner of tough love. I shrug. 'Stuck is in,' I say. 'Stuck is the new impulsive.'

'Jaysus,' she says.

Seventeen months ago, I thought I saw him. It was on a train in Barcelona, the one that goes from the city to the airport. I remembered his brother telling me that he'd gone to work on the continent somewhere, and I thought: *There he is.* He was reading the *Guardian* and he was thinner and had lost the baby fat on his face and he had a look of long-standing tiredness about him. I told myself that when we got to the airport, I'd ask him if he was who I thought he was, and we'd have a moment of charged anxiety, then the shared admission that all the desire was gone, followed by relief that we hadn't thrown in our lot together. I took his being there, his being presented to me for one final inspection, as a gift. Because I was sure that was all it would take, a single moment of reality, for my belief in his perfection to collapse. I thought I'd walk away laughing, shaking my head and chuckling, free of him.

But he got off at a station before the end of the line, far out of town but not yet near the airport, some place that looked like it had nothing to get off a train for. I was angry, disproportionately so. Because it was like having to live through the end all over again. Just left there, in another stupor of unknowing. I spent the rest of the day convincing myself it wasn't him. It was just me, thinking I see people from my past in unlikely places. Trying to make the world smaller than it really is.

As he was leaving me – a rather attenuated process which included his beginning to screen his calls – the ring of his phone took on a different tone. Collusive and unkind. Protective of him. It sounded like the telephonic correlative of a bodyguard. After it was over, on the admirably few occasions I rang him, the tone was different again. Solitary but defiant. I found myself surprised that in his material absence from the world, or my world, this string of numbers and this jingling object should continue to attest to his existence. What did I expect? That the phone company would disconnect him? That his house would be levelled? That if I closed my eyes for long enough, he'd disappear?

Isabella's current favourite book is one about endangered species. Veronica's sister, who works for Oxfam, gave it to Isabella for her birthday. It's one of those books you can grow with: first the pretty pictures, then the stories of imminent demise, then the desire to contribute to Friends of the Earth. There are photos of all the animals in their native environment. Beside the photos are their vital statistics: what they like to eat, what their habits are. Somewhere on the page is a synopsis of just how bleak things are for them.

> The giant panda is found only in China, one of the world's fastest growing and most populated regions. As few as 1,000 of the black-and-white bear-like animals cling to survival. They are confined to the mountainous bamboo forests of southwestern China.

In the back, there's an index of estimated worldwide populations. *Dwarf Blue Sheep: 200. Yangtze River Dolphin: estimated at forty. Hispid Hare: 110. Golden-rumped Lion Tamarin: 1000. Malabar Large Spotted Civet: fewer than 250 mature individuals are thought to survive.*

I feel a creeping anxiety when I look at the list, thinking of bands of animals cowering in various corners of the world.

Isabella doesn't really understand. She hasn't fully grasped the concept of 'the future', so her sense of dread is incompletely developed, still confined to things like the dark and losing sight of her mother in Tesco.

When she asked me one day what the numbers meant, I said, 'That's how many are left in the world. How many pandas or wild yaks.'

She took it in her stride, the way she would've a lesson in counting from a picture book: three apples, two dogs, one pear.

'Two hundred,' she says, pointing at the number to the upper right of the Tonkin Snubnosed Monkey.

Still, she knows there's something special about these animals.

'Where are they?' she asks.

'Different places,' I say. 'All over the world.'

Veronica goes to the shelf and takes down the World Atlas. We flip from the Yangtze to Ethiopia to Brazil. To Saudi Arabia, where the Arabian Oryx soldiers on; Pakistan, home of the dwindling Indus Dolphin. To Indonesia and Vietnam, where sixty Javan Rhino are holding out.

Today I have a map of Dublin on the light box. I wash it with water. Then I de-acidify it, a calcium hydroxide solution that leaves an alkaline buffer. Then I paint it with methyl cellulose to make the paper less absorbent. Eventually, I get to the repairs, infilling the lacunae, the holes or the odd-shaped chunks missing from the borders. I use lens tissue, then Tonosawa, a Japanese tissue, scoring a piece out to follow the line of the lacunae and pasting outward, the fibres along the edge of the tissue tenacious, holding it in place.

I prefer to work on books. When you take them apart, separate the cover from the text block, undo the sewing, it's like unreeling time, finding the hidden, arbitrary details that explain how a thing came to be the way it is. You see a missed stitch, an eyelash in the glue of the binding, a scrap of paper from a worktable that got trapped in the pastedown. Sometimes they used pieces of thick paper to stiffen the spine. They grabbed whatever was handy and often the paper has writing on it, just three or four words torn from a sentence and always in that elaborate careful script and that sepia tint that has become the colour of nostalgia.

Two weeks ago they thought they'd found her. They were on her trail. A little girl in a baby-blue coat with a fake-fur halo had been captured on CCTV at Connolly Station. She was alone and appeared distressed. The footage was fuzzy, though, and the fur was rather low over her face and she never looked directly into the camera, which was positioned high above her head. The footage went out on RTE. Sophie's parents were interviewed. They said she was wearing a coat like that when she disappeared. They issued yet another plea for mercy.

To think she could be out there, the mother said, *all alone.*

But everybody who heard her must've thought what I thought. If Sophie was still out there, she wasn't all alone.

Anyway, it wasn't Sophie. The little girl was from Portlaoise, up in Dublin for the day with her parents and separated from them for a terrifying ten minutes. It took twenty-four hours to straighten the thing out. The Portlaoise family was on TV then too. The girl who'd been mistaken for Sophie was delighted to be back with her parents. But she felt sad for Sophie's parents and was sorry she couldn't be both Sophie and herself. She didn't say that exactly, but it was clear what she was getting at.

Now the family in Portlaoise have become tireless campaigners for Sophie's safe return. I wondered how the little girl felt, the whole nation mourning the fact that she was herself and not someone else. Isabella was crushed, though it was strange: you could see she envied the girl from Portlaoise. People thinking she was Sophie for a whole entire day.

In front of my house, in the car park that serves as our commons, a swarm of children congregate daily, in various combinations. They play unintelligible games or enact facsimiles of grown-up life, five or six of them standing on the corner chatting, looking, despite their stick legs and skinned knees and dirty T-shirts, like they could be at a cocktail party.

The other day three of the boys pedalled their small bikes around in a circle and whooped and whooped and whooped, revelling in the meaninglessness of it all. When they'd exhausted the possibilities of that activity, they began turning death-defying somersaults on an armchair someone had deposited on the footpath.

I find the children difficult to tell apart, particularly as they are always growing, always changing so fast. There are clusters of brothers and clusters of sisters, and I'm not always sure if this slightly taller child is an older sister of the girl I saw last week or if she is simply an older version of her last week's self. I have the urge to tag them, as though they are cattle.

Then I get the urge to photograph them. I have a camera, a special one called a Holga that I got for Christmas. The leaflet that came with it referred to 'the Holga mystique'.

A Holga is a study in imperfections, and to use it an exercise in breaking free from dependence on technology, precision, and 'uber-sharpness'. The uncontrollable vignetting and peculiar light leaks create a partnership between you and the Holga. These 'flaws', accompanied by your creative choices, result in a quasi-serendipitous art.

It sounded like a religious experience and I was scared to take a picture. I didn't know what to take one of. Nothing seemed deserving. And then I thought of the kids.

'Good idea,' Veronica says, in a way that means *That is a really stupid idea.*

'What?' I say. 'Why not?'

We're out for my birthday dinner. All week, she refused to tell me where she was taking me. *It's a new place,* was all she'd say, *in Blanchardstown.*

'Blanchardstown?'

9

She made me close my eyes while she found parking. Then she led me to the restaurant.

When I opened my eyes, I was standing in front of a place called 'The Disaster Café: A Dangerous Place to Eat'.

'Well,' I said. 'This *is* a surprise.'

'First,' she explained, 'you go on some kind of virtual adventure, or disaster. Then you eat dinner. I thought it would be fun. We don't have to do the disaster bit, though. At least, I don't think we do.'

I looked at her. 'Are you kidding? I'm not coming to the Disaster Café without undergoing some pre-prandial trauma.'

She smiled sweetly. 'Sometimes I forget what a good sport you are.'

We stepped into a square black lobby that was like the beginning of a haunted house. A man checked our names off a reservations list and led us to the door of a small auditorium.

'The programme lasts approximately ten minutes. When you take your seats,' he said, 'you must put on your seat belts. If at any time you feel unwell, you pull the emergency lever under the seat and your chair will stop moving. Any questions?'

We looked at each other. 'No,' we said. He opened the door.

'The disaster du jour,' he continued gravely, his voice gone suddenly like the butler in a horror movie, 'is earthquake.'

Then he turned on his heel and was gone. We groped our way to our seats.

'The disaster du jour,' I whispered. 'That's priceless.'

Veronica smiled again. I could see her teeth in the dark. She was glad I was entering into the spirit of the evening.

A few minutes later, we heard a rumbling. Then a sound like ripping. The floor in front of the seats opened, like a crack in the earth. Then huge screens lit up all around us and we were surrounded by footage of buildings tumbling and people running hither and thither, screaming. Some real people to our left screamed, then laughed. I took Veronica's hand and squeezed it. Our chairs began to shake. I had a moment of actual fear, wondering if the building was structurally able for this nonsense.

There were several minutes of this. And then it was over.

Now Veronica is pronging a mollusc out of her Connemara seafood casserole with Thai aromatics. I'm having lamb shanks with a mild kashmiri curry. Blanchardstown isn't what it used to be.

'Tell me,' I say.

'Tell you what's wrong with it?' she says. 'It's illegal.'

'Illegal? What? Taking pictures of children?'

'Taking pictures of children you don't know.'

'But I do know them. Sort of.'

'You can't do it.'

'You're telling me that taking pictures of children you don't know is *illegal*?'

'That's what I'm telling you.'

'You mean because of . . .?'

'Of course.'

I shake my head and pour us both more wine. 'Amazing,' I say. 'How did I miss that?'

She is just about smiling. She likes bringing me new information. She likes to shock me, because she says it's difficult to do.

'What if you're a photographer?' I say. 'Like Cartier-Bresson or John Hinde? You lose a whole demographic?'

'Dunno,' she says, poking hopefully around in her sauce. 'I think you can get a special licence.'

'A licence,' I say, 'pfft. What about painting them? That too?'

'What? Portraits?' she says. 'Portrait painting isn't exactly in the ascendant.'

'What if you're a street sketcher?'

'Look,' she says, and bundles the linen napkin up in her hands. 'I don't know all the details. I just know that photographs of strange kids are out.'

I try to classify this new data, what it means to me and to us and whether it's a gain for child protection or a loss for the wider world. I put it under loss. Lost: a form of adult innocence.

After dinner, we go back to my place for birthday cake. It's warm and we sit by the open window and look out at the rain that's begun to fall. It falls on the flat roof opposite, my meteorological station. I look at the vehemence or gentleness with which the drops hit the puddles, and I know what to expect. Light rain persists, heavy rain passes.

'No cats tonight,' I say.

When it isn't raining, they do ballet on the flat roof, stretching and mincing, and I watch them through the upstairs window, like they're the feline culture channel.

Veronica's put slices of cake on plates but we haven't touched it.

'Weeelll . . .,' she says.

'Yeeeessss . . .'

'You're another year older.'

I try to smile.

She rubs my back vigorously, as though I'm a child she's wrapped in a towel after swimming.

'Do you ever feel lonely?' she asks.

'Me? Mr Banana? Lonely?'

'Come on,' she says.

'Once a week you ask me if I'm lonely.'

'Not once a week.' She puts her hand back in her lap, then fishes a cigarette out of the pack and lights it. 'I'm only asking,' she says.

I know how she sees me. Like I have carved a circle around where I stand and just haven't fallen through yet. I'm alone like people in traffic jams are alone. I am what the urban landscape discharges, as if people like me were so much pollen wafting through the streets. I go to the movies too often on my own. I prefer the beloved-as-imagined to the demands of the real. I am incapable of unguarded sincerity. I am stuck. I am lonely.

'Not particularly,' I say. 'Why do you ask?'

'Because I care,' she says, in a rather exasperated tone. 'Because I love you and I want you to be happy.'

'What about you? Do you feel lonely?'

'I've got Isabella.'

'Mm,' I say. 'You do.'

'And I'm seeing someone.'

The rain is gaining in intensity. The window gives a little shudder on its latch.

'Oh-oh,' I say. 'You didn't mention it.'

'Yeah,' she says, 'for about a month now.'

'Well,' I say, 'that's good. Now neither of us is lonely.'

They found the girl from Greystones. It's on the radio as I'm heading south through Wicklow on a Sunday drive. It's the top story in the headlines-on-the-hour. This time, they are sure it's her.

An hour later, when I'm stopped for lunch near Glendalough, Veronica gets me on the mobile. She sounds desperate. 'You've got to come back,' she says.

'I'm only in Wicklow,' I say.

There's a silence and then a staticky hiss, like an old radio between stations. I walk a figure of eight, trying to find her again.

'Are you there?' I say.

'Yeah,' she says. 'I'm—'

'I'm losing you.'

There's another hiss and then it's crystal clear.

'I'm here,' she says into the newly clarified air.

I experience the fleeting, disproportionate joy, the intense relief of mobile reconnection, as though we're speaking from antipodes or have spotted one another's smoke signals across an otherwise unfriendly mesa.

'Listen,' she says.

'I'm listening.'

But she doesn't say anything.

'Are you there?'

'I want you to come over,' she says.

'Are you OK?'

'I'm OK.'

'Me too,' I say. 'Isabella?'

'Isabella—' Static again. I look up at the sky, which is all blue above me, and walk in a circle. But walking and looking up at the same time makes me dizzy, so I stop.

Isabella gets on. She breathes heavily but doesn't say anything.

'Hello?'

'Banana,' she says. 'Bananabananabanana.'

'*Mr* Banana to you,' I say.

Then she makes a noise that sounds like someone blowing over an empty bottle.

Veronica takes the phone back.

'Can you hear me?' she asks.

'Yeah,' I say, 'I can hear you.'

'They found the girl,' she whispers.

'I know,' I say. 'I heard.'

'Isabella doesn't know yet.'

'Oh . . .'

'Come over,' she says. 'Be here when I tell her.'

'Sure,' I say. I look at my watch. 'I'll be there by four.'

I get back in the car and head north on the N11. Approaching the turn-off for Enniskerry, I pass the electronic headlines. Sophie isn't there any more. The system – sensitive in its own way – effects up-to-the-minute removals of those who are located or apprehended. Sophie is no longer the disaster du jour.

Isabella takes it well. Her eyes grow wide and she cries a bit but, like in the game of hide-'n'-seek, Sophie's present whereabouts and her no-longer-beating heart are facts slightly unreal to Isabella.

That night, Veronica and I take Isabella to the swimming pool. My favourite part of swimming is afterwards, at closing time, when everybody's out of the pool. I look through the big window in the lobby. I can see the water from there, dead smooth now, a perfectly glassy, transparent shade of blue. I want to lie in it when it's like that and feel what it feels like to have that much stillness surrounding me. But my presence and its perfection are mutually exclusive realities.

Back at Veronica's, Isabella insists on the endangered species picture book. *The Northern Hairy-nosed Wombat: 113. The Seychelles Sheath-tailed Bat: fewer than 50. The Vancouver Island Marmot: 24.*

I look at Veronica. Twenty-fucking-four, I mouth. 'Do they know? Do you think they can feel it?'

She stares at her hands in her lap and thinks about it. Finally, she says, 'I bet they can.'

I look at Isabella and I know something she doesn't yet: that she will probably outlive us, Veronica and me. I don't know which of us will go first, or how, but whoever lives longer will gradually lose the feeling of sitting next to the other. The sensation of hearing the voice or feeling the touch of the hand. We won't grow old enough to know Isabella when she's old. We'll be gone, and then everyone we've ever known will go too, so that someday there will be no one left on earth who has ever met us. But until then, there'll be echoes. There's Isabella, and whatever Veronica has helped to make her, and there's what other people will become in response to who Isabella is. A chain of reactions going so far down the line and in so many directions that they won't even know it, these people, what their own lives are a result of.

The Joke

Roddy Doyle

If he went now, he'd never come back. He'd go and she wouldn't know, or care. He'd come back and the same thing; she wouldn't care. So, what was the point? He wasn't going anywhere.

And that made it worse. And made him more annoyed. And angry. And stupid.

This thing now. It was nothing. The thing itself.

– No, no. He'll come and collect you.

That was it. Word for word. What had him half standing, still sitting, his fat arse hanging over the armchair.

His arse wasn't fat. But there was more of it than there used to be. Not that much more.

Anyway.

They were the words.

– No, no. He'll come and collect you.

The words themselves were harmless. She hadn't even been talking to him.

But that, there, was the point. She hadn't been talking to him. She'd been talking to someone else. She still was. On the phone. He didn't know who. Her sister, her ma, his ma. They were the even-money bets. But it could have been anyone. Her friend, the adultery woman, was another prospect. She was a three-to-one bet.

He wasn't a betting man. Never had been.

She was out in the kitchen; he didn't know who she was talking to. But he did know that she'd just offered his services to whoever it was at the other end.

– No, no. He'll come and collect you.

And that was the thing. And had been the thing for a long time. And he was sick of it.

Sick of what but?

He wasn't sure. The whole thing. Everything. He was just sick of it. The invisible fuckin' man.

– No, no. He'll come and collect you.

That was who he was. What he was. The invisible man. The taken-for-granted sap. As if he was just waiting there. With nothing better to do.

Granted, he was doing nothing. But that wasn't the point. No way was it. He'd been sitting there, doing nothing in particular. But it didn't matter. If he'd been climbing Mount Everest or upstairs in the bed, it didn't matter. It didn't bloody matter what he was or wasn't doing.

It was the fact, the thing. He didn't know how to–

Just hearing it. He was sick of it. And he couldn't say anything. Because it was so small. He could never explain it without being mean or selfish or other things that he really wasn't.

Her friend, for example. The adultery woman. They'd been friends for years. A good-looking woman. Didn't nearly look her age. And the adultery thing wasn't fair. He wasn't judging. He didn't; he never had.

Anyway. He'd been there when she'd left her husband. He'd helped her load the car, *his* car, with her bags and her two kids and all of their stuff. While the husband was at work, or wherever – the pub; he didn't know. And he was glad he'd done it. It had been the right thing to do. He'd never doubted it. Not once. Or resented it, or anything. The husband was a bollix, an animal. She was well out of that situation. And he wouldn't have cared if the husband had come after him. The woman's jaw was strapped and broken, sitting beside him in the car. The kids in the back were pale. It had been a good deed, that one. He'd felt a bit heroic. The wife had hugged him, kissed him, thanked him again and again.

That was the biggest example. The most dramatic.

He wasn't making his point. He was missing it.

A better example. Her mother. Not such a bad oul' one. Harmless really, once you knew her. Anyway, he'd gone out in the pissing rain to bring her home from her bingo. More than once, and no problem. He'd been happy to do it; he'd do it again. And her sister. He'd brought her twenty Silk Cut when she was stuck at home with her broken leg. And a choc-ice.

Errands of mercy. He'd been doing them for years. And here – good – here was the point. Not once, not once – none of them had ever asked him.

She was still on the phone.

– Yeah, I know, yeah. God.

Not once. Fair enough, they'd all said Thanks.

You're great.

You're a star.

I don't know where I'd be without you.

And that was fine. And appreciated. But none of them had ever phoned and asked to speak to him. Not once. Ever.

And it wasn't just that.

It was –

Fuckin' everything. He was sick of it.

But he sat down again. His arms were getting sore, holding himself over the seat. But that didn't mean anything. He hadn't changed his mind; he hadn't made it up. He could get back up; he would. She was still on the phone. It wasn't urgent, whatever it was. He had to clear his head. He had to be clear. He was going to say No when she came looking for him. He had to know why.

It went back. Back, back, back. Ah, Jesus – years. His fault. He accepted that. Yeah. His own fault. So.

But it wasn't about the errands of mercy. She'd called them that. It wasn't just them. He had to be clear.

He'd liked it; he remembered. When she'd said that about errands of mercy. She was drying his hair with a towel. She sat on his lap. One leg each side of his legs, right up at him.

He still had his hair. Most of it.

Lap was a stupid word.

He loved her. That was important.

Back.

Give and take. There'd once been that. Partnership. That was what he'd have called it, although he didn't like that word either. Partnership. Give and take. He brought her ma home from bingo; she sat on his lap. But that wasn't it; that just cheapened it. It wasn't about the sex. But –

That too. Yeah, definitely.

How, but –? How was he going to get his point across without making it look like it was all about sex when it wasn't but, in a way, it was?

He'd deal with it.

Roddy Doyle

Anyway.

Partnership. It had all been part of it. The relationship – another fuckin' word. They'd done things together. Even when they weren't together. He'd do the driving or the shop, clean the windows, whatever. But they'd both be involved. They'd done them together. That was how it had felt. How it had been.

Something had happened.

Nothing had happened. It had just happened. The way things were now.

She was still in there, on the phone. He could hear her agreeing and disagreeing, with whoever. Listening, nodding. Putting her hair behind her ear.

He still loved her.

And the partnership had stopped. Somewhere. He could never have pinned it down; he'd no idea. There'd been nothing said. Nothing done. As far as he knew. But, who knew?

It was a mess. He was. A mess. His anger. Moods.

He wanted to reach out. In the bed. And he couldn't. It wasn't there; he couldn't do it. He couldn't lift his hand and move it, a foot, a foot and a half – less. He couldn't do it. What had happened? What had happened?

He didn't know. He honestly didn't. He didn't know.

It was a good big telly, one of the wide-screen ones. He'd thought they could watch it together. At least that. When he'd bought it.

He was older. Fuck that, so was she. That wasn't it. He didn't think it was.

They'd never spoken about it.

What?

He didn't know. The change. The stop. He didn't know. The partnership. Fuck it, the marriage. And it wasn't true about the sex either, exactly. They still had it, did it. Now and again. The odd time. The hands would meet. The warmth.

What was he going to say? When she came in?

She was still in there, in the kitchen. Still chatting.

He was right but. Essentially, he was right. It was gone. Something had gone wrong. Something small. Something that he hadn't even noticed. It had changed. She couldn't deny it.

And would she? Deny it? He hadn't a clue.

He used to know. He used to guess right, more often than not. What she'd say. How she'd react. They'd smile at each other, because they

18

both knew what they were up to. She'd slap his arse when he passed. He'd put his hand on her hair. Words hadn't mattered; she'd known what he meant. I love you. I like you. I'm glad.

I love you. I like you. I'm glad.

That was it.

He used to – he could tell when she was going to say something. Before she did. Something in the air, in the atmosphere. He didn't have to be looking at her. He knew. And she did too. And he'd liked being read.

He didn't know when it had stopped. The reading. He didn't know. Maybe they still could, read each other's thoughts; they just didn't. He didn't know; he didn't think so. He didn't know her. He *knew* her, but he didn't know her. It had been a slow thing. Very gradual. He hadn't noticed.

That wasn't true. He had. He'd noticed.

But he'd done nothing.

What?

Jesus, it was terrible. Stupid.

He was angry. He was always angry.

He was always angry.

He lay awake, he woke early. It was always there. He didn't know why. Nothing had happened. Nothing big. His fault. He should have known. It was there a long time, the difference. The silence. He'd known.

They'd never had a row. That was true, more or less. There'd never been anything serious. Small stuff. Missing keys, her ma at Christmas. Nothing big. Fundamental. Neither of them had ever stormed out or packed a bag. They'd never shouted or broken anything. There'd been nothing like that. There'd been nothing.

Maybe it was the kids.

He was blaming the kids.

He wasn't. Just, maybe that was part of what had happened. They'd never had time; they'd been too busy. Always ferrying them around, football and dancing and scouts and discos. Then ferrying her ma as well. And her sister, and his ma. And her friend. The one he'd driven away from her husband.

He'd had a thing about her. He'd have admitted that. It had never come to anything. But he'd felt it. A woman who'd had sex with some-one she wasn't married to. He'd been excited. That was true. At the time. Even with her kids in the back of the car. Adultery. Another word that did nothing for him.

The kids but. There was nothing in that theory. They'd been busy, run off their feet – mad stuff. But they'd had the kids in common. Even when they were upstairs, in the bed.

Is that one of them waking?

Don't stop, don't stop.

Where's his inhaler?

Don't stop!

They'd liked it. They'd loved it. At the time. And it had been a long time. Twenty-six years. What had happened?

He didn't fuckin' know.

Did she?

He didn't know.

Probably.

He didn't know.

He didn't know anything.

The telly hadn't worked. Not really. Stupid, again. The idea that a television could bring them together. Even a good one. They didn't even watch telly much. They never had. He liked the football, now and again; he wasn't that fussed. She liked the politics. *Questions and Answers. Primetime.* There was another telly, upstairs in the bedroom. You didn't need a big screen to watch politicians. The whole idea had been stupid.

The football was better on the big screen but.

He felt himself smiling. Like a fight against his face. He let it through. He smiled.

She was still on the phone. She laughed.

Like the old times. He'd smiled; she'd laughed. The way they used to know each other.

Stupid.

He was being stupid. It wasn't like the old times, nothing like the old times – whatever they were. He was by himself. She was somewhere else. There was no togetherness in it. None.

It was nice but. Her laugh. He'd always liked it.

He used to make her laugh.

God.

Could he still? Make her laugh. He doubted it. Would she want him to? He didn't know.

But he'd done it before. He'd tickled her, now and again. He couldn't do that now. Creep up behind her in the bathroom. They were never in the bathroom together. He smiled again. The thought. Creeping up behind her. She'd have fuckin' freaked. And it wasn't the only way he'd made her laugh. Words used to do it. Jokes. Playacting, acting the eejit. She'd liked it. She'd loved it. She'd moved closer to him when she was laughing.

He could give it a try. Now. A joke. Paddy the Englishman and Paddy the Irishman were –. No; it was stupid. There was the one about the guy with no back passage. No. The one about the Irishman at the Tina Turner concert. He smiled. Too long, and she hadn't liked it the first time. He remembered.

What was he doing?

He wasn't sure.

What's the difference between a good ride and a good shite? That was a good one. Short and good. But it was so long since he'd told her a joke. He was just being thick.

They hadn't spoken since this morning.

There's the rain now.

Yeah.

There's the rain now. Him.

Yeah. Her.

And that was nearly – he looked at his watch – eight hours ago. And now he wanted to tell her a joke. It was mad. What's the difference between a good ride and a good shite?

Mad.

Thick. Stupid.

He wasn't angry now but. He wasn't sure why he'd been angry.

That wasn't true. He knew. But he wasn't angry now.

He'd tell her the joke. He was nervous now. It was a good one to tell but. It was short, no story to it. He'd see if it worked as he told it.

What would he see? He didn't know. It was what he wanted to see; that was the thing. Her face. He wanted to see her listening – that was all. See her face, see her listening. Knowing what he was up to. That would do.

He listened. She was out there, in the kitchen. He could hear her shoes. He knew, somehow – he didn't know how: she was finishing up. The way she was moving, like she was leaving. She was going to hang up.

What's the difference between a good ride and a good shite? He couldn't do it. It was too mad, too desperate. She'd recognise it for what it was: begging. A cry for fuckin' help.

That was stupid too but. It wasn't a cry for anything. And it wasn't fuckin' begging. It was only a joke. There it was now; she'd put the phone down. She was still in the kitchen. It was more than a joke. He knew that.

Would she know?

He could hear her now.

She came to the door. She stopped.

He looked at her.

Organ Recital

GILLMAN NOONAN

When Kate made her suggestion it wasn't even like something she lent weight to, more like a musing to herself to which no response was expected. And Bill's response, when she thought of it later, was so predictable she wondered why she had reacted to it as she did. She could have ignored it, filed it away with all the others. After all, the birthday party for Elsie had been no different from any other, unless her mother reaching eighty-six was that much of a dramatic advance on getting to eighty-five. The sequence of events, family members arriving, Father Wilson, the cake, the singing, the wine, answering poor Masie's question 'Where am I? Whose house is this?' for the umpteenth time, was an exercise in management, the mind unchallenged beyond the need to please and serve. A grandmother several times over, Kate had mastered the art of detachment to a point where – especially in her dealings with Joe – it had become a defence against any degree of emotion beyond that of concern. A loving servant to all the family, faithful to the end, she was now most content with her own cup of tea in the kitchen.

Elsie, she knew, would try to set the tone. Or rather, with Father Wilson and a few other cronies in support, the theme. And as surely as one section of an orchestra would stir up another, Joe and Bill would spark the counterpoint, flanking Masie, quietly crooning to her the songs she loved, their old mother now witless but demonstratively loved, pitted against the superior Elsie with all her guff about the state of the world. Anything later than about 1947 had been wiped from Masie's mind but the way her sons activated her, cradled her poor mind in an instant of song and laughter, she shone more brightly as a beacon of all time, of all their lives. Even the kids slurping their juice were drawn to her, crouched at her feet, while across the room Elsie gamely held out in

23

her moral fort against the barbarians. That was the difference, Kate knew well, between Joe and herself. He showed a passion for his mother of which Kate was incapable, no less than Elsie would have shunned any such displays of music-hall affection for herself. Masie lapped it up, as she had done for years on the amateur stage. She was their star still. One evening they had all sat through a showing of *Iris* on the television. Kate could feel Joe and Bill thinking: our Ma will not become like that. We can still bring her to life with a song. When it was over Bill remarked that the young Iris would have been like the mother. Not the other way around. Masie was the benchmark, even for Iris Murdoch!

'Oh, I agree entirely, Father,' said Elsie, delicately removing a crumb of birthday cake from her lower lip. 'You know, I was reading an article the other day in the *Times* that said we're reverting to a kind of eighteenth century . . . what's the word? . . .'

'Hedonism,' said Father Wilson.

'Hedonism, that's it.'

'I read the same article myself,' he went on. 'We complain about the modern excesses but it's a bit like Halley's comet, the same thing comes around again even if it takes a couple of hundred years.'

'And it's not what we used to call the lower orders that are most guilty in all of this.'

'Heavens, no. Apparently it was good sport for young toffs in the eighteenth century to take their beer out on their balconies and urinate down on passers-by.'

Bill reached across Kate for the bottle of sherry on the sideboard. 'A pity,' he muttered in her ear, 'we've no fuckin' balcony here.'

'Don't give her too much now,' she chided him. 'I think she's had enough.'

'Just a nip.'

Their side were tuning up, allowing Masie small sips of sherry. Left to themselves they would have allowed her the odd fag too but in company they didn't dare. Kate watched them buzzing around her like bees feeding their queen. In a sense they were shielding her against the outside world, as her husband had done in the last year of his life. No one had realised how bad the dementia was. When people called he would prime her so that she knew whom to expect, often giving her a crossword puzzle to work on just before someone entered the room. And that was the amazing thing about Masie's brain: she could still manage a crossword puzzle!

'Passive smoke,' said Elsie. 'I know, it's awful. It catches your throat.'

'And clings to your clothes.'

'You know, we all went on an outing last Saturday and . . .'

The buzz in Masie's corner became a croon, Bill's tenor floating in like a lighter shading on Joe's bass. The panic in Masie's face melted in a smile.

> *Only a rose I give you,*
> *only a song dying away,*
> *only a smile to keep in memory*
> *until we meet another day.*

In song, unashamedly, they made love to her. Masie stretched back like an old cat full of its warmth and well-being. She held her sherry glass in two fingers, moving it in the air like a wand. Her voice when it came was like a wavy scratch on the men's veneer.

> *Only a rose to whisper,*
> *blushing as roses do.*
> *I'll bring along a smile or a song for anyone,*
> *only a rose for you.*

'No, thank you, pet,' Kate said to young Jimmy handing around a plate of biscuits. His mother Susie, Kate's youngest, a budding hypochondriac, resumed her account of her friend Deirdre's baby's twisted-gut operation.

'The poor child!'

'Saint Faustina, oh yes,' Elsie battling on gamely, 'when was she canonised again, Father?'

'It was certainly the millennium year . . . Let me see, must have been Easter, musn't it? That was when the pope . . .'

> *Stars shining above you,*
> *night breezes seem to whisper 'I love you'*
> *birds singing in the sycamore tree*
> *'Dream a little dream of me.'*

Each old woman at the heart of her circle. They're like the twin souls of Dublin, Kate thought. Spirits and the spirit, the bawd and the saint. Not that Masie had ever been a bawd but the mimic in her had played at devilry. And perhaps even now unconsciously (for the poor creature wouldn't remember it) the way she lent back in the armchair waving her glass in the air reminded Kate of the Dutch print on her bedroom wall, the lady in a golden dress reclining tipsily in a chair, holding aloft her wine glass. Who had bought it for her? Bill, endlessly cultivating the voluptuous image? And to what degree, even years ago, had he begun to manipulate it to counterbalance the high-minded Elsie?

'Jimmy, don't kick your brother!'

Kate gently separated the two young boys at her feet.

'You terrors,' she said, lifting Jimmy onto her lap.

> *The way you wear your hat,*
> *the way you sip your tea,*
> *the memory of all that,*
> *no, no! they can't take that away from me.*

'It was in the news this morning,' Elsie said. She glanced across to the other camp and smiled. 'The poor thing. She's enjoying herself.'

'Isn't it remarkable,' said the priest. 'She still knows all the old songs.'

'But the new breakthrough now,' Elsie went on, leaning forward into her circle and slightly lowering her voice, 'is that the researchers – I think it's in Uppsala – have found ways of tracing the proteins in the living brain that causes, you know . . .'

'That's important, yes, because up to now they had to rely on analysis of the dead brain . . .'

'Nuns,' interjected tiny Mrs Laverty, Elsie's best friend, 'apparently suffer less from . . . you know . . . than . . .'

'Yes,' said Elsie, 'I read that too. Less stress, I suppose.'

'And diet, of course,' said Father Wilson.

'And less passive smoke, probably,' said Elsie, fanning the air. 'That's for sure.'

> *The way your smile just beams,*
> *the way you sing off-key,*
> *the way you haunt my dreams,*
> *no, no! they can't take that away from me.*

Young Jimmy squirmed out of Kate's grasp.

'Jimmy, would you like to play in the kitchen with Rosie?'

'No!'

'I have every sympathy,' said Father Wilson, 'with a young person from Kurdish Turkey or anywhere else looking to better himself by getting a job in this country but there are rules and—'

'I think we are a soft touch,' said Mrs Laverty. 'My husband says—'

'When my husband, God rest him,' began Elsie, 'was in the Department—'

'Anyone for coffee?' Kate almost shouted.

And it was when the coffee had been drunk and they had all left, kids shouting their pleasure like creatures released from captivity, Masie now fast asleep in her chair, that Kate had said, 'You know, I imagine it could be useful if more old people like my mother were to donate their brains for research.'

She caught the glance that passed between the two brothers.

'Why not?' said Bill. 'Good as new. Hardly been used.'

She had invited it. And there was a time she would have laughed with them. After all, that kind of down-putting remark had been their life's currency together.

They were planning to fill in part of the bay down by the Bull Wall. Joe, spelling out the economics for freight shipping was for, Kate against. From her bedroom window she could just make out the glitter of the incoming tide, Dun Laoghaire pier on the far side like a thin line drawn out into the bay, a boat moving away from it like a fly over water. She had echoed the Clontarf residents' main objection to the plan as the first insidious step towards greater infill, the bay shrinking as developers' bank accounts swelled. Joe had muttered something about the 'stodgy middle classes with their manicured lawns' not wanting to offend their eyes with a bit of industry on their doorstep. She had never won an argument with Joe over business, not since they married and he was expanding his father's old huckster's yard up on Clanbrassil Street into an installation and plumbing empire that spanned the city. That she and Joe ever even dated had seemed unlikely. She was in her nice office in town and he was in and out in his overalls, a guy fixing something. And with a wisecracking lip that had no one taking him very seriously. When he offered her a lift one evening after work (there was a bus strike) in his BMW, cool jazz playing on the car radio, she revised her image of him. She even remembered looking at his thick curly black hair, which later in transports of another order she would grip and hang on to, and think-ing: Why didn't he strike me like this earlier? Was it that you didn't ever see beyond the overalls? And at first Elsie too was taken in by the fancy car that pulled up at the gate, and the slim swarthy-looking gentleman puffing his fag while he waited. When she found out a bit more about

Joe's background she opposed the match with all in her power. Even Joe said at the time it was hard to blame her. She would have expected her only daughter to marry within the social envelope that had contained her family and her governmental husband's. And the young Kate too, on her way to school, had probably harboured an image of her future husband going off like her dad to some department on Merrion Square in his pinstripe suit. But it was an image as ephemeral as one of Elsie's watercolours, all fancy mood with little substance. In the end it was blown away like a leaf in the whirlwind of Joe's energy. After the wedding Elsie went on a pilgrimage to Fatima to regain her spiritual equilibrium.

Masie was now at the centre of their lives. She had arrived like an unexpected child. Not long before that Kate had moved into their son Harry's old room because of the row with Joe over his smoking in bed. The way he had dug his heels in over the issue suggested to her that he welcomed the chance to sleep alone, that in some way now she was beginning to annoy him with her own unrest. They were like two middle-aged people in training to live beside rather than with each other. Masie arriving to be looked after only seemed to cement the breach. And this was it, too: when she thought of the bay infill she had an image of Joe and herself drifting out away from each other to more separate moorings. Part of what they had shared, the easy swing and flow of their lives, all mixed with the routine of family, was filling up with some hard stuff shipped in from a part of the brain activated for just this period of life. For that was what younger people found difficult to grasp, that often the greatest voyages of the mind, and none greater than that back into a forgotten self, were begun at the onset of old age.

It was Bill, of course, who kept it going about Elsie's brain, too good an opportunity to miss. Years earlier, at another birthday party, Bill, the worse for wear, had insulted Elsie when she reprimanded him for using the f-word in the hearing of children. He told her that some of those children were his and he was going to effing use the f-word with them as often as he liked. And she could be Mrs Effing Church Triumphant if she wished but to please stay out of his effing road. Of course it all blew over but the scars were livid to this day. When Bill walked out on his family and set up with a new partner he was only bearing out all that Elsie had thought of him. And Bill rubbed it in by bringing the partner, a flighty blonde called Jane (a bimbo, they all agreed on that) to another family gathering. But Joe had always stood by his brother, continuing to support his family. He bought out a partner in the used-car business and installed Bill as manager. Again his instinct was unerring since cars were the only thing that Bill understood.

They came in from the back after doing a job on Joe's car. Working brothers, their image was always subtly aggressive. Bill, washing his hands at the sink, said to Kate casual-like in a way that didn't fool her for a second, 'What did Elsie say about your suggestion that she should donate her brain to science?'

'I didn't mention it to her, Bill,' replied Kate, casual as himself but feeling her gut tighten up. With his mother so vulnerable it was now clear to her that *any* coupling of Elsie and Masie in the same sentence was fraught.

'I thought it was a really good notion,' he said, smiling at her, drying his hands.

'Yes, I don't see why not? We always think it must be younger people who do this. Would you like a cup of tea before you go?'

'No, thanks. We'll be having a pint.'

Like Elsie's exchanges with Bill there was this formal thing in their own interaction. Where her brother-in-law was concerned Kate was definitely in her mother's moral camp. And Bill knew this. The men left, after a short crooning session with Masie to cheer her up, for the pub. Sport, as ever, was on the cable for the old woman to watch throughout the day. Kate soaked her feet in a basin of warm water and clipped her nails.

'Whose house is this?'

'This is our house, Masie, Joe and me.'

'Am I staying here tonight?'

'You are, love. You're living with us now.'

'Am I?'

'Yes, and now we'll be off to bed. Here's your pill.'

The television was still on. Speedboats whizzed about somewhere. Kate watched, unseeing. All of this, she thought, were she ever, God forbid, to suffer from Alzheimer's, would be wiped from her mind. All that seemed so vital now would be gone. Even that scene between her mother and Bill might never have occurred. Their first trip to France to the holiday camp with the kids would not be there to recall. She might *just* squeeze in her first date with Joe but even that was doubtful. The shutters had come down on Masie's brain long before her own courtship started.

Had she dozed? The brothers were returning, their voices loud with drink. It was as if every time they were in the house together now with Masie in this state they had to keep up a false jollity. Perhaps if their sisters had not all emigrated, Kate often thought, they wouldn't have been thrown so much together. Now Bill was pacing around, looking for something.

'You forgot something, Bill?'

'My keys. I put them down somewhere?'

Kate felt a tingle on her skin like a sudden draught. Had he forgotten on purpose? A little more probing of the imagined slight on Masie's brain? Joe had a worried expression as if Bill had somehow slipped out of his reach.

'Ah,' said Bill, finding the key ring by the sink. 'I'll be off, so.'

'Okay, Bill. Safe home.'

Joe followed him out to set the alarm on the front door. At the last moment Bill turned in the hall and took a step back towards Kate.

'You know, I was just thinking,' he said.

'What's that, Bill? Are you sure you have everything?'

It was like electricity in the air. Kate stood there waiting to be struck.

'I was just thinking, you know, if Elsie is going to do this . . . you know, with the brain and everything . . . why shouldn't she, like, donate a few other things, like . . . I mean, organs are valuable . . .'

He was dismembering her, she thought. Had they sat over their pints in the Yachtsman and carved Elsie up? Anger coursed through Kate like a hot flush but her reply when it came (and for a moment she felt the breath sucked out of her) was cold and flat.

'Well, I suppose I could suggest . . .' She shrugged. It was a thing of nothing. What was Elsie now but a cadaver? 'Elsie, I'm sure would be the first to . . . In for a brain, in for a . . . kidney?'

'That's what I was thinking,' said Bill. 'Or a liver. That must still be pretty sound in her.'

'We'll talk about it later,' said Joe, laying a hand gently but firmly on his brother's arm.

'And of course,' said Kate, pale as a sheet, pulling the trigger now, 'sad as it is, you know, with Masie, you might consider making a similar arrangement. Why not? We're not just all brain, isn't that true? God help us, to be talking like this. But as you say . . .'

But Bill had nothing further to say. Turning abruptly, he left. Joe followed Kate back to the kitchen.

'Why did you say that?' he hissed at her.

'Say what?'

'About Masie. Don't you know the state he's in.'

'Oh, he can attack me through Elsie's brain but I'm not allowed to even mention his mother, is that it?'

'It's not the same.'

'Is it not? Am I not doing what I can for Masie? What gives him the right . . .'

'He's dying of . . . sadness, woman! Can't you see? She hardly knew him tonight when he—'

'And we're not? Does that mean he thinks I have no feelings for Masie?'

'Of course not. He's just . . .'

'He's just your little brother you still have to protect from the big bad female *genteel* ogres of my family, isn't that so?'

'Nonsense. I—'

'He could insult me to my face, as he once insulted my mother, and you'd still put your arm around him and protect him, wouldn't you? And did you sit down there in the pub with him all night and listen to him sniggering over how he'd like to carve up Elsie and scatter her body around the world?'

'I hardly listened to him. I have other things on my mind. The business . . .'

'Bugger the business,' said Kate, and tramped up the stairs.

She could, she thought, get the entire family to sign donor cards. Every man jack of them. Parents signing for kids, guardians for the incapable. It would set a benchmark for organ contribution. The family would be famous. They might kickstart donor activity throughout the world. She would organise a donor-fest to which the entire clan would assemble, perhaps even a small marquee in the garden with balloons and games for the small ones. Father Wilson would say prayers, turning it into a crusade. After all, this was what science wanted, a rational approach to mortality, an acceptance that even the little kids had a contribution to make, however tragic might be the circumstances. And Elsie's friend Whatshisname on the *Irish Times* would come along and photograph them and take down all the details of what organs they were willing to pool. Joe's lungs, definitely. They should make interesting viewing. And what about you, Bill? How have you marked your card? Well, Kate, I was thinking maybe my scrotum, though at present I am still quite attached to it. I think that's an excellent choice, Bill, because you are surely a classic asshole. You would be making a unique contribution to asshole research. And how about you, Bimbo Jane? Oh dearie me, well, Kate, I was thinking maybe . . . You were actually thinking, Bimbo Jane? I was thinking, Kate, that maybe my ovaries would be of interest to science. What do you think? I think they would make a wonderful contribution, Bimbo Jane. Good as new, never been used . . . And you know, Bimbo Jane, last Valentine's Day I peeped into a bag Bill had left in the hall and saw the Kinky Sex Oufit he had bought for you. Isn't he wonderful? Fifty-two and still buying frilly knickers. What a lover! But then of course you had been a bikini bride an' all . . .

'Whose house is this?'

'It's our house, Masie.'

Mrs Horgan the day-care companion had left and Kate was taking over again.

'Am I staying here tonight?'

'You are. And so am I, God help us.'

'Amen,' said Joe, passing through.

All day they had behaved like strangers in a guest house, using the amenities but wordless, indifferent to all but their own needs. Now he was off to a meeting and Kate could again settle down with Masie and watch the sport.

'Oh, look, Masie, the speedboats are back.'

'Are you going to do my feet?'

'Not tonight. We'll just watch the sport.'

'Is my father coming?'

'Not tonight, Masie, love. I don't think so.'

When Joe left she sat erect, feeling the tension mounting in her. She did some of the exercises she had been taught at yoga. They didn't help. In the end she phoned Susie and asked her if she could come over and sit with Masie for a while. When Susie arrived they all had a cup of tea together, giving Masie time to get used to Susie sitting beside her.

'I won't be long,' said Kate, leaving.

'No hurry, Mum.'

The meeting was in the primary school all her children had attended. The place looked deserted but the lights were on in one of the classrooms on the second floor. When she entered she was surprised to find it was almost full. Joe sat with others on the raised area where the teacher would stand. Kate took a seat in the back row and listened to the debate. Definitely, it was one-sidedly against the infill scheme. But Joe and a few others were holding their ground, downplaying the idea of vast incursions in the bay. What was being proposed was reasonable and controllable and in the end would benefit the city. Kate waited for an opening. Someone mentioned a feasibility study. She got to her feet, her heart thumping. The words came to her. Afterwards she saw it as a kind of miracle that they had.

When she heard of feasibility studies, she said, she always wondered who they were going to be feasible for. (Spattering of applause.) She had read an article only this morning in the paper in which a TD spoke of the widespread corruption that existed in this country between the developers and the so-called planners. (Lively applause.) The TD spoke of the greedy, grubby, grasping hand reaching into people's pockets in the name of progress and modernity and being of benefit to the city. We all know who'll benefit! (Even livelier applause, stamping of feet.) She was a citizen of this city, born and bred, and a member of this community, and she was backing the No campaign with all the passion of one who loved Dublin Bay as part of herself, as a treasure of nature that must be defended against the vandals of so-called progress. If they had their way they would tarmac over the entire natural world. *They* should be infilled somewhere, dumped, yes, preferably far away in some other country that might like to use their greedy talents. (Tumultuous applause, stamping feet, banging on desks.)

One old gentleman with long silvery hair swivelled on his chair and shook her hand.

A flash popped in her eyes. She would make the *Clontarf News*!

She waited for him, drying the same cup over and over. Susie had long since left. Masie was fast asleep in bed. His key rattled in the door. She thought she could smell the porter off him even before he entered the kitchen. He looked mutinous, his eyes small and red in their sockets. Her eyes flicked around to see what was within reach for him to smash. It had only ever happened a couple of times. He had never laid a hand on her but wasn't there always a first time? Her chin came up. She was good at outstaring people.

'Brilliant,' he said, snapping open a can of stout.

'What's brilliant, Joe?'

'Your performance tonight. I never thought you had it in you.'

'I surprised myself.'

She picked up the milk jug from the table and put it in the cupboard.

'A pity you're as witless as all the rest.'

'So there are others who think like me? Great, that means . . .'

'That means there are witless people who put forward the same emotional arguments against a perfectly sane and sensible scheme. That's what's witless about it. It's all emotion. Where would Dublin Port be without infill, tell me. Back in stinking slobland, that's where.'

'We know where the slobs are.'

'Our wonderful bay. Every fucking stone in it is sacred. Let's all go down on our bended knees and pray to every fucking sacred stone in it.'

'What's wrong with emotion? If people feel deeply about something . . . They *feel*, Joe, it's human. They don't *like* what is happening. Isn't that as valid an argument as all your fancy economics?'

'Did your mother put you up to this?'

'Oh, yes, blame Elsie now. Are you going to start on her too like Bill.'

'I'll start and finish where I like.'

'As you always have, Joe. But you can't deny the same right to me or anyone. You know, Joe, I have never criticised your mother for anything, anything, she has ever done. In fact, I've always got on well with Masie. But I'm sensible enough to know that you never actually liked Elsie, and Bill even less so.'

'She did put you up to it. But she hadn't the balls to come and say it herself. Pathetic.'

'And don't you ever, ever, say anything unkind or cruel about her again in my presence or believe me, Joe Hegarty, I'll march out of this house and never return. Your own brother showed me the way . . .'

'Pathetic.'

'Elsie for all her ways is a very kind person . . .'

'Pathetic.'

'And in many respects is a better person than you or me or Bill or the pope in Rome—'

'Better? Define better.'

'Better!'

'What's better?'

'Better!'

'What's better about the sanctimonious old cow?'

'Better! Better!'

'Better my angelic Irish arse.'

'Yes, and you might put that down on your donor card as well. An anatomical miracle surely since you usually talk through it.'

'Donor card? What the fuck are you on about, woman? Are you going witless as well?'

'Where I'm going is away. I warned you, Joe Hegarty. Susie will give me refuge!'

'Why don't you try Father Wilson?'

'Maybe I will. He'll find me a women's refuge. Elsie always said I'd end up in one when I married you!'

Smash!

What was it? The small vase. She had overlooked that.

She went for a walk down as far as the Bull Wall. An offshore wind was like a creature snapping at her heels. Coming to a slipway across from the boatyard she stood on it for a while and let the wind whip around her ears. The tide was in. Far out the dark head of a seal bobbed up. She stretched her arms out and part of the motion was a wave to him. You're welcome any time in our bay, Mr Seal. No infill here, thank you.

On the way home she called into a newsagent's and pretended to be studying the magazines while she looked through the local community papers. No, there was no photo of Kate Hegarty at the No Infill campaign meeting. Heading back again into the wind along the front she thought: This is vanity. I'm pushing myself out in a way I never did before. Nearer now, the seal popped up again and seemed to concur, following her with his large doleful eyes.

A series of events took place that suggested to her that it was more than vanity. It was as if she were being punished for her flippancy with people's bodies. First Bill was driving around the city when he experienced a severe pain in his chest. He was rushed to hospital for an emergency operation on his heart. Then Bimbo Jane on her way to visit him put her foot in a pothole and broke her ankle. A few days later the bus taking Bill's eldest son home from a football match crashed and the boy suffered trauma to his eye socket. For a while the doctors even thought he might lose the sight of one eye.

That was already a good proportion of one family in the same hospital. Susie rang and said Malcolm her brother-in-law had been diagnosed with testicular cancer. The beast came closer. Old Mr O'Toole next door fell while putting out the rubbish and broke his hip. Mrs O'Toole, rushing home, tripped over a dog but luckily she didn't break anything. Finally, the dark thing entered the house, as Kate knew it would. Masie woke with a chest infection. Her breathing was laboured. Mrs Horgan rang for an ambulance. In the hospital they said there was a build-up of fluid in Masie's lungs. When they visited her she was covered up behind an oxygen mask. She looked lost and panic-stricken, a shrivelled up little mite. And down the hall they hadn't the heart to tell Bill she was there beside him.

Kate went for another walk along the front but this time she entered John the Baptist's. The church was deserted but several votive candles had been lit. She lit a few more and knelt down in a pew.

O Lord, she prayed, I have sinned in thought against my fellow man. Forgive me my sins. I have thought unkindly of Bill and the fault is in me because I do not understand his grief. He loves his mother in a way that maybe I am incapable of loving mine because I am a shallow person. But You did not make me shallow, it is my sin to have walked with the Evil One saying nasty things about people, and he has conspired with me to do them ill. Whatever we think about Bill and Bimbo Jane— You see, there I go again, forgive me, Lord – all Bill is doing is loving his mother and where would I be without the love of my children? And now through my cantankerous shallow spiteful ways I have lost Joe's love as well. Help all those who are suffering, O Lord. Take poor Masie into Your loving arms and ease her pain.

In the porch she looked back to the altar, adding: And I don't know if You're for or against the infill, Lord, but if You're in favour of it, then Thy will be done in that too.

When Joe came in, close to midnight, he was in a sorry state. Stout had spilled down over his trousers. There was a streak of ash on his lapel. He looked like a hobo. But tonight there would be no row. He sat on a chair in the kitchen and moaned to himself. Kate took his head in her hands and cradled it against her. She had no practice at this any more. It was like balancing a hairy old turnip on her arm.

'We'll feel better in the morning,' she said. 'You've just had one too many tonight.'

'It's not that. I went up to see her. She's going, Kate. Ah jasus, the sight of her. She didn't know me, just sat there like a . . . like a . . .'

'I know, Joe. I know.'

'On the way out I went in to Bill and put my head down beside him on the pillow. We cried together like two babies.'

'She's in no pain, Joe. I don't think she is.'

'It made me regret all the things I ever said about your mother. It's like a punishment.'

'You mustn't say that! If anything it is I . . .'

'You never said an unkind thing about Masie.'

'But I said other unkind things. Like saying Elsie said marrying you I'd end up in a refuge. She never said that, Joe.'

'I know. We say these things.'

'She always had the highest regard for you. She always said you were a great provider for your family. And that in her books . . .'

'Kate, I'll never say another unkind thing about her.'

'That's good, Joe.'

'And you know, what you were saying about her giving her brain to science an' all, it's when you see Masie up there in that state that you realise how true that is, how important it is.'

'I'm sure it is.'

'We must tell her to do it. *I* must tell her. It must come from me. In fact, I'll tell her it came from Bill and me. That will please her.'

'Well, I suppose you could mention it . . .'

'No, no! I mean now, Kate! She might die tonight and it would be too late. We must go over to her. I'll call a taxi . . .'

'It's the middle of the night, Joe!'

'Tomorrow, then.'

'All right, tomorrow. But right now, we'll go to bed and sleep this off.'

She put him to bed, tucking him in like a child. No doubt by the morrow he would have forgotten all about Elsie and her brain. But next morning, looking rather shook, he shaved carefully, put on a clean shirt and one of his better jackets. To her alarm he even dabbed some aftershave on his cheeks.

'We won't need to call a taxi,' he said, sipping his coffee. 'We'll drive. I'm fine.'

He had a kind of mad stare like a man on a hopeless mission. He's losing it, she thought, but she didn't dare oppose him.

They drove past the gates of the Castle. The sun was hot. It was like the first real day of summer. Smart-looking people were turning into the Castle driveway, meeting up for lunch. Elsie often went there for afternoon coffee with her art club mates. Kate had phoned to say she and Joe were calling around. Was it Masie? Had she died? No, Kate said, it was something else. Something Joe wanted to say to her. She said she would be in the garden. She would leave the gate open

Elsie's garden was long and narrow, ending in a rose bower from where one could see the tip of the Castle tower. There she sat beside her small easel putting the final touches to a watercolour.

'It's Bullock Harbour,' she said. 'I'm working from a photograph.'

They stood behind her and dutifully admired.

'Lovely,' said Joe. 'Very nice.'

'Very pretty,' said Kate.

'Of course I only paint for charity now,' she said. 'Would you like some coffee?'

'No, thank you, Elsie,' said Joe. 'We're fine.'

They drew up a couple of folding chairs and sat facing her. She looked the real thing with her smock and palette. It was sad about Bill's heart but Kate said a quick prayer of thanks to God that he was safely out of the way in hospital.

'You mentioned charity, Elsie,' said Joe, never one to miss a sales pitch. 'It's actually along those lines that we came to see you.'

'Ah,' said Elsie, smiling. 'You want a donation.'

'Yes, but of a special kind. We were thinking in the family . . . that is, Bill and myself and Kate but probably most of the others too . . . with my mother's Alzheimer's an' all . . . we were thinking how important it is for all of us, young and old, to donate some part of ourselves to science to alleviate the sufferings of other . . .'

'And you thought of me?'

'Of course we thought of you! Could we leave you out? You're a woman of such . . .'

'Sensibility,' said Kate.

'Exactly!'

'So creative.'

'Exactly! So vital in your commitment to . . .'

'Humanity.'

'That's it! So human. So alive and healthy still . . .'

'What part of me do you want, Joe?'

'We were thinking maybe . . . your brain?'

Whatever sequence of organs may have flashed before Elsie's eyes, and the many seconds she sat staring into space would suggest quite a few, her brain definitely seemed to come as a surprise. She licked her lips, taking a small swallow. The silence deepened. Somewhere a phrase of Mozart escaped from a neighbouring window. A shaft of sun cut through the bower and Kate saw it, the brain, just by that intricate spiderweb, a wonderful gleaming thing like a huge walnut with its ridges and folds. A small bird landed on it, sang a little, and flew off. And there, moving in the leaves, was a hand, Father Wilson's, shaking holy water on it.

'I'll have to think about it,' said Elsie.

'While you still have it,' said Kate, feeling faint.

Next day the phone rang as she was washing up.

'Kate?'

'Yes, Mum?'

'I've decided against the brain.'

'Oh, really?'

'Yes. I was talking to Father Wilson about it. He said he favoured the heart.'

'Ah.'

'Yes, he said I had the biggest heart of anyone in Dublin.'

Kate marked it down on her mental card: One outsize female heart, quite ancient.

'We're all losing it,' she said into the sink.

One night, vicious showers beating in across the bay, Masie lost it. Kate had an image of a small bright stream of life, bright as Masie's eyes had been, silting up, ceasing to flow. The Hegarty clan assembled from all corners of the globe. A few days after the funeral a car pulled up beside Kate as she was walking home. Bill wound down the window. He was looking pale and had lost weight. He handed her out a slim folder from a travel agency.

'Two tickets to Lourdes,' he said. 'I was going to take Masie along with a group of other poor unfortunates. You and Elsie go instead.'

'Are you sure, Bill?'

'I'm sure,' he said. 'Ask Elsie to say a prayer for me,' he called out, speeding away.

And so Kate and Elsie went on a pilgrimage. They prayed for Masie's soul. Elsie lit a special candle for Bill. They helped with the sick and infirm. On their last day they took a tour bus through the countryside, drinking wine in small villages. They joined up with a group of tourists and laughed a lot. For the first time in years Kate and her mother had fun together.

On her return Kate was astounded to discover that Joe had stopped smoking. He was still suffering like someone recovering from shell shock. She took him in her arms. They ended up like young lovers on the sofa.

'Sex in a smoke-free zone,' said Kate. 'It's very topical, isn't it?' He reached for her but she held back. 'Do you smoke after sex, Joe?' she asked.

'I don't know,' he replied. 'I never looked.'

It was an old joke and they laughed. It was like a glimmer in the ashes of their old easy banter.

They continued to sleep in separate rooms but began to go out more together again.

Different City Different State

PAULA CUNNINGHAM

'They're just rats with a-ti-tood.' The fat guy in the plaid shirt enunciates slowly and carefully. 'Rodents.' I don't feel quite the same about squirrels after that but I'm determined to persevere with my project. A single black-and-white photograph every day, like a kind of photojournal. I know the squirrels will get scarcer soon and that before too long they'll all go into hiding. I don't know what I'll photograph then. It's like my way of crossing off the days.

I didn't want to come here. Well, part of me didn't, but when I got the scholarship I kind of figured I should. I persist with the photographs and feel good when, one morning weeks later, I almost forget. By this time I reckon I'm getting a reputation as the crazy campus squirrel photographer and I try to photograph them covertly, pretending my interest lies in pale, naked trees. 'It's something about rebirth I guess,' I say if anyone asks. And it's weird, but people here, strangers, do ask. 'I'm interested in cycles.'

'You've got an accent,' they say, one eyebrow raised, an intelligent half-smile. I develop a stock response: 'So do you.' Which leaves some of them puzzled, foreheads creasing; some laughing. I'm sorry, it just happens so goddam often. I like Americans. Really.

'Ireland, is that part of England?' 'Belfast, where's that?' At first I think they're thick as champ, but eventually I recognise my own arrogance. It's like expecting people to know the capital of Greenland; just because we're a self-obsessed ostrich of a nation doesn't mean anybody else takes any notice. Or should. Our arses, not the sand.

I know fuck-all about American geography, let alone history. And I've never been into politics. They're all the same thing where I come from. Politics geography history. Geography politics history. Histry palatics

41

jography. That's the way they say them in Belfast. His-pal-jog. Hi-pa-jo. Hipajo. Hiya Joe/Jo.

They've given me an office, room 301 in a big brownstone building I keep getting lost in. Office mates too. Jane and Joe/Jo. Joe slash Jo. I don't know how to spell Joe/Jo and it's problematic. Not knowing how to spell Joe's/Jo's name. It's very uncomfortable. With or without the 'e'.

Jane is serious and beautiful, a newly-wed ex-alcoholic and a brilliant writer. Thick shiny hair, shoulder length, the colour of fall leaves only darker. If it came in a packet at home it would be called Autumn Chestnut. She oozes self-confidence, seems way older than me though she's only just turned twenty-three. Calls me 'sweetie' from day one – it takes me a while to get used to that. Loves her husband but it's hard she says. She knew him, *noo* him, at elementary school. Just a boy in her class. His family moved away. They met again as adults through a friend, different city different state. They started dating.

Joe/Jo is also beautiful. Androgynous. Fine hair on the upper lip, cheekbones like small apples. Dark hair. Cropped. Big eyes with slate-grey irises traversed by maps of yellow lines like cracked and glued-back plates. Wears oversize clothes in neutral colours which lend an air of waiflike vulnerability. Rides a bike, a fifties Harley, and works out. Almost thirty-one but you'd never know it. Used to be a carpenter, building decks and garages. Talks about missing the smell and the feel of the wood; fine dust that gets into your hair and under your nails, into the cracks that appear in the skin of your hands when you work out of doors in the winter. Lives in the woods about ten miles from town in a big log cabin with decks overlooking a river. Shares with a guy called Ron. Throws parties and cooks Indian. Vegetarian. Has a big sad elderly dog called Monk who sleeps a lot.

Jane is too absorbed in her newly wedded bliss to notice when I'm disorientated and miserable. Joe/Jo notices and is kind to me, really kind. Simple things. Like lending me a travel iron and borrowing a friend's pick-up to collect thrift-store furniture for my apartment. Spends an entire Saturday morning putting up shelves for me, and misses the ball-game. Cooks for me and continues to do so despite my failure to reciprocate – I've no kitchen utensils and besides I can't cook vegetarian. Can't cook period. Takes me for rides on the Harley to wilderness areas where we walk for hours. Knows the name of every tree and identifies birds by their calls. Tells me that it's possible, if you live in the woods, to smell the first snow for several days before it arrives. Loves Irish whiskey, which I am happy to supply, and develops a taste for Guinness in spite of my protests that it's so much better at home. First time we go to O'Doherty's bar I start snivelling into my Irish stew (they've used beef) and we have to leave. We never refer to my weepy episode, never talk about anything remotely personal.

I don't even know if knowing how to spell Joe/Jo would help. I'm domiciled in a country where colour and favourite have no 'u's, pants are trousers, and a ride is only a lift. Spellings are treacherous; essays and poems return from my tutor, transgressors lassoed in red ink. I suspect this woman writes entirely with her head. Her poems are perfectly crafted little boxes, beautiful to look at but devoid of emotion, a prolonged, dry kiss that leaves you feeling used somehow, and parched. She has pets, favourites in the class, and the rest of us seldom get to read our work. It's like the opposite of school; you're pissed off when you're *not* asked to read.

There's another example. Two. *School* and *pissed*. Here, school means university or college. Elementary-school (primary) and high-school (secondary) are seldom seen out without their prefixes. Pissed here means angry, pissed-*off*. Pissed at home means drunk. Did you know that the Irish language has only one word for sober and hundreds of words for drunk? I can't remember who told me that but it was probably Jacqueline Cleary.

I check it out in the interests of accuracy. The Irish for dictionary is *foclóir*. *Focal* means 'word'. We used to love saying that word at the Gaelteacht. *Focal*. Any chance we got. *Focal. Focal. Foclóir*. Ha ha. *Fuck all folklore*.

Minaclady. That's the Gaeltacht we went to. For Minaclady my spell-check offers maniacally. I've probably spelt it wrong but I don't have a map here.

The boys from St Mary's in Andytown were the coolest. We were from Newry. The Belfast girls wore drainpipes and knew about things we didn't. We were still in flares. Is it true if he puts his tongue in your mouth you can get pregnant? Does it mean he wants to? It all sounds bloody disgusting anyway.

Trouble is I don't know what Joe/Jo is. I've been looking really hard for clues – bumps, swellings, bulges. Joe/Jo wears baggy clothes and the signals are conflicting. Sometimes I think there might be breast, other times there's a bulge in his/her corduroy trousers and I'm not sure whether it's penis or just the zip sticking up the way mine some-times does. I get embarrassed when that happens, usually when I've lost weight, which I do at the slightest whiff of a stressful situation. I get mortified when I spot it and I try to pat it down. Button flies aren't much better.

I check the dictionary. You can never trust Jacqueline Cleary. She's got this earnest face and intones her statements with an authority I've never been able to muster. Then she laughs really loud, too hard, at the next thing that's even remotely funny and you know buck rightly she's been holding the laughter in. I miss her.

My *Collins Pocket Irish* gives two words for **sober**: *sóbráilte*, which, because it sounds like an English import, doesn't really qualify, and *stuma*, which really means sensible. Under the entry for sober is **sober up**: *bain an meisce de* (literally meaning to remove, take away the intoxication/drunkenness) and *cuir an mheisce díot* (get rid of/get over drunkenness) and *tar as meisce* (come out of, escape or recover from drunkenness). I satisfy myself with this for now; I've fat chance of finding a fat Irish dictionary here.

I call Jerry over to investigate. He's Irish-American, lived in Belfast for a year on a student exchange, and I met him through friends. He lets on he's coming to visit to see how I've decorated my office. I've covered my window with autumn leaves in various stages of undress, from red through orange and brown to that crinkly, almost see-through fawn. I've stuck them on with double-sided Sellotape. They call it Scotch tape here. And Durex in Australia. Honest to God. My sister's been there. Imagine. You could end up in a sticky situation. Loads of cards and photographs as well, and paintings my brother's children made for me leaving. Things with the power to prevent and give rise to the longing for home. And to make me feel a little better when I *am* homesick. Which is most of the time.

I introduce Jerry to Joe/Jo and idiot stares and squints and frowns and looks away and squints again. He circles round, looking Joe/Jo up and down like he's assessing livestock at an auction. I'm mortified. I give him filthy looks which he ignores and he's all smiles and charm and corny lines and Joe/Jo laughs and doesn't seem to notice, or maybe notices and doesn't mind, and I wonder what the hell is going on. I realise I've seen Jerry like this before and it's usually when he's onto somebody, which, when I think of it, is most of the time. Next thing I know they've arranged to go out for a drink – an oxymoron if ever

I heard one. Jerry is incapable of having *a* drink; I've never seen him stop at less than six – even when he's skint he just saunters up to the bar, chats up some stranger and gets one for free. He's exasperating; the sort of person you want to dislike but can't. Anyway, he and Joe/Jo end up exchanging telephone numbers and Jerry rushes off to a class. He tells me he'll call by my apartment that evening; I stay in and he doesn't show up. I try to relax but I can't, I'm tired but unable to sleep, my whole body aches and I've never felt so homesick. I look *that* up in a fat dictionary in the library. **Homesick**. First coined in Germany, 1756, in German Swiss. *Heimweh.* referring to German sailors who, after long periods at sea, became physically ill with no apparent explanation. **Homesickness**: *a depressed state of the mind and body caused by a longing for home during absence from it.* In 1805, one W. Taylor wrote: 'A cat is as subject as a mountaineer to the home-sickness.'

I even miss the fucking helicopters. I miss my boyfriend at home. Ache for him. I miss the way he always calls me 'woman'. I stop wearing skirts. Dresses. Men at the bus stop hit on me anyway and I buy a silver ring from a Mexican trader which I start to wear on my wedding finger. It doesn't help. I begin to dress like a boy. Dungarees and collarless shirts I find in thrift stores. A guy in the class tells me I look like Huckleberry Finn. Gone fishing. My tits get even smaller.

The course director, an obese Texan woman with a nasal drawl and a moustache, is kind. Also an ageing Irish professor. Sitting it out till he gets to retire. To go Home.

I write to my man, at home, every week. Sometimes twice. Funny Hallmark cards with corny teenage *Miss You Love You* lines. He writes once in two months. When I phone he's often drunk. He slurs he'll write, he'll visit really soon. My favourite word's been *soon* since I was three. I pretend it isn't happening. I keep sending the cards. I don't do angry.

About a week later Jerry calls at my apartment with his verdict. He says he's spent some time with Joe/Jo, listened really hard and looked for clues. I ask him about the nature of his research and he laughs and avoids my eyes. He says he's none the wiser and I decide to believe him. He's from the mountains anyway and could sooner sex a moose or an elk or a bear or a deer than a Jo/Joe.

He tells me that I'm losing weight. He asks me if I'm eating enough and tells me that I'm drinking too much. I ask him if he thinks he's my father and tell him to get the fuck out of my apartment. Which I instantly regret because he and Jo/Joe are the only people who ever visit and it's lovely when the doorbell rings but it's too late and I've a stubborn streak and I stand by the balcony door and watch him reverse his battered pick-up down the drive just as Joe/Jo arrives on the bike with a pizza and six-pack. They do a kind of elaborate high-five as if they've known each other for ever and it's all chat and laughter after that. I open the balcony door but I can't hear what they're saying, and when I sneak back inside the door slams and I know that they've heard me. I take some big breaths and walk about a bit and I go out and call them both inside and Jerry gives me one of his pleading looks and we all laugh and we eat and we've two beers each and the whiskey comes out and they both stay late and drive home despite my protests.

A couple of days later I try going to the gym where Joe/Jo works out – it doesn't help. He/she wears a sweatshirt and has moderate leg-hair and feet which are slightly large for a woman and small for a man. I give up. Jerry says he's given up too and he says it's not important and that gender is an over-rated issue, that there are probably hundreds of genders, that gender is the flat earth of the twentieth century, that Shakespeare and the ancients knew but we've forgotten. Or something like that.

We start calling him/her him/her. Or her/him. We're like that. Egalitarian. The right to bear arms and all that Jefferson stuff. My students – in addition to taking my course I teach composition – are required to write a proposal paper on a topical issue. Of twenty-eight students, twenty-two pen right-wing papers opposing proposed changes to the state gun laws which would restrict gun ownership. One student, the son of a Vietnam vet, argues in favour of the restrictions. Three write fervently on the immorality of a downtown nightclub, right next door to McDonald's, which advertises lapdancing; two write dia-tribes, peppered with biblical quotations, inexplicably containing iden-tical typographical errors, on 'the cuntless evils of homosexuality'. One earnest young man who has never spoken in class writes vehemently on the avarice of the North American food industry and the benefits of a vegetarian diet. I struggle to focus on writing skills rather than con-tent. I organise, in a bout of missionary zeal, a class debate in which some of the students are forced to propose a motion supporting restric-tions in gun ownership. I invite my head of department to attend. The proposition team argue unconvincingly while the opposition team pas-sionately regurgitate familiar arguments. Finally the leader of the proposition team jumps horses in his concluding address – his dad, it transpires, owns the city's largest gun store – and the debate culminates in a fistfight. My teaching career goes down the pan. I resolve to stick to safe subjects: antecedents, verb–noun agreement, dangling modifiers, sentence fragments, gerunds, parallelism, pronouns. The infinitive, split.

Eventually I ask Jane. It's about a week later, a Thursday, and we're alone in the office. Joe/Jo's been off for a couple of days. I've been here ten weeks. I know that because that same night Joe/Jo phones me to tell me the snow is coming, a storm, and I sniff and sniff and I can't smell any difference and it happens two days later and it's beautiful and the squirrels disappear. My photo-journal stops abruptly there.

'Jane,' I hear myself say. 'I've got a problem.' I walk to the phone, by the window. Even with the windows shut fast you can hear the storm howl. The trees are skeletal now; their leaves hover and eddy close to the ground. I can't look at Jane and I know that I'm blushing.

'What is it, sweetie? You can tell me. You've been so quiet lately. We've all been anxious for you.'

'It's Joe er Jo,' I say and the window steams up.

'Speak up, sweetie, you gotta compete with that wind.'

I try again. I still can't turn round and I'm shouting at the window. 'It's the phone, Jane. I've been nervous these last two days each time it rings. I'm not a gossip; I'm open-minded, really. The trouble is, it's a real problem. Today the phone will ring. You'll not be here. It'll be a student for Jo(e), and Jo(e) won't be here and, I'll have to tell them and trouble is I don't know which . . . I've no idea which . . . which personal pronoun to use.'

Jane is sweet. She tells me. 'Jo's a girl.'

By then it's too late.

Harry Dietz

GERARD DONOVAN

Mr Dietz's eyes snapped open and he gasped, clutched the sheets on his bed and squeezed them until he knew where he was, until familiar shapes emerged like ghosts from the dark to reassure him: the venetian blinds slicing the street light across his pants folded on the chair, his ties draped on a coat hanger, his radio with the red 5:34 that burned like embers on his bedside table. He let his breath straighten out in a sigh. Another long nightmare in a short night.

Mr Dietz fixed his glasses, switched on the bedside light, and shut the alarm off, even though it was set for 7:30, because he often forgot to turn it off when he woke this early, and it wasn't one of those new ones that shut itself off, and occasionally when he came back in the evening from work he'd hear the thing ringing even from the parking lot and find an angry letter from his downstairs neighbours, Mr and Mrs Shaw, in the slit of his mailbox. After reading the angry letter he'd go to their door. Apologies, promises to buy a newer model, one that shut itself off after a few minutes. Afterward he would go upstairs, and by the time he had switched on his television, Mr Shaw and his wife and their complaints had faded.

Once upon a time, whenever that was, and he often wondered when once upon a time was, Dietz's moods started to come and go like pages of a book flapping in a breeze, until everything he knew lay scattered like fallen playing cards; but then his brain sometimes flashed, even burned into happy flames, and he felt better and saw each moment of his life, it seemed, back to his first steps as a child.

About ten years ago he had gone to the town doctor, a man with teeth bulging out of a smile under gold-rimmed glasses, and told the fellow that he was waking too early every morning and that he felt down about things. The doctor slapped Harry on the back, and told him to keep his chin up, that things would turn around, to think of all the fine people in his life, that everyone got the blues at some point in their lives. Then the doctor guided him out of the office. Weeks later Dietz went back and this time the doctor gave him some pills, but they made him fall asleep at work, sprawled over his calculator, so he stopped taking them, at least in the morning. He kept them in the fridge.

But this time of the morning was his, and Dietz imagined that Mr Shaw and his wife were still asleep, a few feet under his bedroom floorboards in their long, straight bed.

Five thirty-eight in the morning. Dietz knotted his robe at the front and walked along the dark corridor to the kitchen. When the fridge door opened, a bulb lit his face, and he remembered that he'd only gone to bed a few hours before because of that late-night film and because he had to play with the coat hanger to get a better picture on the television.

Let's see. No milk. No coffee without milk.

Best go to Fred's.

Mr Dietz pressed his feet into his moccasin loafers, pulled his grey jacket over the red bathrobe to offset the chill of a late April dawn, and strode out to his Ford Zephyr. As the Ford bounced onto the street, Dietz went over in his mind how to get to Fred's place, and he pulled up to the store in three minutes.

'Hi, Fred.'

Fred looked up from the floor in front of the drinks cooler where he was unpacking a box and waved. 'Hi, Harry. Up early again I see.'

'Yep. Thought I'd get a head start on those figures for the inventory on Monday.' Dietz fished for coins.

'Coffee, Harry?'

'Yes, and milk, please.'

'Leave it on the counter, Harry. I'll see you tomorrow.'

'I've just got a twenty.'

'Take the change out of the till, bang on it, it'll open.'

'How much?' said Dietz.

'Take sixteen dollars and eighty-five cents.'

'OK, I'm taking sixteen dollars and eighty-five cents.'

'OK, Harry.'

Harry poured some coffee and put his milk in a brown bag. He stood by his car and sipped, looked up once at the first infusion of milk into the night sky. It was as fine and crisp a Saturday morning as he'd seen in a while.

While driving back to his apartment, Harry turned into a small street on an impulse because his headlights caught a street sign that rang a bell, but he couldn't say why until he cruised the row of houses. The shapes suggested images that cleared away the confusion like condensation you rub off a window with your sleeve. The street, he knew, had pulled him to it.

Her name was Mary Norman.

She once worked with him at Beodeker's Electronics in Charleston, Illinois, since leaving high school – they were twenty-one and in love; it was 1962, and after five years of dating, they cruised this street one day and selected the home they'd live in if they were married, and then Dietz had asked her if she'd marry him – not that he was ready to ask, but his dad once told him that Harry thought too much and should be more assertive with people. So he took a deep breath and asked her, *Will you marry me*? But he didn't actually ask her until a few minutes later, when he spoke the words out loud.

Now Harry slowed down as he passed the house with the double chimney, the one he and Mary selected so long ago before he popped the question in the front seat while he sipped on a soda, staring straight ahead. Mary had smiled, looked straight ahead too, said she'd think about it. But the weeks turned into months and Mary never said yes; she put it off, never explaining why, until one day she told him nervously in his office at the store that she had found someone else, another friend, someone who made her laugh, and that she was sorry to let Harry down like that, but that laughing was important in a man.

He'd never found anyone else. Not after that. Mary Norman, it turns out, was dating and eventually married the store owner, Mr Beodeker. Harry had thought about speaking to Mr Beodeker, but he couldn't figure out how to bring up the subject. *Mr Beodeker*, this customer wants to know why his record keeps skipping, and after you've handled that, I'd like to know why you stole my girlfriend.

Harry kept her photo in his wallet clipped to his driver's licence.

He turned onto another street. He'd lived in Charleston all his life but most of the streets were not familiar to him. He figured that the next turn would bring him back to Fred's, and from there he could get home again and have his coffee. That street, however, did not bring him back to Fred's; instead he found himself driving on bigger and longer roads, and soon he had to shield his face against the rising sun, so he changed direction, moved down a ramp onto a highway, and the sun swung to the right and the road opened wide like a grey flower in front of him.

He was heading north.

The highway sign read 'Chicago 195 Miles'. He liked the idea. *Chicago?* Why the hell not? Why not? It was as good as lounging around the apartment. He tasted his coffee and felt a lift but quickly braked it down to fifty-five. The car behind him swerved. He hadn't driven on a highway for the longest time, hated it – too many people speeding and tailgating – but today the highway invited him like a warm canal. He pressed to his head the hat he kept in the glove compartment, wrapped his hands over the steering wheel and pursed his lips, glad that he'd decided to do it, and anyway, it was the weekend. As he drove through the flat fields of southern Illinois, he rolled down the window and smelled the fertiliser. Bits of the landscape rolled across the windshield: gas-station signs on towers, exit ramps to small towns off the interstate, a pick-up that was broken down on the shoulder with the hood raised and a red rag knotted on the antenna. It felt good to be on a trip, much better than he felt earlier, but why did he have to drive to feel better? And his dressing gown blew about his face so much, despite the jacket, that he wondered why he didn't go back to dress in regular clothes for the trip.

Cars passed. He saw drivers shaving, combing hair, applying make-up in the rear-view mirror. One driver read a book.

A few miles down the highway, Harry slammed the brakes and stopped in the slow lane. The line of cars behind him squeezed into a tight squeal of brakes and fought each other for lane space fifty yards back. Faces shouted at him as they passed his driver's-side window. He put a finger to his lips and frowned; he had stopped because he remembered that when he was pouring the coffee at Fred's he'd glanced at the morning newspapers wrapped in a bundle on the floor. On the header he reread in his mind the words, *Friday, April 24 1999.*

Friday! Harry drove off to the shoulder and sped up again to fifty-five, mortified that he was driving to Chicago on a work day. Friday! Mr Beodeker would not be amused. Seven miles later he pulled off the highway, drove up to a gas station, and called the store while the attendant filled his tank.

'Hello? This is Mr Dietz. Is Mr Beodeker there . . . He's busy? OK. Can I leave a message? Tell him that, that I'll probably not be in today. No, I'm not sick – yes, yes OK, I'll call later, in an hour.'

He shook his head as he replaced the receiver.

Someone spoke behind him: 'You going my way?'

He turned to the voice. A thin boy of about twenty, looking at Dietz's bathrobe.

'I'm just out for some coffee and milk,' Dietz said.

'I'd really appreciate some help,' the boy said. He stood at the window of the station diner. 'In fact, I'm kind of hungry.'

Harry studied the boy's face. He looked familiar.

'Did you work at the store a few years back?'

The boy swallowed. 'What?'

'Beodeker's in Charleston. I think I remember you.'

The boy steadied himself. 'Yeah, I worked there for a couple of weeks. I got fired. You've got one hell of a memory.'

Dietz said, 'I owe the station ten bucks, but I'll put it on my credit card; that leaves me some cash. Let's get something to eat.'

'I'm John,' said the boy, and shook Dietz's hand.

'Mr Dietz,' Harry said.

They sat in the diner. The boy talked about his plans as he ate. Upwardly mobile after a tough year. Sick and tired of Charleston. An investment idea involving cell phones. Dietz nodded occasionally, dipping his eyes to take a bite out of his burger.

'You still working for old Beodeker?' John said.

'Yep. Still there, never left, never will.'

'Earn enough?'

'Enough to live on, for what I need.'

'I'll bet the old bastard is still paying you six bucks an hour.'

'Eight. I went up to eight four years ago.'

John had bright eyes, and Harry remembered them: they made the young boy very appealing. John had worked in his department but was different from the other college boys that the store hired part-time, most of whom laughed at the idiot Dietz when he asked them questions about how the new electronic gadgets worked. Life had been fine in the late fifties and sixties when he could take apart a Zenith or a Hotpoint and make a day's work out of them, but now the store was full of MP3 players, notebook computers, and God knows what, and he spent most of the day in the office, tapping his calculator, refilling his coffee cup. When customers asked about a new product, he'd call one of the boys over and excuse himself. He often wondered why Mr Beodeker hadn't fired him.

But dependable John had helped, always coming into the office and patiently telling him what to say to the customer, even writing responses for him on a slip that Harry could read from the counter as he assisted the customer. He was sorry when John got fired.

Opposite him, John's mouth was moving, and the words assembled in Harry's brain.

'What do you call a boomerang that doesn't come back?' John said.

'I don't know: a boomerang that doesn't work?'

'No,' said John. 'A stick.'

For the first time in twenty years Harry laughed from his belly. The steel clock on the diner wall read 11:04, and John sat back, patting his stomach.

'Thanks, Mr Dietz. You were always a decent guy.'

Harry went to the restroom. When he returned, John was gone.

Harry sat down and waited for him to come back. The waitress sauntered over and stabbed the check under the pepper mill. She eyed his gown and moccasins cautiously.

'Are you lost, sir?'

'No, I don't believe so. I'm just out for some coffee and milk, that's all.'

'OK, just asked.'

He decided to check the restroom again, but it was empty. He called John's name in the hope that he was in one of the cubicles, but some man shouted angrily, 'No, leave me alone!' and so Harry went to the front of the diner and pressed his face to the glass, where he scanned the lot. No sign of John.

He turned to the stares of customers and reached for his wallet to pay the check, but he'd left it in his jacket, and the jacket was gone. Harry walked back to the restroom to look for it since he'd just been there. Nothing. He looked under the cubicles and the angry man flung open the cubicle door and pushed him, asked him what his problem was. Then Harry went back to the front of the diner and stared out the window and watched his Ford for a few minutes because it was the only thing he recognised.

His father had given a Ford to him around the time he was courting Mary, so Harry bought another Ford when he needed to replace the first, which strangely enough had stopped working the year his dad died. That was the time Harry had an argument with Mary because she had opened the bag in which he kept his father's record collection. This happened a week after he asked her to marry him, when she was still thinking about his proposal. He had caught her sifting through his father's old 78s on his settee one morning and grabbed them from her. With the records in one hand he stalked the room looking for the bag. He shouted his accusation bitterly: she had opened the bag and let the smoke out, the smell of the cigarettes his father had smoked. The bag preserved the smell that was in his father's house the day of the funeral, when Harry had securely packed and sealed the records. He had shouted at Mary for a long time and she had cried. He wanted to seal them up again but it was too late because the ordinary air had mixed in. She told him never to speak to her like that again.

That's when she took up with Beodeker.

'Sir?'

Harry turned from the diner window to the waitress who held the bill out to him.

'Would you like to pay for your meals?' she asked.

'Yes, but my wallet is gone. My jacket is gone.'

She shrugged. 'You want me to get the manager, is that what you want?'

'If you wouldn't mind.'

'Stay right there.' She went to the rear of the diner and spoke to a young man, who wound his way through the tables and looked Harry up and down.

'You'll have to pay. You ate the food,' the young man said.

'Of course I'm going to pay.' Harry reached into the pocket of his robe and retrieved sixteen dollars and eighty-five cents. The manager turned to the waitress. The waitress took the money from Dietz's hand.

'Are you sure you're OK?' she asked. 'I didn't mean to be rude just now.'

Harry smiled. 'You're doing your job. I'll be fine. I'm on an unexpected trip.'

'That's nice,' she said, and lifted her hand in a goodbye as he left the diner.

After another hour on the highway Harry grew tired, as he always did in the early afternoon. He pulled over into a rest area and dozed in the front seat. When he straightened himself up, the sun had moved left of centre in the sky, and the shadows of trees in the fields lengthened towards him.

Walking over to a payphone, he fumbled a coin into the payphone slot and dialled the store.

'I'm sorry to call this late in the day, Mr Beodeker, but I wanted to explain – I don't know what happened—'

'What? No, Mr Beodeker, it's not the third time – Mr Beodeker, I don't know what you're saying – Of course I still work there, Mr Beodeker –'

Harry rushed to the car. For some reason Mr Beodeker was angrier than usual and seemed to think that Harry hadn't worked there for a month, that his position had been filled two weeks ago.

Maybe that's why he had driven all this way today. Yes, that was it, he'd show Mr Beodeker. Harry pulled out of the rest area and chugged over to the fast lane without signalling. The highway behind him gyrated with pressed horns, fists out of windows.

After another hour the signs for Chicago grew bigger and the traffic seemed to close in around him. People switched on their headlights as the light drained from the west. Harry drove in the fast lane and then slowed back to the speed limit. People flashed their headlights behind him. He turned the AM radio up loud to keep himself alert: a talk-show host interviewing a man who had written a book about alien abductions in the Chicago area, and Harry heard the man say on the air, loud as you please, that viruses weren't the only threat facing Americans.

'What do you mean when you say that there are other threats facing Americans?' the interviewer said. 'My listeners want to know.'

'The Russians are what I mean. The Russians, with the help and assistance of our President, are conducting secret training camps in western Montana. These are crack Russian troops.'

'What now, you mean the Russians are coming?'

'No, sir, that's not what I'm telling you. I'm telling you that the Russians are here.'

'What's the purpose? I mean, what do they hope to achieve?'

'To strike at the right moment. We're weak now, with the war and everything, fighting on so many fronts.'

'Frightening,' the host said. 'This is truly monumental. Folks, our number is 800–456–9982. We'll take more phone calls after these messages.'

Harry gripped the steering wheel and looked around him. The sky balanced between day and evening, and lights swarmed in the rear-view mirror. Cars overtook him filled with shapes hunched over or lying back fleetingly in his vision: soldiers, agents, advance people. His mouth hung open and his eyes widened as he swept the mirror with glances. Russians?

Harry remembered his father calling to him from the doorway: he was nine, and they had bought a fallout shelter. His father hurried him to the bottom of the yard and asked him where to build it. Harry pointed to a bunch of big green nettles. The communists might drop a big bomb on the town, his father said, but Harry and he would survive in the shelter for months if it happened. His father swung his spade and dug and dug, yelling at Harry to go into the house and bring him water, or to take his handkerchief and wipe his forehead. *The communists won't wait for us to finish. Look up at the sky, Harry. Look up at the sky while I'm digging. If you see a trail of smoke, it's the atom bomb coming for us.* So Harry watched the sky until his father yelled at him again for something else. He smelled the wooden kit boxes and the wet-cement stink when it was finished. The next week was boiling hot, and one morning while Harry stood in the garden with his toy airplane, his father ran out of the house in his long black pants and jacket and yanked him by the shoulder. *Quick! Quick! The shelter! We've less than a minute!* Harry dropped the plane and tried to look up into the blue but he lost his footing as his father dragged him along. Harry said, 'But Lucky. I want Lucky to come too.' *Lucky can't come. The dog will foul the air. We have to seal it tight. Get in there, Harry.* And his father pushed him in and closed the door between them, the door with the three yellow triangles, and all of a sudden it was pitch-black and Harry's breath bounced in his chest so hard it hurt. *Daddy! Don't stay outside!* And he bent so that his head was between his legs and waited for the world to disappear in a big wind, like his father said, as he hid among the body bags, the gas masks, the dehydrated and canned food, the evacuation procedures, afraid and small in the dark. An hour passed, maybe three or four. No flash. No wind. Maybe it was a silent bomb, and he'd have to check outside to see if it had landed or maybe destroyed another town down the road. And then he heard footsteps, knocking, and his father stood in the breach and took Harry and hugged him tightly in the ointment of sunlight through the trapdoor.

Harry eased off on the gas pedal as he smelled the aftershave, felt the bristles of his father's beard against his cheeks, heard his father tell him for the hundredth time: *The bomb will make everything you ever knew go away – your friends – nothing left at all*. And young Harry Dietz wanted to know what losing everything might feel like but got a headache from trying.

Someone flashed their headlights right at his bumper and he pulled off the highway, narrowly missing an eighteen-wheeler as the driver jammed his brakes. The long sound of a blasting horn and the smell of burning rubber. No wonder those people had been so frantic earlier on the highway, putting on make-up and reading the newspaper while they were driving. They had to keep moving.

There, a payphone in that gas station: The 800 number.

'Yes, folks, and now we have a Mr Dietz calling from a payphone in the Chicago area.'

'Yes, this is Mr Dietz.'

'Go ahead, sir. Your question.'

'Where did you say these Russians were?'

'I said they're in Montana, secret training camps, funded by the United Nations' International Monetary Fund pals.'

Harry breathed into the handset.

'Caller, do you have another question?'

'I can't see any Russians. I've been driving for most of the day and I didn't see one of them.'

'You're making fun of our guest, Mr Dietz—'

'—and what are they wearing? I want to be able to see them coming. I don't want to be caught off guard.'

'Caller—'

'Have they landed in the past few hours? How come I heard nothing about this, and how come nobody's doing anything about it? I don't want to be captured.'

The handset swung as Dietz ran to his car.

The highway brought him to the Chicago skyline, and he followed the traffic until the road split around elevated train tracks. He drew to a stop on a well-lit street near the river and walked along the pavement, his bathrobe blowing in a stiff breeze. He'd sleep in the car tonight, get a job tomorrow, and try to stay ahead of the Russians.

A doorman stared at him from the entrance to a carpeted lobby. Harry approached.

'You can't come in here.' Arm with a red band on the sleeve blocked him.

'I just want to get warm.'

'No, you can't.' Second red band.

'What's the world coming to when I can't get warm?'

When the doorman threatened to call the police, Harry went back to his car and stretched on the front seat, tired from the driving. He wondered what time it was. Perhaps he had already been sleeping in the car. And then a good mood charged at him in a moment of glory: weeks now since he'd been fired, but worth it just to have seen that mean bastard Beodeker's face turn pale when he, Harry Dietz, leaned into Beodeker's office and screamed at him that just because he was the damn boss it didn't give him the right to steal another man's girl all those years ago, and that just because Mary Norman was now his wife still hadn't given her the right to sneak around and steal a dead man's smell. Harry lay on the seat and remembered the silence in the store, the way the cops came and escorted him out, the sick way everyone stared as Beodeker walked behind him, shouting, 'Fired, fired!'

Harry shivered. It was cold here. He watched the evening crowds slide by his windshield, snatches of conversation, laughter, music blaring as pub doors opened. He felt the carton of milk: it reassured him, and then he thought of Fred.

When he woke it was still dark. He gasped and sat up. The car was parked under a sidewalk tree, and birds coiled themselves around the branches in bursts. Harry held his breath, waiting for familiar things to reveal themselves. He groped his way out of the car and walked the pavement, holding his robe tightly against the wind.

Harry Dietz strained back to look up at the city lights reflecting off the skyscraper windows, each one telling him a different story. One told him he was cold, another said he was hungry, another said he was a boy, another said it didn't recognise him at all. Then they all got together and said nothing at all. He strained to listen for the sound of the 78s – Caruso, the big bands – and for the smell of cigarette smoke, and for his dad to appear out of one of those windows, waving at him.

The windows of the shops were lit and he was drawn to them. He paused at an electronics store window and checked the display. The glass flashed blues and whites. He watched the reflected shapes emerge from the lights, and he shoved both hands deep into his gown pockets.

Russians. The men on the radio were right. Now it was all too late.

He said, 'OK, you've got me.'

One of the shapes said, 'The doorman called us.'

'Your English is very good for a couple of Russians,' Harry said.

The other shape took his left arm. 'Let's get you to the station, friend.'

The desk sergeant glanced at the officers, then at Harry, and pointed with her pen to a chair. After a few minutes, one of the officers sat beside him.

'We're making some calls, Mr Dietz. We traced your plates. You're from Charleston. We're waiting for a return call from the police there. They'll see if anyone can come pick you up.'

'Fine.'

The officer left and the desk sergeant's pen scratched the silence from the air. Harry pointed to the wide shelf on the wall behind her.

'A Zenith.'

The desk sergeant said without looking up, 'Very good. Still working. My dad gave it to me.'

'That's a 1967 Zenith, seven tubes, model N731, I think.'

She turned to the radio. 'Hey, that's right. You can see that from there?'

'I used to work with radios. It's got an aerial built-in for both AM and FM, so you'll get a good sound, even in here.'

'I used to get the local stations when it's not busy, which is never, these days. But it stopped working. Haven't listened to it in a while.'

'Your father bought a good model. He knew his radios.'

She left her pen on the table. 'Yes, he did.' Then she smiled at the man in the gown and the moccasins. 'Would you like some coffee?'

'I'd love some coffee. Do you have milk?'

'We have everything. I'll get some. Back in twenty seconds.'

Officer Kearns poured Mr Dietz a hot mug of tea in the staff canteen. She used one of her own, from a can of tea bags she brought to work from her kitchen at home.

A cop just come on duty dropped his hat on the table and sat down, sighed, and pulled out a notebook from his breast pocket. He looked at her.

'I need to be at home. Got this cold coming on.'

'Don't we all.'

She wondered why he still worked as a cop. Every evening, same line. I should be at home. *Go home then.*

'Jane, what's with the guy in the gown?'

'That's Mr Dietz. He's lost, I think. Charleston. The local cops are getting hold of his neighbours.'

'Oh, yeah? Well he was tinkering with that old radio of yours. Said something about a loose tube.'

'Oh, I better get out there,' she said. She backed into the swinging door with a steaming tea in each hand.

'Mr Dietz? Did you fix my radio?'

Officer Kearns stood in the waiting room of the Chicago Third Precinct and heard The Drifters.

'Mr Dietz, where are you?'

Mr Dietz was not where she had left him.

She looked at the shelf on which her father's Zenith was playing for the first time in eighteen years, since he switched it on in the evenings in the seventies after he came home and tapped her head with his newspaper, saying, How's my sweetie?

But she'd been gone barely long enough to boil the water.

'Sitting in the back row of the movies on a Saturday night with you.'

'Mr Dietz?'

The radio sounded like new, tinny but warm. The dials looked big and confident, and the dust that found the tiny crevices in the grille mattered now – she took a tissue from her pocket and spat on it, wiped the film off. And when the warm brown wood shone back at her, she stood again in her living room, with her dad relaxing after work, fiddling with the radio. She heard her friends singing on the bus home. She felt the hot pavement underneath her feet on Saturday mornings when her dad batted her a ball by drop-kicking it off his foot. She tasted the orange pops on her tongue when she slid the taste along it, cold and sweet on those hot days. She heard the silence when he left without notice, drove a car away to work, and work became five o'clock, and work became seven o'clock, and the calls, and the police, and the silence of the line when she lifted the phone to see if her dad would answer. Months later. Her mother's finger twirling the phone line as if coaxing it into ringing. Her hand on the hairbrush that caught a few strands in the corner of the bathroom mirror. Opening the cabinet. Pills on her palm, on her tongue, in her saliva, in her throat, in her eyes.

She learned that some people want to disappear, and there's no finding them after that. The world is full of the missing. She saw her mother from then on only in bits and pieces, in mirrors, in the car, closing the door to her bedroom. And her father? A face in Vancouver, a credit card handed to a supermarket clerk in Portland, an envelope with ten dollar bills now and then.

And the radio? Dust arrived with tiny suitcases The silent Zenith turned into a large apartment block settled by dust, decorated by dust, silenced by dust. A whole country of radio dust with elected officials, a dust government, a parliament of dust, the dust halls of power, the congress of dust. Calling dust to order.

Harry was careful as he walked the streets. The black was on him once more. He dug his hands into the dressing-gown pockets and kept the gown from blowing about as he rounded the corner and blended in with the crowd. A child pointed. *Look at that man, Dad, in the red gown.*

He slouched the pavement, shoulders hunched to hide his face. Behind him a loudspeaker corded the sky. Clear the way! Move your vehicle! He held his dressing gown up a couple of inches and looked behind him at the sirens. Ahead of him, a woman carried a child down a hole.

His breath ran ahead of him and he couldn't catch up with it. He came to the hole. More people going into it, some running, some apparently not that concerned. All down the stairs to the bomb shelter. He followed them, not daring to look behind him.

Down at the bottom, the light dimmed and a tunnel appeared. Everyone walked without hurry, so he walked without hurry. Some read a newspaper as they walked, doubtless, Harry thought, so that they could hide their faces. He held up his right hand and studied it, where he used to write the answers to the questions. Got to blend in with the crowd. He followed until the people around him were silhouettes in the growing light ahead. Then everyone bunched up. Harry held his breath, did not like people pressing him. He watched as people placed something into the slot and moved through a revolving gate, down a short stairway. He felt around in his pocket and pulled out a couple of dollars, then joined the line for a window where a man who never looked up took the money and pushed a coin back. Harry placed the money between the glass panels, said nothing, and took his coin.

He held it in his fingers just as the people beside him did and dropped it into the slot. Just then a gush of cool air bathed his face and he heard the whine of metal hitting metal. He tried to move backwards but the revolving bars wouldn't go backwards, and the man behind him who carried a small black suitcase in his left hand shouted, 'Come on, we're in a hurry here!'

Harry saw the crush ahead, saw some people emerging from the interior, trying to get out through the bars, and they stood in front of him. He was caught between both sides. If they were trying to get out, that meant they knew something. Too dangerous here. He turned to the man behind him.

'I'm going back. Please, tell the man in the window to make this go backwards.'

Someone shouted, 'Tell that moron to get a move on.'

'Hey, you in the gown, we got lives to live here.'

The man with the small black suitcase said, 'You can't go back.'

'What?'

'You can't go back. Clear the way, please.'

There were more people entering than leaving, propelling Harry along. They came to a moving stairway going farther underground. A very extensive bomb shelter, this. Question was, how long would he have to wait? He moved up to the edge of the platform and looked down the tracks.

Very tired. Would like to go to bed now. His heart moved in his chest like a lizard he'd once caught as a boy that dug into his palm with little darts of toes before he let it go. He closed his eyes and thought of Fred. The wind again, but cool and pleasant. The screech, when it came, made him shout and he staggered back to the wall and hid his face. A train slid out of the tunnel, a long, long train. Harry shuffled through the doors.

All the seats were taken, and as the train moved off he held a strap, just as everyone else standing did. All seemed to find a place with no people where they could rest their eyes. Some looked at the ground, some at the pictures on the walls, some at a book, some listened to radios through earphones.

Harry tapped a young boy on the shoulder. The boy took the earphones off.

'What?'

Harry leaned close. 'What's the situation?'

'What?'

'The Russians. How long will we be here, do you think?'

The boy put the earphones back on.

Harry nodded. 'Don't worry. It's been this way for years. I did this as a child.'

A woman got up and Harry took her place because he was tired. When she left, Harry took her copy of the *Chicago Tribune* and read the headline: TERRORIST THREAT: CITY IN FEAR.

The Vice-President says the threat to our homeland is real. Terrorist, nuclear bomb. It's not a matter of *if*, but *when*. Harry saw the flash of the bomb and felt the match flaring up and he knew that he felt more than the resigned feeling he had when he'd finally given up on the new technology at Beodeker's. He felt the pain again. It searched his body with wiry fingers and pressed on his arms and then dug its nails all in one place.

Another few rose for the following stop. Then there was just Harry and a girl sitting at the other end of the car. When the girl left her seat for the next stop, Harry got off too.

The platform was empty. He heard the girl's footsteps click on the tiles ahead. She turned out of sight. Harry followed through long halls. One turnstile, then another. He followed the sound up the steps, felt cooler air on his skin. Saw the tops of buildings. He was back on the street and it was still night. The girl turned right and knocked on a door. She watched Harry as the door opened.

'Good night,' he said.

The door closed.

Harry gripped his gown and walked past the door the girl had entered. It was a pity that people couldn't talk freely. But anyone could be a Russian.

He passed dark alleyways in which fires burned out of barrels, and men stood over them, drinking. Farther on he saw buildings with parts of walls missing and cracked windows. It was obvious that a bomb must have landed on them. The Russians must have attacked this part of the city.

Harry heard a sharp report and ducked, felt a mixture of excitement and fear. Some people were still fighting. Real heroes, those people holding out in the dark alleys, keeping warm and defying the invaders. A siren moved across the night.

His right ankle grew hot. Harry took his eyes from the sky and forgot why he had been searching it for so long.

'Well look at you.' He leaned down and petted the cat as it twined around his ankle and he felt the heat on the other leg.

'Want to come home with me?' He picked it up. It leaned into his chest and he stroked its head. 'I have some milk for you, little kitty. Well, not here, but later, when I get home.'

'You're lucky she didn't scratch your eyes right out of your head.'

Harry turned to a child holding a doll.

She pointed to the cat. 'That's Moses. She's a street cat. She fights lots of cats all the time. Even dogs.'

'Hello, Moses,' Harry said. 'Strange name for a girl cat.'

The girl said, 'Moses doesn't care. And I've never seen Moses in anyone's arms before. Not even once. You must be a cat-man or something. A man once kicked Moses, and my daddy and another man had to get her off his face because she jumped up and hung on to his face with her nails, like *this*.'

The girl put her hands into claws and brought them together in a vice grip.

'It took a while and the man cried.'

Harry let the cat down.

'Dietz is the name.' He held out his hand but she stepped back. 'Harry Dietz. And who might you be, young woman?'

'Mildred.'

'Well, Mildred, I'm hungry and I am going back to my apartment. And by the way, what are you doing out on a night like this with all this fighting going on?'

'My apartment is too small, and anyway, my mom and dad have been fighting since I can remember.'

'My God. What age are you now?'

'Ten years and four months.'

So it's been that long, Harry thought. One parent against another. Probably a language problem. One parent can't understand a word the other says.

'Mildred,' he said, 'I wouldn't worry too much if I were you. And not a child like you, as pretty as you.'

'Easy for you to say,' Mildred said.

'Why is that?'

'You're lost, aren't you?'

'A little bit,' Harry said.

Mildred looked around her and widened her eyes. 'More than a little bit, Harry. You are lost a big bit. You are a whole lot of lost.'

'I'm a stick, not a boomerang,' Harry said.

'What?' Mildred brought the doll close to her ear. She listened, head cocked, took a deep breath, and said, 'Harry, Mildred says you better get out of here fast.'

'Why is that?'

Mildred turned and pointed. A large man walked up to them. He wore glasses and a cardigan.

'Mildred, there you are. Where have you been? Hey, who are you? What you doing with my Mildred?'

'He's OK, Dad. He's lost, that's all.'

'Is that what the man said to you, Mildred?'

'No.'

'What then?'

'He picked up Moses.'

The man walked up to Harry and pointed his finger across the city. 'Get lost back to where you came from, old man. Be lost in your own place. You can't get lost here.'

Harry said, 'Did a bomb explode around here? This place is a mess.'

'OK, we got ourselves a mouth.' The man shoved Harry against a post, bunched Harry's collar in his fist. 'Talking with my daughter.'

'Dad!' Mildred said.

'Be quiet! Where are you now, old man? Are you in your own place now?'

'No,' Harry said.

'Dad, he's lost. Moses likes him.'

Harry felt the grip loosen and figured the worst was past.

'Moses?' the man said.

'Yes, Dad. He picked up Moses.'

The man sighed and looked sideways at Harry Dietz. Then at Moses.

'OK, I'm guessing you're the luckiest man this side of the city.'

'I'm just lost.'

'Here's what we're going to do.' The man lifted his thumb. 'Mildred, you get back inside, and I mean now. And you, I'm going to bring you out of here.'

'Sounds like a plan,' Harry said.

Five minutes later a beige Lincoln Continental drove up to the curb. The man motioned Harry in. The door wouldn't close right for Harry, and the man ended up getting out again, kicking it hard and shouting at the same time.

'It's a 1979 Mark V, smooth as velvet, but that door won't shut.'

'Can't beat the old stuff. Just don't make them like they used to.'

'So tell me about Moses. How come she didn't cut you up? I can't touch that cat and she lives in my house.'

'I picked her up.'

'Just like that?'

'That would be about it.'

'That cat will not let me come even close. I mean, even if I get too close while I'm putting the food in her bowl.'

'I hear she's got a temperament.'

'Did Mildred use that word?'

'She mentioned fighting.'

'Did she now?'

'Yep.'

They drove through another three traffic lights in silence, until Harry finally couldn't take it any longer and said, 'Do you do a lot of fighting? Is that something you can talk about?'

The man looked at Harry and swung the car over to the side of the road. 'I don't know what Mildred's been saying to you, but there's no fighting in my house.'

'Then Mildred must be very proud of you and your wife if you've been fighting for most of her life. She must be very proud of you both indeed.'

The man looked away and laughed. Harry smiled, waiting for the man to talk about his military service.

'Look, Mildred imagines a lot of things.' The man took a drag of the cigarette and blew smoke against the windshield where he pointed. 'See that tower a few blocks that way? We're at the edge of the neighbourhood here. Just keep walking that way and don't look back.'

Harry followed the man's finger.

'Just keep that tower dead ahead of you and you'll be back in your own place soon enough. You got that, old man?'

Harry got out and slammed the door. The car sped off.

Harry followed the lights that lit the sky above where the man had pointed. More lights in that part of the city. He kept the tower in sight and walked close to the walls, in case any fighting erupted around him. The breeze lifted his gown as he passed a bright window on the edge of a busy street. The flashing sign said DINER. He was under the tower. Inside the diner, a thin woman who looked about eighty sat by the window writing on a notepad with one hand while scanning the street with binoculars.

Just the woman I need. She might know some things. Thin, looked about eighty, Harry thought. Likes to know what's going on. Can help me and make me feel a little better along the way. Get back to my apartment and get the television working, watch *Murder, She Wrote*.

He waved back at the dark part of the city in case the man was watching. Thank you.

He walked inside to conversations, Sinatra on the loudspeakers, heat on his legs, and approached his reflection in the window until he was at her table. With a question.

'You from around here?'

'We're all from around here,' she said.

'I'm Harry Dietz.'

'Good for you,' she said under the binoculars.

Another woman trying to survive. Harry felt sorry for her.

He went to the counter and raised his hand until the young waitress saw him. 'I'd like a coffee.'

'What kind of coffee?'

'A mug.'

She rolled her eyes up and blew hair off her forehead.

'Would you like regular or decaf?'

'Just black. I'm over there.' He pointed to the woman's table.

She rolled her eyeballs again. Maybe she had a disease. To have to go around rolling your eyeballs every minute! People would notice. You'd be conscious of it. What an affliction for a young woman.

'I wouldn't worry about that eye problem. It will pass.'

She stared at him. Bit her lip. Called back to counter, 'Two coffees!'

'I only want one,' Harry said.

'She always gets another coffee,' the waitress said, flicking her head toward the woman. Harry returned to the table and sat down.

'I took a wrong turn. Finding my way back.'

'Aren't we all,' the woman said.

He drank his coffee and looked out the window. The diner light flashed. He thought about Mildred and Moses. It was a good thing for him that Moses liked him. Harry felt his face and imagined Moses' claws in his eyeballs and then, in the middle of all that pain, trying to pull the cat off his face. Then not being able to get the cat off and asking for help with the cat on his face.

The woman sipped from her coffee and trained the binoculars on a building across the street. Then she wrote on her pad.

She noticed Harry watching her and put the pencil down. 'I'm minding my own business,' she said. 'Do you mind?'

'I understand.' Then he whispered, 'You've got to keep ahead of them. I was sent here by the man.'

The woman's face brightened. 'A man sent you here?'

'He said I should come to the tower.'

She clapped her hands. 'I didn't think he was interested. Thought I was a pest making all those complaints. You never know with the police.'

Harry said 'Yes' because he wanted to be polite and keep the woman happy. If she were happy, she might make him happy.

'I've got something for you,' she said.

She moved beside him. Harry lifted the mug to his lips. This was good coffee. But no pills.

The woman shoved page three of the *Tribune* under Harry's face. 'In case you don't already know, my name is Phyllis.'

'Hello, Phyllis. Harry here. Harry Dietz.'

'Harry, listen to this.' Phyllis put her finger on the page and read from it:

And in the park, a fourth woman assaulted in four weeks. The victim described the man to police as about sixty years old and tall, who asked her the time as she walked on the park's main trail. She said that he spoke in a gentlemanly fashion before jumping on her. He wore a loose white shirt and green pants, with a sweater draped around his hips.

The woman said, 'What I'm saying is, I called the police because I think I know who's doing this.'

Harry lifted the mug again. His coffee was colder and he wanted more. He looked past the thin woman to the waitress, who leaned over the counter reading a magazine.

Phyllis said, 'Mr Hugh Greene, late of the state of California, who appeared in my apartment block four months ago with barely half a van of furniture and belongings. In fact, one armchair was all the furniture Mr Greene brought with him.'

'One armchair,' Harry said.

'What kind of man brings one armchair to Chicago?' she said.

'Beats me,' he said. 'That's a bit strange.'

'The rest of what Mr Greene brought was clothes, a set of gold clubs, three large bags, and fifteen large boxes. I heard from the van driver that the boxes contained mostly books, though there were also many photographs of Greene's family – a woman and children and what may have been grandchildren.'

'Grandchildren,' Harry said.

'Now what the van driver told me is what Mr Greene told *him* on the trip to Chicago, because Mr Greene drove with him in the van, and Mr Greene talked about his family for much of the time.'

'Mr Greene talked about his family,' Harry said.

'Evidently Greene met her in England when he was training for the invasion of Normandy, sixty years before. Which would make Greene eighty years old.'

'That's interesting,' Harry said.

'He went to Harvard after the war. Became a lawyer. Made a fortune.'

Harry kept his eyes open because he wanted to find the right moment to ask the woman where he was in relation to his apartment. He should listen to her story first. It was polite to do that. He often listened to people at work.

'I find out that Greene's wife is dead, and his children live overseas. So this man,' Phyllis said, 'this rich man comes from California to our apartment block.'

'Yes, seems that way,' Harry said. He watched the waitress wet her fingertip and flip a page.

Phyllis leaned over and spoke in a pointed whisper. 'But this isn't a place where rich people go,' she said. 'And anyway, after his wife dies' – she leaned low and whispered with her hand cupped around her mouth – 'what kind of man brings one armchair to Chicago?'

Though tired now, Harry closed his eyes as if listening, a trick he'd learned at Beodeker's.

'So I decided to observe Mr Greene; his apartment is opposite mine, I leave the door open a chink. He never suspects a thing. Always greets me in the hallway, asks me about my family, always questions.'

'He likes to converse,' Harry said.

Phyllis opened a notebook and read:

He leaves every morning between 8:00 and 8:45 for this coffee shop, stays here, reads the morning paper until about eleven. He sits near the counter and talks with the staff. Seems popular. I ask my friends at the weekly card game to help with surveillance. I outline my suspicions. I don't feel comfortable with a new man on the floor. These days, I tell them, you never know. In fact, the first assault happened in the park six weeks after Mr Greene's delivery van pulled up outside the apartments. He was out of his apartment at the time. I tell them I have already spoken with a Detective Murray, who advised me to lock my door. Greene is a suspect, my friends agree, based on his strange behaviour: his offers to carry their groceries. His sudden presence when they can't find their keys, wanting to help. His requests to play gin rummy on Friday nights. His white hair, his watery eyes, his general lack of family. How he paces at night.

The woman drank from her cup and said, 'Well, what do you think?'
'My God,' said Harry. 'He's your man.'
'I imagine, a man in his eighties that driven.'
Harry searched for his pills in his gown pocket. Maybe they were in his jacket – he could drive back to the diner in case that young boy John felt guilty enough to bring it back.
Phyllis got up. 'I have to leave. Mr Greene may be watching.'
'OK, Phyllis,' Harry said.
As Phyllis left, the waitress glanced up. Harry caught her eye and lifted his mug. She waved the bill. 'You'll be paying for the coffees?'
'No, I don't think so. Don't have any money, not with me.'
Harry noticed that this time the young woman's eyes did not roll up but stayed where they were, on him.
'Eric,' she called.
A man with a towel over his left shoulder came out of the kitchen.
'Says he doesn't have any money. Four coffees.'
'I only had one,' Harry said.
The waitress said, 'Your lady friend had three. You wait here.'
She and Eric went to the cash register. Harry stood and left. He heard Eric shout. Harry looked up. On every side, those skyscrapers. Every window with a story, even when the lights went out.
Come get me, Dad.

Cold Front

BLÁNAID MCKINNEY

It's the swirl of the maps that gets me the most. That voodoo-assed, digital, mathematical swirl of clouds and sunny faces, and the jagged choke of barometric lines, going up and down and round-a-bout, and the sweet and dapper swoon of all those diagonal rain-lines, and the diplomatic peeping of sun-behind-cloud, and snow-under-sun, and rain-after-frost.

All those gorgeous symbols. I love them, believe me. But they're driving me crazy. I feel like a Teletubby, standing in front of all that stuff. Except I'm not. It's all blue screen. It's not really there. I only see it when I go home and watch it on the telly. That's when it drives me crazy. I do a job that I know is stupid, but I don't know how stupid it is until six hours later.

It's crazy. And I'm quite rich. And it's crazy. But I'm quite rich. OK, it's not stupid. It's important, what I do. I've probably saved lives. I know I have. At least I assume I have.

If I say there's a storm coming and some dunderhead decides to take a drive anyway, then it's his own bloody fault if a tree falls on his car roof.

Bad stuff happens. It is not my fault.

But sometimes, I wonder. I wonder why I can't always get it right. I don't believe in Acts of God; it's just the weather. It's just a thing. We should be able to predict *everything*. We've had ten thousand years of watching and observing and taking notes. Ten thousand years of watching the skies and the seas; ten thousand years of listening to the dinky, groaning rhythms of the earth and its various layers, of clocking the moody dementia of the clouds and of the winds. Ten thousand

73

years of practice to get it right. I don't believe in Acts of God. I don't believe in God. I believe in me. I believe in science and I believe in cleverness. I believe in the evidence of my own eyes, and in the evidence of the gorgeous array of machines we have at our disposal, and in the dazed, romper-room conviction that everything is measurable, provable and solid. I am good at my job. But I want to be better. I want a world where everybody pays attention to what I say, and where everything I say is right. To hell with God. I want perfection. When I stand in front of that blue screen and say that there's going to be severe thunder, I don't want some dumb-ass bastard's three-year-old kid having hysterics just because he was too fucking stupid to be a good parent and turn it into a game, or tell her that it's playtime in the elephants' heaven, or something – anything, just as long as it shows he's been paying attention.

I guess I'm just tired of being the add-on, the 'bit' that comes on after the news, when most people are off making a cup of tea.

When they should be paying attention.

People think it's not important, but it is. Name me one occasion, *one occasion*, when what they heard on the news, caused anybody to change their plans for the day. You can't, can you? Because people only *think* the news is important to their lives. It isn't. But the weather is. The weather can lift you up and drag you down; it can turn a corrosive, creeping day into a sublime and nutty epiphany. It can take a tomfool of a night and noodle it into a sobbing shambles. It can swerve a cool and perky afternoon into an antiseptic blank. It can sear your eyes and soothe your skin, assault your ears and desiccate your tongue, soak your toes and soften your fingernails, ruin your hair and turn your very soul into a cute and predatory contraption.

No, the news doesn't matter.

Unless the news is about the weather.

I just wish that everybody felt the same way I feel. It's not just pointing a stick, or a forefinger at a stupid magnetic symbol on a blue board. This is life and death stuff, here. Honestly.

I'm not sure how I got into this game. Television, I mean. I worked at the Met Office for eight years. It was a serious job, but fun. Then I saw an advert for the BBC and, well, that was me – I got the morning weatherman job, and I've been at it for two years now. It's trivial but easy. But I've never quite been able to shake the notion that my former colleagues are laughing at me. Laughing at the dancing puppet in front of the blue screen. A man who once had some credibility in academic circles, reduced to idiotic banter with the blonde girl and the so-called 'patrician' guy who read what is laughingly called the 'news', and exchange lollygagging claptrap for two hours. Ah, well. Never mind. I know what I'm doing and I know it's important.

I just wish other people did.

Swine.

I have predicted every damn weather phenomenon there is. I have never made a mistake. Well, almost never. Michael Fish in 1987? Not his fault. Not really. But even so . . . That's not a mistake I would have made. I would have checked and re-checked and double-checked. And then pestered my friends at the Met Office and checked the whole damn thing again. Twice. Three times.

But even with my mug in their stupid faces, and my voice in their ears, and my chilly but splashy body language all over their living rooms, some people just don't bloody listen. I get it right 99 per cent of the time. And they still don't bloody listen. They still insist on pretending that the weather is just some benign, lowlife, lightweight and fluffy thing, a thing that has nothing to do with them, a thing that can't touch them.

There was this storm about two years ago. I predicted it. Not just taking the information from my erstwhile colleagues, but doing my own research too. I've got most of the gear I need in my office at home. I just confirm this and confirm that, and, once again, cross-check like a right maniac, and then I put it out there, on the telly. That's what I did that morning. I told them. I told them. No peppery wind or cloggy flood or sandblast sun or jagged hailstorm is going to get the better of me.

Never.

It's not my fault if people don't listen.

That storm was fabulous. It was utterly gorgeous. It killed seventeen people. It was effortlessly beautiful. It was fantastic.

Most people haven't a clue what a storm is. They know nothing of twelve-mile-high cumulonimbus clouds. Enormous amounts of energy are released, as water vapour condenses then freezes inside the clouds; the resultant rising air currents swirl upwards to the tropopause. The wind sculpts the top of these clouds into an anvil, and then – well, all hell breaks loose. And that's not including the lightning. What people don't know is that the electrical charges are produced by collisions between ice crystals; the positive charge fixes itself at the top of the cloud, and the negative charge at the base. A positive 'shadow' charge builds up on the ground beneath, and an electric current is then discharged in a flash between ground and cloud. A weak spark known as the 'stepped leader' reaches down from the cloud, and a positive leader rises to meet it. The main discharge, which we call the 'return stroke', and what the rest of you dumb fucks call 'lightning', takes place from cloud to ground along the channel created by the two leaders. So there you have it – 55,000 degrees Fahrenheit, 186 miles per hour, and 1.5 million volts. When lightning hits a tree, it's not the violence of the blow, as it were, that causes it to split – it's the heat which instantaneously vaporises every molecule of fluid in the trunk and causes it to *explode*. Brilliant.

There were a couple of grandmothers in Brighton, a few schoolkids in on the South Downs, three couples out walking and a bunch of other people. I don't remember. I was too busy collating the data and drinking. I had predicted that storm down to the last breeze, more or less. God, that was a great night. That was a beautiful storm.

And the next day, the *Daily Mirror* is blathering on about 'tragedy' and 'chaos' and 'families torn apart' and various other slabs of crap, with their stupid, hackneyed pictures of trees ripped up and cars overturned. Christ, they just love that stuff. And, of course, there's always some 'hero' or other – some witless bonehead who's rescued a dog from 'the rising waters'.

Anyway, seventeen dead. No big deal. They should count themselves lucky.

Roy C. Williams, an American guy, was struck by lightning seven times over a period of thirty-five years, and escaped with minor injuries every time. But he was a nervous wreck at the end of it, and hardly left the house. He should have realised that his God loved him so, He wanted to mark him out as special target, as a sweet and ballistic lightning conductor for His fishy and excellent love . . . whatever. But he didn't. And died a broken man. In his bed.

But the thing that annoys me the most is that nobody ever just stands back and says 'Wow!' Nobody ever thanks their God for astounding them in such a fashion, for bruising and bristling their so-called faith, for bestowing upon them the gift of rage, the gift of a doubting tantrum, the gorgeous gift of svelte desperation. Nobody ever thanks their God for chugging them out of their gurning, gormless, starved and dreary little lives by sending them a big fuck-off *storm*, a huge and mesmeric monster, a hefty thing. Nobody ever thanks their God for killing them in the most elegant and truthful manner possible. Nobody ever thanks Him for that fanciful and ghostly thing called the weather. They all just whine.

Nobody ever takes the long view.

Except me.

And I warned the stupid fuckers to stay indoors.

On their heads be it.

Anyway, storms are the least of it. Storms are not, shall we say, subtle . . . there are a dozen ways in which the weather can take people out, and most of them are a lot less noisy.

No matter.

Hail. Now that's a different matter. I wasn't able to warn them about that because, well, it happened in Japan, and we haven't quite hooked up our systems with Kyoto, but, well, never mind. Seventy-three people dead, most of them clobbered on the head by hailstones the size of golf balls, and with pretty much the same killer density. Excellent stuff. Top of the anvil stuff. The wonderful thing about hailstones is that they don't just fall; they collect moisture as they fall, which freezes as they are carried back up to the top of the cloud on the upcurrent; they fall again, and this damn procedure is repeated over and over again, and each trip through the cloud adds a new layer of ice. Unfortunately, the hailstones eventually become so heavy that they have to fall to earth, otherwise that marvellous dance could go on for ever, up and down, just getting bigger and bigger and bigger . . . never mind. Seventy-three dead. That's something of a victory. If you look at it in a certain way. My way, that is. And all of them were out walking in the streets and in the parks – just walking around, like a bunch of dimwits, even when they were told, even when they were warned. But hail doesn't have to hit you on the head to kill you. Most bad (or rather, good) hailstorms occur in north-east India, where entire fields of crops can be devastated in minutes. So, a good hail can starve you to death, too. The best we ever got here in Britain was in 1959, in Wokingham.

Tennis ball-sized.

No casualties.

I was never able to explain any of this to my kids when they were growing up. They thought *snow* was cool. Snow. Jesus. Snow is bullshit. Snow is vulgar. Snow is a big, fluffy nothing of a thing. Snow covers the city and makes it pretty. Snow covers all the dogshit until the moment you walk it into your living-room carpet. Snow makes you believe that a great and paved and ruffling glaze can make all things beautiful. And then it melts. Then it turns every pavement into a brown and muddy sewer. It turns the city into a puny, brawling and oozing slut, a horrible and apologetic thing. Apologetic for having ever fooled you, for making you believe, just for a moment, that the world is a sturdy and elegant place.

I hate snow. Ordinary, domestic snow, that is.

Ice.

Now that's the ticket.

Ice is the thing.

Five years ago, I dragged my two kids, kicking and screaming, to Lapland. Christ, that's where Santa lives – you would think they'd have been ecstatic. But no, they just whined and bitched and complained about the cold. Never mind Santa; if I'm honest, it wasn't for them, it was for me. I didn't give a flying fuck about my kids and Santa. I just wanted to stay at the Ice Hotel in Jukkasjärvi, 200 kilometres north of the Arctic Circle. It's made of 3,000 tonnes of ice and 130,000 cubic metres of hard-packed snow. It has sixty rooms, an ice-screen cinema, its own art director, lasts for a few months and then, in April, just melts back into the Torne River, whence it came. The Torne is so clean, even the ice cubes in our vodka come from there. Anyway, that hotel is an engineering marvel. I loved it. The kids hated it. Their mother was off in Crete, lying on the beach, baking herself in the sun, which she did five times a year. I warned her about that.

Whatever.

So I parked the kids in the Ice Hotel kiddie crêche for three days and just enjoyed myself with the ice sculpture shows. I love those things. I've been to a dozen ice sculpture competitions over the years, and those damn things just get better and better. In '96, I attended the International Snow and Ice Sculpture Competition in Breckenridge, Colorado. Teams from ten countries had under three days to sculpt a twenty-tonne block, using chainsaws, pickaxes, blow-torches and huge hammers. I was drunk most of the time – everybody was, including the competitors – but Christ, it was gorgeous. The British were whimsical, the Swiss geometric, the French romantic and the Russians – well, the Russians were as mad as a box of frogs. But the Canadians won, with a twelve-foot-high abstract chestnut, symbolising . . . something or other. And one member of the Moroccan team was taken off to hospital with altitude sickness. We all enjoyed that one. (I like the Plymouth, Michigan competition too, but when the Japanese team used 200 two-tonne blocks to reproduce a scene from Disney's *Aladdin* last year – well, that kind of ruined it for me . . .)

So there it was. The perfect marriage of form and substance. Big, terrifying monsters that melted before our very eyes under the warmth of a beautiful and radiant sunrise. It was truly magical. It reminded me, as if I needed reminding, that nature can build us up and it can tear us down. It can build and destroy and rebuild itself. It doesn't even really need us at all. We are just passing through an unwinnable and unrepentant vortex of power. We are nothing.

And then, of course, I get back to London and every damn BBC party has ice sculptures. Swans and eagles and pumpkin heads and miniature polar bears like the ones out of that fucking Coke advert, and dinky little swans and doves, and 'ice-cube men' and some hopeless, happy couple's initials. And some effete 'artiste' swanning about like a big queen, tweaking and preening his 'creation' with a fucking nail file and a pair of tweezers, and bowing to his adoring bunch of C-list celebrity pals. Like he's a real artist. Well, just because he's 'created' an open clam shell for Madonna, Michelangelo's 'David' for Julia Roberts, two-foot Grecian urns on plinths for Elton John and a mini-Pegasus for the bloody Queen, does not make him an artist. He thinks he's in charge. Well, he's not. When his kit melts, all that is left is a bunch of drunken bimbos and bruised egos, crazed paparazzi, a few crotch shots and another week's worth of material for *heat* magazine.

Christ on a crutch. That's the problem with us and beauty. Before it gets out there, a thing of beauty has to pass through the hands of snobs and philistines who, between the pair of them, are capable of destroying anything.

Anyway, I had a good time in Lapland; I really didn't want to come home. Pity the kids never got to see Santa. I was never actually so cruel as to tell them straight out, but they could probably tell from my general demeanour that Santa doesn't exist. Ah well. They have to grow up sometime; it might as well be now. That was last April. They live with their mother now. The sun worshipper. Sand worshipper.

Remember that song '(Everybody's Free To Wear) Sunscreen?' The one by Baz Luhrmann? I always liked that one. And not because it doled out a bunch of dumb platitudes to a bunch of (probably even dumber) high-school graduates, but because the first and last lines were the best thing about it. Wear sunscreen. Simple as that. (And FYI, that lovely, stentorian voice isn't Baz Luhrmann's either – it's some poor, underpaid American sap called Lee Perry.)

Wear sunscreen. As high a factor as you can get it. I've been saying this for years, but the only people who listen, and nod, are Australians. They know about these things. Germaine Greer was on a chat show, this one time, and she told the story about how she and all her girlfriends would cut out the letters of their boyfriends' names in paper, and lay them on their bellies as they baked in the sun. A melanoma named *Bruce*. Nowadays, every expat Aussie with an ounce of sense dives for the sunblock and the shades at the first hint of sun. But not us Brits. No, we just lie there, loving every lovely, vile and vicious ray, adoring that unholy chorus of light and warmth and, ultimately, death.

But I do like sand. Not in and of itself, of course – it's just pulverised rock and coral – but I like it when the professionals get to work. Rather like the ice sculpture competitions. Two years ago, I took my daughter to Hardelot, a coastal town near Boulogne, where they hold an annual sand sculpture competition. (As you will have gathered, I like these things.) My son refused to come and his mother refused to force him. His loss. Her loss. It was great. My daughter wasn't allowed onto the beach while the professionals were working, obviously, but once I'd explained it to her, I think she took it rather well. After she'd stopped crying and whining like a bloody banshee. But the competition was great. It started off as a numpty local council idea and evolved into a permanent part of the tourist calendar, as much by accident as by design. Well, whatever – good for them. That year, there were ten artists, from Scotland to Singapore, in competition for a lousy £3000 prize. Each one was given one week and 750 wheelbarrows full of special sand shipped over from Belgium. I know. Belgium. Go figure.

Apparently, Belgian sand has the innate advantage of youth, not having been rolled into spheres by countless years of countless waves; under the microscope each grain is a perfect little cube. In other words, working with ordinary beach sand is like trying to arrange a pyramid of marbles, but Belgian sand stacks up like a million tiny bricks. Each artist compacts the sand into a forty-foot-high triangular pile and then chips away from the top down, using spades, chisels, knives and pokers. One guy created a representation of Poseidon, another Aesop's hare and tortoise, and yet another Ariel, the Little Mermaid (what is it with these people and Walt Disney?). Well, it was a great day out. It reminded me of the old story of the Golden Sands of Pactolus, the small river in Lydia, Asia Minor (does anyone even use the term *Asia Minor* any more?), which was famous for the amount of gold in it. Midas bathed there apparently . . . My daughter ran through the judges' barrier when the whole thing was being judged, and I had to smack her on the arse for that. She said later, when she'd stopped crying, that Ariel's fish scales felt as hard as rock. She didn't like that one bit. And she didn't like it when I wouldn't let her lie in the sun. She was only seven. I wasn't going to let her burn like that. If I can do anything, I can do that. She hated me for that. I don't care. I'm not so stupid as to defy the sun. People just don't get it.

They don't get the power of the sun. It's 'nice'. It's 'pleasant'. 'It's a nice day,' they say. They have lost every iota of mythology. Trust me, we were all a lot better off when we worshipped something we can see with our own eyes, when an eclipse really seemed like the end of the world, when crops lived or died according to what the sun was doing. When we lived or died. The Assyrians and the Babylonians had *Shamash*, the Persians had *Mithras*, the Aztecs had *Tezcatlipoca* (*Smoking Mirror*), the Egyptians had *Ra*, the Romans had *Phoebus* and the Greeks had *Helios*. They had fear and quivering terror and endless gratitude for the swollen power of their god; they had the cannibalism of the fan, they had serious applause in the night, they prostrated themselves, joyfully, before the flip and frazzled grandeur that was their bitch of a god. They had a panic and yelping adoration that filled the trajectory of their very existence.

They had a life.

And what do we have?

We have traffic jams to Brighton every Bank Holiday. And skin cancer.

Their mother died last year. Her father didn't want me at the funeral. I don't know if that was because he never liked me in the first place, or if it was I had been badgering the stupid bitch to stop sunbathing so much. Either way, I did show up, and hovered around on the edges of the cemetery, trying not to be noticed. I don't know why I even bothered to put on a proper black suit. My kids were being held by their grandmother, in a vice-like grip that wasn't entirely comfortable. They were squirming and crying and trying to get away from her.

It was a really cold day. The mourners were gathered around in a miserable, hunched, bunched circle. I recognised about a third of them. I could only hear snatches of the service, depending on which way the wind was blowing. The priest's voice was a thin and reedy thing, a thin and soft and ineffectual growl, a thing of reasonable pallor. The kind of voice, the kind of kindly drone, I suppose, that comforts the uncomfortable.

The wind. I once tried to teach my kids about the different winds – the Arctic, the Anatole, the Hesperie, the Cryere, the Mesembrine, the Galerene and the Sirocco, the Besch and the Garbino; all those magical words and ways – but she stopped me, partly because I was boring them, but mainly because she hated my job.

Mainly because she hated me.

I don't know why I went to the funeral. That marriage was over long before it was over. Nobody wanted me there. Maybe that's why I went. To see if anybody would see me. To see if anybody would see me and come charging after me. Nobody did. I mean, they saw me, but then they just filed past me, in a dull, black-coated and resentful line.

Nobody even paid me the compliment of flinging a few choice insults in my general direction. Even the kids ignored me.

It was as if I was invisible.

I *told* her about sunscreen. I bloody well *told* her. I even played that fucking song to her. Ten times a day. Thinking the woman could take a hint.

But by that stage, everything I said – well, she would just do the opposite.

More fool her.

Damn.

Anyway, I just went back to work. The kids live with their grandparents now. I thought about trying to get custody.

But I realised that I didn't have a chance in hell of winning.

I realised that they were probably better off with their granny and grampa.

I realised that I was scared about sacrificing my career.

I realised that I didn't actually didn't give a dead dingo's kidneys about my kids.

Fair enough.

No point in being a hypocrite about these things.

So I just went back to work. As television's best-known weatherman.

Sometimes, in the middle of all the cheesy bullshit, I try to inject an element of realism into the proceedings. Sometimes, in the middle of the ordinary, everyday, bullshit-type weather – the kind of weather that requires nothing more than an umbrella and an expression of polite forebearance – I try to make people aware of what *exactly* is going on around them, even though they don't know it.

I try to slip in a few things about what goes on, for example, at sea.

If people knew what goes on at sea, they sure as fuck wouldn't be whinging about a little shower, dampening their brows and spotting their shoes, while they're out shopping for their organic whatnots at Sainsbury's.

Cretins.

Now, out at sea . . . well, that's a different matter.

In my first year with the BBC, I did a little moonlighting on Radio 4 for the Shipping Forecast. That was fun. I mean, it was hard work. I wasn't reading the stuff, just putting it together – I don't have the voice for radio; I'm just about pretty enough to be on television, but it was good solid work, and it was nice to be in daily contact with my old friends at the Met Office.

Anyway, there was a mistake one day and, after a couple of hasty, nasty meetings, they decided to put me on the telly full-time. I think they were just covering their arses, rather than punishing me. There was nothing to punish. It wasn't my fault.

It was just a breakdown in communications. Besides, it isn't as if a job on telly is exactly a step down. Well, I don't think so. OK, it's not exactly brain surgery, but it's easy work and well paid. If I don't have to use my brain, then so much the better.

But the sea. That's a bugger. People have no idea what goes on out there. They have no idea what it's like to be out in a trawler in a Force-10 storm, just so that they can have their fish-fingers on a Friday. Christ, most people don't even know how big a fully grown cod is; they probably think it's the size of a fish-finger, when it is, *in fact*, the size of a fucking coffee table.

The biggest recorded wave in history measured 112 feet in height.

Not on my watch, thank God.

I probably would have just lied about it, gone home and gotten heinously drunk.

But that's the great thing about the sea. If some awful disaster happens, the evidence disappears. It's not like an earthquake in Turkey; there are no interesting heaps of rubble to poke through. There are no teams of aid workers and sniffer dogs and no makeshift refugee towns of tents, no photogenic kids and their grandparents weeping and wailing for the cameras, no clouds of dust and flies and dirt and bad sanitation, no reporters doing their 'noddies', no nothing. Nothing but the calm blue and utterly flat sea, once the hurricane has disappeared. All evidence is gone, gone, pulverised and drowned. And that's the great thing about hurricanes. They devastate low-lying coastlines with four-metre waves, but on the lee side of the eye, the sea level actually falls because of the blow-back winds. So your pleasure boat can be left high and dry, while your cousin's house, forty miles away, is floating in the Pacific.

Great stuff.

Don't get me started on tornadoes. They're just cartoon things. Picking up cows and barns and shit. Too many movies. No, the sea is the place to be. The sea is where it began and the sea is where it will end. People ask me about climate change. Sure, deforestation and whitened coral and desertification have something to do with it. A bit. But when the end comes, it will come from the sea. The glaciers are dripping water. Is there a worse sight than that? Glaciers dripping fucking water. They're supposed to be ice harder than rock. By the time all the earthbound problems become *real* problems, it won't matter, because we'll all be under twenty feet of water.

Result.

I don't know why, but I really like that idea.

At least, when we go, we'll all be cleaner than the day we were born.

But folk just don't appreciate the horrors that can come from the sea. They think of seaside holidays. They think of sand (in its mundane and spherically grained sense), sun (in its fat, carnal and beatific sense), water (in its softly swaggering, staggering sense), and breeze (in its slovenly, unfussy, alchemical sense). They never think about Venice, the sea-born city, or England, the sea-girt Isle, or the Euxine Sea, or the Bride of the Sea, or Sea-green Incorruptible, or anything else. It's just water. The same thing that comes out of our taps, filled with chlorine and various other chemicals.

They never think about the gods of the sea.

They never think about the Nereids, the Sirens, the Oceanids; they never think about Amphitrite or Glaucus or Tethys or Portumnus or Nereus or Leucothea or Triton. I don't believe in a main and mighty God, but I believe in lots of minor gods, and it really pisses me off that most people don't. They expend all their synaptic, hi-hat energy in prostrating themselves in front of some seemingly wrathful, ingeniously bitchy and yet imbecilic Almighty. A paean to numbness, dull and shabby. And they ignore the little ones. The important ones. The ones that bestow upon us something a little chill, something lacerating, sublime and tangled, something melancholy, terse and sensible.

The small deities that allow us to be calm and perplexed and joyful . . .

The gods of the earth. The gods of the weather itself.

Well, I haven't seen my kids since. But that's OK. I was never the best parent in the world. I never pretended to be. I brought home the bacon.

But sometimes, sometimes, I get so weary. Sometimes, I'm lying in bed and I can't get those pictures out of my head. The sight of her coffin being lowered into the ground. The sight of my kids averting their eyes from mine. That horrible, deadpan crunch of avoidance. That look of pouty, tearful spite; a look that said that they didn't need me any more, that they had never needed me, a look of flushed stalemate, a swerving glance that said that a haphazard and hokey hatred wasn't the worst thing that could happen to a poor and immaculate bastard like me.

OK, so I made a couple of mistakes. So I fucked up. So the Shipping Forecast thing went a little west. I misread a few figures and, well, a trawler got into some difficulties. A couple of young men died. But they knew what the risks were. Christ, those guys were pulling down over a thousand pounds a week. Not that I'm saying it was their fault. It wasn't. I don't mean that the way it sounded. It's just that everybody in that business knows what could happen out there. These things happen at sea. Worse things happen at sea. I don't know what happened. I was kind of new at it, and I guess I wasn't paying attention to the figures.

Anyway, I gave out the wrong details. I made a mistake. But that doesn't make it my fault.

Bad weather is everywhere; if they'd avoided that storm, and taken the right precautions, they just would have run into another bloody storm, probably an even worse one, a few days down the line. It's just a matter of time, and luck, out there.

Anyway, I'm not working at the moment. I mean, I'm still on contract with the BBC, but they're a little skittish about having my mug on the telly, what with me being out on bail at the moment. I'm doing some gardening, reading a lot of books, watching re-runs of *Cheers* and *Frasier* and *Friends*, and just generally lounging about. I got away with the Shipping Forecast thing. I don't mean 'got away with', because it wasn't exactly anybody's fault, but the kid . . . well, I guess that's a different matter. It was three weeks ago. I'd only had four beers, so that wasn't the thing. It's just that I'd run out of milk. And cigarettes. It was pissing down, and I could tell, just from the sky, that a storm was on the way. I like technology – I like it, but I'm experienced enough to be able to get by without it. I'm able, if I'm forced, to use the evidence of my own eyes. I don't need charts and printouts to tell me what's happening on the Beaufort Scale.

I need only to sniff the air and get a good gander at the horizon to be able to tell whether it's going to be a Force 8 (that's 43 to 51 knots), or a Force 9 (52 to 60 knots), or a Force 10 (61 to 68 knots), or a Force 11 ('Violent' – 69 knots or more), or a Force 12 ('Hurricane' – you don't want to know). I can tell if what's coming is 'imminent' (within 6 hours), or 'soon' (between 6 and 12 hours), or 'later' (more than 12 hours), just by using my eyes and my nose.

I can tell whether the weather coming up is going to be a little, cheeky guttersnipe of a thing, or a brassy, beautiful saviour, a superfly graphic that tales your day from a gibberingly rubbish heap into the realm of redemption, where you feel more kindly towards your fellow man than you normally would, and more kindly towards yourself than you ever, ever should. I can smell a meat-'n'-two-veg calamity on its way, and a soft breeze after the wreckage of that; I know when the sun, or the wind, or the frost, or the rain is going to be a piece of polite twaddle, or an addled spring-heel of a creature, or an absolute and banging bastard.

It's a process of osmosis.

I can feel it on my skin.

I know the weather.

I know the weather better than I know the inside of my own mouth.

But I needed some cigarettes. It was a bad storm. But I needed cigarettes. And some milk.

I was only doing about 40 m.p.h., but that was enough to tumble that stupid child into the grille, onto the bonnet, flush into the windscreen, over the roof and into the air, just like a little broken bird. It was strangely beautiful. His limbs went all akimbo, and when he hit the ground – I saw him in my rear-view mirror – it was with a soft implosion, as if every bone in his body was broken. Which, pretty much, every one was.

But at least he was dead before he hit the ground.

So that was a blessing.

At the very least.

That one was my fault. That one I can claim as my own.

I read books, these days, and watch television, and don't do a great deal of anything else.

I saw the weather coming.

I knew what it was going to be like.

But I ignored all that and got in my car anyway.

So there you have it.

Sometimes, I wish I had stayed at the Meteorological Office. Sometimes I wish I had just stayed a humble civil servant. Right there, in Bracknell, Berkshire.

Sometimes, at night, I think about the kid. But I think about the fishermen more often. That Shipping Forecast was a poem, a sweet and evangelical mantra. I guess I just fell in love.

I guess I just got carried away with the names, the sheer bloody poetry of those place names – *Tiree, Butt of Lewis, Sunburgh, Fife Ness, Greenwich Light Vessel Automatic, Valentia, Ronaldsway, Malin Head, Scilly Automatic* – and that was just the observation stations. By the time I got to the forecasts for the coastal sea areas – *Viking, North Utsire, South Utsire, Forties, Cromarty, Forth, Tyne, Dogger, German Bight, Humber, Thames, Dover, Wight, Portland, Plymouth, Biscay, Trafalgar, Finisterre,*

Sole, Lundy, Fastnet, and all the bloody rest of them – well, I barely knew what I was saying.

I wasn't even thinking straight.

No wonder the figures swam before my eyes.

It was poetry that did for me

It was poetry that did for those sailors.

And the child?

It was a moment of carelessness that did for him.

Just a gentle and unholy dynamic that no one could have predicted.

Well, you can't predict everything, can you?

P.S. I've just remembered – that sea coastal area isn't called Finisterre any more. It's been renamed. The Met Office has renamed it Fitzroy. They named it after Captain (later Admiral) Robert Fitzroy, the Captain of HMS *Beagle. He took Darwin to the Galapagos Islands and beyond. He was a very devout man. He suffered the torments of hell for years afterwards, because he believed himself to be responsible for introducing the ghastly gospel of evolution to the world.*

Evolution.

The thing that shook the religious world to its very core.

He believed himself to be an insult unto God and the unwitting instrument of the Devil.

Fitzroy was a good, conscientious and intelligent man.

He was a good man.

In 1837, he was awarded the Gold Medal by the Royal Geographical Society.

In 1841, he became an MP, and in 1842, the Conservator for Merseyside.

In 1843, he became the only Governor of New Zealand who took any notice of Maori rights.

In 1854, he became the first director of the Meteorological Service (now known as the Meteorological Office).

In 1865, he committed suicide by slitting his own throat.

I suppose God just got the better of him.

Faithless-heart

CÓILÍN Ó HAODHA

He could never remember exactly when he had fallen in love with the ghost that lived in the shadow on the half-landing of the second stairs. The attic stairs, where a bare bulb hung on a long flex from the high ceiling. And though it was real love as far as he could tell, it wasn't love at first sight. Not then. It would be a long time yet before a bulb swung or there could be eye-love and self-conscious hands would shake, and it was even before you knew what you could do with any of them.

It was still in the age of hands busy to distraction: the right one holding a frightened candle in a chipped, handleless mug, and the left cupped close to protect it by screening off the dark from its aghast look. Just at the end of the time, the nights, his mother sat in the dark at his side and told him a favourite story of the girl with different coloured eyes. One blue and one green, or one green, one brown: one any colour, and one always green. The eyes of a girl who would take his hand softly in her softer one and smell of flowers, swing him up behind her on a horse, behind her fire-hair, and take him away with her, from her, to a place from where he wouldn't want to come back. Because he would be so happy there, with her. And, falling voice, sleep falling, she would be so sad, *do you know that, son?*, without him there. It was the time for asking questions just like that, and like if you knew *what colour are my eyes*. Asked innocently, without checking or minding if he looked. He didn't, hadn't first, and when he did it was difficult to decide. So in the end he said they were just the same as far as he could tell. Not different, just the same. And she smiled at that.

And not long after, it was the time for knowing better his mother said, about what had gone before is what she meant. About whatever might come ahead as well. But that was him putting words in her mouth and making her say things like *clever-clogs* or *be careful, you'll get a swelled head* or *son, you've got a lot to learn yet*. She never spoke them harshly but exhaled them in such a small tight voice that there was always room for a doubt or two to seep out into his stunned breath and settle there on the edge of her quiet thoughts, in the short air between them.

And it didn't matter to him that when he told her about his first love, the one who lived in the moving shade, that she had said it was all in his head. That it was all nothing more than a fickle candle spreading a lie through the corner-banister of the stairs and painting it on the wall, blinding his eyes from seeing or, really, hearing that the noises breaking in the early night as he made his way up to bed were nothing more than his own feet landing on the steps, and taking off again. He knew, knew, there was a ghost there. And he got to know her – since she was definitely a girl, the girl she had told him would one day come, the girl he had to wait for now alone. He got to know her a whole lot better all through a year, until the fateful day he had woken up suddenly but fully, and caught sight of the vacant corner on his way down to the kitchen and remembered for just how long it was he had forgotten her. And she, he supposed later, musing over a half-glass of foggy water and watching the chickens wake, she must have thought he didn't love her any more, and gone away. *No way.*

Nothing could have been further from the truth of it. The fact that she always curled back to the edge of a flame when it nudged closer, just out of sight, or that her voice sounded a bit like the blind on the small landing-window clipping the frame in winter, like an invisible bird hidden and singing in the tall trees in summer: all of that could not shake his faith. Nor was the suggestion, that the moan which slipped out from under the attic-door on wet days was just some wind being trapped in the eave-gaps or the wall-spaces and feeling sore, a good enough explanation for him. Not enough to convince him that she wasn't sad about something (and that was probably about the way most people didn't think she was there), or crying for something that was really missed, presumed dead: long hair, a brightly patterned dress, someone, some boy, to call a friend? There had to be something more to it for him. And it was her. And her only for him as well.

It was a long way back from the red-cheeks of his embarrassed forget-fulness to how cold he had felt the day he decided to follow through on his long-considered plan, and catch her unawares. He was sure that if he had met himself in a mirror then, he would have been the thin blue shape in the middle of a patch of unpainted walls, shivering into a blur in the evening-light of half-five on a February day. In socks, so as to make no noise, and holding the key that had been so under-used it had begun to think of rust, holding it tight against his trouser-leg, he crept up the last six steps on the attic-stairs. And when the slanted door swung in, there wasn't a sound. *She hadn't heard him then?* Tracking because he had the nose for it: the smell of dry-rot, husks of mouse-droppings and sweat: thinking of definite foot-prints and wide-eyes and wet-back shuddering.

What he thought of first as laughter quickly dissolved itself back into the pumped wash in the water-tank, and the mumbling might have been whatever had managed to float its way up through a ceiling from downstairs. But he found nothing feeling around in the dark with shy hands, over the loose tops and split sides of stacked boxes, or on the rough surface of cross-beams under his feet which he placed firmly but carefully everywhere. Nothing until he was sitting in the corner, facing into the widening line of light cutting across from the open door with his back growing colder against the gable-wall, when he put his hand down into the yellow insulation he had helped to lay and found a piece of paper rubbing against his fingers and crinkling as if to say: *this is what you're looking for*. Then came the hurried thudding back to the door and the breathlessness (both of which he had to deny boldly to his mother later on), back into the last of spring-light to see what was there: a photograph – young girl, bright dress, long hair. And a smile to say all the rest, what wasn't shown there. He knew she had left it for him to stumble over, in the one place he couldn't miss. And when it turned warm in his shaking hands, his sharpened breath, he thought of it as a kiss.

By now, by the time the hens had shaken themselves awake and were pecking hopefully at frost-thaw earth for scraps, an empty glass swinging loosely in his hand, by then, he was laughing at himself. Kiss: his mouth made the shape naturally at the sound of it: kiss. And laughing turned his cheeks red again, the cheeks he had to, had to now, shave every second day. Something in the roll and drop of a solitary laugh (a little nervous, perhaps?), reminded him of the way she laughed, and more, of the last day she had laughed that way. She found the photograph bent over the left-shoulder of the bed-frame, where it had slipped down from its pride-of-place under a feather-pillow and the corner of an eiderdown. And laughing, tucked the split ends of her greying hair under the collar of her cardigan and tried a smile and flushed then. When he had, he thought, stammered all the way from a rushed denial into an ignorance that was almost strong enough to convince himself he waited for what she was going to say. Waited, and was taken completely by surprise by the quiet which was broken only by breaths made difficult. Made difficult by what? Then, even the son of such a mother, who told him much more often now how much he had to learn, could see that she was preening and blushing furiously at an image in a mirror of her younger self. And he was old enough now, the sound of a glass smashing on the cold ground fracturing his thoughts, old enough to know that red could also be the colour of shame. *No way.*

There was nothing to be ashamed about in it. Even later, when he knew the story had become another classic, another favourite, he didn't blush. Not when he thought of it himself nor when the woman, who he barely recognised and who had was-it? three children now, skipped through it quickly for him in the shop. The story about how a son could be blown or thrown away from a father's heart and head. Feel himself flying through the air, wind-rush on his face, from the kind of father who would grunt once for disapproval and twice to say he'd have a hot drop of tea. *Don't you answer your mother back.* And only much later, coming to himself again, in the nick of time to catch himself from falling into his mother's arms and staying there for ever, or at least until they were stripped bare and melted away. And though all those elements were swirling in the kitchen with a floor of broken glass and a window that looked out onto a decrepit yard, a wild hedge: a wordless father and a laughing mother and someone who felt very like himself: all of it there, he was just as sure that the story wasn't theirs; and hoped desperately that it wasn't his.

For one thing, he had been so young: young enough not to be bothered by feeling her hand on his head and ruffling his hair when he hunched over the good table, a mat spread under, hurriedly doing his homework in the front-room just off the foot of the stairs. Young enough not to have to worry that the turned-in end of the curtain was hiding a class-mate, a school-friend, who might be drinking in this act of terrible affection with greedy eyes and running off with a swollen mouth to tell the others just what he had seen, that *she still and he still did she? kissed him did he? and kissed her*, before lifting the latch on the hall-door and making a break through scattered rain for the school gate. That all came later. Like now, coaxing the last pieces of the glass into a dust-pan with a small-handled brush that had been chewed away by rough tiles, like then, he was back to kissing again. And, calmer now, or being older, he was no longer ashamed.

And for another thing, it wasn't real love, no matter what age you were when you thought about it: not the grabbing hands of a girl with one green and always different coloured eyes; not the grace of the ghost's movements floating around for a year; not the eye-love from the girl with no-matter-at-all hair and dress who came much further away and much later on.

Still, it had been frightening to be kissed good-bye by a mother who didn't seem to notice, or want to notice, that you were getting old enough now to be in a real love all on your own. Like the love he felt, he gave, looking out through a bedroom door left only slightly ajar and hearing his head-hummed serenade to a girl he didn't know very well being answered by an applause that sounded like the gentle drumming of rain on the stairwell window. The sound that could just as easily have been dried, pressed petals rattling onto the floor in the dark, cast down from a balcony hidden somewhere high up there. But she never understood how big he'd grown up then, and never could, he thought. Big enough to make her shrink before his eyes, with longer arms, strong enough to hold her at the end of them.

None of it was ever enough though: arms tiring and cramping with the strain of asking questions in the guessing-game of his father's mutterings, and trying to get away from her as he got older and she got smaller, more vulnerable, and clinging to him: to save her from the passing years, the what-would-happen-then, and what would happen them. *Don't leave. Stay here – if you try, you will find your other heart and be happy just here.* To save her, when he couldn't save himself? He had to leave them, her, him, then. *Don't ever answer your mother back like that.* But not before he had spent day after day – six years, if you counted them – searching in a playground, classroom, study hall, for the hand that might have cast petals with the grace of light rain falling, a face which, even turned away and around the corner of his eyes, was smiling at him. A hand that would have his, take his. A face that would have the word *kiss* written all over it.

And after six years of forgetfulness, the ghost moved back in with the sound of breaking glass, of a bulb bobbing on the end of a long flex. Everyday, in every double-edged smile one of the girls from school might flash at him, or in the pleading look his mother wore now, day in, day out, like a faded dress worn out, her power grew darker over him. Until he didn't think his arms could hold out any more. Until she had become so substantial that every creak in the ceiling on a calm night became a threat: *You will never find me if you stay here.* Until she literally weighed upon his mind, and once there, sat and laughed. Laughed even when his mother said *don't leave, don't leave us to go dumb and blind and deaf altogether, like this, all together* – and he couldn't think of anything to say back.

And there was no going back the day he left. It was as simple as that, or so he would be able to think for a long time yet. Left the very same day she told him that he was the only thing that she really cared about any more. Left without a kiss at the front-door. And without one look back at a wordless, dismissive wave or the fountain of tears that rolled onto the porch-step. Without his usual blank-face, know-nothing smile for the girl-next-door who leaned over the gate and demanded to know *where he thought he was going off to with his bags packed?* And he went without one thought for the ghost that lived on the attic-stairs and who, from the very beginning, with the promise she had made to him of a one-true-love with different coloured eyes, had been the cause of all of it.

But no matter how far away he went the shadow stayed. As it had always done. From the time of its first stirrings in a slightly scared candle making its way, one step clipped after another, up the stairs. And all the time when the ghost had gone away, it was there, painted into the bare corner of the wall that blocked his sight every morning on the way out his bedroom door. Even when she was gone. Right through to the time when a glass, empty of a dry-mouth morning water, was let drop and crack itself up. And to the day a bulb was let fall from a workman's hand and fall jerkily until it snapped taut at the end of the long cord, and blink in shock for a moment till it had gathered enough composure from the new electric hum to just hold light.

And away into the future, much later on, when he knelt on the cracked plinth of their twin grave and felt in every bump of gravel-clay, heard in every tough weed bursting weakly through for air, the sound of her voice telling him that he had a lot to learn yet by the look of him.

The long look she took of him from the place where she was sitting then. A shadow spread even when she was gone, and plastic petals rotted patiently on her face (old and young), his closed mouth, her hands, his turned head, her laughter-lips. Telling him *have I ever told you this? –* if once, one thousand times – *your father and I, we, fell and stayed in love here. Here, in this very house.* She wouldn't let up. Not even when he beat down on their shared gravestone with his bare fists and shouted *I know it all now* for anyone who might be close enough to hear. Or just far enough to swerve quickly and begin to walk the other way. But he was the one who had to turn away unanswered, not even with a grunt, and slouch-walk out towards the road to hide the tears that galloped down his face: not tears of grief, and only tears of rage. *Don't leave, son.* He left, and the graveyard gate slammed closed, and swung open. Waiting for him to come on back in again. Back in out of the rain.

But, at the very least (if this was the only comfort for the dying years, so be it), at least, he had gone away. To all the countries where the sun shone as a matter of its course, as a matter of a country's pride. No rain to fall and play a game called havoc with your heart. And, being careful and watching where you placed a foot, you could see the shadows lying and spreading from far enough away to avoid them all. Moving from front-to-back-to-front in his mind all the time was the thought that he might just find her, somewhere out here. Thinking and grinning to himself at odd moments when he thought no one was looking at him. And this was the man, the grown boy, who didn't need to be reminded that one false step, a trip stopped before the fall began or ended, could bite his tongue and turn a grin into a grimace with a curse. And once his lip let something like that slip – *damn! –* then she might have enough time to run away and hide from him. *Damn it all.*

After all the days-after-days, it came from nowhere, the day a threat was carried out: *you'll never find me if you stay here.* Not from the sun-spin regular as clocks, nor from a page flipped over calmly in the book of life. The girl darted right across an empty room before his very eyes, eyes she pierced through once as effortless as smoke, and as stinging, and stuck. And once in, settled herself for the longer or shorter wait on the nerves in his head. It didn't matter that she had decided to do this in a country far-flung under the sun and in a restaurant that was too busy disgorging itself of evening trade to notice that anything else was happening there. Especially not anything as mind-boggling as this. And nothing that had gone before mattered any more to him:

the leave-taking of which he couldn't, wouldn't think or wandering stranger-streets in search of work or hearing old trains rattle uncertainly homewards, past dirty windows in his first lodgings near a park. Nor did it matter that he never knew her name. But when he added it all up: her colour, the way she did her hair and her bright dress, her father and her mother and her husband and her faith: all that was left was a sum total that said she could never be his. And placing it on well-tuned mental scales, she swung up. There was no way of balancing it with his sense of fate.

And then nothing mattered but the smile she gave, no wave, as he made for the door – last out as usual – and for the small bar at the end of the only village road. And no laughter, just a small crease on her cheek when her lip moved up, pointed out the arrow-eyes that were fixed on him and looking in such a way as if to say he was the only thing that mattered to her then. Or anymore. Nothing mattered but the colours of her eyes: blue and green and brown and grey. As if to say to him: *don't leave.* And though he had to, he left a little lighter, holding the memory of her quivering on the back of his eyes: sharp-pointed, with the feel of feathers. It was just his luck that, as he was stepping over the thin beam stretched across the base of the door to keep a flood or a stray animal out, his mind tripped and his body stumbled and she had rushed to right him. Held his elbow with her right hand, her left hand was full of flowers, and set his hat back onto his ruffled hair. And it was just more luck when she had to say good-bye and he heard the word that meant it lick her foreign tongue and lips, the sound escaping exactly like a kiss.

She sank in straight away, tingling down his spine from his head and shooting through tight lungs on her way to his heart. And once there, she drove everything else out: a girl laughing in the attic in the frozen and moaning dark, a mother wearing a hungry look like an old dress, begging for just one more stitch to hold it all together over thinning arms and a melting waist. For ages after that, he thought of her, their meeting at the store-front last thing on an ordinary night: the ignorant walk he'd taken up a clay, stony hill, leaning into the dusky restaurant lit by an oil-hiss and warmed by candles flickering, eating food unknowing, food she might have prepared for him. And then paying, a tip dropped carelessly onto the dirty table-cloth; the movement of her taut face, across the room it came again like a bow pulled tight, the point of snapping in. And falling into flowers, handfuls of them.

But it was never going to last, it was never even going to start, as he watched the sun go down with a merciless glory for such an ordinary evening. It was never meant to, bitterness had taught him that. And it never did – *Life is the great teacher, son. Remember that.* And who is it that teaches bitterness: how to turn talking into stalking, words following and following and never letting up? *And never answer back.* Again, no answering. She was dead, and he was dead before her, before the question had even occurred to him as good enough to ask.

If it was over before any of it had begun, it was his own fault for wearing her out by running it all through his head, over and over. He wanted to be back like a shot to the look in her eyes. The difference of them. But it didn't matter if he took a whole stretch out of the dark road winding in his head or cut every possible corner on the rocky path from the pub to a dim-lit restaurant door, he never got there soon enough. And if a finger touched a finger in light leaking from an oil-lamp to form a warm pool, and if a breeze swept silk-soft in through an open door on a quietening night, it was just a story told about someone who sometimes looked like him – a story ghost-written by himself. Sunrise, sunset hot day, cold night: it went on. Went on and on until he decided to go back home, battle-worn and sore, and settle who was right and who was wrong, for once and for all.

He turned his head to look over his shoulder at the curl in the high road, just where it became all excited and scattered stones at the thought of the long free-wheel just around the bend. He could have let his breath be taken away by the view of the valley-floor perfectly arrayed and ready for summer. He would have let it go, if it hadn't already been taken hostage and cut up by a steep climb and thinner air banded together. Breaths made difficult by the thought that maybe she had been right about forgetting everything that went before, that maybe eye-love wasn't something that you searched for shyly and uncertain and then found by accident in the dark. Maybe it was something that you had, or didn't have. Maybe, and this was bitter now, maybe it was something that you lost. *Remember that.* Was that what she meant? – that things weren't always as they looked and sometimes you just had to grin and bear it, or just laugh? He turned to go, not seeing in the midday cloud-rollover someone skipping pages in the book of life to find out what happened in the end. And faster lightning-teeth with lips cutting both ways out, flashing a smile for him.

Jolting over the crest of another hill, he looked down on everything. On a village dropping from a height and scattering all over uneven ground, just to stake a patch; on trees, houses, streetlamps, stuck-up and whitened, waiting for night to settle in the middle of a winter afternoon. His knuckles whitened on the bar of the seat in front of him and held back his reply when an old woman leaned over his shoulder and said: *you're the one who went away and wears a beard now, coming back.* And later, whispering into the back of the bus where other ears leaned out (and not for his): *he broke his mother's heart, going away and never writing like that.*

But her heart was beating steadily, a little fast, when he swung down off the last step over a puddle of rainbows to the stop, and was wrapped suddenly in her arms. Arms wrapped in cold, black wool. *See, the black sheep is home. It always happens. And they always take them back.* He stayed there long enough for her to say *lamb* in her wet cheeks and bright eyes for every one to see. He stayed there for her sake, didn't he? to shield her bodily from the conspiracies that were gathering in small broods, finding reasons to hang around and watch them meet each other after the unwritten years apart: a frayed thread, a loosening button, to sort a bag or check the time, anything.

He wasn't sure the kitchen-clock was right, that it was half-five to the clicked wheeze of broken chimes, because he heard no door-opening or foot-stamping or coat-hanging or smothered cough. But he wasn't ever coming home now. She had told him that right after a burst of cold rain had taken pity, stopped the play and cleared the crowd away out of that: that he had died a few months back. A heart attack and peacefully, without a sound. So while she was tearing rashers one from another with a twisted fork and reminding herself in a low voice that *he'd be needing the two eggs and not one*, he was wondering about how quiet the house had become. Without him there.

And it was as if he wasn't, not there, the way things went their daily round, the round she was swept into from the moment she felt the fading carpet under her feet until she lifted them slowly and swung them in, struggling with a blanket and hoping they'd be warm. *Keep warm, there are plenty more blankets in the hot press.* As if he didn't know. Things went on like that. Except now, of course, she had an arm to lean on. Something to squeeze if an innocent, neighbourly remark cut too close to the bone, *oh! he's back – I didn't know you there*, or she needed to steady herself and catch her breath halfway in, halfway back, with her free hand.

In the shops: bread, tea, butter, sausages, eggs: a canvas bag full of habits that she carefully doubled for his benefit. He liked to watch the way her face changed slowly to make the numbers up. The same number of steps down an aisle to check the tag on something she was never going to buy. Just to have a quick look. A quick look at him to make sure it was alright to hold him like that, as if he had somewhere to go soon and had to be there on time. Then queuing at the till, screwing up her face as if she was trying to tune the invisible radio to an old song, and finding when she got there, or close enough to the thinnest crackle, that she couldn't remember, didn't recognise, the words anymore. While he was doing his best to return the cheered *hello* from a tired woman who used to have a girl-next-door face and make-up on: dyed hair drying, a stained uniform and a swelled chest saying *I have three children and a faithful husband now.*

On the way back, the graveyard. To see him, she said, to see that he was doing okay: nipping weeds in a green bud, dumping dead flowers, brushing muck from the stoop of the stone that bore his name, with more than enough room prudently, thoughtfully, left for her own. *It'll be no trouble at all. It'll be grand.* Then leaning down and head bowed talking to or talking for a man who wouldn't, or was it couldn't? answer back. *Don't ever.* And when a sudden gust of wind sent leaves scuttling up the path to the gate, it was like the sound of a young girl laughing in a photograph waved in a nervous hand. Of a lone woman having a cry all to herself, all for herself, rattling beads and fingering rings, behind a hearse.

He didn't know how or when but somewhere along the line he had found the strength not to run away. And he stayed the whole way, eyes-down, palms-clasped, from the long, front row of the church through the slow march to a slower bell, all the way through to the movement of his hand sprinkling soil down into the drop and covering her name. His name. His name. And even afterwards when people grabbed his hand and tried to catch his eye and say how sorry they were, they all were, and what a wonderful woman (and mother) she was, she was, she was. Even then.

And even when it was all over, he couldn't, didn't want to think of leaving them. Or of ever finding love. It was hard if he thought of it: he'd had love at first sight and then, and then he'd had no love and no sight and, in the end, nothing. Nothing, and nobody to blame. And if it was anything, it was that made breaths more difficult. Which was why he tried never to think of the things that went before. For days after, he opened cupboards, painted walls, lifted carpets, soaked rust out of forgotten keys and cut grass. Sunrise, sunset: things went on. Until he was yesterday's, last week's, last winter's news, and was forgotten. Forgotten everywhere except in a cluttered shop where a woman brightened, straightened shoulders at the cash-desk for his sake, and saved the paper with a *yours is the only copy of this we get around here* said without a trace of laughter. For his sake, kept a newspaper that came out *only once a week!* or a postcard from abroad that someone sent – all white strands and palm trees – so she could ask him about the place. And maybe a short story about the kids that might be nice to tell. Just nice.

That was it: just nice. And nothing like taking an arrow through the eye and being happy, happier, still. But that was all behind him, battle-broken and alone, like a bulb hidden behind a lampshade at the top of a house so it spread no shadow. Like a tiny pile of broken glass that was buried somewhere in a compost-heap that was too busy colonising the yard to grow a scar. Like feathers scattered in the dirt and made to look like a split-fletch arrow abandoned by some Indian brave, brave in the night-raid and cowardly escaping before every dawn attack.

And no sign either: not a sound from the attic when he'd sealed all the eaves; not a photograph that he'd found again and fed to hungry flames along with everything else; not a word from the old man who, even if he'd spoken and even if he'd listened, he might never have understood. And she was silent too. Himself as well: well settled into the odd smile, the odd walk, the odd talk and the odd laugh. But he usually just stayed quiet. He'd learned enough now not to even try and answer back. *He broke his mother's heart.*

Except on a damn-it-all day when he forgot, and a graveyard gate might be slammed angrily in his wake. And let clang open defiantly as if to say *don't leave, come back.* A day when he might say he knew it all now when what he really meant was *what about mine?* When what he really meant to say was his heart. Heading for home with no revelation waiting for him at the bend in the road, blurred-eye blind and swearing slurred. For anyone near enough or far enough to listen. And for himself. Swearing never to speak out of turn again.

Hy-Brasil

Mary Burke

It is not down in any map; true places never are
Moby-Dick

This tale is told in an irreligious age. Doubtless, you are an unbeliever. So you may, if you wish, take this story for a fiction. It is the wisest option and an illusion that saved the lives of many from the firing squad in the days of the War of Brother against Brother. But more of that later. This is the story of a place that once existed. It was called The Region. You could find it on a map if you cared to look scrupulously (for in truth it was an inconsequential spot only documented by its nearest neighbour). It had train timetables and many such other evidences in favour of its existence, and were you to take a train that named a town of The Region as its destination, it would drop you in a place whose name conveniently matched that listed in the timetable and the map. It had all the trappings of a real destination, though it was believed that its true name could not be invoked for fear of re-igniting the ancient dispute of its tribes over this very question. In those days, it would have appeared peculiar to have stood on street corners in neighbouring lands proclaiming that The Region did indeed exist. If a destination was listed in the transport company's handbook, then all agreed that it existed.

That was, then, an Era of Belief. On Sundays the preachers of this region had intent congregations. In their crowded, bright houses of God they boomed against the sins of illusion, violence and rival interpretations of the Holy Handbook. There was great emphasis on the danger to the soul of metaphorical darkness. And because everyone was locked inside cosy, well-lit churches listening attentively to sermons and concentrating on saving their souls, nobody noticed that outside it was growing dark. All the while the darkness crept from the hinterlands around the murmuring penitents and the edges of the map began to curl up as if being gradually devoured by the slowest of holocausts. And nobody noticed that outside it was growing dark.

But there was another sinister change seeping into the soul of The Region. And of this shift the people became aware, though it occurred gradually.

For as long as the people of that domain could remember, the past had at times interfered with the present. Sometimes at dusk, ghostly battalions of straggly, ill-equipped soldiers glided silently between the alleys of the tenements. The battles of corner boys who played out their fathers' muted curses against neighbours with sticks and stones would respectfully cease while the foggy spectacle flowed quietly across the no-man's-land of the alley separating enemy lines. Their vehement little mouths, which had prematurely learned to be economical with opinions, remained set as their fleet eyes followed the shadowy battalion as it passed and slowly faded. Then, as if on cue from their restless ancestors, they raised their sticks once more and re-enacted old battles. The boys accepted these ghosts as part of the living world; sometimes an inattentive man went out for milk, shuffled into the ghostly domain and wasn't seen for days. When he returned, incoherent and damaged, his mute, stone-eyed wife tended his bruises and denied to the neighbours that he had ever been away. The people accepted this enigma as a fated curse, which they had called down upon their own heads long ago. (A family member must always invite the vampire in.) The King's soldiers were never called in to investigate such mysteries. To suggest calling in the King's soldiers would have brought a bitter smile to the bruised and skinless lips of the man concerned, for such trauma induced eternal suspicion in victims. Very occasionally, a man went out for milk and never came home again. The King's soldiers were never called in to investigate such mysteries, since they too began to vanish in great numbers.

The rules of time and space had thus gradually become skewered in The Region (so do not rely on the events narrated having been told sequentially). At first, the community tried to understand this troubling mutation, but ceased probing for fear of the explanation. Besides, the alteration was, mercifully, invisible to those dazed travellers who occasionally wandered through from neighbouring lands. The line of time began to curl inward at the edges (as if being gradually devoured by the slowest of holocausts) and this folding made time circular. The past and present merged confusingly. At the marketplace or on a street corner, a hazy, slow-motion scene of an event that had occurred hundreds of years previously would sometimes hover inches off the ground like a film reel projected onto a wall. The burghers of the town would cease their activity and wait patiently for the vision to disperse. Bizarrely, the outcome of one notorious battle from the annals of The Region, which appeared again and again, had varying outcomes depending on the audience. The cause of this spectacle was unknown, and, if truth were told, on the whole the people stopped caring why it was so. They had goods to sell and work to do, and the occasional invasion of the shuffling, decayed, mute hordes of the dead was tolerated as one of the peculiarities of a far-flung, foggy, mountainous land. The peoples never feared that the past would engulf them or obscure what appeared to be permanent (on most days at least).

And so, for generations, the people were oblivious to the fact that their land was being imperceptibly unanchored from the world and the present. They remained implacable when returned wanderers told them that the names of the towns of The Region were one by one disappearing from the annals and timetables of the adjacent territory. One insistent traveller was stoned by a derisive rabble of boys (who had been hurling rocks at each other until that point) when he could not produce a foreign atlas in which he claimed The Region had ceased to be included.

The cataclysm that eventually overcame The Region started as a harmless trickle. Simply, people in neighbouring lands began to forget that it existed. Geography teachers unintentionally neglected to teach it, and history teachers found themselves ignoring it. People stuttered when they attempted to say its name, and no one at all would now admit to remembering its earlier forbidden names. Those who covertly researched it found their thoughts constantly wandering and references well hidden, perhaps because The Region's language, once shared with its neighbour, became increasingly marbled with babbling phrases, as if subterraneously grazing other tongues. Everyone found it hard to recall any concrete facts about the place and could only dredge up meaningless gibberish, as if a radio dial, which had rested on one station for years suddenly whizzed at demonic speed. Each presumed that the growing haziness was their own particular block, since, of course, they could never remember to discuss the problem with another. They didn't realise that it was a sinister process all were undergoing simultaneously. By the time of the cataclysm, however, The Region wasn't completely forgotten. It had just come to occupy the dusty, seldom-consulted position of a far-off barbarian kingdom in the consciousness of its neighbour. Such strange ripples in the reality consensus are not allowed to exist for long, lest humans enquire too scrupulously into the imaginary rules they exist under. And so the contradiction caused by The Region in the consciousness of its neighbours and in the sense of reality of its citizens was quite simply rectified. It disappeared.

In one fateful instant, The Region was murdered away from the memory of its neighbours. It vanished as if someone (in a delegation to God) had simply signed it out of existence.

Some took this for the work of a strange angel while others spat that it was certainly the work of a fiend. But most were secretly relieved that their own land, at least, remained what they referred to as Free. The Region was now a blank space in the maps of The Neighbouring Region, a black hole on earth. A very few in the adjacent territory had doubts, but had to suppress them when they could not find any references to The Region in schoolbooks, travel timetables or maps. Throughout the households of the land, rebellious young men muttered against the assurances of their brothers and against all the evidence of the ('newly revised') travel guide and the ('recently updated') atlas.

They muttered, brooded and bided their time.

Most, however, were willing to accept this as proof that The Region had never existed, though there remained a very few poets and madmen who persisted in the delusion. And at the time of the Disappearance, a few believed in their heart that the land had once existed, but said nothing for fear of being perceived to be a Rebel Against Reality. In the end, these seditious mutterings burst into an inferno of hate that the people after named the War of Brother Against Brother. And after the war was over and the Rebels Against Reality had been lined up and shot by men who had shared school desks with them and by boys who had courted their sisters, it was only the mad and the reckless who stood on street corners insisting that The Region had once been in every map and in every schoolbook. When it was pointed out to them that no such fact appeared in the latest editions they were without answer.

Does it exist now? Where did it go? Some say it was simply swallowed up by another land. Others that it had belonged to that same land to begin with and had only imagined itself separate. Some say it merely slipped irrevocably into the past. Or the future. Some were heard to say that the fairies have taken it 'and it's been theirs for so long, that I don't think we'd recognise it if it suddenly appeared out of the mist'. Recently, there have been outlandish and discredited whisperings that the rulers of neighbouring lands have launched an investigation into the possibility of the existence of The Region. And recently, too, corpses of those tortured to death by a phantom rebel army began to disappear from the wantonly dug graves into which they were purged. Those who quarried where the bones should have been found nothing. Perplexingly, relatives of those who had died swore they saw images of their kindred materialise as grey, flickering figures in the background of television shows discussing the mythical Region, silently opening and closing their mouths and gesturing rabidly to those around them to whom they were invisible and without voice. Poets and madmen still claim to be able to occasionally see The Region hovering a few inches off the tops of the waves, reflected like a film reel from the days before Reality onto the shimmering mists of the coastline of The Neighbouring Region – the coastline they imagine used to be a boundary between two lands.

Postscript: This document will have passed through the hands of many translators and editors before it reaches you. Do not trust any imputed clues or congratulate yourself when you detect seeming contradiction, for all apparent slip-ups are perhaps carefully designed cul-de-sacs. Most of all, distrust apparently obvious interpretations. Question the motives and loyalty of those who offer an interpretation freely. Most of all, question the real source of those beliefs that seem to be your own. This is, after all, an era of unbelief. There is no such thing as a real source, though much Trouble is caused by that which claims to stem from such. And finally, distrust this narrative. Where did I get this information? After all, you know nothing of me or of my motives.

Surrender

WILLIAM WALL

Thus we went down, circle by circle, things closing in as we went. Go to the Molo Bevorello, he said. Pay at the little kiosk. There will be a ferry waiting. Do not fall asleep on the seat, in the shade, or you will visit each island in turn and come back to the same place. When you wake you will have passed through the past, the present and future and you will have to begin again.

Or perhaps he did not say so much.

Now I see him standing on the quay with the fishing co-op as backdrop. Men are taking boxes out of cars and passing them into the darkness. A *paranza* with its weighted net is unloading. The little buses and cars wait for us to disembark. When we step ashore we will enter another world. I feel the shiver of the crossing, the shifting paradigms. Everything will be the same and different on this shore. When we turn to look back at the ship we will be looking outwards: though the same crossing will be there, we will notice something uncertain in the light, or a ripple in the air. A turn in the tide of the fluid we breathe. The world is always novel from an island.

Noisily, amid the cacophony of homecomings and departures, Jim embraces Terry, then me, and leads us to the golf cart that is the island taxi, the only thing small enough to negotiate the narrow streets and lanes. How often has he told this one detail in his letters that are themselves like poems? The *vicoli* of the island so narrow there are no real taxis. They drive like crazy. And I have rehearsed the discovery so frequently that when I see them they are unreal. From the back seat we smile like pilgrims at everything while the driver swings between crooked houses, in and out of the sun, and there are times that if we placed our elbows on the armrest some wall would clip them off. Lemons glow like weak bulbs, small intense oranges reach for the hand. Garish pelargonium, bougainvillaea, hibiscus, gardenia. Every once in a while the sea winking like broken glass.

At the hotel the *padrone* and his wife greet us. They are gracious, welcoming. We are led upstairs to the rooms which are bare, clean and full of light from the big ill-fitting windows. A tiny balcony looks out on the middle branches of an ancient bougainvillaea. On the corridor between Terry's room and mine we embrace in solemn silence. A brief symmetry.

Jim has his work. Or so he tells us. He lives in a room in a different hotel. It has become his by occupation: he calls himself the colonial power. The room faces down across a courtyard of uneven slabs and down a corridor that becomes a side-entrance to the hotel. He has everything he needs. A shabby, arthritic laptop that groans and whistles when he saves something onto a disk, that drops dead without warning when the battery runs low, the screen faded so much that it is difficult to read what he writes; a line of books separated from the line above it by a plank, the bottom row holding up the top, the whole topped by a weighty *Cambridge Italian Dictionary*; a small camping cooker on which he heats coffee and other things. A variety of bottles of wine. Only two glasses. He asks us to steal one from our hotel. 'They'll give you glasses in the bathroom. They'll never miss one. Say you broke it.'

Terry says it sounds just like the shabby flats we used to have when we were in college. Broken beds and chairs whose joints had come unglued and mice. We all remember the beds.

He has lived there for three years. He's clean, apart from a little weed. The book is coming along nicely. He earns a crust by teaching English. 'And of course,' bowing to Terry, 'there is the generous advance.' The room is cheap because he occupies it all year round, though it can be cold in the winter. Dawkins sends him things. Reviewing brings windfalls.

'Did you do your reading?' he wants to know on the first evening. 'Did you do your homework?'

Yes.

'*Nel mezzo del cammin di nostra vita,*' he recites aloud, '*mi ritrovai per una selva oscura, che la diritta via era smarrita.*'

People turn to look at him. A smartly dressed woman smiles. He continues into the second verse, standing up, the scraping of the chair imposing a partial silence into which the beautiful ordinary *terza rima* falls like the ingratiating words of a seducer. The waiters purse their lips and raise their eyebrows at each other. He ends at 'So bitter it is that scarcely death is worse, but I will speak of the good I found there and also certain other things I learned.' There is polite clapping at the other tables and he bows and smiles, bows and smiles. Terry pulls him back into his chair. She glares in mock exasperation.

He sits and the smile fades quickly. 'They all learn Dante at school, excerpts in every textbook, the way we had Shakespeare,' he says. 'They all know that part.' He stares at the heaped rings of squid on his plate. 'The middle of the walk of life,' he says. 'The heart of life. It's the first line. Perhaps *because* it's the first. Seven hundred years have turned it into a cliché. I don't know what to do with it. The middle of the footpath of our life? The crown of life's road? Halfway in the stroll of existence? The shortcut to death? The inside track?' He laughs bitterly. 'It's such a banal opening.'

'How far did you get?' Terry asks. He hears the professional undertone.

'The book will be ready in a month. I'm at the tidying up stage.'

Neither of us believes it. He stares defiantly.

Terry says: 'I think you said that last year in your October letter. I think I have a copy in my bag in my room.'

Around the tine of his fork he hangs a piece of squid so white it is almost artificial. He holds it up for a moment then puts it in his mouth.

'My printer is shagged at present. I'm waiting for a new one to arrive. It was supposed to be here today. Tomorrow at the latest. I'll run it off for you then.'

'That would be great,' Terry says. The tone is acid. 'They said to me before I left: Get him to show you what he's done, otherwise he'll lie about it. So . . .' Something leaves a bad taste in our mouths. Not the squid.

Terry pays for the meal in the Bar Dal Cavaliere, carefully folding the receipt into a section of her wallet and this simple transaction gives her the right to insult him, to challenge his credibility. The night is thick with electricity.

'And you, Charlie,' he says. 'What do you have?'

I tell them about my job. I tell them about the in-fighting and the campus politics, the small triumphs of academic life. My last paper. A projected study of Irish political poetry. The students I can boast of. I do not tell them about the careful pattern that has become the geography of my days: the streets I do not walk, the bars I do not visit. About how nobody calls unexpectedly, because an unexpected knock on the door could mean death. About the meta-language in which the name of a street or a school or a friend establishes an entire history, a tribe, a politics, a future. There are no innocent words where I live. The weight of meaning is unbearable and so the decent thing to do is to mean as little as possible. I do not mention that I heard the Omagh bomb explode as I went to visit a colleague that Saturday morning. That I had the window of the car open. That I knew it had to be a bomb. But, I notice, my hands shake as I talk.

As we walk home, boys race Vespas down the hill at terrifying speed. They bump and twist over the uneven basalt slabs that make the road surface. Couples stroll towards us. A family group. Three grandparents, two sets of parents, two children. One child runs into the shadow between the lamps calling insistently that the other is afraid. *Hai paura. Hai paura.* I recognise the words. Grandfather remonstrates: Be quiet, he says, people are asleep.

And the sound of someone tidying cutlery comes down from one of the high blank walls where the houses turn their backs on the passer-by.

'I don't ever wish I was married,' he says, 'but I surely wish I had kids.'

'How's your Italian?' he says to me, and I tell him that it's coming back slowly since I came. 'I stopped doing the courses a long time ago. I got lazy.'

The hotel is asleep. The night duty is thrown across three seats in the lobby, the television flickering at him, its blank back towards us. We take our keys from the desk and tiptoe to the stairs. He calls a sleepy *buonanotte*. The marble wall is cool to the touch. In my room the window has been left open. There is lightning along the coast towards Cumæ – the sibyl crackling about doom, thunder in rapid salvoes. Delicate lightning in the blue gloom. The great black peak of Ischia, at its base a thousand lights. I can make out traffic signals, cars moving down a hill. There is no breeze even up here so high above the beach and the streets. The lightning flickers and dances and the drums roll like marchers warming up for the advance. Far away in Ireland, a mile, two miles from my office, they would be standing in circles beating out the rantan, the huge hollow bellies that farted anger and spite. Warming up for weeks for the Glorious Twelfth. Tradition. There were other traditions too – like beating Jews, like raping Moslems – that were founded on hatred: nobody was queuing up to give them 'parity of esteem'.

She rises, sleepy and heavy with the heat, at half past eleven and suggests we spend the afternoon at the beach. Jim is to get on with installing his new printer and running off the first draft of whatever he has finished while we spend a few hours sunning and swimming, relaxing and talking over old times.

It is, I recognise, part of her strategy. 'Come with me, Charlie,' her phone-call said. 'It'll be a bit of a holiday.' And I thought it would mean a few days, a week, alone with her after all this time. And she may have been thinking the same.

But most of all she knew I was the only one he trusted. He would never trust her. Now she would take me down to the sea, to soften me up, to keep me onside. And when we get back to the hotel the first draft as far as Canto XXVI will be waiting for us. Then we can begin in earnest. 'He must do it, Charlie,' she said. 'I'm afraid he'll self-destruct any minute now. I've spent years on this.'

Terry sitting in her office, making calls, dictating letters, *she* has spent years on this.

We each hire a chair and an umbrella, the first we find. The matronly ladies who bring their children down slightly later all move further along. The lilting sound of the unknown lulls us and we sleep with our feet towards the ancient sea, our heads towards the crumbling pumice cliffs until I am awakened by a dream in which I can smell rotten vegetables.

The smell is still there. A breeze has developed and small waves are pushing an object towards me that I had originally assumed to be a small rock forty feet offshore but is now clearly a dead turtle. The shell is there, forming a bowl in which the meat putrefies. The underside, some kind of softer armour, is broken. There is no head, no flippers. When it surges on a wave it provokes a tiny storm of dark sand, clouding the water. The sun has come round to shine in our faces under the brim of the umbrella and the soles of my feet feel hot.

The women are departing, gathering bags and children. All along the beach the chairs that had been filling when I fell asleep are emptying now, their angles pointed back towards the village. Where has the day gone? A man in pale-blue overalls comes down and strips in a single elegant procedure to a fragment of cloth that I take to be his bathing trunks. He walks forward purposefully and then launches himself at the water. A boy comes down the steps behind and begins to clap the chairs closed. He is careful not to make noise, seeing Terry sleeping in the shade. He unties the strings of the umbrellas and they fold down suddenly, silently. He smiles at me.

I wake Terry. I see her tumble out of some happy place. She sniffs the air and makes a face. 'It's the dead turtle,' I say. I point. She stands up abruptly. 'Jesus Christ! Why didn't you wake me? For fuck's sake!'

It is no use to protest that I am just awake myself. She gathers her things and stuffs them into a net bag. She pulls a cardigan on. She walks past the careful boy and up the steps. I give him a thousand-lire note and say *ciao* tentatively. He says *ciao* back.

I try to keep up. I watch her sandals – the way when she tilts forward onto the ball of her foot the strap at the heel slips down and a gap develops briefly. The way the tendon at the back of her calf becomes a smooth curve of muscle, a bent bow. Two tendons work the hinge of her knee. I have been falling behind for ten years now, publishing less, relying on older and older notes, old friends, the same places. A failing college professor. A forgettable teacher. Whereas all impediments have failed to slow her down or have been discarded. She is the commissioning editor now, the peak of her profession, a successful woman with a string of major publications. She talks about her list. The things that are on her list and the things she would like to have on it. Jim's translation, for instance. Every now and then she flaps the edges of the cardigan she has thrown over her bikini. 'Jesus Christ,' she says, 'I think that smell is still in it.'

The window of Jim's room is open and we can see a brown cardboard package on top of the stack of books at the far end – the printer still in its case. In the outdoor dining area on the right of the passage Jim is talking to a very old man and there is a bottle of wine on the table. The rattan roof throws a slatted shade on them. A lizard scuttles for cover as we pass. His tail is twice as long as his body. Jim waves us over with an empty glass but Terry carries on. 'I'll see you at our hotel,' she says, moving on quickly, and unspoken is the implication that he is my responsibility. That she has delegated him to me.

'That man,' he tells me excitedly, 'is a genius. Do you believe that, Charlie? He tells me stories, amazing stories . . .'

'You can't keep this up, Jim,' I say. I have been told to say it. I know I am letting him down. 'Terry is pissed off. She told me to tell you she doesn't believe in this project. They may ask for the advance back.'

'Fuck that. They never ask for their money back and you know it. What are they going to do? Sue my computer off me? They can have it. I'll still have a pen. They won't be able to stop me. And if they do the contract's off. I'll be able to hawk the book around. Penguin would be interested, maybe Faber. It's going to be sensational. Fuck *Beowulf* man! This is about God and love not some fucking giant alligator.'

'They won't pay the next advance.'

Dignity then. 'I never expected it. The contract says *on delivery of manuscript.*'

'But you wrote asking for it.'

He explodes. 'For my fucking printer! Not for me!'

'Terry says give it to her on disk and she can read it on her laptop.'

Silence.

'Jim?'

'That'd be the same as giving her the manuscript.'

'Exactly.'

Very quiet. Looking at me. 'No.'

In the humidity our clothes are sticky. It is like being covered in a fine layer of sweat. Her blouse is loose at the waist and every now and then she lifts it and flaps some air in. We sit on the terrace under a bougainvillaea in full purple flower and watch the lizards waiting for flies behind the lights. She is drinking a limoncello and I am drinking water. I have decided I need to be careful. She is tipsy and sentimental, talking about old times. I notice that her language has coarsened in melancholy. Fuck this and fuck that. Or perhaps it is the drink. She keeps her knees spread but closes them with a snap sometimes to circulate the air. We laugh over distant escapades, close shaves, stale jokes. There is nothing like old times to soften the hard rim of the here and now.

'Charlie, will you help me?'

Her face is close to mine. I can smell the wine and the sweet limoncello.

'You saw the sample pieces he sent. It's going to be something, you know that. He trusts you, he always did. I'm an editor not a friend, I know that. But I do so want this book to come out. For him. It'll make his name. But he must finish it. The time is right. Will you help me? You're his friend.'

'That's what you brought me for,' I say. 'I'm at your disposal.'

'But do you believe in this book? Do you have faith in him?'

'There's too much faith in the world, Terry. But what you showed me – I know what I saw. It's his best work yet.'

I watch as she fiddles with the thin glass. And flaps air under her shirt. What I have said is not enough.

'How can you stick it, Charlie?' she says. 'Up there. Aren't you ever afraid?'

'Are you?' I say.

'Don't give me that London-is-as-dangerous-as-Belfast crap, Charlie.'

'How long is it since you took the Underground at night?'

'That's true for every city.'

'I like the place,' I said. 'And a lot of the people. They're interesting. They're direct. Honest.'

'Fuck honest. You mean they don't say enough to tell lies.'

'Which of us does?'

Later I said: 'You may not be able to understand this, Terry. I kind of feel I've gone this far and I'd like to see how it pans out. There's a cease-fire now, you know. Peace talks. Everything is different.' By which I mean they use baseball bats instead of guns, tyre-irons instead of bombs.

Jim tells me that I was once a completely crass person. The implication, I think, is that I haven't changed much, that the word *completely* might no longer be necessary. He now refuses to let me into his room on the grounds that I am of the other camp. I knock and he responds by calling me False Sinon. You brought the horse in, he calls, and then you opened the gates. Torture yourself that all the world knows it. And then I hear him laughing.

Like most things he says I sense a passage behind that I cannot at once locate. It gives his speech a bizarre, slightly hollow, echoing quality.

He keeps me waiting at his door and I am suspicious of the sweet smell that comes through the cracks. When he comes out he is unnaturally cheerful. 'You recognised the allusion?' he asks. 'Sinon was the guy who opened the gates of Troy. He's way down in hell, according to my man Dante. No offence, Charlie. No offence, man.'

I try to see his eyes but he looks away.

'Let's go for a swim,' he says.

The beach is called Ciracello, he tells me, famous for being the only beach on the island that has never been famous for anything.

On the way down the hill he is preoccupied. He hums and talks to himself. Sometimes he beats out a rhythm in his palm. He greets a leathery old man outside the vegetable shop with *Salve Tommaso, eh?* And the old man replies with *Salve, Jim*. How long has he been living here? And how can he survive?

'I'll never do the *Paradiso* or the *Purgatorio*,' he says suddenly. 'They just don't interest me. Hell is where it's all at. Next I want to write a play about Paolo and Francesca. And that bastard Malatesta. It has all the ingredients. When she says, you know, *nessun maggior dolore che ricordarsi del tempo felice nella miseria* I truly believe it. There is no greater pain than to recall a happier time in a time of grief. That'll be the last line of the play. Curtain. It'll be about love and memory. That's my next project after I get the monkey off my back.'

The monkey is the translation. Terry says it is not uncommon for authors involved in long projects to feel resentful, even though the project is paying their wages. They have already mastered most of the difficulties and are anxious to move on to the next challenge. It's human, she says. I detect a note of disbelief, as though she does not believe in the humanity of writers.

The beach is crowded because it is Saturday. Close to the steps there are the chairs that Terry and I hired on our second day. Young women with impossible bodies lounge on them, trying to avoid the shade of the umbrellas. Some are topless and their breasts have paler triangles, the nipples set off-centre. Jim stands and surveys the throng. 'Conveyor-belt beauty,' he says. 'When you come to Italy first you can't take your eyes off them. The beautiful women with the perfect hips and perfect legs and asses. You think the gods have indeed smiled on them. After a while you start to wish for some individuality, for someone with a little more flesh or small breasts. Notice the number of bottle blondes? *La bella figura*. They're obsessed with surfaces. It's a plague of clones. The Italian for girlfriend is *bimbo*, or was anyway.'

He swims very far out. A line of orange buoys marks the limit that boats are permitted to approach the beach. He swims out there, so far that against the sun I can hardly see his head. I follow him by the occasional splash. The beach underfoot is too hot. I spread my towel as far as possible and sit hunched to avoid touching the burning sand. Where the water washes in it is black. The peak of Ischia is in the distance, suggesting the immanence of holocaust, the dormant Epomeo trailing a wisp of cloud as though it smokes. At our backs, somewhere behind the hill, twenty miles away, are Vesuvius and the fields of fire in which a man is petrified where he falls down and a dog dies at his post watching the black ash and the smoke. It was no surrender there too, and duty and the fearless few. Pliny taking his notes, the whole thing too good to be missed for a historian. I have known a few of those.

I am aware of the whiteness of my skin against the black sand, the brown and black bodies. The flab at my waist. It feels sinful, not in the way of great sinners, but truly sordid and unpleasant. I should take care of myself. This woman that is between the two of us, driving him, frightening me: so beautiful still, so desirable. Nothing has been resolved in all those years. I fell in love with her at twenty-five.

I am beginning to resent my intermediary status and our morning and evening tactical conferences. Is he writing? Has he shown me any of the text? What does he say about it? Has he discussed the technicalities? There is something more here than I can fathom. As before, I am out of my depth.

He tells me nothing, I say. We talk about women, the way men do (this exasperates her). We went swimming and he told me he intended to write a play about Paolo and Francesca. He quoted a line about there being no greater pain than to remember a happy time in a sad time. He went too far out, beyond the safe marks. I worried.

She rejoins sharply. 'A time of misery. I know. That was in the sample section he sent us. It's Canto V.' She seems disturbed. 'Why does he keep going back to the same things?' she says. 'Why can't he move on? I so want him to finish this. It'll make his name. Make his reputation. We all know he deserves more than he's got. This'll put him centre-stage again. It'll be his *Beowulf*.' I have noticed that she thinks like this: the new *Bonfire of the Vanities*, the new *Longitude*. When she talks about the books she is working on she is always enthusiastic – it's always *the new* something else. As though each thing that is valuable belongs to a template stamped out by someone more original.

And I want to say that Dante is not sexy, with his big hooked nose and his flap cap and his talk about angels and punishment and his desire for revenge on the people who sent him into exile from his beloved Florence. Monsters and dragons are in, God is out, I think. This will be a fine translation but it won't have him giving readings in a football stadium. And I am worried about his state of mind and whether he is looking after his health. 'There's ants in my computer,' he told me yesterday. 'They come out of slots in the casing. At first I thought I'd evict them, but nothing shifts the bastards. I'm thinking maybe they'll figure something out. You know the way ants have this kind of collective mind. Maybe they'll get at the mother-board. Or figure out a way to make themselves heavy enough to press the keys. What if I start to get messages? Jesus, I couldn't take it if the fuckers started to write about me.'

I never know when he is serious now. Never know when he is taking the piss. I am lost.

'Why did he do this to himself,' Terry says.

She drinks too much. Two *aperitivos* before dinner. A full bottle every night at our table. Afterwards a night-cap or two. Grappa for her, a kind of Italian poitín and sometimes limoncello. When she drinks she asks searching questions. 'Why haven't you found a woman, Charlie?' Why hasn't she found a man? Not men, but a man. 'I don't want to be a serial shagger,' she says. 'I want to settle down. It's almost too late for kids. What happened to us all? How do people work in this climate?' Between twelve and four she sleeps. 'When I'm at home I never sleep during the day,' she says, 'why am I sleeping so much?' Then Jim comes out of the shadows. He is wearing plastic sandals, a dark T-shirt, grubby grey trousers. He is a little out of breath climbing the short slope up to the terrace. For the first time I notice the strange pallor under his tan, the rings around his eyes, the way his hair seems to sit lifelessly on his head like some kind of rough cloth. 'We are going to a concert,' he says. 'Come on, no slacking.'

The island band is playing for St John's night in the little village of Corricella. The streets are full of strollers, couples arm in arm, families, single men or women. This evening walk is the quintessential Italian thing for me, the mothers and daughters arm-in-arm, the boys on Vespas or in small cars, revving the engines and waving. It is a familial chaos, the crazy art of community. They call to each other or to people in windows or on stairways. This is a different life. 'I want to stay here,' I tell him. 'Find me a job teaching English and I'll stay for ever.'

'No you don't want to stay here,' he says. 'You're a kind of Narcissus, falling in love with your own mirror image. You're better off up there in Belfast with those hard-arsed Free Presbyterians in that God-forsaken place you're teaching This is the kind of life you would *like* to want, Charlie. But it would be a different you that wanted it.'

'Fuck you and your bullshit,' I say, surprising myself. Since moving to Northern Ireland my expletives have weakened and fallen silent. Blast, I say. Or Damn. Sometimes even, Goodness. The old words feel wet and hard in my mouth. 'What do you know about Belfast? No more than you see on TV. What do you know about the people there? You haven't a clue.'

'No,' he says, not in the least affected by my outburst, 'you belong up there all right. Up in the hard North where a bargain is a bargain and nothing over. You'd be ripe and rotten here in a month.'

Steps lead down a sheer cliff and the crescent-shaped village is below us, sheltered from the open sea by a concrete reef. The pastel-coloured houses are joined at the top or bottom or by fantastic staircases, or shared doorways, stepped up three or four or five floors with their back against the cliff. Some of the rooms must be cut into rock. The buildings are crazy but the boats are neat and orderly and the nets lie in piles along the quay. The music has started and the sound of a cor anglais rises to meet us. We stand at the top and watch Terry stepping neatly down into the darkness. Her light skirt swirls as she drops. There's a change in the air, a breeze ruffling the darkness out by the breakwater. The boats are sawing on their moorings. It has come suddenly, whatever it is: sudden and unprovided for.

'It's too late, Charlie,' he says. 'It takes years before you're any good at living in a place like this. I'm only starting now. And it's probably too late.'

He's right. And Terry too. Where I live it is better to say as little as possible. Careful sentences, practised and positive, modulated. We live with the fear of other people's faith. A false word could cost a life or a leg. People have been killed in error. *In error*. Afterwards nobody apologises. My next-door neighbour lost three fingers of his left hand when a sheet of plate glass took them off. He had been evacuated from the travel agent's office where he worked, but the bomb exploded prematurely. He never talks about it. We pass the time of day but he doesn't wave. It helps to be polite. Better again say nothing. I am tending in that direction. A day will come when I will walk to the pub for my evening pint and walk home again without uttering a word. The silence is a tangible thing. People take sustenance from it and wear away in the process: in the consanguinity of bloodbaths. I take a deep breath and push out against the silence.

'She means what she says, Jim. She's not doing this for herself. I mean there's no money in poetry. You know that. She's had to fight off the marketing people and the money men to keep you in the list. She believes in you. She believes this is going to be an important work.'

The band strikes up 'Colonel Bogey' and suddenly there is a spring to his step. 'Come on, man,' he says, 'we'll miss the best of it.'

'You're working for her, Charlie, you know that. I know it too. I forgive you.' It's the following night and we're watching the activity in the port. A ferry is coming in at high speed because of the cross-wind. Suddenly it sweeps up a tight circle and drops its anchor. Then the water is boiling forward from its stern. Bright lights shine down onto the after deck where a handful of passengers watches us. A man appears on the quay and waits for the rope to be thrown. Late into the night the ferries move between the islands on a bottomless sea: by day they are purposeful white shapes among the pleasure-craft.

'I'm not working for anybody,' I say. I am aware of a momentary equilibrium: the slightest motion and I fall. 'I'm just lost. I agreed to come because I thought I could persuade you to finish the translation. I'm not making a secret of that. She rang me up and asked me. You're his friend, she said. He'll trust you.' I look steadily at him. I want him to understand. 'First of all I believe she's right. Secondly, it's important for you. When Terry sent me the draft copy I knew exactly why she was so anxious to get you to wrap it up. It'll make her name and it'll remake yours. It's as simple as that.'

He laughs and shakes his head.

'It's true,' I say.

'You talk a lot of bullshit even for a college teacher. You always were full of it.'

'You have to come home.'

'Fuck that. I am at home.'

'Look – Jim, please.'

All day a sirocco has been blowing over the back of the island; a thin, high layer of cloud; the sun a pale orange light behind clouded glass. It was difficult to decide where the horizon began and ended. The sea on the south-eastern side was rough and waves broke white: but where we sit now, in the lee of the port-captain's hut, it is pleasant enough, although a fine dust settles on every surface. 'Forget it, Charlie,' he says. Then suddenly 'Are you fucking her?' I shake my head and stare at him. 'Are you sure?'

'Look, Jim, if I was, I'd know, all right?' He pats me on the back. 'Poor Charlie Kennedy. She's not for you. See what she has become. It would be like fucking a rope or . . . anything functional. She's a machine. She has no feelings. She's a unit in the system.'

I tell him once again that he doesn't know what he's talking about. That she's my friend too. And he apologises. 'You know,' he says, 'I'd like to love her. In a way I do. I'd like to want her, but I don't. I don't really want anything or anybody. It's not her, it's me.'

He has reached the end of some kind of tether, I see. The skin is looser around his eyes and taut over his cheeks. He seems even thinner than when we saw him first ten days ago. I have the strange impression that a metamorphosis has taken place in him between strength and weakness, the first becoming the second in the reaction. And I know too that he is lying: that after all these years he still remembers her body the way a bird remembers the summer.

'Look at these guys.' He nods at the people spilling out of the ferry and into the tiny orange bus that will take them home. 'They work on the mainland but they live here. They think they have the best of both worlds, but they're as thin and as flat as paper. One touch and they tear. Either you live on the mainland or you live on the island. You can't belong to both. Did I ever tell you my father ran out on us? When I was ten?'

'It's in your bio. Half the world knows it.'

He gives me a suspicious look, then grins.

'Tomorrow I'm going to show you something. I want you to see it before you go back.'

When I get back to the hotel the wind is shaking the lemon groves, the gloomy bougainvillaea. There are brighter windfalls in the dust. A curious musical whistling noise pervades the hotel. *La casa delle fantasmagorie*, Vincenzo the night duty says, imitating the sound. He points to the ceiling. *Il vento*. He is apologetic.

I knock on her door but there is no answer. I hear only the hotel's eerie whistling. I want to tell her that I think there is something seriously wrong, that I think he's losing it, that maybe we've pushed him too far. I am prepared to believe in her sleep. That she lies on her bed in something light and cool, dreaming her dreams, with one hand under her cheek, or lying along the pillow. I tiptoe along the corridor of the house of the phantoms.

But sometime after midnight the silence wakes me. The wind is gone and the room is stifling. I open the shutters and step out onto the balcony. The bougainvillaea looks enormous in the darkness. There is no moon. For no reason I can explain I am aware that Terry is watching me from her balcony. I turn and look at her. She is there for a moment then she is gone. I go back to bed. Then I hear her tapping at my door.

She shakes in my hands. 'Be nice to me,' she says. 'I can't stand it.'

As I fuck her I think of the Trojan Horse. But it is not like fucking a piece of wood or a rope. There are things he does not understand. And afterwards we console each other with silence, by our even breathing, a kind of peace. A film of moisture separates us where our foreheads almost touch.

In the morning we drink from the only remaining glass. She sits with her back against the wall, the sheet rucked across her lap. I hold one breast and circle my thumb around the nipple. She looks down and smiles. 'Come to London with me,' she says. 'You'll find a job. Get out of that dead end you're in. Go someplace that has a future.' And I agree, not wanting to lose this moment.

This is Pozzo Vecchio, he says, this is the most beautiful place.

A tiny circular-domed church at the same level as the road, then rank after rank of stairs, the walls lined with marble graves that swirl downwards circle after circle. The stairs relate to each other in complex ways, intersecting, parting, blending, twisting, paralleling – like an Escher print. Down on the flat at the bottom of the last set of steps, almost at the same level as the sea, is a conventional graveyard with the usual mix of ordinary and extraordinary headstones – flat marble slab or angel with trumpet, simple crosses, bas-relief of the resurrection, Calvary, or the Virgin Mary. Beyond the wall people play in the sand. There are children's voices, the sound of a football and brave goal-keeping and spectacular passing. He stops there with his back to the sea. Look, he says. The strange geometry rises steadily towards the little church, the graves mounting or descending according to point of view, and at the top leaning curiously on the wall and looking down on us, a man in blue overalls.

He begins to recite.

> *Above those gates I saw a thousand shadows*
> *Haled from Heaven, who bellowed at us:*
> *What are you who, without passing,*
> *Travel in the kingdom of the dead?*

The man in blue overalls is straining to hear. The simple lines echo among the marble slabs.

Jim pauses for effect, or perhaps to listen for echoes.

'The funny thing about translating,' he says, 'is that the closer you get the more you realise that the gap between you and the work is unbridgeable. It's this tiny space where everything is so intense, so concentrated that if you stepped into it the forces would tear you apart. The space between two languages is too small to be crossed.'

The man in the blue overalls is smoking and a translucent cloud surrounds him like a glory.

'I've made arrangements to be buried here,' he says after a time. 'With the priest. He doesn't know anything about me except that I come from Ireland. Ireland is a very devout place, as far as he's concerned, famous for its resistance to heresy. He doesn't know about your crowd up north, Charlie.'

Terry chuckles. 'It's going to be a long funeral. I hope you don't expect us to carry your fucking coffin from Ireland to here.'

Her words shock him. I see him shiver. He begins to recite the same lines in Italian, louder this time, as though to reach the workman overhead. *Chi è costui, che senza morte va per il regno della morta gente . . .*

'Come off it, Jim,' she says. 'You're giving me the creeps. Finish the fucking book and stop messing me around.'

'I have finished it.'

'You have on your ass.'

He chuckles. 'It's a long time since I heard that particular colloquialism.'

There is a real smile tugging at the corners of her lips – the first one I've seen since we came. Once I thought they were made for each other. What happened to them?

She begins to lecture him. 'You need to get back home,' she says. 'You need to get a fellowship somewhere or a residency. Better again, start lecturing. Jesus, you could lecture on the influence of Dante on someone.

Anyone. *The Waste Land*. They'd fall over themselves to get you. Try the States. You need to get a grip on yourself. Finish the book. Once it comes out they'll all want you . . .'

Gently he repeats, 'I *have* finished the book.'

She steps in front of him, her face flushed with anger. 'For fuck's sake, stop! Stop lying! Do you know how much I have riding on you? My fucking reputation, that's what!'

He takes a computer disk from his trousers pocket and hands it to her. I see that it is neatly labelled *The Inferno – Dante Alighieri, Trans. James Henchion*. She takes it from his hand and turns it over as though the underside would reveal a rotten substructure. She stares. Then she looks at me and I shake my head, a tiny stiff movement meaning he never told me, I knew nothing. Maybe I detect a tear in her eye, maybe not. 'Jim,' she says softly, 'you didn't rush it? Did you?'

'As a matter of fact I finished it months ago. I just couldn't let go. How many years am I at it now?'

They laugh together, easily, warmly. She takes his hand.

'Thank you.'

'No, thank *you*. You drove me this far. I'd never have kept going but for you. I wouldn't have done it for anybody else.'

'Is there anything special you want . . .? An epigraph or anything?'

'Yes. I want the words I just quoted, in both Italian and my English under my name. I'll write to you about it. I have cancer. A bad one. I'm not going home. When you pay me the rest of my advance I'm renting a small house just up there. So I'm in the parish. I may even start going to mass in that church. The *padre* is going to be pleased.'

At four in the morning the island is buried in fog. Prospero is at work. And even in sleep the isle is noisy. At the first wink of light the sparrows start to hope. A cock crows somewhere. An engine turns over down the hill in the port. Fog in the morning is a sign of a good day, my father used to say. But here it is never anything else so no signs are necessary. I move her hand and she shifts a little and murmurs something incomprehensible. I cannot resist the thought that I am the one she came to after all these years. Although I don't know why and the possibilities are worrying. And now I know I am going to lose her, the stubborn Northern cold surfacing in me at last, the no surrender. I try to think how I will tell her, and I wonder too if it will matter to her now that she has her book. I open the French windows and sit on the tiny balcony and look out towards Ischia and wait for things to lift. My heart is a sparrow. I try to work things out but I cannot escape the feeling that there is something shameful about all of us. We are going home because we have what we want. What we came for. And he is afraid. The fog is beginning to burn away. Already the spine of Vivara is visible. Houses are morphing out of the grey. The colours remind me of home. Two pink houses, a gold house, a yellow house, a grey.

They Need No Motorcars

Julia O'Faolain

At last the builders turned our house over to us.

For half my life we had been making trips to see what had started as no more than a plan pegged out with string. Later we had earthworks to admire, foundations with an interesting crawl-space, then reassuringly solid walls which, however, made passers-by stop and exclaim.

'Djez see,' we'd hear them marvel in the village shop, 'the new bit they're after buildin' onto that queer, new house?'

1937 was a bad year for novelty. Offended by the exposed beams in our open-plan living room, gawkers gave it short shrift.

I, though, was barely five, so to me the world was new and novelty pure promise. Too good a promise? To be on the safe side, I crossed my fingers. Electricity amazed me. Having known only oil lamps, I thought of electric ones as storing captured lightning. Or genies. My hopes were radiant – and yet the house surpassed them. For months after we'd moved in, Aunt Annie and I kept wondering how we had ever managed to survive in the old, unwired one on the edge of the Wicklow bog, and congratulated ourselves on the comforts available in south County Dublin.

Aunt Annie, who was not my aunt but my mother's, was frail and small-boned with hair like bog-cotton and a wardrobe full of buttoned shoes and high-necked dresses made of white-sprigged silk. She had come to live with my parents and me when she was eighty and I was four, and I think now that she feared being a burden to them. Perhaps they horrified her? Their cigarettes and laughter and my mother's lipstick? The opinions they'd picked up when living abroad? I don't know. I was too small to know, but I felt the intensity of her concentration on me and the demands of an alliance which I wasn't sure I could afford. Or rather, I welcomed it, then found that I seemed to have contracted for more than I knew.

Telling me bed-time stories was her one contribution to the household chores, and she made it with such zest that, when she'd taken my candle and left me to digest what she'd read – it was always laced with horror – groping my way to an unlit lavatory was often beyond my nerve. In the old house this could lead to my wetting the bed, then to shame and discomfort as the hot pee turned cold. But I still begged for the stories. They were spine-chilling and I was a fear addict.

Now, though, all I had to do was reach for the switch, and hey presto, the primrose walls of my new room swam into sight. Freshly distempered! Shadowless. Clean! They made me cocky and sure that the witches, infesting the house we'd left, could not hide here. Anyway, now that I was learning to read myself, I lost interest in them. I had joined the library and discovered the *Just William* books and light-hearted sagas about English children.

Aunt Annie took no interest in these. She was turning in on herself and, in spite, or because of the electric light, was now the one afraid. Well-lit mirrors disheartened her, and our house move soon struck her as rash. Change, in your eighties, was a risk, and unfamiliar sounds could be omens. There was a foghorn. The tolling of the Protestant church bell was close and loud. Cows, a slow, overweight bull and a braying donkey patrolled two sides of our garden which, until recently, had been a stretch of tussocky pasture. Now that it was fenced off, the vegetables and uncropped grass on our side tempted them. Munching loudly, they leaned into the new palings, sometimes broke through, and were apt, when shooed back, to panic, bolt in the wrong direction, then plunge clumsily down the fresh earthworks around the house. They churned up the freshly laid lawn and smashed rose bushes, and my father worried lest one break a leg and he be liable. Might their owner 'have the law on us'? In my head these words took on the magnitude of Aunt Annie's alarms – which now came home to roost.

At dusk one evening, hearing us shout at the stampeding animals, she looked out her window and saw a car drive down a lane two fields away. The headlights were masked by a windy hedge, and she screamed in terror that 'they' were coming to take her away. My mother thought she meant an ambulance, but Aunt Annie said, no, she meant the fairies or, as she called them, the 'good' people whom it was unwise to describe by any other name. 'Those are their lights!' she whimpered.

'Will-o'-the-wisps! It's them all right! That's the headless coach! *An cóiste bodhar!*' There was nothing benevolent about fairies in Aunt Annie's book. They were an ancient, angry, dispossessed people animated by venomous schemes. '*O vo, vo!*' she wept, for she was getting more old-fashioned by the day and had started using Gaelic words like an old country woman although, to hear my mother, she had lived all her life in Cork City and knew no Gaelic at all. Maybe she was in her second childhood and remembering words some rural grandmother had wept over her cradle? Reverting? Turning back in time? My mother took a firm tone.

'Aunt Annie, those are motor-car headlights.'

Aunt Annie wouldn't have it. 'Those are no motor cars!' she wailed, stubbornly intoning the words. '*They* need no motor cars!' Then, as if to annoy us, '*Wirrasthrue!*'

When I laughed about this later, my mother said I had no heart.

'Can she really believe in fairies?' I wanted to know.

'Maybe not. Maybe she's too afraid to name her real fear, which', my father guessed, 'could be the fear of being sent away.'

'Where?'

'Never mind,' said my mother.

'To . . .' My father opened his mouth, but my mother put a hand over it.

'Be kind to her,' she told me. 'Remember how kind she was when you were small.'

Sometimes I was kind. It was agreeable to be praised for this.

'God bless your eyesight, child,' said Aunt Annie when I threaded her needles. Now that she no longer read to me she was trying to make herself useful by mending, but her stitches were erratic and often had to be pulled out.

I did her favours, fetching her bottle of Guinness to spare her old legs, and plunging a reddened poker into the glass to make it fizz. This earned her gratitude, and I was flattered to hear my parents say how good I was with the old woman. Sometimes, though, I teased her, for it was interesting to see how easily she could be reduced to terror. I can only suppose, as I consider the behaviour of that small, alien person whom I must still call 'I', that I was timid and felt called on not to be, and was testing the limits of fear.

'You could have given her a heart attack!' my mother scolded one day when I had gone too far. 'She could *die*! She's old. That's what she's afraid of. Didn't you know?'

I hadn't thought of this. Yet I had seen death: stiff-legged blackbirds lying on their backs, a drowned, hairless, half-rotted dog and, more worryingly, the carcasses which in those days hung on meat hooks in butchers' shops. Their connection with Aunt Annie's fears shocked me.

'I didn't mean to frighten her,' I protested. 'I wasn't even thinking of her at first.'

'Well,' said my mother, 'it's time you *learned* to think. You're nearly eight years old!'

I was! The three years since our move had changed me – and not, my mother said, for the better.

'Don't let me catch you doing the like again.'

What I had done was dangle a doll called Angelina over the upstairs banisters. Angelina had been a gift from friends in Boston and, in keeping with our notion of America, was big – as big as myself, though, being dressed in a pink cheerleader's outfit, she did not resemble me at all.

In spite of this, Aunt Annie, peering near-sightedly from the bottom of the stairwell, mistook Angelina's dangling feet for mine. She had been expecting disaster! Here it was! Foreboding blinded her to the blatant make-believe of the pink leatherette boots. 'Help!' she screamed. 'Quick! Someone! The child's hanged herself. Or she's falling – falling from the top floor!'

Next she felt a constriction in her chest while I, up above and, naturally, unaware of this, was egged on by the drama to jiggle the feet and yell that, yes, – 'Help! Help!' – I *was* losing my grip!

Aunt Annie let out a shriek and collapsed.

This alerted our maid, Bridie, who burst from the kitchen followed by Mrs Kelly, the char, and when I got down to the hall, my father was there too, and four pairs of shocked eyes were condemning me as heartless and possibly murderous.

'It's her fault,' they told my mother, who now came in from the garden. 'Her with her doll.'

'The old lady's dying,' cried Bridie, who enjoyed trouble. 'Fright put the heart across her!'

It was a false alarm, and Aunt Annie recovered.

I was punished and Angelina confiscated, and though I felt badly for a bit and sorry for Aunt Annie, I was resentful too, for who but she had taught me to relish fear? On Good Friday, when she asked me to do the Stations of the Cross with her, I made an excuse. The Stations of the

Cross provided her – and had, in earlier years, provided me – with something between the chill of a horror story and an orgy of companionable tears plus, in her case, I suppose, hope. We had pictures of each Station to look at while saying the prescribed number of prayers and working up our feelings.

I'd been wanting to give up the practice anyway, for, though Aunt Annie's fear of death must have kept her piety on course, I was aware of profane, slyly pleasurable elements in mine. The Jesus figure in our pictures had a red gown, long hair the colour of my own, and looked like a woman. Blasphemously, I imagined *being* him and had, rather half-heartedly, tried scratching the stigmata on my feet, then found that this had none of the thrill of my imaginings. Soon I began to feel guilty, since our sins – among them play-acting with the stigmata – had helped drive in the nails. Best, perhaps, to give up the Stations. In the later images, where the gown was removed, the stripped Jesus was too clearly male for me to imagine myself as him anyway. But I knew that Aunt Annie's bellowsing fervour could still work on me and pump up that hot, inner bloat which God must surely find disgusting. I feared His contempt.

'We're doing the Stations at School,' I told her. 'I don't want to do them twice.'

'You don't like being with me any more,' she reproached me, and nodded her stubborn head with pique. Nod, nod! Confident as a judge's gavel. 'You're not my girl any more! Aha! That's the real truth! It is! Isn't it? Admit you've turned against me.'

I denied this, though my feelings were indeed on the turn, soured by her wheedling need. Even today, when I hear the phrase 'eager to take offence', I think of how her offence-taking was a plea for things to be made well, like a kissed bruise. Things nobody could make well! 'You're not my friend,' she'd wrangle and look ready to cry.

A pretence? A tease? Adult tears sometimes were, but Aunt Annie was too easily hurt to rank as quite an adult. So I said, 'It's not that, Aunt Annie, honestly. But I have homework to do. I'll read to you later if you like. I'll read you *The Cork Examiner*.' We got this paper so that she could finger her way through the 'Births, Marriages and Deaths' and see who had died in her home city. By now almost everyone she had ever known had. No wonder she couldn't bear to lose a friend.

I recognised the feeling because of what had happened with my godmother, Molly Fitz. She, I had been warned, would not be visiting us any more, nor sending me gifts. My father had published an attack on the government party for which her husband worked. So she'd cut us off. What choice had she? my mother demanded and answered herself. None! Molly Fitz was not the one to blame!

'No fraternising!' my mother quoted bitterly. 'That's the rule. Don't tell me,' she reproached my father, 'you forgot?'

They had been cut off before. Twenty years ago, he, she and Molly Fitz had been on the same side in the Civil War, and old opponents had ostracised them ever since. Soon old friends would do the same. We would now be cut by *both sides*, said my mother! Molly Fitz's desertion would be read as a signal.

To me the blow was personal. She had been a generous godmother and for my last birthday had sent me two French dolls, a prince and princess, with china faces, eyes which opened and closed, and real hair. The prince wore satin knee breeches and the princess a crinoline. Nobody else got gifts like these.

'Well you can kiss goodbye to such things!'

My mother was sure people on our local bus were refusing to meet her eye. 'We're pariahs!' she told my father, who let out a guilty laugh, kissed her and skipped impishly out the door.

He had been building again and now had a wooden hut some way from the house with a telephone extension and electric power. It had a verandah where he sometimes let us join him for meals, which felt like picnics because of the nearby fields in which we could see a pond, wild rabbits with white scuts, a stately heron, and of course the cows, which no longer bothered us now that our hedges had grown thick and thorny enough to prevent them.

Most of the time, though, we kept away from the hut. Inside it he and a few friends were getting out a magazine, which continued giving offence to the authorities and, by extension, to passengers on our bus. From time to time there were libel threats, calls to lawyers, whispers and great gusts of possibly nervous laughter. I, carrying trays of refreshments from the house, caught shreds and echoes, and was viscerally on his side, though I could not have said what was at stake or why there were sides at all. Maybe, to use a word of Aunt Annie's, he just liked being contrary?

'He thrives on it!' said my mother, who had thrived with him in the glory days of 'the scrap', as they had called the struggle for Independence. Now they and the century had turned forty; life was drab; comforts like sugar were in short supply; the Second World War was on and neutral Ireland had no jobs. As people thronged to England to find work, the ones left behind must have felt as if the city's energy had drained away. My father had his magazine. What had she?

These notions erupted in murmurous spurts, half out of my hearing. Aunt Annie heard them too. 'Ha,' she murmured under her breath. 'Feeling sorry for ourselves, are we!'

Her tone surprised me. It was one she usually reserved for me. 'Pull a sour face,' she'd scold in just that voice, 'and if the wind changes you'll be stuck with it.'

The new changes brought back memories of how, long ago, when my mother's mother died, Aunt Annie had taken charge and – her story – selflessly devoted herself to rearing her dead sister's children. A wild brood! But my mother remembered *her* as a hopeless housekeeper who burned porridge and served rashers raw. In friendly moments, the two sang songs they'd sung then. One was about a small girl to whom they sometimes gave my mother's name and sometimes mine. What, I wondered, if the wind changed and I stayed stuck in their bickering past?

'You be good now,' Aunt Annie warned me, 'your mother's got enough troubles.'

'What troubles?'

'Never mind.'

Adult secrets! Well I'd known my mother was restless, if only because we were trespassing again.

This had been a hobby of hers and mine when we lived in Wicklow. During the Slump – it was worse in Ireland than elsewhere – that county had a lot of estates whose owners, unable to keep them up, turned keys in the doors and left for London. Soon neglected greenery exploded; tennis courts became meadows and yew walks tunnels. Wildlife slithered and whirred, and my mother and I, defying rickety signs warning 'Trespassers will be Prosecuted', eased our furtive way up and in, over high walls topped with broken glass. For me it was like stepping into a story by the Brothers Grimm. In her the decay aroused a mix of rebelly triumph and awe. In her youth the Great Houses had been targets for arson. Now, as the lines of their formal gardens softened and blurred, they acquired a savour of doomed romance. Inhaling this in a pot pourri of ruined roses, we were, she somehow conveyed, repossessing what, centuries ago, had been stolen from the native Irish – us – by planter stock. Cromwellians and the like.

But she wasn't consistent, for we were friendly with two old ladies from that same stock who still hung on in one such house. They gave us tea, when we called on them, in thin, Belleek cups. My mother's seamless politeness on these visits shocked me.

Could she, I wondered, be as two-faced with me? She *was* with Aunt Annie, but then so were we all.

'Don't upset her. Keep bad things from her. Remember her weak heart!' These house rules had been laid down by Doctor Condon, our GP.

Aunt Annie could not be told of our trespassing, which anyway we had given up. Once petrol became unobtainable, and returns to Wicklow had to be by bike, there was no time for it. This was because, at last and three years late, my mother, who was busy making a kitchen garden to keep us fed, had sent me to school.

Though punctilious with the Cromwellian old ladies, she was, in her own word, bolshie with my school nuns. Maybe, having taught me herself till now, she saw them as rivals? At any rate she flouted their prime rule, which was that pupils must fit in. I had the wrong uniform. She had made it herself in the right colours but the wrong shape, and though, as a concession to the hard times, I was let wear it, I had to stay out of sight on official occasions.

'Why do you care?' she asked when I complained. 'Why,' she marvelled with genuine wonder, 'would anyone *want* to be like everyone else?' She was sure that when *she* was young nobody did.

Well, *I* did. I just did and, what was more, I tried to keep my classmates from meeting her in case she disgraced me by talking about a person's duty to think for herself and not be a bourgeois conformist. None of the other parents used words like that! Ha! said my mother, they didn't because that was what they were!

Were they? At times I agreed with her, but fearing she'd say this to their faces, I intercepted and tore up all invitations to parents to attend school events. I was now nearly nine and what I wanted most in all the world was a shop-bought gym slip and a school tie.

Then the trespassing started again. Quite near our house, the grounds of a locked and barbed-wired, Victorian Gothic castle had been let revert to a wilderness which abutted on woods where we often walked. Perhaps there had been talk of ghosts? Had lights been seen? I refused to listen for I now distrusted and tried to check my mother's flights of fancy. Don't even mention witches, I told her. My father backed me up. So she talked instead about the old days when he used to make bombs. Bombs? Daddy?

'You're fooling?'

'Ask him.'

'But wasn't it a secret?'

'*Then* yes. Not now! Now everything's public. Now he's a gadfly!'

This was a stab at his attacks on de Valera, who was himself attacking and interning his own hard-line followers. But her annoyance – I knew, I guessed – had more to do with my father's having new friends, one of them a woman, whom she didn't like.

Some of our visitors defended Dev, saying the hard men wanted to put bombs in English postboxes. And Dev had to keep the English sweet lest they seize our ports. I heard this on evenings when my parents held open house and I was helping serve sandwiches, barm *breac* and tea. Liquor was too expensive, so we offered none, but excitement rose without it. Having open house meant that enemies could drop in and come face to face. Sometimes there were rows. It was interesting and confusing. But I kept wondering – *could* my playful, mild father have made bombs?

'Oh, but that,' said my mother when pressed, 'was twenty years ago!' She regretted bringing the matter up. 'Anyway,' she added airily, 'he only made them. He never threw them.'

'He didn't?'

'No.'

This was somehow worse. Chancier. Double, double toil and . . . Unused bombs were trouble! Where were they now? I imagined him stirring a bomb-cauldron. Maybe it wasn't true? I asked my father who said, yes, he'd made bombs. Someone had to.

'We were fighting a war.'

It had, he said, been an uninteresting job. I didn't dare ask about the woman friend.

'Your mother,' he told me out of the blue, 'is in a bit of a black mood just now. A bit under the weather. You should try and cheer her up. She's the racehorse breed. Takes things hard and needs her mind taken off them.'

Did she? What things? Did trespassing take her mind off them? Was this because fear, like the valve on our boiler, was a release? Or was she testing her nerve?

She and I climbed the wall around the castle and dropped into an orchard where leaf mould muffled sound, and fruit, falling in a buzz of wasps, rotted plumply. Further on, autumn flowers were in rampant bloom. There were red-hot pokers and purple Michaelmas daisies, but she picked none. Her pleasure, as in visits to a waxworks, was in airing accounts of long-dead landowners who hid mantraps to catch poachers and break their legs. All her tales featured brutal gamekeepers and black-hearted magistrates and had probably been told to her first, long ago, by Aunt Annie. I was giving a dismissive shake of my head when a corner of my eye caught a movement among the apple trees to our right. I grabbed her hand.

'Mummy, a gamekeeper!'

She was looking in the wrong direction. 'In those days,' she mused, 'they—'

'No! Now! Here! There's one. Look!'

'Hey! You!' called a voice. 'You over there!'

A man was advancing on us, carrying a gun. He wasn't pointing it and it wasn't a gangster's gun. Not a revolver but the sort my father had used for shooting rabbits when we lived in Wicklow. The man wore corduroy pants and a tweed coat so rough and prickly it brought to mind the withered nettles goosegirls spun and wove in Aunt Annie's stories. His eyebrows were an erect yellow stubble and his face lumpy as though stung by nettles.

'Hullo there!' He was now quite close and my mother had seen him.

'Let's run,' I shouted to her. All scepticism gone, I bolted and didn't turn until I reached the place where we'd come in. She wasn't with me. Where was she? I retraced my steps, then, slowing, hid behind a bush to see what was happening.

He had a hand on her arm. Was he taking her into custody? That was a word I knew from newspaper stories. No. He was handing her – what? A notebook in which he had just written something? He screwed the top back on his pen.

Moving furtively from tree to tree, I got close enough to hear my father's name and that of his magazine.

She was *chatting*! As if the man were a guest at one of her open-house evenings! Catching sight of me, the two began to laugh. Sheepish and baffled, I sidled forward to hear him say he was one of the men whom de Valera had led and then let down. He knew of my father's attacks on Dev and wanted her to take him a message of support. As for our trespassing, well, no harm if this was the end of it.

'The old people used to say,' he quoted, 'every dog is allowed one bite!'

As if to apologise for the comparison, he presented her with a bag of apples which he must have filled earlier, for it was lying on a bench. Next, looking her in the eye, he warned gravely that we should not come back, then, leading us through a shrubbery, and down an avenue to the gate lodge, opened a door and let us out on the road.

On the way home my mother was unusually silent.

When I asked if the man *was* a gamekeeper, she said, no, a caretaker and that we mustn't breathe a word about what had happened. 'I'll tell your father,' she said, 'later.'

'Did the caretaker write a message for him?'

'Yes.'

'Which side is he on? The caretaker? Molly Fitz's or the other?'

'No side,' my mother said. 'He has no side. Now I want you to pay attention. You're to say nothing about what happened. Have I your promise?'

'Yes.'

I was confused. Why, just when her credibility had been boosted, did she want me to keep quiet about it?

'We'll not be going back there,' she told me. 'So mum's the word, eh?'

'I promise,' I told her, but two weeks later I broke the promise. I don't know why. Maybe all this anarchy and secrecy were too much for me, and I needed to take charge? Make them mine? Or maybe, like my father, I was just being contrary?

He was out dining with what she called 'his new friends', and I was playing ludo with Aunt Annie, when I heard raised voices below. Looking over the banisters, I saw the top of a bald head and recognised Mr Lynch and trouble. Mr Lynch was the park ranger and not the sort of person who called on us. It was not his job which prevented this. If he had been a reader or would-be writer, or had had political interests, he would have been known as Jimmy Lynch and welcome at our open-house evenings. But he did not. He had no interesting interests at all. Why he was here – I knew with instant guilt – was as the father of my new friend, Una, with whom I had climbed into the castle orchard earlier that day and stolen apples. Nobody had seen us and I had hidden my share in our turf shed, but Una must have been careless with hers. Mr Lynch, who was violent in the drink, had clearly been drinking now.

'Breaking and entering!' he cried in righteous disgust, and said he was going to give Una a hiding. No relative of his ever laid a finger on what didn't belong to them! The bad influence hadn't come from his side, and Una would not be spending time with me any more. Was he making himself clear? She and her mother were at this moment lying low in some neighbour's house. Keeping out of his way! But they'd have to come home some time and when they did . . .

'Mr Lynch, why don't we sit down and talk about it?' My mother's voice was coolly cajoling. 'Let me get you a cup of tea.'

He said there was nothing to talk about, and she said he'd got the wrong end of the stick. The stick, he said, was what was needed.

'No, *no!*' My mother, who had advanced ideas about child-rearing, was horrified at what she'd started. It wasn't a matter of trespassing at all, she told him. The caretaker was a friend and must have given the girls the fruit. 'Tea?' she offered again and led Mr Lynch out of my hearing.

Shaken by what I'd started myself, I went back to find Aunt Annie suffering from palpitations. She had not been able to make out Mr Lynch's words, but his voice had frightened her. She now read almost everything as a portent, and what could such fierce rumbles portend but the day of wrath which she had so long been expecting? Twice already she had been anointed, then recovered.

We had grown used to her frets, so I gave her her pills with a glass of water and did not call my mother, as this would have meant confronting Mr Lynch and backing up her lie. I hadn't the nerve.

After a while, though, I began to worry. What if Aunt Annie died from lack of attention? I crept downstairs and hid in the hallway where, through the kitchen door, I could hear the wrangle still going on. It was quieter now, and I knew by the stops and starts and the odd rattle of a spoon that tea was being drunk. Mr Lynch said we had climbed the orchard wall. He'd got that much out of Una before she and her mother ran off. We had not gone in the front gate or any gate, so we were trespassers. He was sticking to his point, but sounded chatty and almost as if he were enjoying himself.

'Oh, Mr Lynch!' My mother's voice was amused. 'Did you never play at being a cowboy when you were their age? Or an engine driver? But you weren't one were you? It's a game. A bit of excitement to take their minds off the dreariness of . . .' She drew breath and stopped for the tiniest instant as if changing her mind. '. . . school,' she finished weakly.

Mr Lynch laughed. A chair scraped. They were coming out. I doubled back halfway up the stairs. She had calmed him!

'Forgive them their trespasses,' she was saying as they opened the front door.

He laughed again and I backed up the stairs to find that Aunt Annie too was calmer.

My mother never mentioned Mr Lynch's visit to me, and when trouble came it was from a different quarter.

The milkman told the gardaí that something queer was going on at the castle. The caretaker, a lone man living by himself in its gate lodge, was taking too much milk. A crate? Two? I forget. But the place was raided and – shades of my father's old bomb-making days! – it came out that bombs were being fabricated there by a rump IRA which was in opposition to the government.

'Twenty men they found!' Aunt Annie, who had been talking to Bridie the maid, revelled in shock. Bridie was on a network. She talked to other maids, some of whom had come from the same orphanage as herself.

'I heard six!' My mother, drawing on my father's experience in *their* war, thought six quite enough for a bomb factory. But nobody knew for sure. It was a great time for hugger-mugger and keeping things out of the papers.

Aunt Annie insisted that bomb-making had now grown more terrible and complex. She seemed to be pleased rather than frightened by this, just as she was when listening to the war news on the BBC. Perhaps she thought of bombs as lightning conductors for the random evil that threatened us all. Some of this had now been averted. 'Two crates of milk bottles!' She began counting on her fingers. They'd only use it in their tea. 'Two crates! Enough for fifty men!'

Did the bomb-makers belong to the pro-German or Communist wing of the outlawed movement? Either way, my father had no sympathy for them. Perhaps the wings combined? I never knew, but my mother's claim to be friends with the caretaker sparked insinuations and, though the gardaí took no interest, passengers on our bus did. It wasn't true that they cut her. Gossips were too keen to probe to do that.

'How's your mother these days?' people would ask me. 'Busy gardening? She's great at that, isn't she? Keeps ye in spuds all year round, I'm told, and in strawberries and raspberries too! So ye get the jam-maker's special allowance of sugar! A great woman! I heard she used to get cuttings from the man at the gate lodge down the road. It must have been a shock to hear what he was up to?'

'Yes,' I'd say. 'She's gardening I don't know about cuttings.'

'And your grandaunt? Failing, I hear? Ah well, she's a great age, isn't she?'

Aunt Annie was finally rushed to hospital just as she'd known she would be. She died there, and I was not taken to the funeral, though my mother described it. Petrol was still scarce, so the hearse and cabs following it were all horse-drawn, and the horses' heads bore black plumes.

'They need no motorcars,' I quoted.

'What?' My mother had forgotten.

'It's what she said that time when she was talking about fairies. Daddy said then that she was really thinking of something else! And he was right! She was thinking of her own funeral.'

'Oh, *poor* Aunt Annie!'

'Yes,' I agreed piously, 'poor, poor Aunt Annie.'

Secretly I didn't think she deserved too much pity. She had known how to keep her mind off her real worries. She'd used stories the way my mother used trespassing. Una and I had now definitely given *that* up. We didn't need our minds taken off anything, and our new, burning interest was in being picked for the junior school play.

Matters of Life and Death

BERNARD MACLAVERTY

The boy sat on one of the divan beds for almost an hour without moving. At his feet the shopping bag with their pyjamas and things in it. His younger brother lay on a rug on the floor between the beds turned away from him. Nothing was said. Sounds drifted up from downstairs – the wireless was on, a mixture of distant music and talk. Doors opened and closed. Traffic hummed from the main road. At one point there was ringing.

'Telephone,' said the boy. His brother nodded. High heels clicked across the hallway and the ringing stopped and the doctor's wife spoke. Sometimes his younger brother made a noise like a pig – snuffing back and swallowing green stuff. It was revolting and he wanted to kill him. Then the boy heard someone coming up the stairs. The doctor's wife came to the half-open door and tapped it lightly with her fingernail.

'Can I come in?' The boy sat upright on the bed – his brother rolled around and looked over his shoulder at the door. The doctor's wife stepped into the room. She leaned forward and put her hands on her knees so that her head was on a level with the boy's sitting on the bed. 'So – Ben and Tony – have you settled in?' The boys nodded.

'Do you want to go outside?' The boy thought it seemed somehow wrong.

'No,' he said. 'Thank you.'

'Into the garden for a bit. Get a bit of fresh air before lunch.' The boy had already made his decision and he felt it would be rude to change it.

'I'm OK.'

'Whatever suits. Also I was wondering if you had any likes or dislikes for lunch? Either of you. It's coming up to that time.' No. This time both boys shook their heads. 'Some boys can be very picky. I have nephews and nieces who would run a mile rather than eat a soft-boiled egg.'

'Some eggs have elastic bands in them,' said the boy's brother.

'Pardon me?'

'In the white bit – some brown rubbery things. Eucch.'

'Well the eggs we get here don't have anything like that in them.' She laughed. 'So what would you like?' The boy sitting on the bed raised his shoulders in a slow shrug – he'd no idea. 'A boiled egg? With plenty of hot buttered toast?' said the doctor's wife. The boys nodded. When they had a boiled egg at home their mother spooned it from the shell into a cup and mashed the bits up with some butter so that the yellow and the white mixed evenly.

'Very well, then – it's too early but let's go.' She ushered them out of the room and down the stairs into the kitchen. They walked quietly in their new surroundings. There was a tall refrigerator purring in the corner. She sat them up on stools at a table and bustled around putting on a saucepan of eggs, dropping slices of bread into the shining toaster, setting salt and pepper on the table. She promised that they could make flavoured lollipops later on.

'What's your favourite flavour?'

'Orange,' said the boy. His brother said, 'Milk.'

The doctor's wife laughed, said it was impossible to make a milk lollipop.

She was dressed as if she was going out for the evening – a silky green frock, pearls around her bare neck, high-heel sandal shoes. She lit a cigarette from the lighter she used to light the gas and bit down hard on the first intake of smoke.

'Dr D'Arcy and his wife – they're always immaculate,' his mother said. 'For all the world like Fred Astaire and Ginger Rogers.' Dr D'Arcy wasn't their doctor – just a friend of the family. Ben and Tony's father and Dr D'Arcy were both in the Young Philanthropists. Their own doctor was Dr Gorman. Dr Gorman was the one who came to the house when anyone was sick. And to the hospital after you had had your tonsils out.

'Ice cream – and plenty of it,' was the medicine he prescribed.

The boy had seen photos of Fred Astaire and Ginger Rogers dancing in the movies. His mother and father were very keen on supper dances and would go to one or two every year – mostly ones run by the Young Philanthropists. For days beforehand the house would be full of excitement. On the night, the boys would be in the kitchen with

Miss McKay, the babysitter, and upstairs the bathroom would be going full tilt, the steam and the shaving and the powdering and perfuming all going on at the same time along with shouts of *Are there no laces for these shoes? Where are the cuff links? They'll be where you left them last year.* Dr D'Arcy would be picking them up by car, or a taxi would have been ordered and the ones getting ready would always be running late. And then they'd arrive into the room for the 'showing off' with his mother saying, 'I'm as ready as ever I'm going to be.' And she'd swish and twirl around the kitchen, the dress and her petticoats taking up most of the space. She'd touch the necklace at her throat and worry that it didn't match her diamante bag. His father would straighten his black bow tie at the mirror by crouching his knees. It was set at the correct height for their mother. And because it was a special occasion they'd kiss the boys goodbye and tell them to behave and so on and not give Miss McKay any trouble. Their father smelled of shaving soap. And their mother would decide at the last minute not to wear a coat because it just sat out and made the dress look silly – her wrap would be warm enough. And the doctor's car would be honking its horn outside and suddenly the door would rattle and slam and they'd be gone. Silence. And Miss McKay would be sitting there smiling, waiting to play cards. The next morning when the boys woke there would be balloons and paper hats and cocktail sticks shaped like tiny sabres or brightly coloured swizzle sticks on their bedside chairs.

'You poor things,' said the doctor's wife. Her long red hair gave the impression of being unruly – standing out as it did from her head. She fought a constant battle with it, combing and sweeping it aside with open fingers.

'Four minutes?' she said. 'To be on the safe side?' She looked very tall and glamorous as she stood waiting for the toast with one hand on her hip and a cigarette in the other. Her fingernails were painted. Even her toenails were scarlet – peeping out the front of her high-heel sandals. When the eggs were ready she set one in front of each boy. They stared at them but didn't move.

'Let me.' She sliced the top off each egg and set it on a plate beside the egg cup. 'No bits of shell,' she said. 'Clean as a whistle. And apostle spoons. What's keeping you?' The boy scooped a little egg white from the lid and put it in his mouth. His younger brother did the same. The doctor's wife took a seat on a stool and leaned her elbows on the table staring at her guests. She looked long and hard at them then smiled.

'I would just love two boys like you,' she said. There was a sound of crunching toast and chewing. She made a platform for her chin with her fists and looked from one boy to the other. The younger boy chewed his food with his mouth open. His brother watched in disgust as he rolled the mashed up food around his mouth. Occasionally the younger boy stopped for breath – breathed in past the mush and then would continue chewing.

'So what would you like to do this afternoon?' The boys continued to eat and stare defiance at each other. 'We could do something in the garden.'

'Like what?' said the boy. He must have thought his reply sounded rude because he added, 'That'd be OK.'

'What games do you play at home?' The boys stared down at their eggs then looked at each other. The boy said with a smile,

'Cricket in the yard.'

'I'm afraid we have no yard here.'

'Slow-motion football,' said his brother.

'And what, may I ask, is that?'

The elder boy tried to explain: a round balloon – the pitch was the hall – the goalposts the stairs. His younger brother got off his stool and began to move in the kitchen with heavy limbs demonstrating to the doctor's wife. He was smiling, remembering. 'Like you're in syrup when you head the balloon – it's slow-motion – like in the pictures.'

'I'm sorry but we have no real toys – not even a balloon.' The kitchen darkened and spots of rain appeared on the window pane.

'We'll have to think of something else. Would you look at that?' She nodded outside. 'How I would love to live somewhere like Spain or Barbados. Somewhere you can *depend* on the weather.' The boy's brother took a spoonful of egg and looked down into the shell. He made a noise in his throat – he didn't spit – but he allowed the egg along with some half-chewed toast to tumble out of his mouth onto his plate. He drooled strings of liquid stuff after it. His brother turned away.

'Is anything wrong?' said the doctor's wife.

The younger boy was leaning forward, swallowing and swallowing. Then he regained his composure.

'An elastic band,' he said, looking down into his eggshell.

'No. There's no such thing.' The doctor's wife swivelled off her stool and came to see. The child pointed at a small brownish spot deep in the white of the egg and curled his lip up in disgust.

'Would you like a banana?' She took the plate with the mouthful of mush and tipped it into the bin as if nothing had happened.

'Thank you,' he said when she set a banana on his plate. He peeled the skin back and scrutinised the white of the banana for flaws or ripe spots. Finding none, he bit into it.

'I hope the rain's not on for the day,' said the doctor's wife. 'More tea?' Both boys refused. 'When you're finished in here – you can just wander about the place. Explore the house.' The phone rang in the hall and she hurried out. They heard her talking for a long time. When she came back they had finished eating.

'You can go anywhere you like, boys, except the surgery. Dr D'Arcy sees his private patients in there. Need I say more? Needles and things.' She gave a little shudder. 'It's the only room we keep locked. Let me show you around.' She ushered them out of the kitchen and led them along a parquet hallway. She left wafts of lavender in her wake.

'Oh, this is what we call the dance hall.' She pushed the open door and the boys looked in. It was a yellow wooden floor. There was a large bay window which made the room seem very bright. They all walked into the room and suddenly there was an echo to every sound.

'This is a maple sprung floor – our one extravagance. It was put in by the same people who did the Plaza Ballroom. Feel it move with you.' She let her hand rest on what looked like a sideboard. 'The radiogram. The piano is for visitors who can play. Can either of you?'

They both shook their heads. No, they couldn't. They went to the next room.

'This is the library but not many children's books, I'm afraid.' She pointed to one side. 'Mostly medical stuff. Not very nice. Promise me you'll avoid that side.' The boys agreed. 'But the good doctor likes the occasional detective story.' She waved her hand at a complete bookcase full of green-banded paperbacks. 'Most of all, Agatha Crispy.'

'Christie,' said the elder boy.

'Just my little joke.' She smiled and pointed out some of her own childhood books, but they looked school-girlie. The telephone rang and she rushed to answer it. She shouted over her shoulder, 'I'll leave you to it.'

The boy and his brother stood staring at the detective stories. The boy turned to the medical books at the other side of the room. They had titles he could barely read. Words that meant nothing to him – ologies and isms. There were *Lancets* and *British Medical Journals* – many books about 'the Catholic Doctor' – shelves full of Maynooth and Down and Conor quarterlies. He took down a large book and opened it. It had some black-and-white pictures illustrating diseases. Misshapen men stripped to the waist. A person with a blackened hairy tongue thrust out. A bare woman with droopy chests covered in spots. Then babies stuck together – then things so horrible he slammed the book shut and put it back on the shelf. He went into the dance hall, hoping to get away from such images. But they were in his head. He knelt down on the smooth floor to look at the records. They were neatly stored in heavy books which contained paper sleeves with a circular window so that the label could be read. Decca, Columbia, Parlophone and His Master's Voice – the rich red behind the white dog. The radiogram had a cupboard at one end and the door was not properly closed. The boy looked around then eased it open. Bottles and glasses. A bar stocked with gin and whisky and other stuff.

He turned round and his brother was standing there with his hands in his pockets. The boy pushed the cupboard door shut.

'What are you standing there for?' His brother pulled a face. 'Why don't you go somewhere else?'

'I'm all right here.'

'Why d'you always have to follow me?'

His brother didn't move for a while. Eventually he sidled off back into the hallway.

There were more things to do in the library – so the boy went back, hoping his brother had gone elsewhere. Beside the detective books were the yellow spines of countless copies of *National Geographics*. Pictures of naked African women were to be found in these. The boy sat down on the carpet and pulled out a magazine. Photos of Norwegian pine forests with light fanning between the tree trunks, parrots and seas sweeping onto beaches in Australia. Something on the bright lights of Broadway with the headline saying for every light there's a broken heart. Photographs of the American Civil War with dead bodies sprawled everywhere.

It was good to be rid of his brother. His very presence was an annoyance – the way he spat out his food in front of the doctor's wife was terrible. But it wasn't just that – it was a continual thing. His sniffing. His mouth noises. He did sneaky farts. Sometimes you heard them, sometimes you didn't.

The rain had stopped ticking at the window and the sun came out. The light fell in warm squares on the flowered carpet. The wallpaper was strange and posh. He had never seen anything like it. It had a pattern of flowers – maroon against a creamy background. But the flowers were made of velvet. He reached out and touched the pattern with his fingers. It was soothing in a way. He loved the touch – the way it gave with his pressing – and he continued touching with the palm of his hand as he looked down at the page. The words seemed to move. He found them difficult to read. His eyes wanted to close. He was tired. He hadn't had much sleep. What with people running up and down the stairs all night. Sometimes loud voices, sometimes whispering outside his door. At one point he'd recognised the priest's voice. When he'd put his head out to see what was going on – his mother had pleaded with him to stay in bed. 'For me,' she said and her face had had a look he had never seen before. On anyone's face. So he stayed put with the eiderdown pulled over his head. His brother had slept throughout.

He put his head down on his forearm and closed his eyes. And he drifted in the warmth of the sun and the carpet and his fingertips singing after contact with the wallpaper. When he woke he smiled – then he remembered and his face went solid again. He didn't know how long he'd slept for, but he had drooled on his arm. He rubbed it dry and looked around him. What must have wakened him was the slam of a car door because the back door of the house opened and a voice shouted, 'Hello!'

Dr D'Arcy, still wearing his hat, stopped at the threshold of the library and saw the boy lying on the floor.

'Hi,' he said. 'What a sad, sad day.' He came and hunkered down in front of the boy. The doctor reached out and touched him on the shoulder. Then patted him on the head as he straightened up. The boy did not know what to say. He was on the verge of tears but did not want to show it. 'You're making yourself comfortable, I see.'

'Yes.'

The doctor stepped back out into the hallway. His wife came to him and offered herself for a kiss. He took off his hat and kissed her. The boy looked away.

'Not lonely today, eh?' said the doctor.

'I have my hands full.'

'Where's the other boy?'

'In the garden.'

The doctor hung his hat on the hallstand. He was tall and thin and wore a dark pinstripe suit with a pink shirt and a maroon bow tie. His thinning hair was Brylcreemed flat to his head. In high heels she was almost as tall as her husband.

'The weather's wonderful now.' The doctor's wife beckoned the boy. 'Let me show you the garden.'

All three of them went out the back door. The garden was surrounded by a grey stone wall, but the boy could see other gardens with hedges and apple trees.

'It keeps the heat in and the wind out,' said the doctor's wife. 'Do you like flowers?' The boy said he did. 'Dahlias and chrysanths are my favourites. I put so much work into my flowers.' The doctor produced a packet of Craven A and he and his wife lit cigarettes.

'I suppose you're a bit young to start,' he said and they all laughed. As they walked around the garden she pointed out various plants and told him things about them. 'Eternal vigilance when it comes to snails,' she said. 'Japonica here. And night-scented stock. Ummm . . .' She cupped a russet chrysanthemum and inhaled its scent while making swooning noises. The boy looked at her. The parting in her hair was straight. The skin of her scalp was blue-white shining beneath her auburn hair. The doctor walked with his hands joined behind his back.

Down behind a garden shed they came across the boy's brother.

'Is that where you are?' said the doctor's wife. The younger boy stood up and looked sheepish.

'It was nice and warm here,' he said.

'What age difference is there between you?' asked the doctor's wife.

'I'm ten and a half and he's twelve and a half.'

'I know what we can do,' said the doctor.

'What?'

'A little archery.'

'No.' She seemed taken aback.

'The boys can use *your* bow. They could draw that. Easily.' The doctor walked away towards the garage and came back with a bow and a quiver of six arrows which he gave to his wife. Then he went back and came out with a target which had obviously seen better days. He walked past them and set it three-quarters-way down the garden.

'Adult toys,' he said when he came back. Then he straightened his face. 'This is *not* a toy. People could get killed.' He dropped his cigarette and trod it with his toe into the grass. His wife took one more inhale and did the same.

'Ask King Harold,' she said.

'He got it in the eye,' said the boy. His younger brother clapped his hand to his eye and staggered about gasping, 'Agghhh.'

'OK – enough. Enough. Who wants to go first?' The boy shrugged and indicated his younger brother. The doctor's wife sat down on a concrete step and crossed her legs. The doctor talked them through the equipment in such detail.

'Watch carefully. Everything I say to your brother also applies to you. This groove at the bottom of the arrow is called the nock.'

The boys just wanted to be firing arrows. Eventually the doctor took one from the quiver and notched it onto the string. He pulled the bow and aimed at the target.

'Make sure the string touches your lips.' He released the arrow and it flew silently and stuck in the edge of the target. 'I'm not used to your bow, darling.'

'Nothing to do with the fact that we haven't shot for about five years.'

He laughed. Then fitted the younger boy up to shoot.

'At least move the target a little closer,' said the doctor's wife. Whenever the younger boy did shoot the arrow, it slanted into the grass well to the left of the target. His brother laughed and sneered.

The doctor noticed this and said, 'I hope you can do as well.' The doctor handed him the bow, then an arrow. It had a brass tip which looked like a bullet. He notched the arrow on the bowstring and drew the bow just as he'd been shown. There was a great feeling of power – like a spring wound as tightly as it would go. He shot the arrow and it ended up in a flower bed at the foot of the wall.

'Not bad at all. Better distance,' said the doctor.

'Turn and turn about,' shouted the doctor's wife. They continued practising for some time and they all cheered loudly when the older boy's arrow stuck into the straw at the outer edge of the target. The telephone rang in the house.

'Just a minute,' said the doctor and hurried back into the house. It was the older boy's turn to shoot. He allowed the bow to straighten and waited. The doctor called out to his wife and as she jumped to her feet the boy saw the white undersides of her thighs. She ran inside leaving the boys alone in the garden. The boy drew the bow and aimed at the target. He held fire. The thought in his head was that it was possible to kill his brother here – in this walled garden, away from everyday life. Then there would be two funerals. He could say it was an accident. He hadn't meant it. He had seen arrows thwhack into the bodies of the US Cavalry at both the Lyceum and Capitol cinemas. He could see it now – this one in his fingers piercing his brother's pale-blue shirt. With its tiny, flat mother-of-pearl buttons. The blood welling and gathering around the shaft of the arrow as it protruded from his scrawny chest. He slowly turned the weapon towards his younger brother, who stood there with his mouth half-open, mouth breathing. He was squinting his eyes against the sun.

'You're not allowed to do that,' he said.

'Where's your brother?' asked the doctor.

'In the bathroom.'

'Good.'

'So everybody's hands are washed?' said the doctor.

'Including mine,' said the doctor's wife smiling.

The younger boy came to the table with the backs of his hands glistening where he had neglected to dry them. The doctor said grace and they all bowed their heads after the doctor's wife bowed hers.

'What are you interested in?' The doctor shook out his white linen napkin and looked first at the smaller brother, then the older boy. The silence was there until the older boy felt he had to say, 'Dunno.'

The doctor spread the napkin over his lap.

'You're at the grammar school?'

'Yes. Going on to second year.'

'Have you any hobbies?' The boy didn't want to say he didn't know again so he said, 'Yes.'

'What?'

The boy thought for a while. Then said, 'Painting by numbers.'

'That's interesting. How many have you done?'

The boy hesitated and the younger boy said, 'One. He's done one. But he never finished it. He only did up to four.'

'I did finish it. I did all the colours.'

'He only did two of the blues and two greys.'

The doctor's wife interrupted, 'Now, boys, I'm sure it's not worth fighting over. What was it of?'

'A garden.'

'How I would love to have this all the time. Bickering and refereeing. You are wonderful children . . .'

'Phyllis . . .' said the doctor and she stopped talking. She looked down at her plate. The doctor lifted his spoon from the white tablecloth and began his soup. The others did likewise.

'And you, little man? What school are you at?'

The younger brother sucked in the hot soup with a slurping noise.

'I'm not a man,' he said. 'I'm in Primary Seven.' The doctor's wife smiled. As did the doctor. There was silence at the table when the two adults refused to ask any more questions. Eventually the doctor spoke:

'Your father was a great man,' he said. 'It's so seldom one person can make a difference.'

All their spoons chinked against their plates and nobody said anything for some time.

In his single bed his younger brother began crying. But he tried to disguise it – keeping it in. This started the boy off too and he cried into his pillow trying to cloak the sound he was making – a silent kind of open-mouthed girning, with tears wetting his face and the pillow. He stopped to hear if his younger brother had stopped. Silence. Except for downstairs. There was music playing. He didn't know what time it was. It was still quite light. He didn't know if he had been asleep or not.

After dinner they had played cards. Knock-out whist, twenty-fives, beggar-my-neighbour. Then the doctor had left to drive down to the boy's house to pay his respects. The doctor's wife said it was her duty to stay at home – not to babysit, they were far to old for *that* – but to just keep an eye.

The boy listened hard and heard the regular breathing of sleep coming from his brother's bed. He was thirsty. He'd have to get up. Did too much crying make you thirsty? The loss of moisture? He didn't want to call out as he might do at home. And he needed to pee. He got up and went to the bathroom and flushed the toilet after him. He stood at the head of the stairs and listened down. The music had stopped long ago. Lights were on all over the place but he couldn't see anyone. He could be down and get his drink of water from the kitchen and nobody would notice. Where was the doctor's wife?

He began down the runner of carpet in the centre of the black staircase. The boards creaked a little but nobody came to see who or what was making the noise. In the kitchen there were glasses in the draining rack. He filled one and sipped from it. With the glass in his hand he moved out onto the parquet tiles of the hall. There was a ticking noise coming from somewhere – not like the ticking of a clock, it was too slow for that. He walked towards the sound. It was in the room with the dance floor. He looked in and saw the doctor's wife sitting in a tall armchair – at least he saw her legs. Her back was to the door. The lid of the radiogram was up and a record was revolving slowly – clicking in the overrun. The room was full of twilight from a yellow band in the sky. There was something about the way her legs were sprawled that looked strange. He walked towards her. Was she dead? Was it something to do with the light? He peered around the wing of the armchair. She was fast asleep, her mouth half-open, her head slumped. She would wake with a sore neck if she slept like that for long. Still the record clicked regularly. He turned and with his right hand lifted the needle off. The noise stopped. Then she wakened. At first she looked glazed and bewildered, as if she didn't know where she was. Or who he was – a boy in pyjamas standing in front of her. She opened and closed her dry mouth several times.

'Oh, how thoughtful of you,' she said. She raised herself in the chair and took the water from his hand and drank it. She gulped it down and sighed when she had finished. 'Thank you. Just what the doctor ordered.' As well as cigarette smoke there was a strange smell in the air. Not perfume – but like perfume. She set the empty glass down on a low table beside her chair. There were several bottles on it – a half-filled green bottle, a wine bottle – empty glasses, a half-filled ashtray. 'I'm such a mess.' She sat forward and double-handedly scratched her fingers through her hair. 'Where's Gabriel? Is he not home yet?' The boy didn't know so he shrugged. He didn't even know who Gabriel was. 'What time is it?' She squinted at her watch. 'Oh my God. A quarter to a lemon.' She turned to the small table and finished the drink in her glass and smacked her lips. She poured another drink from the green bottle and lit a cigarette. That was the perfumed smell. 'A gin is not a gin without ice,' she said and levered herself up from the armchair. She came back from the kitchen with her glass ringing and the cigarette in her mouth. 'I feel I want to dance. Will you do me the honour?' The boy didn't know what to say. 'Can you do a quickstep?' The boy shook his head. He couldn't be rude to people who were looking after him. But he wanted to run. 'I thought not. But it's really quite easy. Let's shed some light on the proceedings.' She switched on a red side light and stood in front of him. 'Right. To begin at the beguinning. That's hard to say at this time of night.' She went to the table and stubbed out her cigarette. She placed her hands on his shoulders and showed him the steps. Looking down she realised he was in his bare feet. 'I don't want to trod on your tootsies.' She unhooked her feet from her high-heeled sandals and kicked them to one side. Then she stood with her feet together and sighed 'Ohh I have such bunions.' She continued to teach him the steps and move him. He felt ungainly and reluctant. His head was almost to the height of her shoulder and he could smell her perfume and another strange smell like onions. When he made mistakes with his feet she laughed uproariously – doubled over at times. He didn't see what was so funny. His face was hot and he was sure he was blushing. Once or twice she grazed his cheek with her breast. It was a soft feeling. It gave and he wanted to touch it again out of curiosity – like the wallpaper. 'Now music will sort the whole thing out. Listen to the music – really listen – and the dance will come to you.' She turned away from him and played the record on the turntable. The music breathed out. '*Heaven, I'm in heaven.*' She began to sway in time to the singing voice. '*And my heart beats so that I can hardly speak; and I seem to find the happiness I seek when we're out together dancing cheek to cheek.*' She laid her hands on his shoulders and pressured him into moving 'No – don't look down,' she said. 'You're good – you're getting the hang of it. Move to the music.' She crooned the words along with the singer. She said, 'Gabriel says dance is about *not* getting in each other's way gracefully.' Then she added as if it was an afterthought, 'I think it's about knowing – about knowing each other. And wearing gorgeous clothes. There is no sight in the world to beat a man in black tie and tails. Love is everything.' The boy tried to humour her. She made him attempt to dance again. His bare feet scuffed and bumped against the springy floor. He trod on her but she seemed not to notice. She seemed not even to be speaking to him. She said, 'For me dancing is a matter of life and death. Can you imagine what it would be like to be in an iron lung?' Somewhere a door closed but she seemed not to notice.

The doctor stood in the doorway of the dance-hall room and switched on the main light, which was shaped like a chandelier. She blinked and stared in his direction. He slowly removed his hat and hung it on the hall stand.

'Gabriel,' she said. 'I'm just teaching our guest the rudiments of the quickstep.'

'Ot-way are-hay oo-yay ooing-day?' he said.

'Othing-nay.' She took her hands off the boy's shoulders. The record came to an end and began ticking again.

'Oo-tay uch-may ink-dray.'

'No, only a little. I felt so sad when they went to bed.'

'My parents talk that language too,' said the boy.

'Of course,' said the doctor, smiling. 'I forgot – it was they who taught it to us. They said it was a code for talking in front of *you*.'

'But I got to know what they were saying.'

'We speak it even though we don't have any children,' said the doctor's wife.

'Ime-tay or-fay ed-bay, oung-yay an-may. You have a difficult day tomorrow. Your mother sends her love.'

'Gabriel, dance with me. Let's demonstrate the quickstep for him.'

'Phyllis – you're being . . . The time is out of joint.' The doctor's glance went to the boy.

'Please,' she said. 'There is no time like the present. For this.' She lurched to the side of the floor and got into her high-heeled sandals. From the window sill she took a box and sprinkled something from it, whispering onto the floor.

'Lux perpetua,' she said and turned to the boy. 'Soapflakes – to allow the feet to glide.' She put the record on again. 'A bit more volume.' And raised her hand to invite the doctor to dance. He stared at her and nodded his head a little in disbelief. '*Heaven, I'm in heaven*,' and they were away across the floor, their bodies close, their feet in time. The doctor, when he turned, rolled his eyes to the boy – to let him know he was just humouring his wife, who was being more than a little foolish. The fingers of their upright hands were interlaced. The doctor's hand at her back was cupped as if holding something precious. Their feet skimmed and her dress swished and outlined her thin body as she traversed the floor. The boy now knew the tune and knew where it was going. They moved as one person, their legs scissoring together to the music. They had variations – sometimes dancing side by side – sometimes swinging out away from each other and sling-shotting back together again. She threw back her head and her red hair fell and swayed. The doctor's back was straight, his chin elegantly proud. The boy felt as if he was watching his parents. If they didn't dance like this – and he had never seen them dance at home because they had rugs on the floor and the room was too small – it is how they would have *wanted* to dance.

He felt he couldn't leave the room and go back up to bed because the doctor and his wife covered so much of the floor so quickly. He would be trampled or would at least cause them to interrupt their dancing, and he didn't want to do that. So he stayed where he was and watched.

Something moved in the doorway. It was his brother. The loud music must have wakened him. His face looked crumpled and sleepy and he stood with one bare foot on the threshold.

'Dance with your brother,' shouted the doctor's wife.

'That would look stupid,' said the boy but not loudly enough for it to be heard. It was enough that at that moment he was glad he hadn't killed him in the garden earlier.

The music stopped. And the doctor and his wife ended their dance, he mock bowing and she inclining her head in gratitude for being asked. The only sound now apart from the ticking of the record was their loud breathing.

'I see we are all here now,' said the doctor looking at the boy in the doorway.

'I couldn't sleep.'

The doctor, still panting, went over and squatted down before the boy standing on the threshold. 'I'm not surprised. At her volume,' he said and looked at his wife. 'Now, boys, you have a difficult day tomorrow. You'd better get some sleep.'

'I'll waken us all at half eight,' said the doctor's wife.

'And I'll run all of us in for ten o'clock mass.' By now the two brothers were together at the foot of the stairs. The doctor was touching each of them on the shoulder. 'Oh I forgot to say. It is now definite. The Bishop *will* attend the funeral. Not many people *that* happens to. You should be very proud.' The Bishop had confirmed him – tapped his cheek at the altar rails and declared him a soldier. The hand had smelled of cigarettes and perfumed soap.

'Goodnights apiece,' said the doctor.

The boys began to climb the stairs. When they were halfway up the elder boy looked round. The doctor's wife was in tears, watching them climb.

A Good Turn

GEORGE O'BRIEN

1

Jack the factotum took a dim view of the Dutchmen.

Mr Devanny was not surprised by this (very little ever pleased Jack), deeply deplored it, wished he could ignore it, but it was no good. Whether it was cheese for breakfast, stench of cheroot, the weight of the sample cases or the dirt of their Land Rover, Jack bared his bad teeth at it. 'The thin edge of the wedge, Mr D,' he was wont to declare in his phlegmy baritone. 'The thin edge of the wedge.'

It being both his nature and his calling to act the good neighbour (he was not an insurance man for nothing), Mr Devanny initially tried to give Jack some friendly advice about handling the new arrivals. First off, it would do no harm to bear Ireland's tradition of hospitality in mind. Then there was the principle of the thing – he himself, Mr Devanny explained, was a firm believer in living and letting live. And thirdly, what about self-interest? Wouldn't Jack be much better off opening his arms to the guests, in a manner of speaking, instead of putting up his fists to them? He would of course. 'A word from the wise. Those lads have euros to burn.'

But instead of practising what Mr Devanny preached, Jack turned on him. Cornelius Klutterbuijk and Wim van Damm might be as welcome as the flowers in May to Mr Devanny, but to Jack they were work and more work and jump-to-it, bossy buggers, room service at all hours . . . 'And don't be talking about money. They're worse than women at tipping.' Though, mind you, when it came to women, they didn't let the grass grow under their feet, did they? A right pair of laughing cavaliers they were. Jack supposed Mr Devanny knew about . . .? Here, under the Commercial Hotel's very roof, if you don't mind!

As a matter of fact, Mr Devanny did mind. He didn't want to hear about it. Scandal and gossip were, in any case, beneath him. He hoped that was clear. Jack cocked a knowing eye at him and leered a thin-lipped leer, as much as to say . . . But no, the thought might come in handier later. He broke into his usual rant instead: if only those two buckos would kindly stick their drilling gear and geothingabob up their hole and feck off for themselves the better off everyone else would be, adding, as he turned to go, that if some people weren't so fond of that gin of theirs they might not be so *céad míle* bloody *fáilte*.

Mr Devanny blanched and bridled at Jack's departing back. Of all the confounded neck . . .! Someone ought to teach that fellow what his place is. But he remembered his position and took a deep breath. He would not lower himself. His was the high ground. He must never forget that.

Some weeks went by. Mr Devanny nursed his much-abused other cheek, feeling as usual increasingly pleased with himself, as time went on, for having turned it. And he cagily steered clear of Jack as well, which also pleased him.

Then came a certain Sunday, one of Mr Devanny's fishing-with-the-Professor Sundays, days that always turned out to be a chore and a bore in their way, but which he preferred to regard as corporal works of mercy, really speaking. And he liked the early start. The mild air, the unassertive light, the sleeping town's composure seemed to mirror his own best qualities: the equanimity, the modesty. To preside over his native Desh without anyone seeing him, invisibly keeping an eye on everything, that, sure enough, was an insurance man's dream. Also, of course, the Professor was an early bird himself, and a cranky one at that, although Mr Devanny certainly could not disagree with him that punctuality was the politeness of princes. He looked again at his watch. He was all right. Everything was under control

Jack was sneaking a smoke amidst the Commercial's porch foliage.

'Morning, morning,' Mr Devanny called civilly without altering his brisk pace.

Jack, however, was as usual feeling far from civil. 'Did you ever see the like of it?' he said.

'I beg your pardon?' Mr Devanny was trying to keep cool, keep his distance. But he heard the flaw in his voice, felt the sting of the key ring as he gripped it too tightly for comfort.

'Her Nibs,' Jack intoned lugubriously. 'Did you see the feck of her last night? Lord God! It beat all.' He sucked deeply on a fresh cigarette, emitting in a splutter of smoke his disgust at this new evidence of how out-of-hand everything had got. But Mr Devanny had no wish to discuss Her Nibs and her feck, not now, not ever, not to himself, not to anyone, above all, not to any underling, though to his chagrin he had seen Miss Luby, the Commercial's manageress, the previous evening.

That is, he had seen the transformed Miss Luby, as she tacked uncertainly past him towards the lounge on heels unfamiliarly high. It was not the first such sighting he'd had recently, and every time her appearance was more excessive than before: short skirt, deep decolletage, huge hair giving her a semi-electrocuted look, swags of gold chains. But last evening was his first exposure to her in full fig, all sails hoisted and her course set: he could no longer deny that she was doing a line with Wim or Cornelius. With both? With each in turn? My God! Mr Devanny thought of what he'd heard of Amsterdam, and felt running up his spine that involuntary shiver which meant someone had stepped on your grave. She was the same age as Mr Devanny himself, forty if she was a day, and until the coming of the Dutchmen she had struck most as being more flint than flesh. Now she looked like an explosion in a haberdashery. Was it courage? Was it madness? Marvelling even as, with embarrassment, he paled, Mr Devanny would have dearly liked to know.

But all he could do was stare at her like a cow at a train. And as she disappeared from view, the steak dinner he had treated her to at the Saddle Room of the Fison Lodge Hotel, Knocktoppery, no less, came back to him with a brutal pang, and how, over coffee, toying with a spoon, as he did his best to steer the evening in a certain direction, she had asked, more loudly than was strictly necessary, if he would ever kindly do her the favour of taking a running jump at himself.

'Of course you saw her,' said Jack, with a moist little chuckle. 'You should have seen the look on your face! And did you get the smell off of her? She's the smell of a hoor's handbag.'

The front-desk phone began to ring. Mr Devanny said, 'That's the phone ringing,' and made to move. But instead he felt Jack's heavy hand grip his arm, saw that Jack was working on something else altogether.

Eyes squinting spitefully and with a malicious smirk on those knife-blade lips of his, Jack looked Mr Devanny slowly up and down. Long-lashed, wide-awake eyes of cornflower blue, drink-reddened cheeks, a short, smooth, round and blubbery trunk, he's a doll, Jack said to himself, grinning; if I poked him I'd puncture him. Still, even if it only amounted to giving a cheeky youngster a clatter across the ear, Jack was glad of the chance to take the wind out of Mr Devanny's sails. Who did he think he was, love-thy-fecking neighbour when they're Dutchmen but turn his back on the staff, the old reliables?

'You weren't there,' said Jack, leaning in confidentially. 'But I seen her, after. I seen her going up them stairs. A fright to Christ, as God's my judge. The whole length of the legs of her there for all the world to see. Not that you need to see that, of course. You were *there*, as you might say, ha-ha. A sly dog, in your way, eh, Mr D?' Jack tightened his grip. 'It must be hard for you now, though, having your eye wiped in front of your face, like that, eh?'

Smoke breath. Stale sweat. Scrawny thrapple. Jack's proximity was suffocating. The phone, still shrilling like a mad thing, struck Mr Devanny as much louder now, piercing, drilling. He held the key ring so that it really bit. But he would not let his revulsion and humiliation get the better of him. Never. Self-respect demanded no less. Jack was agog, waiting for him to squirm. But Mr Devanny pulled his arm free. Raising his eyebrows as his one rebuke to Jack's effrontery, he said mildly, 'If you ask me, Jack, it's the thin edge of the wedge.'

His flask was in his pocket, his Astra stood gleaming in the car park, faithful Sally Wallace was making up the sandwiches, the Professor was fussing with the tackle. These things Mr Devanny could hold on to. It was Sunday. It was going to be a good day. But, absentmindedly brushing the sleeve of his blazer, he acknowledged being shaken. The likes of that fellow blackguarding me, he thought. And I twice the man he is, seed and breed!

And the worst of it was, he'd made a mistake. He should have kept to the high ground. Even now Jack was knocking at her door with her tea and toast, ready to report him, putting his own very words into Mr Devanny's mouth, no doubt, the bad-mouthed wretch. Which she would undoubtedly tell Wim and Cornelius. Who would defend her, needless to say. So they might well turn their back on him, leave him high and dry, any chance of their maybe doing a bit of business together gone down the drain, not to mention the hopes he had that they might help him make some sort of European connection, all the drink he'd stood them to float the possibility and prove his *bona fides* gone for nothing.

He stuck his split knuckle in his mouth and began to suck. The sting was just about gone, but the sucking was soothing. Desh passed him by, unseeing and unseen. The smooth Astra lullingly purred along. He took a nip from his flask, then another. The Dutchmen were good lads, though. Men's men. Open. They knew him. They'd know that he meant no harm, that he was, in fact, a gentleman. And, truly, he was a great believer in keeping the sunny side, up, or out, in the art of the possible, and so forth.

But oddly, instead of going straight on out over the bridge to the Professor's, he made a left onto the Island Road, an equally, if not more, familiar route of his which found him, before he fully realised it, in the middle of the large empty car park of Mrs Fitzpatrick's Select Lounge. In all the visits and revisits to this day he made long afterwards, to the day that all his troubles began, asking himself over and over what happened, the one thing he could never, ever, understand was what possessed him to make that wrong turn.

2

The Professor Flynn hung up the phone and, turning to Sally Wallace, his niece and housekeeper, extended his hands and intoned in a slow screech, 'The sparrow has landed! Thanks be to you, God!'

Sally cringed, as she always did when her uncle did his holy voice and hallowed gestures. She knew he couldn't help taking himself seriously – what man could? All Desh, indeed, knew the fits of self-importance that periodically overcame him (nicknaming him 'Professor' accordingly). Sally could even acknowledge that the lifetime he had spent amidst the priests and pupils of Mourne Abbey would be bound to leave a legacy of swelled-headedness and lording it. The town, however, could afford to laugh him off as all mouth and trousers, like a clown. But when the Professor was puffed up like he was now it put Sally on the defensive. If she had learned anything in the three years since Mourne Abbey shut up shop and he became her boarder, it was that when her uncle had big plans big trouble followed.

So Sally kept mum and stayed where she was, screened off behind the haze of cigarette smoke and newsprint indispensable to yoking herself into another day as her uncle's nursemaid and cook-general. But it was no good. He was as thin as a cane (his complexion even had something of a cane's yellow finish), but slight as he was when he was this full of himself he was too much of a handful for her. Later, when this mad idea of hosting an asylum-seeker – sparrow, indeed! – blew up in his face, like all his other high notions, and he, Humpty Dumpty, relied on her to collect, again, the shattered pieces of his lofty thoughts, his lily-white principles, his impeccable motives, there would be all the time in the world to contemplate this latest adventure into righteous-ness and doing good. But the way his high horse was prancing now, there was nothing for it but to give him his head, although ever since she'd accidentally learned of it Sally thought this scheme his crackedest one yet.

Some months before, when serving tea, the fishermen having once more laboured all day and caught nothing, as the Professor repeated until they dutifully laughed, Sally had overhead him spouting to Devanny in his most professorial manner about Bosnia, Serbia and all the rest of it, the refugees, 'the Department', official policy and public spirit. She had made some faint demurral – language difference, some-thing like that. She scarcely remembered, because the memory of how the Professor had turned on her was so much sharper. He'd brought up Wallace and everything, carrying on at such a rate about speaking and being spoken to that even deadpan Devanny soon lapsed into what looked like – dammit! – pity.

That was what had carried the extra sting – whiskey-breath Devanny taking it all in, while his presence made no difference to the Professor. Alone, she could have treated the outburst as just so much weather, rumble and crack and a sudden downpour. But with Devanny looking on, she couldn't simply pass the rant off as routine, one more example of how it was the Professor's second nature to lash out, how Sally lived with being seen but not heard. It was humiliating that Devanny saw her stand there like a donkey, taking it. Devanny was no longer one of her uncle's fishing accessories now (flat like his tweed cap, empty like the wicker basket for the catch). He'd learned something of herself and Wallace, a subject too shaming to be mentioned in public, or mentioned at all. Had she not, without either planning or preventing it, allowed her uncle to take over her life, to occupy her waking hours, her house, her finances; had she not allowed him to believe that he had saved her and that only for him she'd be on Stubb's List, out on the street, a charity case; had she not endured his tantrums and tall orders, fixed his hot-water bottles, fed him his pills, all in the unspoken hope of desertion and the bastard Wallace being stricken from the record?

The Professor didn't know enough to see what he'd said. Sally smarted too sorely to tell him. Life went on in sullen silence, a climate to which they readily adapted, not for the first time. On subsequent Sundays the Professor expatiated on his Balkans strategy behind the closed doors of the front room – the study, as he called it, since that was where he kept all his old newspapers. Whatever his crusade *du jour* was, from the Tidy Towns Competition to the children of Chernobyl, one of the inevitable turns things took was a retreat to the study for interminable committee meetings (and sandwiches). This time there had been no group, no fighting, no split, no pyrotechnics, just some brown official envelopes and long phone calls, so Sally let him piddle along. The whole thing – sponsorship, fostering; the little she picked up from eavesdropping didn't make it clear – struck her as pie in the sky entirely.

To her great annoyance, it now appeared that she had been quite mistaken, and that she would have to pay attention to him whether she liked it or not. Sally might wish to hide from the voice of command which now assailed her, but he could not run. That was Donie (the Professor's past pupil in the Department) phoning up just now from Dublin. The boy was being put on the train this morning! Make sure you tidy the study, that's going to be the classroom and we'll be starting first thing in the morning. But don't touch anything! Everything was all in order. This poor devil (by the way, we'll be calling him Milo, best to be informal) might not be rightly housebroken – and small blame to him. But that's all the more reason that we set a standard. It was part of his instruction, how to live civilised. They too should be taking this opportunity of putting their best foot forward and start as they meant to go on, just like their guest. This was a new day for everyone, if only they had the wit to take advantage of it. But he had to leave this very minute for the Junction. Where in the name of Paul was Devanny, the one morning he could come in handy? And why wasn't that scut Jack answering the phone? Air out the room. 'What else?'

'Did you take your pill?' said Sally.

He looked like he needed to, with the hectic stride of him back and forth across the kitchen. His eyes had an electric glow. A sheen of perspiration varnished his sallow complexion. He picked up the phone and punched the buttons viciously. He banged the phone down.

'You won't be wanting sandwiches, so?' said Sally.

The Professor marched out of the kitchen. The front door slammed. Sally pulled her dressing gown tight around her and stubbed and stubbed her half-smoked Silk Cut until every last spark of it was black.

3

'No,' said the Professor, explaining the absence of rods and hamper. 'Today we are fishers of men!'

'Aha,' said Mr Devanny, game but clueless.

Knowing of an old date, however, that the main thing always was to match whatever mood the Professor was in, and that sooner rather than later he would receive a fuller explanation of this departure than he really needed, Mr Devanny took the old familiar path of least resistance.

Apart from giving directions to the Junction, however – which rubbed Mr Devanny the wrong way; it was like he was a stranger, a cabbie, a servant (a Jack, for God's sake) – the Professor was silent. This was odd. But as they crossed over the incomplete Desh by-pass, Mr Devanny realised that it must be their route that had struck the Professor dumb. He could certainly understand; he'd be speechless himself, under the circumstance. For it was somewhere hereabouts, nice and handy for the new road, that that swindler Wallace wanted to build his executive bungalows, the great scheme that had taken everybody in, Sun Life, the Bank of Ireland, Sally . . . and probably the Professor, too, come to think of it, since for all his brains he wanted a piece of a good thing, the same as everyone else, and just like everyone else, had no head for business. They, as Mr Devanny well knew, did not grow on trees.

Nevertheless, it was most unlike the Professor to deny himself the pleasure of hearing his own voice. Indeed, he didn't seem himself at all, face sweaty, eyes burning, staring dead ahead as if to add will power to horsepower, clenching and unclenching his hands, wrenching his mouth around oddly, like a dog with a toffee. A couple of years ago, when he was fighting either the head office of the teachers' union or the Desh Against Sellafield crowd, the Professor had confided in him that the heat of the moment would do for him, surely. Often he was sure he had a turn coming on. It was caring too much. Not that he was ashamed of it (he cited the gospel on faith without good works). And if the heart gave up, wouldn't the soul go marching on? Would he not have laid down his life for his friends?

Mr Devanny wondered what friends those were, and looked across at the Professor, fervently hoping that he wasn't in for this long-threatened turn. And to try to lighten the mood, when they came to Scrake Cross, Mr Devanny said, 'Oh, the townland of Scrake, where the goat ate the clergyman.'

'Bike and all,' was the time-honoured rejoinder. But it never came.

Mr Devanny sighed. The boot, he saw, would be on the other foot all day today.

But just then, the Professor broke out with, 'Look at that! Isn't that a digrace?'

Mr Devanney's gaze followed the quivering finger pointing at a makeshift hut, surrounded by mounds of earth, standing in the middle of a thistle-strewn field.

'Oh, that,' said Mr Devanny. 'That's only the Dutchmen. The EGS, don't you know – European Geognosic Survey. Was I not telling you about that? The two surveyors are staying at the Commercial. Fine fellows. Friendly and natural. And good will come of it, too, I'd say.'

'Nice company, I'm sure. You should get out of that place. Settle down for yourself. But what was I saying? Oh, yes.' The Professor's voice gathered force. 'Tell them friends of yours to clear up after themselves. Turning the countryside inside out and leaving an eyesore like that as their mark and seal – they should be had up.'

'Oh, I don't think they're finished out here yet,' Mr Devanny said knowledgeably.

'They're finished all right,' said the Professor solemnly. 'They were finished before they started. But even if there was something there, digging and drilling and dirtying everything isn't the way to get it. You talk about progress. I'm sick and tired of telling people that the only progress is in their hearts and souls. Those are depths enough for anyone. But who has the equipment to bore down into them? That's where people like you and I come in. We must lead by example. Why d'you think we're here?'

'On this earth, like?'

The Professor glared at him.

'Oh, I see. Milo. Oh, yes. Oh, I see.'

Deftly Mr Devanny punctuated the squall of nostrum, dictum, motto and tag that the Professor now let loose. 'Errand of mercy.' 'The greatest is charity.' It might have been one of those interminable, drink-free Sundays in the study, except that of course today the Professor was bracing himself for the big time. A miracle, a blessing, certainly, certainly; and one which brought a definite and not necessarily welcome change to these Sundays, Mr Devanny realised. And so, just at the moment when he should have given the Professor the gentlemanly equivalent of a pat on the back, he felt unable. Not only was there the thought of a change, but an unexpected eddy of uncertainty clutched him at the mention of the Dutchmen. He just simply had to block everything out until the buzz of another little nip could take care of him. So he gripped the wheel tight, straightened up in his seat, stepped on the gas, and wheeled into the Junction in a dust-raising, bird-scattering rush, almost flattening Milorad Vranič, who was standing in the car park clutching a SPAR plastic bag, the image, as Mr Devanny said afterwards, of the itinerant he unquestionably was.

4

Ordinarily, few sounds were sweeter to Sally than that Sunday slam of the front door. It was the official signal that she could now call her soul her own for a few hours. She could luxuriate in a vaguely sluttish surfeit of Silk Cut and Maxwell House, loll in the living room with her dressing gown as loose about her as she pleased, lap up the letters in the agony column, their heartfelt quality an acrid sort of pleasure which oddly put her in mind of bonfires. She could paint her toenails. She could have a bath.

After the bath she liked to look at herself, not only to hunt for lumps but for other forms of reassurance no less vital. True, she was getting leathery around the neck, but apart from that she liked what she saw well enough. The breasts were firm but not flashy. It was said that big ones were best, but Sally was glad hers weren't flabby. The rose of her nipples was so modest, so unsullied, and the stippling around their aureoles reminded her of little buds. Belly quite flat; behind within reason. And she liked the way droplets of bathwater glistened like little jewels in her bush. Though nobody but herself could see why, she could still call herself a girl – well, girlish, anyhow. Sometimes, even, the thought of what a girl might like occurred to her, and she would throw herself on the bed, then, and was not ashamed that there had been times when she had let herself go entirely, before she got as far as the bed, in front of the mirror, even, there being something irresistibly odd and daft in letting the mirror take your place (or so it felt); in fact, at those times, laughing, moaning, madly shaking her head, she wouldn't have cared where she was, bed, floor, study sofa, or in front of the hurling match on television with the crowd cheering and cheering.

Today, though, there could be no losing the head if she was to do what had to be done. So as soon as she saw the Astra pull away, Sally got busy, thinking that building up a good head of steam would get her through. And if the place looked well it would keep her uncle at bay, too, although he was the least of her worries, since with him she had only to remain as she'd been since he'd cut her with the Wallace cut before Devanny.

Yet, when she'd finished mopping and dusting and hoovering the downstairs and there was only the room to air out, Sally still wasn't ready to face it, and scrutinised intently all the gleaming surfaces, trying to find something easier. Dinner. Sparrow he might be, but this – refugee, asylum-seeker, alien? what should she call him (chancer?) – was also a man, so first and foremost wanted feeding. The Professor was a great bacon-and-cabbage man, but that might not sit well, Sally thought, with a Balkanian, or whatever they were called these days. She'd go up to the SPAR.

The advantage of *Manresa* being beyond the Beverley Glens housing estate was, as the Professor liked to point out, you had your privacy (some of the estate crowd were very undesirable, really). But the disadvantage was that Sally had to shop by bike. The strip of stores serving the estate was only a mile away, but with the lunatics now driving, and the local sport of buzzing – driving as close as possible to others on the road, cyclists especially – getting there was an ordeal. And then with the crowd at the shops (it being Sunday afternoon there was nothing else to do), Sally couldn't leave her bike in the usual handy spot and had to queue for ever while an unappetising nuisance in an anorak had it out with the cashier. Variously pierced adolescents passed the time with a spot of shoplifting, while their younger brothers and sisters fought and squabbled and jostled, effing and blinding like jailbirds, the cross-eyed Romanian young one giving as good as she got, Sally saw, by way, no doubt, of teaching the ways of freedom to the half-dozen compatriots who'd evidently sprouted up alongside her since Sally had seen her last. Then, no sooner did she finally get outside, than bearing down on her came Stella Harty with her brood, new baby Jade and all.

Sally waved and called and leapt on her bike. 'I must fly!'

Jade!

Tossing the dinner of frozen macaroni-and-cheese and a Bakewell tart onto the kitchen table with a wooden bang, Sally plopped herself down on a chair, panting. She was bet, too tired even to put on the kettle for herself. And not only that. She also felt a strange wave of angry disgust break over her, though what had given rise to it – those seething youngsters at the shop? the squad of Hartys? the buzzing cars? – she couldn't tell. She made a pot of tea and ate the last of the Jaffa cakes and, almost absentmindedly, smoked three cigarettes in rapid succession. But still the feeling sloshed unsettlingly around her.

It was only when, after a quick shower, Sally found herself trying to find something to wear, that what the matter was came to her. The clothes were part of it – all of them relics of the Wallace era, the calf-length tartan skirts for the office, the navy-blue suit in which she nearly melted when they landed in Crete for the honeymoon: what the successful businessman's wife is wearing this half-century, fit for a spinster of sixty, maybe, and not for a woman half that. But the clothes were not the whole problem.

The whole problem was that although the sun of Heraklion was dim and gone these three years, something of it lingered, like a pang, like a burn. And it wasn't dressing herself that brought this home to Sally, but dressing the bed in the room.

The spare bedroom was never called anything else but the room. But the wallpaper's teddy bears and alphabet blocks spoke, however, of the different name that Sally once upon a time intended for it, obscured though they were now by box upon box of invoices, statements, blueprints, minutes, solicitors' letters and bank correspondence. The Professor had insisted it all be kept – 'in case we can sue', he said, when it was only the mercy of God that it was he and Sally who weren't sued. But the boxes still dustily stood there, to Sally an archive of all that had been taken from her. The very thought of having been left so comprehensively in the lurch made her fit to puke with loathing and rage. She threw blouses and cardigans vehemently hither and yon. She cursed and she swore and she growled like a mastiff in the name of her wrongs and her rights.

5

When Mr Devanny saw Sally he stopped short as though poleaxed.

Milo brushed by with the Professor following fussily and, Mr Devanny noted, not a word of thanks, though he had to let that go for now on account of being literally knocked from his horse by this blinding vision.

For just a tiny little moment, he did think, admittedly, first Miss Luby, now this. But he quickly retracted. Sally was in a different class entirely, as was evident from her having no gold chains, the gracious poise with which she held the door, her solicitous welcome – 'Is that your bag? Wisha, God love you . . .' And, most of all, the suit, if suit it could be called and not a coat of paint; blood-red, severe and exquisite in its contour-affirming cut, profound and uplifting in its neckline plunge. Mr Devanny could only gawk, and as he did so the scales fell in jig-time from his eyes. This was a woman and a half he was looking at – again, but for the first time. And he reflected not only on the truth of the old saying concerning those none so blind but also on what a remarkable day this was turning out to be, after all.

When Mr Devanny made to follow his two passengers into the house, however, Sally, with a complicated gesture combining apologetic shrug, wry smile and toodle-oo flutter of the fingers, indicated that he should stay where he was. The door shut in his face. Mr Devanny had noticed the Professor speaking to Sally as, with her hand on his back, she pressed him to go on ahead in. His head was nodding rapidly, always a sign of rattiness, and Mr Devanny understood. They needed an hour to settle in, and as he slowly returned to the car he cast about for phrases to do with the making of allowances. Nothing particularly charitable came to him, so he sat for a moment, raised his flask, and muttering 'Good luck', drained it, and drove off.

Luck, indeed, was exactly what the Professor would need over the next little while, if Mr Devanny was any judge, because as far as he could see, Milo wasn't much of a prize. There wasn't a pick on his bones. That Bayern Munich windbreaker of his was as wrinkled and stained as a floorcloth, and the black singlet under it was, if anything, worse. To tell the God's honest truth, Mr Devanny thought, this Milo looked like he'd fallen off the back of a lorry and not someone fresh from government keeping. And another thing that wouldn't help was that he looked very foreign. Mr Devanny had expected not so deep an olive complexion but something browner, like Dominic Savio's in the picture in his missal. Milo's face was narrow, tapering to a pointed chin. A knife of a face. And the eyes were slant, like a goat's, with oval sockets and pupils dark as sloes. Gypsy eyes, thought Mr Devanny, shifty, liquid; deep waters and an inward cast . . . If he had a moustache, now, he'd be the dead spit of a right Balkan bandit, though no doubt the men from the ministry had thoroughly examined him to make sure he was no more than his tinkerish self, not an arms czar or drug baron or carrying any of the other ailments which, to Mr Devanny, made up the steep but obviously worthwhile price of progress.

Still, Milo seemed a clever fellow, Mr Devanny would give him that. He had some words of English, and put them in the proper place as often as many of the palookas frequenting Mrs Fitzpatrick's. Apparently he had German, too – 'German better,' he said matter-of-factly when Mr Devanny complimented his gift of tongues Mr Devanny didn't quite see how German came into it, though of course the education system on the continent was streets ahead of anything here (anything the unions would permit, that is, Mr Devanny might add, the Professor concurring) . . . And of course Milo had come this far, which also showed he was no daw and knew what side his bread was buttered on.

Nearing town, Mr Devanny felt increasingly mellower and decided that, all things considered, there was no need really not to make Milo entirely welcome. He had nothing to lose, and perhaps a certain something to gain. He would let himself be prompted by Sally's impressive cues, and be said by her. How very fine she looked. How very fine indeed. Could it be at all, he wondered, that maybe her flutter of fingers, which strictly speaking was unnecessary – her other signals were perfectly obvious – was meant to say something else, that within the clear-cut cheerio a tentative come-hither coyly lingered? Now there was a thought! And with it to guide him he let the Astra amble round the streets of dormant Sunday Desh, past Oisin Frozen Foods (M. T. Fitzpatrick, prop.), a valued client, and Hanrahan's Pharmacy that was, now a video rentalry, a good client also; past his own little office opposite the chapel, its livery of green and gold the worse for wear, but still strong inside, where it mattered, and finally back to the Commercial via Wood Street and the ample house where he was born but couldn't bear to live in after Mammy died and which now provided a nice rental income. All these were hopeful signs as well. All things were buoyant.

Speaking of clever fellows, by the way, Mr Devanny, sitting over an early pint in the Commercial lounge had to hand it to the Professor. What exactly he had to hand him might not be entirely clear at this very moment. But there was no getting away from the fact that once Milo was on board, the Professor seemed all business, would hardly indeed allow Mr Devanny to get a word in. He was a man with a plan without a doubt. Milo . . . House-room . . . Mr Devanny sipped and sipped and cogitated and by the time he'd reached the heel of his second pint he saw it all. The department, the government, the minister, Bertie himself

– every man jack of them would be going down on their knees in thanks to the Professor for solving their refugee problem. For good as the turn being done Milo, it was surely only the tip of the iceberg. There was no shortage of Milos. And what made more sense than turning idle Mourne Abbey school into a place where the poor unfortunates could make themselves at home! For a fee, of course. At EU rates, too, no doubt. Mr Devanny took a long sip of his fresh pint and sighed with a kind of fulfillment. Ah, my dandy fine smart Professor, he said to himself, in on the ground floor of a copper-bottomed growth industry – and with your old pal at your right hand to insure you!

Not to take anything away from today's particular good turn, not a bit of it. That was what everybody needed now and then, a leg up, a helping hand. Do unto others and so on and so forth (the Professor would have chapter and verse for it). In fact – here Mr Devanny felt inspired yet again, and he beamed out at the empty lounge – that was how to handle Jack. He would ask Wim to give Jack some regular, soft and tippable task. He would ask him now, this minute, strike while the iron was hot.

A very tousle-headed Cornelius opened Wim's door a crack to Mr Devanny's knock, and from behind him came the dull slump of something heavy falling and a screech of female laughter.

'Later, OK,' Cornelius whispered breathlessly, leaving Mr Devanny mumbling, 'Sorry, sorry,' to the hastily closed door.

An American wandered into the lounge eventually and Mr Devanny spent an instructive hour with him discussing soy beans. But the American apparently didn't understand the idea of a round, and besides maintained he had to be in bed by ten – it was some sort of self-controlling system he had.

Mr Devanny had a brace of nightcaps for himself, then, but neither Con nor Wim showed up, which was all for the best, really, as after his big day he found himself now nodding off.

In the middle of the night Sally Wallace came to him dressed, for reasons best known to herself, in just a skimpy plastic apron. Her breasts were very much larger than he'd imagined, and she sashayed back and forth near where he was sitting, moving at such angle that he could see that she was mighty, only mighty, now, in all respects. She had a bottle of tomato sauce with her with which she sometimes posed coquettishly and which she sometimes fondly stroked, smiling broadly throughout.

6

The Professor had it all worked out, from schedule of meals to eternal reward, just about, and in the first few weeks everything went according to plan and he was all hosanna. Placing a reliable shape on Milo's day, so important for the young man's obvious need for stability as well as for the life that was to come for him, had the Professor rejoicing in his natural aptitude for command, which he discovered was not dead after all but sleeping. He welcomed the return to those certainties of what, where and when to which the Mourne Abbey curriculum and timetable had habituated him, though of course years of trying to save schoolboys from themselves was mere childsplay compared to his present undertaking.

Early to bed and early to rise went without saying, naturally. Less natural was ensuring that Sally toed the line. Let her stick her tongue out a mile at him when his back was turned (his hackles, too, he found, were in excellent fettle), it was a new day and a new way at *Manresa*, whether she liked it or not. And to be fair, she did, when asked, desist from pot-walloping to take in his express desire and wish she not mammy Milo or in any way look on him as a sad case, a lost soul, an orphan of bad blood and wicked fire. He was not some charity case from the North of Ireland. On the contrary, Milo was a gift, and should be treated accordingly, the Professor said. The bounty that was Milo was in their keeping to be properly reaped and winnowed for the good of all, said he, holding forth again in that holy tone of his, and adding, 'Now the dinner has to be at twelve sharp, if I'm to take my pill as prescribed, and have my nap and take Milo for his walk.'

The walk was an absolute must. Milo had to be *in corpore sano*, of course, and beside he mustn't feel confined to quarters. He had to realise that all that was behind him now, and be encouraged to have confidence and trust. Besides which – and more importantly – he had to see and to be seen. The plan demanded that exposure be on the same footing as instruction. Indeed walks were the classes' essential public compliment. The first Sunday evening at mass, when all eyes were on them, was proof positive of visibility's value.

And really, everyone was very nice. The Professor had the distinct impression that all along Main Street hatchets were being buried, as though Milo was in the nature of a peace offering. The dole officer, Delaney (a big noise in the Vincent de Paul), acted as if that painful imbroglio about the raffle tickets had never taken place. Father Condon 'couldn't stop', he said, but his grin seemed genuine, and he did shake Milo's hand. Even people about whom the Professor thought little and cared less were civil. Fagin of the AIB, with his pink-tinted specs and Mexican moustache, crossed the street to speak, having gathered over a quick one with Mr Devanny that some money-spinning scheme was in the works. It did somebody like Milo good – a nobody, really speaking; a man from God knows where – to find himself welcomed and wondered at. And it did the Professor's pride no harm to point out the Desh top ten, Doctor Casey, Laffin the solicitor, Fitzpatrick the Frozen Foods king, their Mercs and Beemers, and their ox-blood-brick chateaux in the fields on the road to Knocktoppery.

Old Mrs Fitzpatrick gave Milo a Crunchie. Miss Luby stood them a drink and spoke warmly and welcomingly about how good foreigners were for the town, with their lashings of tin and no fear of spending it – though the Professor had a tricky time trying to fob Jack off with pleasantries. All that remained, really, was a picture in the paper with Tom Tomelty, T.D. But Tomelty's surgery was worse than rush hour at Lourdes, with its constant slew of anxious supplicants (all in dowdy soccer-club regalia, for some reason). So the Professor, not wishing to be too conspicuous, let the photo go for now. Besides, it would do even more good later on, when phase B of the plan came to masterful fruition. As it surely must. He had read with pleasure and deep pride about how the Irish saved civilisation. Had barbarism determined that that hour had come round again? If God willed it. He himself was ready. And although he tried not to walk with breast expanded, he had the very pleasant feeling that it was, which gave him a sensation not dissimilar to being at prayer, uplifted and significant.

The town took note and christened Milo 'the Greyhound'.

7

'So I heard, anyway,' said Mr Devanny.

'I thought it was the Sparrow,' Sally said sarcastically. This habit Devanny had been making lately of 'just dropping in' when the others were taking their walk put her out, and the reek of Old Spice off him did not improve her mood, it being what Wallace wore.

'Ah, it's because he's thin, I suppose,' Mr Devanny said diffidently.

'It's this bloody town!' Sally exclaimed.

Her uncle's inclinations towards harnessing and leading, she knew, were lifelong and incurable, so it was only a matter of time before he, somehow or other, made himself a laughing stock again. Being proof against the folly of men, Sally took that in her stride. Yet still the nickname stung; made her feel obscurely apologetic and embarrassed. Since she had no way of showing – to Milo, to herself, to anyone – that she was any different from whoever thought up the name, it was as if she was a party to the naming. The thought struck her with an unpleasant clarity. And rudely telling Mr Devanny he must go only helped a little.

Gentleman that he prided himself in being, Mr Devanny accepted implicitly (though it seemed unusually sudden) that Sally had things to do. Yet as he turned out of the driveway he confessed himself disappointed. She should not have taken what he'd told her with such a crestfallen air. Loyalty to her uncle was an admirable trait, certainly. But had it not been clear that he had only brought the matter up to place her on the alert? He himself had laughed heartily at the nickname's aptness when Jack had mentioned it, and while he could hardly expect that of Sally, she ought not to be so prompt to shoot the messenger. A little smile wouldn't have killed her. Nothing would please him better than to bring a smile to Sally's lips, after all she'd done for him lately (just the other night he was allowed to fold her underthings while she pranced around him superbly in the buff).

Bloody fool! Sally thought. She lit a cigarette and sat staring vacantly out beyond the smokescreen of it. After a while, Milo's face presented itself to her, or rather, not his face but his eyes. His extraordinary eyes. Sally hadn't really felt their presence until quite recently when she'd had the bright idea of fixing Milo up with some of Wallace's old duds. 'Tenk you, tenk you,' Milo had said. But the way his deep, dark, liquid, languid eyes moved – shy, embarrassed, pleased – as she skipped around him with her pins and inchtape told her many other much more complicated things. Such sad sincerity, such piteous gratitude, such patience with the world. His strength of feeling had taken her quite unawares, and troubled her. And as she had watched, then, afterwards, Sally had seen too how Milo's eyes could flash as the Professor prescribed something on the home life of the tapir or the larynx of the toad for their long evenings of television. Fire eyes, deer eyes, eyes of Al Pacino . . . Sally giggled girlishly. She stubbed her cigarette out and sighed. It was a shame, really, about the language barrier. She wished she hadn't been right about that. She would have loved to talk to him. And they had plenty of time while the Professor was napping.

For his part, Milo would have liked to talk to Sally, too. At least she might be able to tell him what was going on, because six weeks after his meeting at the Junction he was still at a loss. His host, though plainly crazy, was harmless. Indeed from his daily barrage of verbiage Milo was picking up the odd word of English. Compared to Nuremberg, the town of Desh was dreary and pedestrian. But Milo had seen worse, far worse. Besides, he wasn't turning back. Going on had been his faith and focus for too long to stop now.

Initially, all Milo could imagine was that he had been drawn into some labour racket. The official who had hustled him to the train – working on a Sunday, Milo noted – was probably planting a Serb here, a Kurd there, a couple of Nigerians somewhere else. Unspoken supply meets unuttered demand for a very modest surcharge and the less said the better. Milo found the prospect neither pleasing or displeasing. It had happened in Germany. It had happened in Antwerp. He'd seen it happen to Letts, Greeks, Maghrebi, all sorts, all wandering and wondering, the same as himself. And, if anything, better this way, Milo thought, if all staying at home meant was shooting or being shot. They laughed at him in the hostel, called him a dreamer and a nancy-boy, as they put their heads together to go south for the proper slaughter, the big Mercedes loaded down with treats for kids and old folk, and underneath the Glocks and Walthers. Lost and lonesome though he sometimes felt, Milo had kept moving in the opposite direction, until one raw North Wall morning he tumbled from the back of a Dutch truck to land in what was turning out to be a never-never land in which he seemed to be a *gast* but which had neither sign nor light of *arbeit*.

The days, strange as they were, had assumed the pace and pattern of normality. Milo could see no hidden agenda. On the contrary, the Professor came across as excruciatingly well meaning, Sally obviously wanted to be kind. Yet, relieved as Milo was to be no longer working as a janitor, and though at times it struck him that his luck must have turned, the very virtues of his hosts made him feel as trapped as ever he'd felt with bucket and brush. This was a gentler entrapment, of course, but in a way that made it more unreasonable, because it was more difficult now to know if this was a dead end too, and what he was required to do was so obscure. And when he put this line of thought aside as unproductive and, besides, unworthy, he found the state of mind replacing it – his unspeakable boredom – to be just as big a problem.

He had seen in town large numbers of youths in Glasgow Celtic shirts (and had not much liked the hulking look of them) – but where was the soccer field? Where the *Kino*? Where a drink ? Milo would have liked to talk to Sally about these things. And as if the daily round of dull Desh and the stultifying television evenings were not boring enough, what turned him most immediately to stone were his classes, so much so that the Professor caught him out a number of times and Milo had not been able to repeat as required.

The mistakes made the Professor grind his teeth and sigh sorrow-fully. But, with an effort, he remained calm, reminding himself that he wasn't dealing with a child here so a clip across the kisser would prob-ably be counterproductive. The Professor wouldn't mind but the thing was simplicity itself. '1014, Battle of Clontarf.' Show battle picture. 'Clontarf, Dublin 3.' Show map of Dublin. 'Dublin 3, post code.' Show letter. 'Letter.' Show, e.g., brown departmental envelope. 'Read.' And so on. Recap every half-hour by dictation.

'And he seemed so willing early,' the pained Professor said, Mr Devanny having merely inquired if everything was all right, seeing from his office window the Professor leave the chapel.

'The spirit is willing,' Mr Devanny observed idly.

'What's that supposed to mean?' the Professor snapped. 'The flesh is weak, is that it?'

Mr Devanny drew back, effusively protesting. It was just . . . He groped. He fumbled. 'It must be a great responsibility,' he said, soberly, although it did occur to him too that the Professor still had not confided in him the Mourne Abbey plan, which was, in fact, unfair.

The Professor grunted. Little did Devanny know how solemn the call-ing, how grave the mission, how worrisome it was that an inattentive Milo would put the kibosh on phase B.

Tense dinnertimes became more frequent, Sally noticed, the Professor's graces grew longer and placed a greater emphasis on grati-tude, and Milo sat with his eyes cast down the whole meal through, although she could swear that there was fire in them. He has his pride, she thought. He has his passion. She'd read in a magazine story that lads from his part of the world had their fiery side.

Yet when the Professor retired for his nap, Milo was as natural as anyone could wish, took his coffee at his ease, helped clear the table, brought out the rubbish to the bin. And it was true, around Sally he did feel relaxed. He liked to watch her as she went about her chores. She'd say, 'It's cold today,' and rub her hands, going, 'Brrr,' which made him smile. She used the words for ordinary things, pointing to them on the dresser, on the stove. He learned them quickly, glad of their ordinariness, their usefulness. She signalled him to translate, and handed him a cup. '*Šolja za čaj*,' he said. 'Cha!' said Sally, delighted to hear the peculiar echo of what she called tea. She held up a soup plate. '*Dubok tanjir*,' said Milo, laughing at how welcome and how strange the words felt.

Sometimes when she baked, Sally saw his hand reach out, involuntarily, it seemed, take a remnant of dough and absentmindedly knead it until he'd made a little house, a little animal, a ridge of tiny, jagged mountains. Sally watched his long, strong, slender fingers flex and ply. She looked into his poignant eyes. She thought how lost he looked.

She thought – He thought – But when later on they tried to work out the what or why, they weren't able. It just happened. Sally was washing, Milo was drying. Sally turned, for some reason, and at just the same time Milo turned as well, and their eyes met, creating that telltale moment of stillness, that inhalation, from which there is no turning back, and the next thing either of them knew they were kicking up their heels on the sofa in the study, while upstairs the Professor slept the nap of the just.

8

There then followed a period of intense culinary endeavour by Sally in which just about everything she served was mashed – the spuds, the turnips, the parsnips; she'd have mashed the chicken nuggets if she could – the better to conceal an extra pill, ground up, in the Professor's helping, so that her afternoons of love could go undisturbed, and even be, with luck, prolonged. The Professor, rising late and groggy from his naps and not at all inclined to walking, made his feelings known about this unwelcome sense of stupefaction, although, as expected, he got nothing out of Sally. 'See the doctor,' she said.

'Stress,' was Mr Devanny's verdict. 'You're doing too much.' Would the Professor hear the insinuation that it was time to think about a helping hand? Mr Devanny sincerely hoped so. Wim had told him in strictest confidence (not wanting Miss Luby to know yet) that he and Cornelius would be pulling out for Spain before long – though he pleaded a pressing appointment when Mr Devanny then tried talking business with him. We'll all be left high and dry, Mr Devanny thought, with something like a shudder – no good turn for Jack, Miss Luby seduced and abandoned, no Europe opening up for me. More quickly than he'd bargained for, he was in need of movement on the Mourne Abbey front.

'Take it from me,' he said, mustering his best man-to-man tone.

'Maybe you're right.' The Professor emitted a slow sigh of bafflement. The very thought that unexpected and inscrutable forces were insidiously loosening his grip on his days and ways struck him as an intolerable injustice, entirely out of keeping with the spirit of his motives and the generosity of his vision.

'All work and no play . . . ' said Mr Devanny.

'Pray? But sure I do pray, dammit!'

Mr Devanny moved swiftly on. 'I have an idea,' he said. 'Why don't you let me treat the three of you to dinner at the Commercial? The lamb isn't bad. I'll ferret out a civilised Bordeaux . . . ' Mr Devanny checked himself before the idea's brilliance went to his head entirely. It was exactly the kind of thing, he realised, that he should be doing much more of. Cast your bread upon the waters. There was his Fison Lodge initiative, of course. But that was in the dark ages. Now there was Sally, the inexhaustibly versatile Sally, with her nurse's uniform, with her lion-tamer's lash, his undeclared dividend, his very own sleeping partner, lighting up his nights.

The Professor hemmed and hawed and strongly hinted to Sally that what was needed was less the pleasure of Mr Devanny's table but more prayer from himself. But Sally was not to be put off a night out – an official one, that is, since she and Milo had a couple of times risked slipping up to The Last Post on the estate for a drink before closing. To be seen down the town with Milo would be a mighty thrill. So she maintained that to turn Devanny's invitation down was neither nice nor fair. There wasn't much Devanny could do, God love him, so why not let him do this much?

'Oh, Devanny has his uses,' said the Professor, unable to admit he agreed with her.

'And I don't know about you,' Sally added, 'but I get tired of the taste of my own cooking.'

The Professor yielded. 'Yes, well, a change is as good as a rest, I suppose,' he said.

Better, said Sally to herself, a thousand times better! And she laughed heartily. There was little anyone could say these days that didn't put her in mind of herself and Milo.

The Professor, however, having made, as he thought, a major concession, retaliated by decreeing that 'this famous dinner' would not take place until the following Sunday fortnight, and that during the interim, beginning immediately, the nightly family rosary would be said. In fact, he chastised himself roundly for not having made the rosary a firm fixture sooner. But then he had to go easy on the boy, find out if he was of the proper timber. It wasn't just any Joe Moke who could be ordained, he told himself, as we know to our cost. And if saying the rosary now risked rushing the liturgical agenda, so be it. No more pussyfooting!

'Sunday fortnight it is!' Mr Devanny sounded delighted. 'And d'you know, Sally, I was thinking we might make a day out of it. Take a turn in the car, see a bit of the country, get a breath of fresh air. Our friend would like that, I think. Tea and scones, something stronger perhaps for the gentlemen, ha-ha . . .'

'Grand. Right you be,' Sally interrupted, and rang off, before his excitement made a bloody fool of him altogether.

But he was right. Milo should be shown the country. Everything she had he should be shown. All – she was that daft about him – she had was his. His image came to her when she was chatting with Stella Harty, when she was swabbing the floor, when she eavesdropped outside the study, hearing only the Professor slowly intoning. Twenty, fifty times a day he came to her, and every single time Sally was reduced to a clatter of gooseflesh.

It was no longer a matter of Milo's fine, young, limber, surprisingly sallow thingabob – his wand, his dousing stick – though God knows she struck oil as far as it went, powerful, magic, glorious . . . But now that she had got to know him too, the whole thing was so much more than a fling, seeing what he'd gone through, poor boy. She would bind his blazing wounds, though, never fear. She would salve his scars. The pity that she felt was, she was sure, true love. He was quiet, and of course she liked that too. And he was brave as well, and clever, which she admired in him, naturally, even if he was inclined to be a bit too unassuming – look at the way he'd brought out the story of himself to her . . . First, last and always, though, was the loving kindness, the heartwarming tender sadness that she felt. He, too, like her, had been damn near done out of life, the poor sparrow. She wished she could thank him for making her see that. She wished she could tell him that. She fed him bars of post-coital chocolate, smoking and humming: the whole of her humming. She wished she could crawl into his ear, lever herself some way down his gullet, fill him from head to toe with her. Lose herself in him for ever and ever, amen.

Milo yawned until his jawbones crackled and made a little bow of apology to the Professor – sorry, but he couldn't help it.

'Again,' said the Professor, not very encouragingly. 'Who made the world?'

Milo shook his head. It was no good.

The Professor's face was sulphur-yellow, sweaty with exasperation and the uphill struggle. 'God made the world!'

No doubt, thought Milo, this religious business – the rosary beads, the holy picture, the book with the answers whose name he hadn't grasped – would have had him yawning all by themselves. But they were not the problem. Sally was the problem. Or the two together were the problem – Milo could hardly think straight. But no sooner had the prayers begun than Sally wanted him at night as well as in the afternoon. She wanted them to go into a field on the way home from The Last Post. She came to his bed. She took him to hers. He mimed tiredness, but with closed eyes he looked so deliciously saintly that it would be a sin, as Sally saw it, to leave him be. He mimed soreness, pointing at himself and grimacing. Sally made to kiss it better ('and the eggs, how's the eggs?' putting her hand under them). He wished he could explain himself, but for all the words he now had, none were the right ones. He wished he could say that this was not how he imagined earning his keep. He wished she didn't roar as she came, because she would surely bring down the house one of these times, though he loved her going all out, and him with her, him with her . . .

He had to tell her that, yes, *liebchen*, he was indeed having the time of his life, but that really she could not go on like this, leading him by the *kurac*. He should have told her this when he felt the first surge of delight and release ebbing and he found himself able to think about himself, not just about his circumstances. Now, afraid of what she might come up with next, they simply had to talk. He sat up in bed, satisfied, dissatisfied. Sally had just padded away, her face bloated and blotchy, as though ill from her exertions. But Milo lay wide awake. The dark was thick and heavy, a negative, oppressive afterglow. Soon, he thought, he would fear her. Then hate her. Such was the strength of her need. Such was the power of her powerless life.

He turned on the light and rummaged through the box files for blank paper. His hand moved freely and unconsciously and he began to draw.

'Look,' he said. It was the following afternoon. Sally was hoisting herself moistly onto his lap.

'You're such a good boy,' she said, 'I got Black Magic.'

'No,' said Milo. 'Today we talk,' and pulled the sheaf of drawings from his jacket pocket.

The first one consisted simply of a sign. Nürnberg.

'Oh, Nuremberg,' said Sally, 'is it? Did you ever see that picture *Judgment at Nuremberg*? His Nibs,' pointing upstairs, 'thinks it's the greatest picture ever made.' She laughed.

Milo sighed impatiently, pointed to the sign, then to himself.

'Oh, I see,' Sally said. 'You're from Nuremberg? But I thought . . . ? Oh, you were *in* Nuremberg, ah right . . .'

The next picture showed a man on the ground with three youths around him kicking. 'That's very good,' said Sally, smiling up at him. But she saw with alarm from the flare in his eyes that this was not what he wanted her to say at all. He shoved the next sheet at her – someone in bed – then, quickly, the last one, a man running. Sally looked at him again. For the first time in a long while Milo saw something tentative in her expression. Does she see? he wondered. 'Is that you?' said Sally, pointing to the last picture.

Milo didn't mention the Hauptbanhof where he and his pal Dusan had gone to find a whore, or the chill of empty Eilgutstrasse by the Sheraton-Carlton near where the yobs had set upon them or the wait for the ambulance and for the *polizei*, the wait for nurse and doctor at the Martha-Maria, and after that Milo not waiting at all, the liability of suddenly becoming visible, of being named and questioned, all too clear. After that, running away.

Sally took his head on her breast, stroked his hair and his face: 'It's all over. It's all gone.'

But after a very little while he broke away from her and gave her a direct look, as much as to say, I don't want to be babied, I don't want to hide, these are the things that somehow or other I must live with, which must not prevent me from living. Sally looked at him, surprised, and got down off his lap, dressed herself fully slowly and quietly and went back to the kitchen. She is upset, Milo thought, that is good. Now she would take him seriously, instead of night and day boiling his *jaje*.

He made more drawings. Sally saw a house on fire, a woman in black, a mound with a lopsided cross on it. There were more running pictures, too, running from his home by the Tara, through the Drina's burning flood plain, across transient frontlines, shifting borders. Sally was in tears. Milo didn't know if that was good. Perhaps he'd gone too far. The respite which he thought he wanted quickly turned into a different form of involvement, as demanding as the one he had, for the time being, escaped. Now he could only draw. Now Sally could only look, teary and numb.

One day after dinner, instead of clearing off the table as he usually did, Milo took his plate and began to wheel it round and round.

'Stop,' Sally mimed, 'you're giving me a headache.'

He chanced handing her a fresh sheaf of drawings. She saw him sitting at a pottery wheel. She saw him sitting in a studio. Then there was a house, with mountain peaks and shafts of sunlight.

Sally thought back to him fingering the dough. She put the drawings on the table. He was trying to explain, turning the plate again, pumping his leg as though to propel it, then making shapes slowly with his fine-fingered, sure-touching, earth-moving hands.

'*Mein Traum.*' Milo shyly smiled.

Sally nodded slowly. She understood. She'd seen that he'd done the drawings of old Wallace bills. The cleverality of him! Ah yes, but it was just like the gentle, understated ways of him as well, to know the thousand words' worth of a picture.

How long they sat there looking at one another they couldn't say, it didn't matter, Sally thought the silence said it all, and Milo supposed it had to, not knowing quite what else to think, and not being at all sure why Sally seemed so solemn, since the pictures were his dream of happiness. She should be smiling.

An explanation of Sally's seriousness was soon forthcoming, however – as soon, in fact, as the Professor rose, had tea, and announced that as he'd planned to go over their day out's final details with Mr Devanny that afternoon, he'd as soon leave Milo at home, if that was all right.

Seeing the Professor turn him aside with a raised hand, Milo's heart sank. Sure enough, as soon as her uncle left, Sally scampered up the stairs. But it was not what Milo thought, because as he made his leaden way up after her, down she came against him carrying one of the box files from his room and indicating by complicated head movements that he was to do the same.

There was an old tar-barrel – another Wallace remnant – in the ruined back garden, and into it they poured the files.

'Whoo!' Sally went, clapping her hands as the flames shot up, and hopping from one foot to the other. She looked at Milo as directly as he had lately looked at her.

'Now!' she shouted.

What did that mean? Milo wondered, gazing at her flushed and beaming face.

9

'Now,' said Mr Devanny, very businesslike, 'let you two gents sit in the back, the way you, sir,' to the Professor, 'as our guide won't have to be turning around the whole time with your commentary. And you, Sally, sit up here with me. You're my co-pilot!'

It was two o'clock on an afternoon that looked every inch of Sunday – a day of rest, cloudless and calm. 'A glorious day, thanks be to God,' said the Professor piously.

'Amen,' said Milo, a solecism at which the Professor could only sigh, having little energy any more to do more now where Milo was concerned. Was the fight going out of him? Was Milo being not thick exactly but just diffident, indifferent – agnostic, that was it – on purpose, neither wishing to be saved: nor to save himself? Not for the first time, the Professor peevishly asked himself why it took the patience of Job to do any good in the world. But that's God's way, he reminded himself: test, test and test again, like the powerful teacher He is.

Mr Devanny smiled across at Sally, motioning with his eyes to the back seat, as much as to say, condescendingly, the odd couple. 'You're looking very nice,' he ventured, thinking, as his eyes rested on her bust, not as nice, though, as in that strange conductress's outfit, with its interesting belts and dotey little pouch for the money – a sporran, that was it – with your 'Pay up and look happy!' Cheeky thing . . .

Sally said, 'D'you know what we ought to do?'

'What's that?' Mr Devanny said, keenly.

'We ought to have tea at the Fison Lodge. That place in Knocktoppery. I hear it's very good. And I was never there, imagine.'

'Well, we could.' Mr Devanny was now less keen. 'They get very busy, of course. And we shouldn't spoil our dinner.'

'Yes, Mammy.' Sally lit a cigarette.

Now that stung. But Mr Devanny rose above it by dwelling on his driving, bevelling around bends and scorching along straights like a past master, the Astra obedient to his every touch, even if he was going too fast for Milo to see anything. Not that the hillocky fields had much in them to see – the odd ruin, the odd clump of cows, the odd heap of dirt and lean-to marking the progress of the Dutchmen and earning anathema from the Professor's running commentary. 'This will interest you, Milo, this is historical, and you know I often think your history is much the same as our own. The religion, the fighting for your freedom, the yoke of the terrible Turks. You're one of us, sure! That fine-looking house down there used to belong to the Murphys, a Catholic family, but begod didn't the eldest son marry one of the Earl of Shotover's nieces . . .' The long story was not interesting. But when at length the Professor, by nodding off, released him, leaving Milo to look beyond this meagre ground, he could only think of the various other nowheres he had known, the gutted remains of the family home, his murdered mother, his futile dream of the turning wheel, the frail hope of making something out of clay. It seemed so stupid, this need of his for some simple, harmless object. So stupid. So far off.

Sally's smoke had filled the car. Milo let down his window. He was suffocating.

After many a silent mile, during which Sally was afraid to say anything to Milo, for fear Devanny caught her drift, and Mr Devanny was afraid to say anything to Sally, for fear Milo did likewise, they came to a T-junction.

'Left or right?' said Mr Devanny, the arms of the signpost having been broken off. 'I think this is it.' He turned right.

'This is what?' said Sally. It was not Knocktoppery or anywhere like it.

'You'll see, now,' Mr Devanny said, explaining that, on account of his forty winks, there, the Professor wasn't able to conduct his tour as planned, so this would be a nice surprise for him.

The overgrown avenue along which Mr Devanny sped was not, however, Sally's idea of a nice surprise, and Milo, sunk sullenly into the corner of his seat, looked about the way she felt. It was the Professor who looked lively when the Astra slewed to an abrupt halt on a gravel turnaround before a long, two-storey, grey-stone barrack of a building. He sat bolt upright.

'I must be dreaming,' he said. 'This,' he turned to Milo, 'is where I spent my life. Mourne Abbey. The upper storey is the dormitory. My room was in the far corner, there, the last window. I was in the nature of what the English call a housemaster, though naturally we had no truck whatsoever with English ways . . .'

Enthusiastically strolling ahead, the Professor only noticed that it wasn't Milo who was attending him but Mr Devanny, and that Milo and Sally were nowhere to be seen – had in fact, at Sally's instigation, slipped off around the other side of the building and were heading hurriedly towards the fields beyond.

'Now where did that pair go?' said the Professor crankily. 'This is educational.'

But the disappearance could not have been more perfectly timed, as far as Mr Devanny was concerned. He had been slightly worried that, once he got the Professor to what he had increasingly taken to thinking of as his field of dreams, he would not be able to get his full attention. Now it was as if Sally had cleared the necessary space for him – had read his mind, indeed – like the good angel he knew she was, deep down. She wouldn't regret it; he would not be slow to seize the opportunity; she would have her reward (dinner this evening was only a start).

Mr Devanny began with an oblique approach, noting the surprisingly good condition of the school building and the monastery behind it and the various outbuildings, all entirely suitable – indeed, ripe – for development by the right man with the proper vision, respectful of the past but also forward-looking, a leader with a sense of social responsibility, and so on and so forth (he spoke at length in this vein, as though experiencing difficulty in changing gears). In fact, he said at last, to come to the issue at hand, what with the Professor's own obviously excellent contacts up in Dublin, of which Milo was an embodiment, a prototype, but also he would go so far as to say, a symbol of hope for the future, he could readily foresee the Professor being an inspiration and the head of Mourne Abbey's rebirth as an IRC . . .

'A what?' said the Professor suspiciously, though up to this point he had been listening to Mr Devanny with pleasure and interest.

Having made up the initials himself – he'd read an article on the power of positive initial utilisation – but not having rehearsed his flow being interrupted, even temporarily, Mr Devanny floundered. 'Induction and Re-education Camp,' he said.

'Camp?' The Professor's whine had something of a bite in it.

'Centre,' Mr Devanny hastily amended. 'Centre,' adding wildly, 'They're all over the Continent. And here with the service sector, for example, crying out, literally crying out, for labour . . .'

'Labour?'

Mr Devanny found himself drifting, coasting, his hands no longer on the wheel, so to speak, and a stone wall dead ahead. 'What did you . . .?'

'If I told you once, I told you a thousand times,' the Professor barged in, evidently inspired by his old pedagogical stamping ground, 'if what I represent – what Milo is to be – turns out to be a miracle, which it very well might, by the way, it'll be no economic miracle. It's a matter of God and Mammon, man! We have Mammon. But God is in the ha'penny place. Or would be only for me trying to do something about it.'

'You mean . . . ?' But Mr Devanny dared not admit what the Professor meant.

'I mean,' said the Professor with asperity, 'that Milo is being prepared, by me, for the priesthood – in a preliminary way, of course; when he's ready I'll turn him over to a seminary, naturally. Which will free me. Because I also mean Milo to lend his name to an organisation that I will shortly be discussing with Donie of the Department. MILO. May Ireland Lead Others!'

'Well, see, my idea . . . ' But Mr Devanny might as well have been talking to the wall.

The Professor was in another place. Gazing up at the window of his old room, head raised high, body rigid, as though honouring a leader or a flag, while somehow feeling himself to be both, he was uplifted by the thought of past and present meeting in him, as now they were, how through him each would make the other speak. Devanny had put it very well, come to think of it: vision and tradition, and what's this else he said? Not forgetting, by any means, the Blessed Virgin, who had also greatly aided him attain this restorative confluence. The Professor did not neglect to utter a few ejaculations thanking her, even while reflecting what a damn shame it was that he hadn't thought of saying the rosary sooner.

Neither man noticed Sally and Milo return, Sally checking the back of her raincoat for twigs and brambles, and wearing a broad grin of triumph for having at last met a long-felt want to have sex in a field plastered across her face. Indeed, caught up in the day's differing outcomes as they were, Sally would have remained the least of Mr Devanny's and the Professor's concerns at dinner, too, had not Jack – their waiter that evening, proving to perfection, Mr Devanny noted with some bitterness, the point he'd forcefully made about the service industry's crying needs – inquired of the Professor if a word with him in private would be possible.

This was at the end of the main course of what had been an indifferent dinner – the roast beef too stringy, the Bulgarian Merlot an inky disappointment – and Mr Devanny was already annoyed at the way Jack hovered around the table as they ate, his eye particularly on Milo, as though not quite believing that the guest of honour, whom Mr Devanny had toasted as such, knew one end of a knife and fork from another. But between acting the convivial host and wondering what his next move might be, Professor-wise, Mr Devanny had quite enough on his plate. Jack he would leave for another time, for the Jacks, he sighed, were always with us. And then, just as Milo and Sally had, at Miss Luby's invitation, gone to join Wim and Cornelius in the lounge, and Mr Devanny had decided to press a superfine liqueur on the Professor in hopes of finding a fresh initiative for himself, Jack butts in. Mr Devanny was alone.

The wine was truly terrible, metallic and thin, utterly devoid of finish, and Mr Devanny grimaced as he gulped down the last two glasses of it, resolving that if there was pavlova for afters he would call for Muscadet. Something sweet and crisp, a hint of titillation, a genial libation . . .

But although he could hear himself singing Muscadet's praises to his guests' amusement and edification, Mr Devanny never actually sang them, because with a face of mustardy – even, Mr Devanny thought, alarmed, a bilious – yellow, the Professor broke in on his vaguely rehabilitatory reverie and commanded: 'Get the car!'

Mr Devanny half-stood, as though weak-kneed. 'Dessert? Coffee?'

'Is it deaf you are,' the Professor demanded, 'or just plain stupid?'

'But Sally and—'

'They're ack-acking away at the German, the Grey . . . your friend and them,' Jack put in, as though shocked.

And indeed they were. Sally had to take a back seat, of course, and make small talk with the Luby one. But Milo, sweet boy, smiled over at her now and again, and the other pair gazed at her appreciatively, as well, if in a grazing kind of way, smiling and nodding, so really it was all very pleasant and civil, if not quite the gloat-inducing success Sally had anticipated, had vaguely believed she deserved, though the afternoon field was, she smiled, some compensation.

'I don't give a gypsy's mickey,' the Professor snapped. 'Take us home!'

10

And so it was that a little before midnight that same Sunday, the Professor's tantrum, ignited by Jack, stoked in the Astra by the seething silence of all concerned, and raging out of control once inside *Manresa*, produced at last the turn to which the Professor had long believed his open-heartedness made him prone, as a result of which he had to be unceremoniously carted off to St Dymphna's, Desh, where he was listed in critical condition.

Prior to falling, however, the Professor made sure that he did himself and his principles proud. But since all he had to go on was that she and Milo had been seen at The Last Post – Joe Harty, husband of Sheila, nephew of Jack, was a part-time lounge-boy there – Sally was not at all worried. Of course the Professor rained down his customary fire and brimstone. They'd abused his trust. They'd wiped the floor with the good name of Flynn. It pained him to find that his dead sister's only child was a trollop, a tinker, a tramp. But he was not surprised – and here the tricker Wallace was yet one more time wheeled in for a guest appearance, this time in the unfamiliar role of being more sinned against than sinning, Sally being such a scarlet woman, which brought from her a derisive snort of a laugh.

In fact, the whole thing was funny – the tiptoeing like naughty children away from the house, Milo's efforts at ordering a drink and slipping him the money for it, the stroll home that resembled a three-legged race for slow learners. Even the spectacle of this puny maneen in the middle of the kitchen floor, spouting and quivering and making odd motions with his hands, the kind of sermonising performance Sally had always abhorred and ignored and feared somewhat, now struck her as simply comical in its execrations and exaggerations. And she had to laugh as well to think that Milo was, at last, seeing this pompous, God-Almighty teacher of his in at least some of his true colours. So she leaned against the draining board, smoking and smirking, looking for all the world to Milo like the saucy, insouciant ladies of the

Hauptbanhof, which did not please him. And he tried to signal to her, too, not to roll her eyes so much or add laugh-suppressing crinkles to her nose. But Sally just patted the air beside her – keep calm. To Milo, however, whatever the Professor was raving about must be serious because this was family business, and Milo knew that it was in families that killing began, not the physical kind only, though he had seen that, too, but the living death of estrangement, bitterness and loss.

Submit, comply, and thus deflect, that was how Milo dealt with the authorities when, through rare misfortune, deal he had to, and this was what he wanted to do now when the Professor turned the onslaught in his direction, and he moved further into the shadows around the broom closet. 'I had such high hopes for you,' the Professor wailed. 'But you let me down. You let me down. You're nothing but a cur, after all, just like all the rest of you people, making the most of the soft-hearted, simple-minded Irish. Flea-bitten curs and parasites. I took you in. But by the holy Paul it was you took me in!'

Sally could not believe her ears. 'Well, of all the blasted . . .' But no. She would not try to match the Professor either in outrage or theatrics. This wasn't funny. She would get a grip. So, with quiet menace, she said instead, 'Leave Milo out of it.'

Now it was the Professor's turn to laugh, which he did with a mirthless squawk. 'Out of it?' said he. 'You don't know what you're talking about.'

'Oh?' said Sally, mockingly. 'And what are you talking about?'

But, to begin with, at least, she was sorry she asked, because that was when it all came out – the Professor's motives, the Professor's plans, the remaking of Milo (as though, thought Sally, he was a mere lump of dough), the making of MILO, the salvation of the country, the solution of the Church's vocation crisis (the least he could do in recompense for his Mourne Abbey career), the alleviation, God willing, of the State's refugee problem, and above all, the Christian duty to be of use, to help, faith without good works being not enough to save us, while obviously, as he used to teach his pupils every day, *laborare est orare*, there was no getting away from that . . . All this, the Professor soberly concluded, Sally had brought tumbling down.

Sally could see by him that he meant every word of it, monstrous and absurd as the whole thing was – the dream, the mission, the pride, the righteousness. Perhaps later on she'd look back and feel sorry for him, but for now she'd be damned if he'd make her feel guilty.

She crossed over to where Milo was attempting to merge with the wallpaper. 'Come here to me, Father,' she said, and drew him by the hand out into the light.

Then, with Milo behind her, Sally abruptly stuck her backside into his crotch and began wiggling it around, around and around. 'This is what you believe in, isn't it, Milo? – isn't it, my fine diviner?' She turned and began to eat the face off him in that necessitous, untender way she had, crushing him to her. She said, 'And I believe it too, so I do. The two of us believe it. Together. See? So you can stick your clergy and your salvation army and all the rest of it in the highest rafter of your bony arse!'

'Oh my God!' the scandalised Professor exclaimed. 'You're either mad or drunk.'

Sally gave Milo another rib-crushing hug, sighing, 'Oh, I'm drunk with *love*,' sultrily pronounced *loaf* in a rich, though strange, contralto.

'Stop it this minute.' The martinet in the Professor now tried to take charge. 'I will not have this type of exhibition, exhibitionism, in my house.'

'My house,' said Sally, laughing gaily. 'And you're a bit late, I'm extremely pleased to say.'

She gave Milo one of her frank, delighted smiles.

But Milo had no smile of his own to give back. By now he was all too well aware that whatever they were fighting about, he was in the middle of it. But, untenable though it was, and ardently as he hoped the ground would open and swallow him, he wasn't exactly thinking of his position literally, so he was utterly taken aback when the Professor sprang forward, grabbed him by the arm and began to pull him free of Sally's grasp. 'See sense, boy,' the Professor panted. 'Be said by me.' And then Sally, crying, 'Leave him alone. He's mine!' pulled Milo by the other hand.

Back and forth, for a time, they went. Then the Professor let go of the arm and grabbed a hold of a leg, and Sally reached over to the rack of implements above the Aga and raised a ladle high as though to strike.

'Leave him alone!' she cried again.

The Professor cocked a furious eye at her dangerous height, her towering rage. 'How dare . . .' he began and tried to take a swipe at the menacing ladle. But his reach exceeded his grasp. With a startled look, and in the grip of a searing pain in his arm, he collapsed on the floor before them.

'Sally, Sally,' Milo went. But then his next thought, very quickly, was of Dusan, and of how this incident here was much more serious, in a house, with a woman, late at night, drink a factor (probably), ambulance now, police unavoidable later, and perhaps forever. 'Sally!'

But Sally was oddly bent over the Professor, whether concerned for his condition or to ensure his continuing immobility her body language didn't rightly say. At any rate, she wasn't responding. Milo saw that he was as good as on his own. He thought quickly.

Cornelius sounded sleepy, sullen (in the interests of planning ahead, Milo had asked for their business card, which had their mobile phone numbers on them), but he soon sized up the situation once Milo blurted out what happened, and in next to no time – after a despairing *'Komm doch!'* from Milo, followed by a flurry of *rechts faren* and *links abbiegen* – Cornelius and Wim drew up outside *Manresa*. The Professor was breathing shallowly as they loaded him into the back of the jeep.

Milo conferred intensively with them as they waited for Sally to get her things. Finally she was ready. Milo turned to her, touched her arm, shone his large, sad, sweetly-meaning eyes on her.

'Now,' he said, gently, helping her on board.

Then, throwing his Bayern Munich windbreaker and all his drawings into the tar-barrel in the back garden and helping himself to an ill-fitting Aran sweater of Wallace's and some other odds and ends – a flashlight, an apple, the remaining half of a Bakewell tart – Milo, following Wim and Cornelius's directions, rode off on Sally's bicycle to the hut on the Knocktoppery road, where, tomorrow or the next day, they would pick him up and take him with them, if he wanted, to the hills between Estepona and Ronda in Andalucia.

11

'Sally' – Mr Devanny half-rose. 'To what do I owe the . . .?' But the phrase died on his lips because he could tell by how awful she looked that her surprise appearance in his office was not a pleasure – though, by the same token, she was hardly here on business . . .

She really did look frightful, her eyes bleary and her hair astray, the clothes thrown on her any old way. Mr Devanny understood, of course: from all Jack had told him, she must have had a dreadful night. He wondered if Sally agreed with him how strange it was that the Professor had taken the turn he had long, and in Mr Devanny's view hypochondriacally, feared on the very day he had declined an offer to move with the times? Not that Mr Devanny thought the Professor's collapse somehow vindicated his own vision of Mourne Abbey, not at all. On the other hand, he thought, it made you think . . . He would try to ask her.

'But I understand your uncle is resting comfortably now,' Mr Devanny said. 'And Sally, if you don't mind me saying so, so should you be. You must be all-in. Sit down there and we'll have a cup of tea, and I'll run you home. And I'll tuck you in, and I'll do a bit of house-work while you're sleeping, and when you wake up I'll have the soup ready, the sausage rolls heated, the chips gold and sizzling in the pan, and you can tell me everything.' For as he spoke, it became blindingly obvious why Sally was here (he could have kicked himself for being so slow). She looked to him. She knew she could rely on him. She knew his heart, of all the hearts of Desh, was going out to her, to her alone.

He came around to her side of the desk, pulled out a chair for her, and with a courtly gesture, bade her sit. Was this the time to put an arm around her, or would she appreciate it more in greater privacy? He made a vague gesturing movement for her to sit, then fussed around with the Teasmade. His heart was racing.

But Sally didn't sit. 'Don't bother about tea,' she said. 'I'm in a bit of a hurry, actually. I just looked in to see if you could answer a question for me.'

'I'm yours to command, Sally.' His voice was strangely strangulated.

'Was my uncle insured?'

'Ah, now, that's a good question. I'm sure he was, being above all a practical man, as you know.'

'But not with you?' Sally said – you dull-witted, thick-headed bloody fool.

'Ah, no,' said he. 'I don't do life.'

'Shit,' said Sally. 'I suppose you don't know anyone who'd take the house off my hands?'

Mr Devanny turned around and looked at Sally very carefully.

'If I had the money we could do something, get a place, set him up, like,' she said. 'Then there'd be no more running away.'

She spoke as if explaining something, but it was plainly gibberish, Mr Devanny said to himself. Exhaustion and distress must have the better of her. Nobody in their right mind just ups and sells a house. He drew back a little from her, reluctant suddenly to offer her a hand, much less to extend a sheltering arm, and contented himself merely by indicating that, needless to say, he knew she needed help at such a terrible time but that it didn't do to be too hasty, and that, after all, her uncle would probably be released soon, and would need her more than ever . . . He faltered here, however, seeing that the scenario he'd just drawn up left little room for himself.

'Oh, he'll not be back,' said Sally, matter-of-factly. 'He'll be off to the Regional before the day is out, and he'll be kept going there for a while, I suppose, with the machines. He won't last long. He's as good as gone.'

Later, Mr Devanny wondered if that was surely the now or never moment for a hug. But at the time he was unable to move, stunned not only by confirmation of the Professor's condition or by Sally's cut-and-dried, indeed unfeeling, tone, but by the confusion created by her, almost in the same breath, asking in the same casual way, 'By the way, he didn't ring you, by any chance, did he?'

'Your uncle?'

'Milo, you fecking eejit! Milo! He's after running away on me. But if I could get the money I could get the wheel. What good is a house to me . . .' Now! Mr Devanny told himself. But Sally brushed past his open arms, tears flying from her.

This was at ten. Within the hour, Mr Devanny had drained the full flask of Paddy whiskey that was supposed to see him through his day at the office – that is, until lunchtime or thereabouts – and had driven over to Mrs Fitzpatrick's. There until six or so he sipped John Power and water slowly but steadily under the unblinking eye of Mrs Fitzpatrick (she was a friend of Mr Devanny's late mother, and knew he was weak). And really he didn't seem too bad – a bit numb in the face as he stared into space, a bit half seas over in his walks to the Gents, maybe. He was unusually quiet, though, in fact, not a bit civil, and he kept buying packets of peanuts. But instead of opening them he just pushed them around the table from time to time, making a pattern and breaking a pattern and saying, 'Peanuts,' every now and then with a very unfunny laugh. Watching this, Mrs Fitzpatrick recalled later, she could tell there was trouble brewing, call it her woman's intuition if you like.

She said as much to her son, Mackey, the frozen food king, when, some time later, he came home for his tea. 'That bloody old soak,' said Mackey. 'I won't be long shifting him.' But when Mackey, accompanied by his mother murmuring soothingly, approached, Mr Devanny, who had been staring stupidly at nothing, suddenly sprang up and emitted a defiant, 'Ha-ha!' Mother and son drew back, naturally, never expecting such a drunk worm to take a belligerent turn. So by the time Mackey had recovered sufficiently to shout, 'You're barred, you bollix!' Mr Devanny was weaving the Astra out of the car park, on route to see if Wim and Con had a yen for a jorum, and fuelled by a feeling of having never felt better.

According to Jack, Mr Devanny turned up somewhere between eight and nine. He had drink taken, yes. But Jack, run ragged by getting that pair of bloody hole-borers ready for the road, found it simplest to serve Mr Devanny the pint he called for (and promptly spilled). Mr Devanny then demanded to know where his 'very good friends' were, and expressed vociferously a desire to buy them a drink.

Jack said, shortly, that he had work to do, packing, so would Mr Devanny ever sit down and shut up.

'Packing!' said Mr Devanny, looking long and deep into his empty glass. '*Pack*-ing. Pack-*ing*,' and then, like a chicken, 'Pack-pack-pack, paaack . . .' Very soon he was laughing, as his foolery hit him. 'Bloody clown,' he said to himself. Then he brooded on that for a while. It was sad. Staggering across the lobby with yet one more sample case, Jack heard him proclaim, 'Everyone's gone!' and gave him a scowl. 'They're all gone,' Mr Devanny repeated. Something told him that he was included, and that there was nothing to be done. So he just sat there, sniffling and sniggering, nodding and swaying, and carrying on an animated though intermittent conversation with himself.

At around eleven, the sound of Wim's hearty laughter roused him, and Mr Devanny struggled to his feet, waving and calling to the three inseparables as they merrily trooped upstairs, Miss Luby playing the drum-major by twirling the tassels of her technicolour shawl (a parting gift). On the landing, all three stood and flickered their fingers at him, whether in salutation or farewell Mr Devanny could not quite make out. Then they turned towards the room.

Unable to decide whether to buy a bottle and join them or consider himself given the brush-off, Mr Devanny stood unsteadily in the lounge doorway. He could definitely do with a drink. 'Jack,' he called, much too loudly. 'Jack!' But who should he see sloping along the passage leading to the kitchen but Milo, who had found the dark and the cold of the hut too much, and his position there, besides, ridiculous.

'Aha!' Mr Devanny exclaimed, as though all was revealed. And off with him in hot-ish pursuit, raising with each step his foot an exaggerated height off the carpeted corridor in the interests of stealth.

When he caught up with Milo, he went, 'Boo!'

Milo just about jumped out of his skin. He was nervous enough as it was, not yet quite believing if the Dutch could be trusted. They had told him he could come if he liked, and where to go if he did. But now this. Even if, judging by the state of him, Mr Devanny presented no obstacle and was hardly part of the plan, Milo still felt very watchful and tense after the previous night's events, especially the Professor's collapse, for which by now he was more convinced than ever that he would face charges.

'See here, my fine southern friend,' said Mr Devanny, 'you and I need to talk. You have a claim, as I understand it, to the woman I love. Well, come on. Put them up. We'll see who's the better man. To the victor the spoils.'

Milo's heart sank.

'Defend yourself, you dishonourable beggar!' Mr Devanny shouted. 'You tinker's whelp . . .'

He poked Milo tentatively on the shoulder, then with a lucky blow firmly on the mouth.

'No!' Milo raised his hands surrenderingly, and began to walk away. Back to the hut. Back to the hole in the ground. He should have known that the more visible he was the more trouble he was in.

'Stand your ground, you . . .' Mr Devanny poked Milo in the back. Every blow increased his confidence. 'Think you can have your swinish way with Sally, my flower of womanhood . . .?'

They were back in the lobby now. Milo turned and Mr Devanny almost fell on top of him. 'No!' Milo said again, this time pushing Mr Devanny away, and he, unbalanced, fell against the bird's-eye maple occasional table (an heirloom) so that the legs went out from under it and the bowl with the arrangement of impatiens smashed and Mr Devanny let out a great roar from amidst the wreckage, and Milo darted away.

By the time Mr Devanny got to his feet, Miss Luby, despite her déshabillé, was on the landing screeching at him, 'Out. *Get out!* And don't come back.' Wim put his arm around her as she moaned, 'My lovely table,' and Cornelius made clucking sounds intended to be mollifying. 'Ah, there you are,' Mr Devanny called. 'Put away that mutton dressed as lamb and take a drink with me, a drop of schnapps, a ball of malt,

a *deoch an dorais*, one for the road, though why just one, I say ...'
By which time Jack had turned up, and catching Mr Devanny by his
blazer collar, marched him across the lobby, through the porch, and
with a heave pitched him down the front steps into the unseasonably
chilly street, directing as he did so a hefty kick at Mr Devanny's behind
which, satisfying as it was symbolically, Jack regretted not having
properly administered years ago.

Mr Devanny sat on the pavement and looked at the emptiness
around him. He was sober now, or at least sober enough to sense that
he'd fallen from grace. The cool breeze cuffed him spitefully. He
couldn't stay here. He picked himself up. Sally, he thought, and made
for the car park. Sally needs me. All roads lead to Sally. Sally – to console, to forgive, to make good. Sally to whom a full report would be
made. They'd call the Guards. That Slovakian, Slovenian, scut would
pay for the trouble he caused, pay in full. Together he and Sally would
avenge the Professor, that dear, passionate, foolish man.

But, somehow or other, Mr Devanny got turned around making a
short cut through the Beverly Glens estate and never got to *Manresa*,
although he managed to be the soul of civility to the Setanta Security
man who found him early the next morning parked at the unhandiest
of angles outside The Last Post.

And in any case, Sally had no need of a report. After leaving
Mr Devanny she'd gone to the Commercial where the Dutchmen, very
gently, gave a shape to what she felt. They were taking Milo with them.
Having heard what the circumstances were, they believed he was quite
right to be concerned for his safety. 'You never can tell how people will
react,' said Wim, and although they agreed with her that it was she
who was indebted to Milo, while Wim and Con owed him nothing,
Cornelius said that giving him a lift was nothing, really, no more than
the good turn anybody would do, and Wim said it didn't have anything
to do with owing. They said they were sorry, then, and soberly shook
hands. She could collect her bike from the hut, they said; Milo had told
them to tell her.

Sally had the notion of cycling up hill and down dale for the rest of
the day, and if necessary, night, to see if she might chance upon Milo
one last time. But that didn't last long. She was tired, and besides, the
days of her daftness were done. So instead she went home and spent
the rest of the day smoking and staring, and to her vague surprise,
smiling. She thought not so much of how now it was over but more of

how great it was while it lasted. 'Lunacy, naturally,' she said to herself, laughing. 'But there are worse kinds of madness.'

After dark, she found herself in the back garden. The night sky put her in mind of her burned papers. The burning had been crazy, too, she reflected. Completely over the top. But she was the better for it. No regrets, anyhow. Definitely no regrets. There was a sprinkling of stars. All so far away, thought Sally, but nice to know they're there, all the same.

She had said to Wim and Con, 'Look after him, OK?' And they'd replied, '*Ja, ja*. No problem.' Sally Wallace thought very highly of the Dutchmen.

Drag

MARY MORRISSY

Clothes maketh the man. Your mother used to say that. Her words stay with you as you riffle through the hanging ghosts in your wardrobe. It's a moment of infinite anticipation. What to wear? The evening's expectations are secreted among the limp fall of fabrics, the yielding crush of shoulder pads, the sly whispers of silk. You whisk two or three recruits from the comradely army in the closet and hang them up around the room – over the mirror, on the twin mother-of-pearl-inlaid handles of the wardrobe, or on the hook behind the door. It makes it seem more like play. Makes more of a ritual of it. Often the bedroom will end up strewn with discarded clothes, denuded hangers, shoes abandoned in the second position and still, you won't have made a choice. You find such disarray intoxicatingly slutty, though nothing could be further from the truth. You're a careful dresser, in fact, discreet, but unambiguously feminine. You don't go overboard, of course. No polka dots, no stilettoes in pre-school colours. But you don't like sober either – otherwise, what would be the point? It is called dressing up, after all. You can't stand calculated understatement, that eunuch look the younger ones go for. Those pin-striped trousers or sober little black suits with a white T-shirt peeking underneath and a bit of underwire cleavage just to tantalise. That really *is* drag. You're doing imperson-ation, not caricature. You'd love to totter around in platforms or heels but there's your feet to consider. And your height. You can't afford to magnify flaws. It's all about disguise as any 'girl' will tell you. The opaque tights are your biggest compromise. With a different anatomy you'd go for broke and wear fishnets. But if you're big-boned you can't play the vamp with any kind of grace. Anyway, you want to look like a woman, not a tart.

Bridge club, you mean, blue rinse, George sneers. Bitch! According to George, you have slender hips – this said with some envy – and a real waist. You like George's fitting-room verdicts, admiration confessed to the mirror. Makes you feel real. Authentic. Your biggest weakness is floral. Not loud, but more the summer garden variety. Your mother used to have swing dresses with pink coins of colour like lily pads dimpling a Monet lake. You used to love those. Maybe you're operating out of sentiment, or nostalgia. Though even you would baulk at admitting that your fashion sense is down to your mother's frocks. But, look, you loved your mother. It's not a crime, is it? Though these days any extravagant expression of affection – particularly for your mother – seems to arouse suspicion. Suspicion of what, you'd like to know. You're not afraid to admit that you idolised your mother – God rest her. You keep her alive this way too, with those blessings of hers. You use them sincerely though sometimes people – including George – presume irony. (You open your mouth and your mother comes out, George says.) Maybe you cling to Mother's memory simply because for so long there was just the two of you.

Your father disappeared when you were two – he did one of those magic tricks. Put his hand in the till and went up in a puff of smoke. Left you both in the lurch, your mother would say. In your mind's eye you saw a drunk on a deserted street, lewd smile, evil laughter, rotten teeth. Something to do with that word 'lurch', as if he had reeled off and blundered into another dimension. Of course, he wasn't like that at all. The family photograph (yes, singular – this was a time when fathers took the photos rather than appearing in them) shows him in a rumpled-looking suit, hair in corn drills, shirt collar askew. He looks like an overgrown schoolboy, his worthy clothes over-tended, unloved. He was a solicitor's clerk. He worked in a chamber of brown linoleum, bentwood chairs, a hatless coatstand, a mahogany desk inlaid with green leather. There was a hatch to keep the public at bay. He worked in the Outer Office, trapped behind towers of thick-lipped manilla folders. Keeper of the cheque book. 'He couldn't even get cheating right,' your mother would lament.

It was the first out-of-character thing he had ever done. For years he had plodded off to work every morning, peck on the cheek for Mother, and the promise of promotion. You were a late child, unexpected, so before you came along there had been years like this of dutiful servitude twinned with the delicious prospect of reward. The honeymoon period, Mother called it. Of course, you don't remember him. Useless was your mother's verdict. And she made him so over the years. What use could he possibly have been? Mother was your world. Authority, breadwinner, confidante. If that screwed you up – as George would put it – then so be it.

The dressing up started at home. Mother did it, and you copied her. She had a wardrobe that housed a future that never came. A ball gown in turquoise taffeta whose skirts seemed tainted with water marks when you looked at it in a certain light. A couple of cocktail dresses, one in black silk, backless, another in plum velvet with a sequined bodice, heavy as a suit of tears. Some of her clothes you can only remember fragments of now – pink netting here, the fringes of a scarf there. The greatest treasures were hidden away. A fur stole, all watchful eyes and snakish tails, pungent with mothballs, wrapped carefully in tissue paper in a hatbox on top of the wardrobe. The wedding dress the light had turned to ivory still rustling superstitiously under a clear plastic shroud from the dry-cleaners. And below in the shadows of frothy hems, Mother's shoes. You remember pushing plump five-year-old feet into a pair of her white patent sling-backs. Cold in there. They bowed in the middle like a sagging bridge and the heels were scuffed and threw you forward into the mousehole of the shoe's spire. And the lovely clatter they made, the slap and clack. It was a trade-off with Mother. If you agreed to have your hair washed and not to scream when the shampoo got in your eyes, Mother would allow you to wear her shoes for a treat after bath-time. Forget satin corsets and sus-penders, you say. The memory of being naked in heels seems to you the ultimate in erotic. Then you moved on to her evening gloves. She had several pairs – ivory, pearl-grey and black. Your little fingers burrowed to the tips – it was like climbing inside her – the scalloped ends bunch-ing around your bare bony shoulder. You liked to rummage in the drawer where she stored her headscarves. Horses and anchors and nosegays of daffodils. You'd toss them in the air and in the sirocco flutter they made, her bouquet was released – Blue Grass. You fingered her floral polyester blouses – cross your heart, fabric-coated buttons, sleek to touch but toothily static. Skirts billowed round your head. No slacks here – Mother didn't hold with them though she acknowledged they were handy if you were a working woman. Which, somehow, implied that she was not. The final frontier was her underwear. The flesh-coloured brassières, the lace-hemmed bloomers, the shivering agony of slips. Even her roll-on, which fenced her in like armour, you made into a straitjacket, your arms and torso encased like an Egyptian mummy. You lay on the floor and played dead.

Mother was on a fixed income. She ran a nursing home and you lived in. You spent your childhood among old ladies, querulous or melancholy, sagging folds of skin merging with crumpled clothes. Their bony fingers with rings they wouldn't – or couldn't – part with twitched on counterpanes or feverishly counted off the decades on beads. There was the accompanying smell – though Mother was scrupulous about hygiene – which is not urine, as people like to think, but the sour odour of organs slowing down. Vapours of decay, in other words. Not the ideal environment to grow up in but it was home. You felt singular amongst all that fading female energy, a buoyant child, beloved.

'Baby,' they would call after you as you dodged past the asparagus ferns in mock-brass urns in the hallway. They always had their doors ajar. 'Baby!' Sometimes it sounded menacing, envious. You were baby to all of them. Some other baby, some lost baby. In her turn, Mother lavished endearments on her patients – sweetheart, pet lamb, even love – and they would invariably soften and wilt, and bend to her will. For a moment they would shed their pruney carapaces and smile beatifically at her. But for you she reserved a special term. Darling, come and help Mother out of her dress. Darling, run and get the bed-pan for Mrs Proctor. Darling, tell Mother that you love her.

Maybe that's why you were slow to make friends. How could the world outside ever replicate Mother love and all those senile surrogates? You didn't feel the lack, not when you were a child. And, afterwards, you had George. Mother and George never met. Well, you kept them apart, didn't you? Mother would not have taken to George's vulgar candour. Is George the kind of friend we'd like to cultivate, darling? No would have been the answer. No one would be good enough for Darling. You feel a stab of resentment when you think of it now, when you stand here faced with a wardrobe full of clothes that echo hers. It makes you wonder. Have you somehow turned into Mother? All dressed up and nowhere to go.

No, not true. Tonight you have somewhere to go. On the bed you lay out a jade velvet skirt, a black sateen jacket, a white blouse with an extravagant ruffle to hide your crêpey neck. They lie there playing dead, as if you were dressing a corpse. You wanted to do this for Mother, to choose a costume for her final journey. The thought excited you even in the midst of grief. The turquoise taffeta, the fur stole? You liked the thought that the fox with its hunter's eye and the long drip of its tails might be buried, and once below ground might reassemble itself and emerge into the night prowling, fully fledged. But no, Mother had left detailed instructions. She wanted a shroud, plain brown from the poor Clares. She was buried cowled like a Franciscan.

Then comes the make-up. You sit at the dressing-table mirror. Mother's too. It was one of the few pieces of furniture she treasured. A matching set with the wardrobe. You used to watch Mother doing this. If your father had stayed around you might have been as fascinated by his shaving rituals. As it was, Mother didn't have anyone to watch admiringly as she powdered her face sending clouds of motes reeling into the air, or applying lipstick – Coral Island – to lips puckered into a luscious pout. No one, that is, but you. You wish now that you had paid more attention. But it was the ceremony that compelled you then. The mask behind which Mother's face disappeared, the glossy lips, the brooding eyeshadow – Deadly Nightshade. You remember only your fascination for all those accoutrements – the tweezers, the eye pencils, the emery boards. The mystery of all the little brushes – what were they for? – the powder puffs, the pale squares of make-up in a box like your water paints set, the tiny bottles of gilded nail polish. Even then you were learning how to be a woman. Now as you try to reshape your over-plucked eyebrows you realise how little you absorbed. You stare at yourself in the mirror and see lipstick that's too bright, and a weak foundation.

Mother used to bring you with her when she went to the cosmetic counters at Hamiltons. You used to love that. Picking up the phials of perfume, lifting the heavy glass stoppers and inhaling the scents – tea rose, verbena, musk – while Mother tested lipstick on her hand, or had her cuticles done. What a pair you must have made. Mother in her starched whites from work – she wasn't a nurse but she said people had more faith when they saw a uniform – and you in your shorts and sandals, a crop-haired urchin. You were going through your tomboy period then. The assistants were charmed that you were so taken with the products.

'Lovely to see a sensitive boy,' one crooned. She had alarming black hair in a Cleopatra cut and an ochre complexion.

'The world will soon beat it out of him,' the other said tartly as she redid her fiercesome lashes. And they both laughed knowingly. You blushed defiantly. Mother was too discreet to point out their mistake. Afterwards, years afterwards, she said, 'But darling, that would have spoiled it for you. You wanted to be a boy then. I knew it was just a phase you were going through.'

You're all done now. Ready for the performance. Roar of the crowd, smell the greasepaint! Well, yes, actually, you can. Despite the numerous times you've made yourself up – how many times in a woman's lifetime, who could calculate? – you've never quite got used to its dusty, caked feel – though everything is liquid these days. But to you, even the lipstick tastes stale. And the look, despite your best efforts, is fake. If Mother were alive today – a preposterous thought; she'd be 108 – she'd say pityingly, 'Look at you, darling.'

Tonight is a special occasion. It's a work thing. A party to launch the new consultants' clinic. Fancy place, atrium preening with plants, a coffee dock, and lifts – a far cry from the old dingy surgeries and tatty waiting rooms. You work for a surgeon. Mr Sugars. He does feet. Portly, self-important. But he's got a right, you suppose. He wears three-piece suits like a lawyer and a handkerchief in his breast pocket – his only concession to flamboyance. He keeps his distance – from you, from his patients. He's like an old-fashioned headmaster. You think he would secretly like to be called sir. You'd be happy to do it, but in this day and age you're not sure if that's not a crime too. So he relies on his bearing and his obvious wealth to command respect. With his fees, that's not hard. He's married, of course, and years older than you, but he depends on you for all sorts of things. His Girl Friday he calls you, which shows his age – and yours, because you get the reference. George says you're like a surrogate 'other woman' for him. George has always revelled in being outrageous. Nothing could be further from your mind.

You met her at secretarial school. She started off as your pal – at least that's what Mother called her. The one with the strange name,

Mother would add as if you were besieged with friends. Short for Georgina.

'What a handle,' she would say; 'I don't know what possessed them!'

'Why didn't you shorten it to Georgie?' you asked.

'Too Enid Blyton. Too Mallory Towers,' she said. 'No, George makes more of a statement.'

George was always brighter than you. Her brisk, brunette manner was a cover for ambitions a well-read girl from her background couldn't afford. You and she started out working in the typing pool at the gas company together. Clackety-clack, ding! A synchronised orchestra like Esther Williams and her troupe on dry land. You went for lunch every day at the Parliament Hotel, and to dances on Saturday nights at the Arcadia, long since demolished. Your first holiday abroad – when you were thirty-two imagine! – was with George. You went to Rome on an organised tour. It was only after you arrived you realised that it was for pre-nuptial couples. You were surrounded by honeymooners, eloping or fleeing their families, or wanting to get a blessing direct from the Holy Father. You and George were the only singletons. That's the word they use now – a production-line term as if you were cartons of milk or an easy cheese serving. George flirted madly with anything in pants, but you were too embarrassed. A pair of the hotel's breakfast waiters, brothers, took a fancy to you. You remember a particular night on the Piazza Navona – the boys took you to see the Neptune fountain. Ridiculous to call them boys, but now you can't see them as men. George was walking ahead, draped around Nando – how lightly she distributed her favours, you thought; what a prude you were then – and you were leaning against the curved lip of the fountain desperately holding off his brother. You remember the hardness of Licio's body grinding up against yours, how insistent his ardour was, and how little it meant. This was what all the dressing up was for.

'Cara,' he breathed.

And suddenly you thought of Mother. No, not suddenly. You were always wondering what she would think. Perhaps if you had succumbed then. What? Perhaps you could have banished Mother altogether. But you couldn't. And then you dissolved. Not discreet ladylike weeping, but something more akin to the fountain beside you, as if some inner hydrant had been opened and was spraying everywhere, drenching the bystanders. Licio backed away, hands aloft in defence, then thumping his breast in Latin exasperation saying 'I do nothing.' Mother was only dead six months then.

'What on earth's the matter?' George asked after the brothers had sloped off fearing your hysteria was contagious. You shook your head. Ashamed as if you had acceded to some squalid backstreet encounter. And miserable that you had spoiled George's night.

Despite that, she stayed. Despite her beautiful kissable mouth (she has always known how to make the most of her best features), and her sauciness and her proud, uncompromising name, she never married either. You felt sure she would. So here the two of you are – twenty-five years on – still girls together, though others might snidely call you companions. She will be at the party too – for back-up. Nothing worse than wandering around these drinks and finger-food functions without an anchor, without someone to go back to. That's what George has become. The woman you go back to. Like Mother, really.

There, ready. Except for the jewellery. Mother's locket, with that picture of Father cut down to size. You thread her wedding band around the chain. It wouldn't be right to wear it on your finger. On your breast a costume brooch – also hers – like a spray of baby's breath.

Exploitation, George calls it.

'I wouldn't do it for my fella,' she says hotly. Hers is the president of a bank. George plays golf with hers; she dresses down for casual Friday.

But you don't see it that way. The surgeon's wife is sickly – now there's an irony, George – and can't often attend these things. Nothing Mr Sugars can do about it. (Her feet are perfect, apparently.) So you're roped in. You're happy to do it. You see it as part of your job. You collect his dry-cleaning, you make him tea, you arrange his appointments, you order flowers for his wife. Soon you'll be doing the rounds of nursing homes recommending the best one for her particular needs. Well, you do have expertise in that particular area. So what's the big deal about swanning around in your finery for an evening, playing the role of hostess? Although you'd never admit it to George, you actually enjoy it. You enjoy being mistaken for his wife. You like the way he steers you about the room with his hand lightly at your elbow and introduces you as merely Pauline, as if you two were so intimate that no further explanation was needed. That's why you have to look the part.

That's why the impersonation has to be perfect. You are not playing yourself.

Perfume – always the last thing before you leave. A quick spray at the ears and the wrists. It buoys you to the door like the splash of holy water the ladies at the home used to spray you with. A good luck charm, a way of warding off evil. Blue Grass. Mother is with you.

The Berkeley Complex

NEIL JORDAN

I am an actor, although what that means is never quite clear to me. Some days ago, for example, and I can't remember how many, I was in a line at the supermarket, Dunnes Stores, I think it was. And note how I affect a certain vagueness as to which supermarket. Of course I know it was Dunnes Stores, it's just that speech with me never quite works like that. I declaim, I become the mode of address I'm using, I speak in character, and that character can never be my own. I had entertained a lady friend the night before and hoped to surprise her with breakfast, I was in the line as I said, behind a group of women with my meagre purchases, a melon, I seem to remember, and six free-range eggs, when the girl behind the cash register, dressed in some kind of maroon, rayon smock, as they all are, it was Dunnes Stores after all, blushed at my approach.

She was serving a mother in a pink tracksuit, with an infant perched in the infant part of the supermarket trolley. I am generally quite unmoved by children, but this infant was, by any standard, divine. The mother was a different matter, she had that irritating certainty generic to young mothers, radiating not only a bloom of health but an exclamation mark. Look at me! I have a child! I am a mother! I am proud! Of this tracksuit! Of this bum too large! It is evidence of my fruitfulness! My nurturing! So the mother, needless to say, noticed nothing, but the infant, the divine one, that was a different matter. The infant noticed all the glitter on the cash register, the music of its opening and closing and the finger of the thin-faced, sallow creature in the maroon rayon whose job it was to operate it. Now you might expect, in fact you would expect, with a probability of certainty of 90 per cent, that young maroon-covered Cinderella operating the till would reciprocate the attention of the child.

The magnificent certainty of its mother. But no. She didn't even glance. Her eyes drifted from the shopping on the moving belt, past child and mother, to beyond the mother's pink shoulder. And she noticed me.

I was gratified, I will admit that. Recognition is, after all, the staple of the actor's diet, the cogito of his sum, not so much the reason for his being as the ground his being moves on, we live to be seen, exist to be seen and the awful possibility then presents itself – do we exist when we are unseen? But more of that later. Yes, I was gratified, but not surprised. I had trodden the boards. I had done the soaps some service. My *Othello* – text stripped to the bone, two lovers, one voyeur, and a handkerchief – was not without renown. Surprise, therefore, was not an issue. But I was surprised, if you will, by how gratified I was. That blush, you see.

That blush acted upon me like the first drops of water on a parched landscape that had never in its past lacked rain. And note the rather studied use of metaphor. I am an actor after all. The landscape had once been showered with bounties, had been verdant, fruitful, lacustrine. During my *Othello*, Jane and I had moved onstage and off in the blissful assumption of being admired, observed. Then the run ended and the big drought began and her Iago turned out to be a glass eye in a gabardine trench coat. Even the parts dried up.

So of course I was gratified. That fragile hint of recognition. I had entertained a lady friend the night before, as I said – and you believed me, of course you would, the slightly rakish tone, the hint of concupiscence, the mirror before me, the profession – actor! – but I hadn't, merely wished I had or wished you to think I had, wished you to think I had not been walking in this desert, but through a verdant garden continually renewed by rain. No, there have been days when that statement would have been effortlessly true, but those days were long gone. I had spent the evening at the local pub, drank a little too much, found my way home in a blur I don't remember, woke to the memory of a tangle of limbs around mine, but found myself alone, with a yen for scrambled eggs and a slice of melon. And here, in the supermarket line-up, the young girl behind the checkout desk blushed when she recognised me.

You see, I have of late been suffering from a complex. Now I could have said that differently, I've been suffering from a complex lately, lately I've been suffering from a complex, but I didn't, did I, and why I didn't is part of the problem. And that problem is the stage. The 'of late', again with its ever-so-slight archaism, its basic mechanism, which is one of delay, and delay, you will find, believe me, if you are ever stuck onstage before an audience of anything more than one, artful delay, is of the stage's essence. And if you've read your Dr Freud, which I will admit to doing, fitfully and intermittently, but enough to register unease about some of the more basic facts of living, and if you've ever acted, you might one day find yourself playing the part of Oedipus and thinking of Dr Freud. You may one day find yourself playing the part of Oedipus and wondering at the fact that the most pivotal trauma Dr Freud posited about our passage through this sorry spectacle we call life is based round a theatrical reality. A part. A character. A play. A story, so outlandish, so symmetrical, so complete, that it could never exist without the stage. And you may find yourself wondering about the stage and the world, wondering which is the mirror of which. And you may be wondering now, is that the essence of my complex, some delusional reversal of stage and life, of mirror and reality? And I'm way ahead of you, and will tell you no, my complex is by no means delusional. Nor is it Oedipal. But it is even more profoundly wedded to theatrical realities. I have a name for my complex, a private name. And I'll share it with you. The Berkeley Complex. And it has of late returned. And when the girl behind the checkout counter recognised me, she blushed.

They are both related, bear with me. When she blushed I was gratified, so gratified that I surprised myself. So gratified that I was relieved. Now think about this. The surprise I understood, but whence the relief? As if a hidden hand clutching my chest had just unclasped, a transparent plastic coating over my mouth had just imploded, I breathed for the first time, it seemed, as young girls say, in yonks, I breathed, felt relief, and only then knew I had not till that moment been breathing. And I recognised my Berkeley Complex. Berkeley – the bishop, that is, not the choreographer – the Trinity Divine who wrote the sentence that expressed, with bleak and inescapable clarity, the actor's condition.

Esse est percipere.

To be is to be perceived.

Think of it.

We actors exist to be seen.

And the corollary is, of course, terrifyingly simple.

When we aren't seen, we don't exist.

Even as a child I suspected some dissonance at the heart of things. I had a loving mother, too strong maybe, brought up in that old house out in Greystones, where the peeling veranda on the porch looked out over the Irish Sea. Something colonial about it, as if the rains that washed that yucca tree were somehow tropical, but they weren't of course, they were cold, constant, and damp. Mother too strong, definitely, father ineffectual, wrote pamphlets on a variety of social issues, issues of – what's the word – civic concern. Inveterate letter writer, to the *Irish Times, Independent, Bray,* and *Wicklow Peoples.* But the details are irrelevant, really, suffice it to say that when I woke at night, with the waves doing their business outside and the old house creaking, my greatest terror was that in that dark I was not, in that dark I did not exist, whatever had existed had diminished with the visible universe to what I could see at that moment, which was, precisely, nothing. I would blunder, chest constricted, through the doorways, out the hall, through the other doorway into that animal-odoured room with the large brass bed where after an eternity her bangled hand would turn and switch the side-light on and my relief would be her eyes, seeing me, knowing I was seen. A peculiar child you might say, yes, not for me the snuggle under that blanket of maternal warmth, the Oedipal burrowing of my thin body between his and hers, no it was the eyes that did it, those brown orbs under the long dark lashes, illuminated by the yellow light under the shadow of the trembling lampshade. The plump hand with its bangle reaching out to me, the sweet port-sodden breath, all those were irrelevant, it was the eyes I wanted, always to be within the angle of their gaze.

An awareness of the blessings of mirrors came at an early age. Yes, mirrors definitely helped. They were all over that draughty house and when she finally died, bequeathing it to me, I moved back into that mirrored heaven. Jane of course moved in with me, made an uneasy truce with my familial ghosts. For he had died first, odd how it goes like that, first Papa, then Mama, who never seemed to notice him when alive but was devastated by his absence. There was nobody, you see, to notice her. So she lost all the vital juices, lived in a cocooned memory of the days when they both noticed, even, dear God, loved each other. The old embers, Lord did she rake them over, bringing each memory out of the grey dust until it had given her whatever warmth it had accumulated. The memory, you see, of being looked at had now to serve for the fact. That day in Portrush, she would say, he looked at me, and I would listen, I would listen of course because she had to look at me. Then the sight went, cruelly, two days before she died, she was there but her eyes were no more, and a voice, eyeless, is hardly a voice at all. And the day she died, the most amazing of facts. How life, even at its bleakest, retains the capacity to surprise. One of those eyes, those eyes that so long sustained me, was made of glass.

I had the undertaker remove it. Both lids peacefully closed, in the open coffin. But one of the sockets empty. And to those of you who shudder with revulsion I would say, Do you think the body will arise on Resurrection Day complete with its pacemakers, balloons of silicon, plastic limbs, ceramic teeth, and glass eyes?

Mother. Did the drought begin then, Mother, the day I was thrown back upon the world, with nothing but a glass eye to sustain me? No, later . . .

A glass eye, though, on a bedside table will strain the happiest of unions.

Jane, damn her eyes – blue-green, with long brown lashes, an odalisque droop toward the corner – took severe exception. But then again, perhaps we had never had the happiest of unions. The arguments didn't so much begin then as increase in intensity and frequency, until eventually an endgame was reached: It's either me or it.

How typical of this impossibility we call life to present a choice between the disastrous and the unthinkable. But, let's face it, you do not lose your loved one for a glass eye. So I walked out one tempestuous day, having swept the glass orb from the bedside table into my coat pocket, and strode down the howling gale that the South Pier had become, with every intention of flinging it into the Irish Sea.

But I couldn't. Sitting on the wet metal of the Napoleonic cannon, I looked down into those uneasy waves. I imagined the eye sunk in the silt a hundred yards from the harbour, among the conger eels that slunk out from the gaps between the granite blocks. Alone, unobserved and unobserving, it seemed a fate quite literally worse than death, since death would have placed it secure within my mother's hollow eyelid, in the oaken coffin, the graveyard on Bray Head.

I returned home to Jane's unblinking gaze. Did you do it? she asked. I did, I lied. You know, I've been worried about you lately, she said, and her eyes seemed to soften. She blinked, finally, twice. You're dealing with a lot of issues, I suppose. Issues, I echoed. Yes, she said. Does it hurt to talk about them? Hurt, I echoed. Yes. This house, Gerald, I mean is it the healthiest thing to stay on here when . . . When what? I asked. When so much baggage comes – with it . . .

She was moving closer to me, blinking as she walked. Her eyes, which had seemed dull for months, had regained that blue-green sparkle. I remembered that sparkle, that luminescence, her eyes languorously turning towards me, close, supported by my crooked, exhausted arm. It heralded the onset, or the aftermath, of the thing itself. You haven't worked, you've hardly talked, and whatever happened to your *Othello*? My *Othello*, I echoed. Yes, she whispered, as she was up against me now, your *Othello*, you were going to revive it. My Othello is sleeping, I said, awaiting his moment. Well, she whispered, maybe it's time we woke him.

Her eyes turned towards me, later, supported by my crooked, exhausted arm. We should sell this house, she said, move to the inner city while you rehearse your Moor. My Moor, I said. And, she said, we should share a cigarette. And she reached down to my gabardine coat, extracted one packet of Players blue, one Zippo lighter, and one glass eye.

She left the next day.

The drought did not begin immediately. No, there was a period of respite, of relief even when the empty house seemed not blessed exactly but favoured with an unexpected calm wherein the waves outside the window beat for me and for me only, when the glass eye sat calmly and inanimately beside the bonsai plants, a gift to me from her which I watered, of course, too much unfortunately so they soon began to shrivel and the eye, the blessed eye, reflected their diminishing oriental leaves. There was a period wherein I thought, as one would, it's all for the best, the dripping underwear no longer hanging from the shower curtain. We could have moved as she wanted, not to this drafty mausoleum at the end of the Greystones line but to a place, a gaff in the inner city, a reacquaintance with old friends, old habits, the theatre even, our *Othello* even, my Moor, her Desdemona, but it was, in the tawdry argot of the afternoon soaps, not to be.

And one day, there it was, the drought. Strange how it operates, no way to isolate the moment of beginning, all you know is that something has commenced, something is now happening that once was not. The river shrinks, the grass whitens, the leaves curl, a burnished gold, a certain empty beauty at first, then the beauty fades leaving just that, emptiness, a dry well, river bed, fountain, shoreline, whatever the metaphor demands.

Until that blush on the young Cinderella's cheek while queuing with six eggs and a melon behind a mother and child at the checkout in

Dunnes Stores. I was quietly gratified to be reaffirmed in my existence, paid my two pounds twenty, walked through that subcolonial architecture back to my empty house, sliced the melon, left it by the dead bonsai, fried one egg, toasted one slice of bread, dunked a tea bag in a steaming cup, took it out again after a decent interval, poured a splash of milk, drank the tea, ate the breaded egg staring out at the bare, sere emptiness. The sea was so white it was hardly there. And I realised that if the drought hadn't quite yet ended, its ending had begun.

A triangle of sunlight came through the smudged kitchen window, illuminating the dried leaves of the bonsai. The earth inside the brown plastic vase was overflowing with cigarette ash. The glass eye reflected it and me and the segment of melon beside it. I lifted the eye so it reflected them no more, and wondered whether their presence was diminished by this lack of reflection. I saw myself in its convex glare, forehead and cheeks distended, the room behind me curved into its glass circularity. Mother, I whispered. And I placed her in my right-hand pocket, threw on my overcoat, walked out into the world.

Into the unobserving street, onto the empty train, and through the eyeless city. I was alone in my carriage and alone observed the stations interrupt that rolling mess of ocean. It didn't care whether it was seen or not, it pitched and ruffled without even the courtesy of regularity to its movement. Eucalyptus trees soughed past my window, pines, jutting elbows of manicured wilderness, houses, elegant and dowdy, a browning, shuttered swimming baths, a parkland, a sanctuary for birds. Then the roofscape of your average city, a hint of Victorian grandeur in Pearse Station, an escalator that looked like an old version of someone else's future, a fumble with the ticket at the turnstile, a right turn down Amiens Street underneath the Brunelesque bridge that the train I had just vacated trundled over. I walked, having no direction, and found my destination, not having looked. It was the Olympia Theatre. We had planned, in the days when we still made plans, to revive *Othello* there and I wondered on what stage, if any, she was rehearsing now.

Is there anything quite as sad as a theatrical façade abutting a busy street in the early morning sunlight? The metal canopy jutting onto the pavement, the tattered board above it advertising last winter's pantomime. Theatrical flamboyance unobserved. Or, observed alone by me. And I was pondering the mysteries of observance when I observed myself walking at a purposeful clip down Dames Street, turning right beneath the theatre awning and walking through the glass double doors.

That it was me, I was certain. The doors swung back now, just so, in and out with the force of my entry. And that I was standing on the opposite curb observing the doors swing closed again, I was certain too. But of how to reconcile both irreconcilable facts I was not certain at all. So I walked through the halting traffic, across the smoking street to the doors I had just entered, and entered them again.

It was all must inside and damp red velvet. There were large mirrors on the walls and a booth in the centre of the aisle of the alcove. There was a girl in the booth, rearranging ticket stubs. If she noticed that I was making my second entry, she gave no sign of it. I walked down the half-circle that the aisle became, in my nostrils the corrosive smell of damp from the red carpet. The circular aisle gave way then to a door, and the scallop-shaped fan of the theatre interior. I walked through the rows of seats with their velveteen covers, all around me the emptiness of my echoing footsteps. The stage was in darkness with the curtains pulled back. I heard a footstep then and recognised immediately that it was not my own. It was a woman's step, with a dragging heel that sounded familiar.

I thought you left, Jane said.

I did?

Two minutes ago.

Where did I go?

I don't know. Where did you go?

Tell me what I did before I left.

Are you talking in riddles?

No. Please. Tell me what I did.

You kissed me and you promised this time to sort it out.

Sort what out?

See – I knew. Nothing changes.

Her head bowed low, hair falling over her face, and her shoulders heaved. She was crying.

Don't cry.

I can't help it. Hold me.

I walked slowly to the stage and put my arms around her. I felt a rage of unease inside me.

Promise me you'll do it.

Do what?

Please. Please. Her shoulders heaved again.

I promise.

I heard footsteps behind me. For a moment I feared they were my own. Then I heard the sonorous tones of a director.

Now. Desdemona and Iago.

I let my arms course down her woollen cardigan and wondered when she'd bought it. I stepped backward. For some reason I didn't want them to see my face. So I slipped through the flies, blundered through the warren of half-remembered alcoves and out the stage door.

I bought a Cuban cigar which I set between my lips, unlit, sat in a café opposite, and drank endless cappuccinos. I had a feeling he'd come back. Knowing myself as I did, the depths of prevarication to which I could sink, unless he had effected a radical change in my nature, I was sure he would come back. But he didn't. He came out again.

Smoking this time, a habit I thought I had quenched last year. An irritating actorly strut to his walk. Was that really how I looked, I wondered, how I appeared to others, the gabardine sitting rakishly on the shoulders, the sleeves hanging free? Please let that not be me.

But me it was, actor, turning left down Crowe Street through the jumble of Temple Bar. The coat fluttered in the breeze from the Liffey, the empty sleeves were insufferably smug, if the pose was sickening, the poseur was nauseating.

He turned right at the riverside and walked along the busy window of Virgin Records on Bachelor's Walk. There was a kid of East European descent selling copies of *Big Issue* and I stood, ignoring his outstretched hand, staring in the window at a display of Leonard Cohen records. I saw the brown hair crawling over the collar of the rumpled gabardine coat, I saw the thick right hand run abstractedly through it, I saw myself move right, towards the entrance, past the left hand of the kid proffering the rolled-up copy of *Big Issue*, into the huge, pulsing interior. And I followed. I saw myself go from dark to light, into a world of desultory youths fingering through piles of CDs, up an escalator to the Classics section. I walked from the escalator through the lanes of music as he did, I saw him stop by the compilation display and I stopped too. I saw his finger flick over the alphabetical headings until it reached *C*, and I knew in advance what I or he was going to choose. Leonard Cohen, *Greatest Hits*, of course, how unimaginative if inevitable. Jane always had a terminal weakness for that lugubrious two-note baritone voice, he missed her, or if he didn't miss her, he wanted to abide for a moment in the common universe that was her. And I noticed then, how could I have missed it, how how how how? the torque, the half-circle that snaked inside his shirt collar, the two rubberised ear pads at either end, with the cable that coiled from them to his coat pocket, which could only have led to a CD Walkman. And I felt angry for a moment, I thought, how unmannerly, how unlike me or him, to come equipped with an accessory I would never have dreamed of possessing. And he picked up the CD with thick, stubby fingers and rapidly, with a sleight of hand I never knew I possessed, slipped the silver disc into the breast pocket of his gabardine coat.

I was stilled for a moment by fear for myself. I began to sweat suddenly, glanced around behind me to see if anybody had noticed, one of those Virgin Records employees in the maroon golf shirts, a store detective, maybe, then I turned back to see myself walking with an effortlessly casual lope towards the down escalator. And I began to will myself safely out of the store. Don't panic, I said, keep up that lazy, careless demeanour, lean that way, just so, off the moving handrail and that's it, a glance to left, to the right, walk off the last moving step to the open glass doors, to the street outside. I half expected to hear an alarm sounding as I made it through the doorway, into the bright sunlight and then remembered he had palmed the disk, not the cover. And I began to congratulate myself then, following behind at six feet or so, weaving through the crowds down Bachelor's Walk, through the cars that trundled over O'Connell Bridge. A theft, albeit a minor one, perfectly commissioned, the goods sitting snugly in my left-hand breast pocket. I had reached my right hand in to feel the disc in my gabardine coat before remembering it was he, not I, who had done the deed. And I saw him pausing slightly in his journey as his right hand pulled the disc out from his gabardine coat. He leaned against one of the metal uprights of Butt Bridge and inserted the disk into his Walkman. He placed the earphones on his head and turned round, hunching low, to adjust the volume. A train shuttled overhead and as he fiddled with the levels, his eyes glanced up and I swear they caught mine.

As if a mirror had been placed, my eyes met mine, glinting with reflected sunlight, thirty or so feet away, the passing crowds and traffic intervening. My heart stopped or some such cliché, no it didn't stop but the sweat that oozed from my pores once more wasn't caused by the weak, afternoon sunlight. It was those eyes, more knowing than mine, more themselves than mine, infinitely more at home with what they saw, which of course was my eyes, reversed. They met mine, the lines round the corners creased in the briefest of smiles, then the head turned and moved on.

He was making for the Tara Street DART station, of course, he had to be, the slow, crushed trek out to Greystones in the rush-hour crowds. And I followed, as by now I knew I must. There were two impulses to the following: the impulse to follow him, that is me, and the impulse to simply, like a carrier pigeon, return home. I bought my ticket, as he did, a one-way, no return, moved up the escalator into the cathedral of smoked glass above, and ran behind him into a waiting train.

The crush was as expected. What was unexpected was the presence of a gabardine like mine so close to me, the nape of a neck, like mine, two inches from my lips, and the barely perceptible, tinny sound from the Walkman I was listening to, communicating from another's ears. I should have known, of course. That mournful baritone voice.

> *Jane came by with a lock of your hair.*
> *She said that you gave it to her*
> *That night that you planned to go clear.*

The train lurched. I tried to steady myself with the rail but to no avail and was thrown against him. An odd frisson off my knee as it brushed off his, gabardine to gabardine. And then the panic began to build inside me. Does nobody notice? Two identicals, crushed together in the rush-hour crowds, swaying this way and that, borne out along the curve of south Dublin Bay, past Lansdowne Road, Booterstown, Blackrock, Dun Laoghaire, Glasthule, Dalkey, Shankhill, Bray, to Greystones.

The muddy, brown metallic tempered sea coursed by, Edwardian houses jutting against it like elegant teeth. The green concourse of a train station, Guinness adverts, a tangle of overhanging wires, and the sea again. We stared at it like old friends, with identical brown eyes me and him, him before me, me behind. Then the stripling eucalyptus trees by Killiney Bay spun hieroglyphs over the metallic glisten. I noticed two reflections in the dark part of the window and wondered whether he noticed too. Then I realised the window itself was double-glazed, there could well have been two reflections, and his expression in the worrisome glass seemed far more preoccupied than mine. I wondered about his thoughts and had I ever shared them, had I ever in some fold in time, some identical journey, gazed out on the metal sea in just that way. And if I had, could I now remember? No, of course not. And if he was indeed me, would he himself have remembered his thoughts at some future date, thoughts wondered about by a version of him, unbeknownst to himself, standing behind? The tangled knots of illogic piled one on the other, but the fact was that he existed because I saw him. And I continued to see him as he didn't see me

The train swayed to its errant conclusion then, in Greystones Station. The crowd piled out, as it does. We allowed ourselves to be borne along by it, rush hour, the commonweal, fair field full of folk, this anonymous mass of humanity making its way to its separate homes, and I of course expected him to turn right up by the La Touche Hotel, but he didn't, he walked straight, over the patch of grass above the harbour, then along by the harbour wall, the sea-view guest house to his right, the untidy mess of harbour concrete to his left. The light was fading, have I mentioned that? – it was the twilight hour, between the rigours of day and the pleasures of night, between the comfort of day and the terrors of night, whichever is your temperament. Anyway, the light was definitely fading, the movement of waves catching the glitter from the reborn street lamps. The looming shapes of rocks they used for wave-breaks had a presence in the gloaming that I could only call crepuscular. And he walked up the harbour, climbed the steps to the harbour wall, and walked slowly to the wall's end.

I stood below, watching. I had dived from that spot as a kid; the thrill was to hit the murky water and come up into the roiling waves, swim right beyond the harbour's sanctuary into the open sea, and only come to shore at Silver Strand. He shared these memories, he had to, standing there, right hand in his right pocket, staring at the darkening sea. And I remembered, the shock of memory was like heartburn, I was going to say a body blow but no, heartburn is closer. I remembered standing at just such a pier, in a paroxysm of indecision, and I suddenly knew what his stance implied. What indecision he was grappling with. What his right hand was doing in his gabardine pocket. It was curling, as mine did all those months ago, around the perfect orb of a glass eye. The hand wanted to throw it but the soul lacked the edge. The head knew it must be hurtled so but the heart didn't heed. I imagined a stinging in the eyes like tears, a moistness that came not from the spraying waves but from within and then, to my astonishment, against all of the laws of nature, I saw the hand, slowly but with deliberate aplomb, with an almost studied insolence, emerge and stretch backward, as if after a long sleep, stretch to its limit and then whip like a slow sling towards the sky above and the indeterminate sea below. I could only imagine, since the crepuscular light had dimmed so, the trajectory of that glass eyeball as the force of throwing took it heavenward at an angle of forty-eight or so degrees and eventually gravity took it seaward in a precipitous curve like those logarithm graphs I had so misunderstood at school. I imagined it all, since I saw nothing. But I heard. And what I heard was a distant, very distant and barely perceptible splash.

He was off then. An abrupt turn of the heel, a rapid stride down the harbour wall, an almost lissome trip down the steps to the harbour proper, and he vanished into what was now dark night. And I was left all dark and comfortless in the shadow below the harbour wall. I put my hand in my pocket and reached for the reassurance of that ball of glass. But I knew, even fumbling for it, what the result would be. And sure enough there was dust in my gabardine pocket, there was fluff in my gabardine pocket, but there was no glass eye.

Let me be factual here. Let me strip language of its metaphoric pretensions and confine myself, in the way of Thucydides, to action and its consequences. I walked beneath the harbour wall, a distance of, I seem to remember, ninety-eight steps. I reached the small landscaped park that led through the darkness towards the pale glow of the Silver Strand. I turned rightward there, made my way down Main Street, turned right again at the restaurant inappropriately named The Hungry Monk, and kept walking till I reached the Burnaby. I saw my parents' house, a single light glowing in the living-room window. As I approached it, I saw myself inside, my face glowing blue in the glare of an unseen television. I walked silently, if silence is ever possible, through the unhinged gate, made my way round the mess of garbage cans that was the garden to the kitchen door. I opened the door, and silence was achieved with my opening, at a pace that was murderous and slow. I walked inside then, chose the larger of two knives from the butcher's block that was my kitchen table, tested its blade against my thumb, and found it true, if bloody and painful. My feet made less sound on the linoleum floor than the dripping of my bloodied thumb. I was surprised by other feet again, his feet, making their way to the downstairs toilet. I heard a trickle, and then a flush.

Vanity undoes us all. Choose the most incorruptible of latter-day saints, place a camera in front of him, and watch him glance in the lens to catch his own reflection. And he was, after all, an actor. I came behind him, in the toilet, quietly, and so absorbed was he by his own image in the mirror that he only noticed me when I was well within range. And then, as Othello said, I took by throat the circumcised dog and smote him, thus.

The Homesick Industry

Hugo Hamilton

I've got a job in the city now, in a company that manufactures Irish products, both for the home market and for export. Traditional music, language lessons, dancing records, tin whistles, Aran sweaters – the lot. I'm the distribution manager, so I can see these products being sent all over the world. Even as far away as China, there are homesick people who think of Ireland every day. People tearing the paper off to take out the books and start speaking Irish again like babies. People in tropical places like Cairns, Australia, sitting under palm trees in the heat with the sound of strange birds all around them, putting on the dancing CDs and working out the steps – one, two, three, one, two, three. For a moment, you get the impression that the whole world is homesick. I can see them up there in Alaska, wearing thick Aran sweaters under their parkas and holding small tin whistles to their frozen lips. Frozen fingers pressing out the first warped notes and bringing back the faraway feeling of home.

Nothing has changed very much and I sometimes get the impression that I am like my father when he was alive. I might as well be him. I get on the train every morning and sit down with the newspaper. I see the same people around me in the carriage, the same variation of faces, the same silence, the same glances avoiding each other. I get to the office and go into dream, drifting away to remote places.

People would say that's the way the world carries on from one generation to the next, father and son, into infinity. They will think I have just stepped into my father's shoes. Here he comes, they will say, carrying a cool, new shoulder-bag instead of his usual briefcase. He's looking younger, they might say, but apart from the shoes and the hair, apart from the general youthful swagger and the fact that I don't wear

glasses like he did, nothing has moved on at all. I have the same forehead, the same hands, the same smile. I have the same history and I
have become my father in every respect, which is what I had always
hoped to avoid.

I have always refused to be like him. I wanted to be different, to
travel, to forget where I come from. But sometimes when you try
that hard, you just end up being the same without noticing it. You
finally surrender to the songs like everyone else. Maybe you sometimes
become what you fight against.

I suppose that's why they gave me the job as distribution manager,
because they could see that I understood the idea of not belonging.
They could see that I had inherited something from my father, in spite
of the fact that I had always resisted it.

My boss calls me upstairs to his office one day and demands to know
what has gone wrong. He's just like my father in many ways. He has
that look of nostalgia in his eyes. His chin quivers when he speaks. He
wears a pink shirt and the light on his desk keeps flickering and going
out, so he has to tap it with his pen to get it going again. He looks at me
under the arch of the light and shows his frustration. He says he hopes
I'm not just in the job for the money and I laugh.

'What's that supposed to mean?' he asks.

'What?'

'That laugh?'

'Nothing,' I reply.

'You just laughed. I said I hoped you didn't just take on the job for the
money and you just laughed. What's so funny?'

'I didn't mean to laugh,' I say.

He has something more substantial to talk about. He has ordered a
skip which has been delivered outside at the front of the building so
that a room at the back of the offices can be cleared. The room is to be
used to store a new consignment of knitwear from the West of Ireland.
Sweaters that women have been working on for weeks and weeks will
shortly be arriving here, destined mostly for the export market. For
tourists arriving in the summer, for airport shops and various outlets
around the capital. In the meantime, we need to make storage space. He
wants to streamline the knitwear operation, so that it's knitter to wearer
in the shortest possible time.

But there is a problem, because my boss thinks I'm going to
physically go in there with my staff and carry out all those dusty

files and printing junk to the skip. He says it's urgent. He describes it as a crisis. A policeman on a motorbike has already called into the reception to ask how long it's going to take. The skip is taking up an entire lane of traffic. But I've refused to do this kind of work. It's not my duty. I will not be ordered to fill a skip. Skips are not my responsibility.

So here I am in his office once again, staring across his desk. He's wearing the same pink shirt as always, or else he must have a hundred pink shirts which he bought in one place because he likes them so much. He fiddles with the desk lamp again because he can't see me. He's blinded himself as if in self-interrogation.

'Are you afraid of work?' he wants to know.

'I'm not a labourer,' I reply.

He frowns when he laughs. He laughs when you think he should be getting angry. I want to ask him what's so funny, but he's already leaning across the desk, looking at me in the eye.

'If you could only see yourself,' he says.

He smiles. He slaps his desk and looks out the window. Then he looks back and starts shaking his head.

'I wish I had a mirror so you could see yourself,' he says.

I am the portrait of refusal.

Suddenly, he looks at the evening paper on his desk. He asks me what star sign I belong to, but I refuse to enter into this new game.

'Your birthday is this month, isn't it?'

I don't answer. I know this comradeship trick.

'Capricorn, right?'

He reads out the generic little piece of fortune-telling from the paper. 'You will find that your social life will improve dramatically later on this week.'

'Is that all?' I ask.

He smiles and tries to appeal to me as a friend. He's in a bit of a spot, he explains. Could I not make the exception for once? He tells me that he will never ask me to do anything like this again, that it's only because of the extreme urgency of the situation, the traffic outside. It's not the way he would have liked it, but the gardaí have been in a second time, demanding that the skip should be removed.

'I'm not doing it,' I say.

'Please,' he begs. 'Just this once.'

'You can find somebody else to do this kind of work.'

He stares at me across the table for a while longer. I can see his disappointment. He tries something else. He talks about moral responsibility, duty, dedication, laziness.

'Anarchy?' he suddenly shouts. 'Is that what you want?'

It descends into a political argument. He talks about a more equitable, a more socialist society, a fairer, Irish-speaking country. He doesn't let up. He wants a country like the Blasket Islands with nobody owning anything any more than anyone else.

'Nobody owning anything at all,' I say.

He leans forward to make his point. There was a shipwreck on the Great Blasket once, he tells me, and some boys on the island found a casket full of brand new watches. They wanted to keep them for themselves and hid them in a cave. But they were not accustomed to owning anything or having any personal possessions, so by the end of the day, they had given them all away and everyone on the island was wearing a watch, even though they had no real use for them and nobody had any sense of time on the island.

He tries to fix the flickering desk lamp for good this time. He says it's not really socialism he's after at all but democracy. He says democracy is everybody doing their share regardless of what rank or position they hold. It's people paying their fare on buses.

'That's what democracy is,' he says. 'People respecting their country and working for each other.'

Suddenly he loses it. He burns his hand against the shade of the desk lamp. He gets up from his chair in a fury and flicks his wrist around the room. But it's only when he looks out through the window at the empty skip outside and all the cars snaking around it that he remembers why I had come to his office in the first place. Not a single thing thrown into the skip yet, while we're arguing about the solution for Ireland.

'I'll show you,' he says. 'Follow me.'

I follow him down the stairs, all the way down from the third floor, passing by people without saying a word all the way down to the offices at the back of the building. He takes off his tie and puts it into his pocket. He rolls up his pink sleeves and lifts up the rubbish in his hands, old files, printing materials, ink canisters. Out into the street he goes, carrying bits of junk and throwing them into the skip. I stand there and watch him, refusing to touch anything. He doesn't say a word. His hands are black. His pink shirt has gone grey and there are black streaks on his face from some old printing ink. He's sweating and breathing heavily.

I join in and start carrying things out with him. We work in silence, me carrying out the same amount as him, no more and no less, until the skip is full and we both go our separate ways, him back to his office upstairs and me back into the dispatch office in the basement. He doesn't give me those triumphant looks. He doesn't rub it in. If anything, he understands that I am hurt by this, and defeated.

A few minutes later the phone rings. I pick it up and wait. But there's nothing. It's the two of us listening to each other in silence. Then he finally speaks.

'I'll make it up to you,' he says.

But I've put it all behind me. By the following day it's forgotten. The Aran sweaters begin to arrive in big boxes. Larger consignments are on the way. We are overwhelmed by orders coming in and can hardly even keep up with the demand. Knitwear going out to addresses everywhere around the globe, Canada and the USA, France and Denmark, even Italy.

And one day not long after that, it's my birthday. My boss wants to show that he hasn't forgotten. He's a man who keeps his word and comes down in the afternoon with a gift. He and his secretary and two or three others from the department crowd around me in my office with a big parcel wrapped in blue paper. They clap and wish me a happy birthday in Irish.

'*Lá breithe shona dhuit,*' they say, all smiling, as they hand me the gift. They wait for me to open it, but I'm so surprised by all this kindness that I can only stare at the blue paper.

'Thanks,' I say.

'Aren't you going to open it?' my boss says.

I begin to take off the paper. I can smell what's inside before I can even see it. The familiar smell of rough wool is unmistakable. It's one of the hand-knit, Inishfree Aran Sweaters that I've been sending out to so many people abroad. And now, one of them seems to have come back to me as a birthday gift. A big brown, rope-patterned Aran sweater with a ringed collar.

'You shouldn't have,' I stammer.

For a moment, I ask myself if this is some kind of big joke they're playing on me, but they are all very serious.

'Are you going to put it on?' my boss says.

So I thank them again and again, and put it on out of politeness. I can smell the oily sheep's wool all over me and I suddenly feel suffocated. I used to wear one of these big sweaters as a boy. My father bought them for us. My father wore one himself. It's making me ill and I'm already thinking of what to do with it, how to get out of the building without them noticing that I've left it behind. When they finally leave, I wait for a moment before taking it off and replacing it in the plastic wrapper. I put it back with all the other jumpers waiting to go out in all directions, all over the world. Some days later it goes out by post to Spain, to an address in Madrid.

The Forester's Daughter

CLAIRE KEEGAN

Deegan, the forester, isn't the type of man to remember his children's birthdays, least likely that of his youngest, who bears a strong, witch-like resemblance to her mother. If occasional doubts about his daughter cross his mind he does not dwell on them for, in fairness, Deegan has little time to dwell on things. In Aghowle there are three hungry teenagers, the milking and, of course, the mortgage.

Some of the hardship Deegan bears was brought upon himself. When his father passed away and left the place to his sons, Deegan, who was not yet thirty at the time, borrowed money against the place and bought them out. His brothers, who had other dreams in any case, were glad of the money and went off to make lives for themselves in the city. The night after the bank took over the deed he walked the fine, south-facing meadows. It broke his heart to do it but he could see no other way. With the rest of the money Deegan bought more Friesians, put electric fences round the land and installed the milking parlour. Shortly afterwards, he drove to Courtown Harbour to find a wife.

He found Martha Dunne on a Sunday afternoon in the Tara Ballroom. Deegan, sitting there in a brown pinstripe suit with his beard trimmed, watched this broad-hipped woman making bold figures of eight within a stranger's arms. Her skin was pale as a plate and her scent, when they waltzed, reminded him of the gorse when it is on fire. While the band was playing the last tune, Deegan asked if she would meet him again.

'Ah, no,' she said. 'I don't think so.'

'No?' Deegan said. 'Why not?'

'Ah, I won't.'

'I see,' Deegan said.

But Deegan didn't see and, for this simple reason, he persisted. The following Sunday he went back to Courtown and found Martha in the hotel, eating alone. Without asking he sat down and kept her company. While she ate he steered the conversation from the fine weather through the headlines and wound up talking about Aghowle. As he described his home he began to imagine her there buttering swede, patching his trousers, hanging his shirts to dry out on a line.

Months passed and, through nothing stronger than habit, they kept meeting. Deegan always took her out to dinner and to dances, making sure to pay for anything that passed her lips. Seven months after their first dance they walked down to the sea. On the strand gulls' footprints went on for a while then disappeared. Deegan hated the feel of the sand under his feet but Martha's stride was loose, her brown gaze even. She strolled along, stooping every now and then to pick up shells. Martha was the type of woman who is happy in her body but slow to speak. Deegan mistook her silence for modesty and before a year of courtship ended, he proposed.

'Would you think of marrying me?'

While the question was in mid-air, Martha hesitated. Deegan was standing with his back to the amusement arcade. With all the lights behind him she could hardly make him out. All she could see were slot machines and shelves of coppers that every now and then pushed a little excess into a shoot to let somebody win. At a van a child was reaching up for candyfloss. The crowd was getting smaller; summer was coming to an end.

Martha's instinct told her to refuse but she was thirty years of age and if she said no this question might never be asked of her again. She wasn't sure of Deegan but none of the others had ever mentioned marriage so, with her own logic, Martha concluded that Victor Deegan must love her, and accepted. In all the years that followed, Deegan never thought but he did love her, never thought but he showed his love.

The following spring, while birds appeared searching for the perfect bough and the crocus laboured through the grass, they married. Martha moved into the house Deegan had described at length but found Aghowle to be a warren of dim, unlived-in rooms and unsteady furniture. Nylon curtains, mildewed at the edges, clung to the panes. The wooden floors were bare of rugs, the ceilings mouldy but Martha, being no housekeeper, didn't care. She rose late, drank her tea on the doorstep and threw meals together same as she was packing a suitcase. Often

Deegan came home from work expecting her to be there with a hot dinner but more often than not his house was empty. He'd stoop and find the small enamel plate with fried potatoes and a pair of eggs dried out in the little oven.

Martha preferred to be out in wellingtons lifting a drill for onions or slashing the nettles along the lane. The forester brought her seedlings he found in the wood, sycamores and horse chestnuts which she staked about the land in places where the hedges had been broken. For company she bought two dozen Rhode Island Reds and a cock. She sometimes found herself standing in the barn watching her fowl pecking at the seed, feeling happy until she realised she wasn't.

Before a year had passed the futility of married life struck her sore: the futility of making a bed, of drawing and pulling curtains. She felt lonelier now than she'd ever felt when she was single. What had she hoped for? In truth she had hoped for intimacy, for the type of conversation that would surpass misunderstanding.

And little or nothing was there around Aghowle to amuse her. Every week she cycled to the village but Parkbridge was just a post office and a public house-cum-shop whose keeper was inquisitive:

'Is Victor well? There's a great man, a great worker. You'll not find the grass growing under his feet.'

'You must like living up there now, do you? A fine house it is.'

'Where did he find you anyhow? Courtown? Didn't he go far enough for you?'

One Thursday, as she was about to cycle out for groceries, a travelling salesman appeared with a trailer. A tall man with a long moustache, he parked in the centre of her yard and strode up to the door: 'Can I interest you in roses?'

There, in the trailer, the stranger had all types of plants: rosebushes, budding maples, Victoria plum trees, raspberry canes. It was the end of April. She said it was getting late for planting but the salesman said he knew that, and would not go hard on her. She asked how much he wanted for the roses, and the price he named wasn't high. Over tea they talked of vegetables and how, when you lifted the potato stalk it was like magic for you never knew exactly what was underneath. When he left, she collected hen dung with the shovel and planted the rosebushes deep in rows at either side of the hall door where she could train them to climb up around the windows.

When Deegan came home she told him what had happened.

'You spent my money on roses?'

'Your money?'

'What kind of fool did I marry, at all?'

She stopped and considered the question. 'I don't know,' she said. 'I was fool enough to marry you.'

'Is that so?' Deegan grabbed the end of his beard as though he might tear it off. 'What you don't know is that the hard times aren't over. It's all very well for you sitting here day in, day out. You didn't bring so much as a penny into this place. And, by the way, a working man needs more than dried-out spuds for his dinner.'

'You don't look any the worst for it.'

And it was true: Deegan had put on weight, had the bloom on him that men have after they marry.

'If that's the case, it's not your doing,' Deegan said, and went out to milk the cows.

That summer her roses bloomed scarlet but before the wind could blow their heads asunder, Martha realised she had made a mistake. All she had was a husband who hardly spoke now that he'd married her, an empty house and no income of her own. She thought about finding a job but it was too late: a child was near ready for the cradle.

The children Martha bore she reared casually, never threatening them with anything sharper than a wooden spoon. When her firstborn was placed in her arms her laughter was like a pheasant rising out of the bushes. The boy, a shrill young fellow, grew tall but it soon became apparent that he had no *grá* for farming; when the boy sat in under a cow, the milk went back up to her horns. He looked up to his uncles, whom he visited every now and then in Dublin, and it was hardship to make him do a hand's turn. He would get out just as soon as he saw the opportunity.

The second boy was a simpleton. A beautiful, pale youth with a pair of green eyes staring from a shell of dark-brown hair, he did not go to school. He lived in a world of his own and had a frightening aptitude for speaking the truth.

It was the girl who had the brains, the girl who travelled through youth same as youth was a warm stretch of water she could easily cross. She finished her homework before the school bus reached the lane, refused to eat meat and had a way with animals. While others were afraid to enter the bull's field, she could walk up and take the ring out of his nose. And she had taken a liking to her brother, the simple one.

Always she was urging him on to do the things nobody else believed him capable of. She'd taught him how to knot and cast the hook, to count backwards and hold a sneeze.

Seldom did neighbours come into that house but whenever they did, Martha told stories. In fact, she was at her best with stories. On those rare nights they saw her pluck things out of the air and break them open before their eyes. They would leave remembering not the fine old house which had always impressed them or the man with the worried look that owned it or the strange flock of teenagers but the woman with the dark-brown hair which got looser as the night went on and her pale hands plucking stories like green, unlikely plums that ripened with the telling at her hearth. After these stories they were sometimes too frightened to go back out into the night and Deegan had to walk them as far as the road. Afterwards, he always took his woman to bed to make not only her but himself sure that she was nobody's but his. Sometimes he believed that was why she told a story well.

But in that household as in any other, Mondays came. Whether the dawn was blood-red or a damp, ash-grey, Deegan got up and placed his toes upon the bare linoleum and dressed himself. Often his limbs felt stiff but without complaint he milked, ate his breakfast and went to work. He worked all day and some days were long. If, in the evenings his eyes of their own accord were closing while he'd yet again the cows to tend, it was solace to drive over the hill to see lighted windows and the tusk of smoke rising from his chimney, to know his work was not for nothing. Before he retired, the bank would give back the deed and Aghowle would once again belong to him.

The fact that it stood in a hollow, that the walls within it were no thicker than cardboard, didn't matter. Now that his parents were dead and his brothers had gone, Deegan was becoming sentimental. He remembered not how his mother had spent so much of his youth in bed with the curtains drawn or the nights when his father took down the strap saying he couldn't have it all his own way, but simpler things, plain facts. The line of oaks on Aghowle's lane were planted by his great-grandfather. No matter how hard or high his children swung, those limbs would never break. Secretly, he knew that the house had given him more satisfaction than his wife and children ever would.

Deegan is now middle-aged. If it is a stage when some believe that much of life is over, and assume that what's left is a downhill slope to be lived within the restraints of choices made, for Deegan, it's

otherwise. For him, retirement will be the reward for all the risks he's
ever taken. By the time his pension comes, his children will be reared.
He envisions himself in Aghowle with one Shorthorn for the house.
He will get up when it suits him, sort through stones and repair the
orchard wall. He will take out the spade and plant more oaks on
the land. He can already feel the dry stone, the oaks' blue shade, hear
the milk plashing like old days against the zinc. The eldest boy will
marry, have children, and carry on the name. But in the meantime,
before he can take his early retirement and retreat into this easy life he
craves, there are children to finish rearing, bills to pay and years of
work yet to be done.

One wet day while he is working beyond Coolattin pruning a line of
Douglas fir, Deegan stumbles across a gun dog. The retriever sheltered
for the night under the trees and the forester has, in fact, roused him from
a dream of ponies chasing him through a bog. Puzzled at first by the
presence of a stranger, the retriever looks around and then remembers
yesterday. O'Donnell had tried to shoot him but then O'Donnell's rage
was always sharper than his aim. It was, quite simply, a case of the bad
hunter blaming his dog. Now this bearded stranger whose scent is all
resin and cows' milk is standing over him, offering buttered bread. Being
hungry, the dog eats and lets the stranger stroke him.

Deegan does this knowing he will some day – if no owner comes
looking – get a nice turn, for the dog is handsome. Waves of white gold
travel across the retriever's back. His snout is cold, his eyes brown and
ready as the field after the plough. Come evening, Deegan doesn't have
to coax him into the car. The dog jumps in and puts his white paws up
on the dash. With the sunlight striking his coat and the wind in his ears,
they travel down hills towards the open road. By the time they're in
Shillelagh, the retriever has his head out through the open window
greeting people, barking hello.

When they reach Aghowle Deegan is glad, as usual, to see his house
with its chimney sending smoke up to the heavens – not that he believes
in heaven. Deegan is not a religious man. He knows that beyond this
world there is nothing. God is an invention created by one man to keep
another at a safe distance from his wife and land. But always he goes to
mass. He knows the power of a neighbour's opinion and will not have
it said that he's ever missed a Sunday. It is autumn. Brown oak leaves
are twisting in dry spasms around the yard. Exhausted, Deegan gives

the dog to the first child he sees. It happens to be his youngest and it happens to be the girl's birthday.

And so the girl, whose father has never given her so much as a tender word, embraces the retriever and with it the possibility that Deegan loves her, after all. A wily girl who is half innocence and half intuition, she stands there in a yellow dress and thanks Deegan for her birthday present. For some reason it almost breaks the forester's heart to hear her say the words. She is human, after all.

'There now,' he says. 'Aren't you getting hardy?'

'I'm twelve,' she says. 'I can reach the top of the dresser without the stool.'

'Is that so?'

'Mammy says I'll be taller than you.'

'No doubt you will.'

Martha, who is throwing barley to the hens, overhears this conversation, and knows better. Victor Deegan would never put his hand in his pocket for the child's birthday. He's picked the retriever up some place – as winnings in one of his card games or maybe it's a stray he's found along the road. But because her favourite child seems happy, she says nothing.

Martha is still young enough to remember happiness. The day of the child's conception comes back to her. It started out as a day of little promise with clouds suspended on a stiff, February sky. She remembers that morning's sun in the milking parlour, the wind throwing showers into the barn, how strange and soft the salesman's hands were, compared to Deegan's. He had taken his time. They had talked at length. He'd said her eyes were the colour of wet sand.

She has often wondered since where the boy was but her thoughts, that day, were fixed on the prospect of Deegan coming home. When he did come in he sat in to his dinner and ate as always, asking was there more. Martha waited for the blood but on the fifth day after it was due she gave up and asked the neighbours in and told a story, knowing how the night would end. That part wasn't easy.

But that's all in the past. Now her daughter is sitting on the autumn ground, looking into a golden retriever's mouth.

'There's a black patch on his tongue, Mammy.'

That she is a strange child can't be doubted. Martha's youngest holds funerals for dead butterflies, eats the roses and collects tadpoles from the cattle tracks, sets them free to grow legs in the pond.

'Is it a boy or a girl?'

Martha turns the retriever over. 'It's a boy.'

'I think I'll call him Judge.'

'Don't get too fond of him.'

'What?'

'Well, what if somebody wants him back?'

'What are you talking about, Mammy?'

'I don't know,' Martha says. She throws what's left of the barley on the ground and goes inside to strain the potatoes.

While the Deegans eat, Judge, whose real name is Bob, explores the yard. No doubt the place is fine. There's a milking parlour in whose steel he admires his reflection, an empty hen-house with one late egg, and a barn full of hay. He walks down the lane, urinates high on the trunks of the oak trees, shits, and kicks up the fallen leaves. His urge to roll in the cow dung is almost irresistible but this is the type of house where they might let a dog sleep inside. He stands a long time watching the smoke, considering his circumstances. O'Donnell will be out looking for him. He will be cross as a weasel. Judge picks up a sod of turf and, tail wagging, carries it into the house. The Deegans, who are eating in silence, watch him. He drops the sod in the basket at the hearth and, before they can say a word, goes out for more. He does not stop until the basket is full. The Deegans laugh.

'You'd have to see it to believe it,' says Deegan.

'Where did you find him anyhow?' says Martha.

The girl gives him a slice of her birthday cake and mashes butter into the leftover potatoes, feeds him on the doorstep.

While they are down in the parlour, milking, Martha comes out. The evening is fine. In the sky a few early stars are shining of their own accord. She watches this dog licking the bowl clean. This dog will break her daughter's heart, she feels sure of it. Her desire to chase him off is stronger than any emotion she has felt of late. Tomorrow, while the girl is in school, she'll get rid of him. She will take him up the wood, throw stones, and tell him to get home. The retriever licks his lips and stares at Martha. He puts his paw up on her knee. The pads of his feet are soft. This dog is young. Martha looks into his eyes and, being soft-hearted, fills his bowl with milk. While the retriever drinks she sighs and, with an old eiderdown, makes a bed under the table where nobody can walk on his tail.

That night Judge lies there, in his new bed, thinking. Two narrow escapes in one week. He will have to be more careful. O'Donnell will be out looking for him. This thought makes him cold. He rolls onto his back, stares at the drawers under the table. This is a different sort of house but Deegan is clever all the same, will sell him just as soon as he finds the opportunity. The woman he understands: she is just the protective bitch minding her pup. The eldest fellow says little and keeps to himself. The middle boy's scent is unlike any human he has ever encountered. It is something close to ragweed, closer to plant than animal like the roots you'd bury something under. The girl is complicated. Judge, being wary in this strange place, fights sleep for as long as he is able but the kitchen's darkness and the fire's heat are unlike any comforts he has ever known and his will to stay awake soon fades. In sleep he dreams again of finding milk on the second teat. His mother was champion retriever at the Tinahely Show. She used to lick him clean, carry him in her teeth through streams, proud that he was hers.

The next morning the simpleton, who sleeps odd hours, is the first to rise. Judge wakes, stretches himself in his new bed, and follows the boy out to the shed. They carry withered sticks in and the boy, knowing Judge expects it, does his best to light the fire. He arranges the sticks on yesterday's ashes and blows on them. He blows until the ash turns their faces grey. When the girl comes down she does not laugh at her brother; she simply kneels and, in a teacher's voice, shows him how it's done. She twists what's left of Sunday's newspaper, cocks the withered timber, and strikes a match. The boy watches and is intrigued. The strange blue flame grows bigger, changes and, at a certain point, turns into fire. Something about it makes him happy, makes him wonder. He has a capacity for wonder, sees great significance in things his family dismiss just because they happen every day.

When Martha comes down, sleepy and bad-humoured, the door is wide open and there is no sign of the dog. She had hoped, the night before, that he would run away. A cold draught is coming in. She shuts the door and walks into the scullery to fill the kettle. There, on her sink, is the retriever and with Deegan's good china cups her two youngest stand rinsing the suds off his back. This dog is too big for the sink and he is losing his coat. Clumps of hair cling to the wallpaper. Some part of her doesn't really care but the girl sees her and Martha, being a mother, feels compelled to scold:

'Did I say you could wash that dog in here?'

'You said nothing about Judge.'

'Judge. Is that his name?'

'I called him that yesterday.'

'You'll not bathe him in that sink again. Do you hear?'

'He's my birthday present. At least Daddy bought me a dog. You bought me nothing.'

'I suppose I didn't.'

'You're jealous,' says the boy.

'What did you say?'

'Who cares?' he says. It's a phrase he's heard a neighbour use which he thinks is worth repeating.

'I care,' says the girl, reaching again for water.

Martha takes her tea out to the yard. Outside things always seem a fraction easier. No matter what the sky, the morning sun comes out. She looks down the lane. The oaks are losing the last of their leaves. She drinks her tea, takes the stake off the hen-house door and opens it wide. Her fowl rush past in a sweep of red feathers and dust, racing for the feed and the open air. She names them as they pass. Martha understands her hens. They are, to her, creatures of another time, not truly domesticated. She stoops and reaches into their nests, stealing their eggs.

When she comes back in to make the breakfast, she strides, feeling treacherous. She often feels treacherous in the mornings. She wishes her husband and her children were gone. Always a part of her craves the solitude that will let her mind calm down and her memory surface.

On a hot pan she watches the eggs grow white and harden. Never has she been able to eat them. This morning she longs again for sheep's liver or a kidney. She's always had a taste for such things but Deegan will have none of it. What would the neighbours think? The Deegans never ate but the best and he'll not see his wife standing at the butcher's stall, ordering liver. She stands there in her apron on a Tuesday wishing she'd married another man, a Dubliner, perhaps, who would stroll down to a butcher's shop on Moore Street and buy whatever she craved, a man who couldn't care less what neighbours think.

With the pan spitting, she walks outside and, at her loudest, shouts. The desperation in her voice travels all the way down into Aghowle's valley and the valley sends back her words.

'My God,' says Deegan when he comes in from the milking, 'we'll be lucky if we don't have the whole parish here for the breakfast.'

The Deegans eat and, with full stomachs, go their separate ways. The eldest cycles off to the Vocational School. He has just the one year left and will then become apprentice to his uncle, the plasterer who lives at Harold's Cross. The simpleton heads off to the parlour, gets down on his knees and sets to work on his farm. So far he's built a boundary with dead fir cones and marked out the fields. Today he will build his dwelling house. Before the week comes to an end, he'll have it thatched. Judge escorts the girl down the lane to the school bus. When he gets back, Martha places the frying pan on the kitchen floor and watches while he licks it clean. Without so much as a wipe she hangs it back up on its hook. Let them all get sick, she thinks. She doesn't care. Something has to happen, soon.

She takes Judge up the wood. The sun is striking against the hazel's trunk. It is almost ten. Martha can, by now, tell what time it is without ever glancing at the clock. A blue sky is shedding rain. Some things she will never understand. Why is the winter sun whiter than July's? Why hadn't the salesman ever written? She had waited for so long. She shakes her head. Some absurd part of her still hasn't given up. She shelters for a while under the chestnut and asks Judge if he has ever been in love. She says it as though she expects an answer.

Judge is glad he cannot speak. He has never understood the human compulsion for conversation: people, when they speak, say terrible things that seldom if ever improve their lives. Words make them sad. Why can't they stop talking and put their arms around each other? Mrs Deegan is crying now. He comes over to the woman and licks her hands. There are traces of grease and butter on her fingers, perfumed soap. Underneath it all her smell is not unlike her husband's. As he licks her hands clean, Martha's desire to chase him off evaporates. That desire belonged to yesterday, becomes yet another thing she might never be able to do.

Back home, she bathes. She lathers her underarms and shaves them, cuts her toenails, brushes her hair and fixes a wet knot at the back of her skull. Then she finds herself on her bicycle pushing herself all the way to Carnew in the rain. In Darcy's she buys a royal-blue blouse off a rail whose buttons are fake pearls. Why she buys it she doesn't know. It will be wasted in Aghowle. She will wear it to mass on Sunday and another farmer's wife will tell her at the meat counter where she bought it.

When she gets back she changes back into her old clothes and goes out to check her hens. Jimmy Davis told her the fox is about and lately she feels afraid. 'Coohoooo! Cocohoooo!' she cries, rattling the handle on the bucket. At the sound of her call they come, suspicious as always, through the fence. She counts them, goes through their names, and feels relieved. Then she is down on her knees plucking weeds out of the flower beds. All the flowers have by this time faded yet there is no frost in the mornings. The broom's shadow is bending onto the second flower bed. It is almost three. Soon Deegan and the children will be back declaring their hunger, asking what there is to eat.

As she is bringing the fire back to life, Judge comes in and paws her leg. She looks down. His tail is wagging. Several times he paws her before Martha realises there's something in his mouth. She offers him her open hand. He drops something onto her palm. Her hand knows what it is but until she looks at it twice she can't believe it's an egg. And there's not so much as a crack in the shell. She laughs.

'Aren't you some dog?'

Martha gives him milk from the saucepan and says the girl will soon be home. Judge takes the hint and runs down the lane to meet her. She climbs down from the school bus and tells him she solved a word problem in mathematics, that long ago Christina Columbus discovered the earth was round. She says she'll let the Taoiseach marry her and then she changes her mind. She will not marry at all but become the captain of a ship. She sees herself standing on deck with a storm blowing the red lemonade out of her cup.

Back home, the simpleton is getting on well. In the parlour he has planted late, brown-paper oaks to shelter his dwelling house. The boy likes being alone and doesn't mind the fact that people sometimes forget he's there.

The eldest boy returns from the Vocational School stinking of cigarettes. Martha tells him to brush his teeth, and puts the dinner on the table. Then she goes upstairs. She has things to think about. What she is thinking isn't new. She takes her wedding coat out of the wardrobe, opens the seam and looks at her money. She doesn't have to count it. She knows how much is there. Five hundred and seven pounds so far, she has saved, mostly housekeeping money she did not put on the table. No longer is it a question of if or why. She must now decide when, exactly, she will leave.

Deegan comes home later than usual. 'You couldn't watch that new man. He'd be gone by three if you didn't watch him.' He eats all that's placed before him, rises, and heads out for the milking. The cows are already at the field gate, roaring because their bags are full.

That night he goes to bed early. His legs are sore from walking the steep lines and his feet are cold but before he can turn over he is sleeping. In sleep he dreams he is standing under the oaks. In the dream it isn't autumn but a fine, summer's day. A gust of wind blows up out of the valley. It is so hard and sudden – whatever way this gust is, it frightens Deegan and the oaks flinch. Leaves begin to fall. It all seems wrong but when Deegan looks down there, all around his feet, are twenty-pound notes. Towards the end of the dream he is like a child trying, without much success, to catch them all. Finally he has to get a wheelbarrow. He fills it to the brim and pushes it all the way to Carnew. As he wheels it along the roads, neighbours come out and stare. The envy in their eyes is unmistakable. A few notes flutter from the barrow but it doesn't matter: he has more than enough.

When he wakes he looks out at the oaks. They are standing there, as always. Deegan scratches his beard and goes over his dream. Dreaming has become the closest thing to having someone to talk to. He looks at Martha. His wife is fast asleep, the pale breast pressed against the thin cotton of her night-dress. He would like to wake her and tell her of his dream. He would like to carry her away from this place sometimes and start again but these are childish thoughts. He closes his eyes and hopes he will dream about the barrow once again before he dies.

During that mild winter, Christmas comes. The frost is brittle, the birds confused. By this time Judge's coat is immaculate, his shadow never too far from the girl's. Deegan's humour improves for he's worked overtime and caught thieves stealing Christmas trees. The Forestry Department give him a bonus cheque which he spends on new ceiling boards for the house. All through the holidays he measures and saws, hammers and paints. When he's finished with the last coat of varnish, he takes Martha to the hardware and makes her choose wallpaper for the kitchen. She picks out rolls of white depicting woodbine whose pattern is wasteful and hard to match.

Neighbours come to the house that Christmas and remark on how, each time they visit, the house has improved.

'Oh, an auld house is impossible to keep,' Deegan protests. 'You could spend your whole life on it and see no difference before you reach the grave.' But he is pleased, and hands round the stout.

'Easy knowing you have a good woman behind you,' they say. 'A woman makes a place.'

'That's for sure.'

Martha is quiet. She smiles and drinks hot whiskeys but, despite all coaxing, refuses to tell a story.

For Christmas the girl gets an Abba record which she plays twice and commits to memory. 'Waterloo' is her favourite song. Santa slides down the chimney and leaves a second-hand bicycle for the middle child. This is a disappointment. He'd hoped for machinery for his farm – a harrow to put in the early wheat or a harvester, for his sugar beet's near ready for the factory. Sometimes he wishes for rain. Their leaves, which he made out of bicycle tyres, seem dry and are not getting any taller.

The eldest goes off to Dublin for the holidays. Deegan gives him a few pounds so he will be under no compliment to his uncles. It doesn't matter that his eldest boy's mind is on the city. Deegan has willed him the place and knows that Aghowle will some day draw him back. To his wife he presents a sewing basket and, with egg money, Martha buys her husband a pair of Clark's plaid slippers.

On Saint Stephen's night, a fox comes into the yard. Judge can smell him, detects his stink on the draught under the door before he reaches the hen-house. Judge gets up but the door is bolted. He runs upstairs and pulls the quilt off the girl's bed. The girl gets up, takes one look at him, and wakes her mother. Martha shakes Deegan, who comes down in his pyjamas and loads the gun. The retriever's excitement grows. He hadn't known Deegan owned a gun. Together they run out to the yard. A white moon is spinning, shredding the light between the clouds. The taste on Judge's tongue is hot like mustard but they are too late: the hen-house door stands ajar and the fox is gone. He has killed two hens and taken another. Their young look demented. In the chaos they keep searching but every wing they find is not their mother's. Judge stares at Deegan but all Deegan does is fire a few shots off in the air – as though that would make any difference to a fox.

The next morning the forester goes out to pluck the hens. He looks up at the beam where he hung them but there's nothing there, just the bits of baling-twine he hung them with. Martha has already buried them in the bottom of the garden. Her eyes are red from crying.

'Such waste,' Deegan says, and shakes his head.

'We'd be hard up if we had to eat Sally and Fern. You dig them up. You eat them. I'll make the sauce.'

'You never, in your married life, made sauce.'

'Do you know, Victor Deegan, neither did you.'

The nights between Christmas and the new year are long. The simpleton, with bits of ceiling boards, builds hay sheds for his farm, which he crawls through. The girl writes down her resolutions and with her brother's sense of wonder reads the chapter entitled 'Reproduction' in the eldest's new biology book. Aghowle stinks of varnish and there isn't much money. Deegan is uneasy. He keeps having the same dream: every night he puts his hand in his pocket and there his wallet, bulging with all the money he's ever earned, is cut in two. All the notes are in halves but he can convince neither shopkeeper nor bank clerk that they are genuine. Towards the end, all the neighbours stand there laughing, saying there will be no improvements now.

He dreams a strange dream also: of coming home through a blue evening feeling anxious because no smoke is rising, of walking inside and his house being empty. There is a note that makes him sad for a while but the sadness doesn't last and in the end he is a young man again on his knees, lighting the fire. After this dream he wakes and, in an attempt at intimacy, tells his wife.

Martha, still half-asleep, says, 'Why would I leave you?' and turns over.

Deegan straightens himself. Such a strange thing to say. He'd never thought she'd leave him, never thought such a thing had crossed her mind. The house itself seems strange tonight. Martha's roses have, through the years, crawled up along the dash and, in the wind, paw the windows. On the staircase, a green shadow like water trembles. He goes downstairs feeling brittle, to get a drink. Some day it will all be over. He will get back the deed, buy a steel box and bury it under the oaks. Without Aghowle to worry about, his future will be an open hand. Martha, the mother of his children, will be happy for there will be nights in B&Bs and brand new clothes. They will travel to the West of Ireland. She'll eat liver. They will walk again on a warm strand and Deegan won't care about the feel of sand under his feet.

He takes his drink in the parlour. The retriever is lying on the hearthrug, soaking up what is left of the heat. Despite all his attempts, Deegan never found anyone who'd buy him. The dog is wearing a jacket of red velvet which Martha, to please the girl, has sewn during the holidays. His wife has stitched a zip along the belly and trimmed the sleeves. Deegan shakes his head. In all their time together, never once has she sewn so much as a button onto a shirt.

He opens the ledger and looks over the bills. The price of schoolbooks is beyond reason. The thermostat in the cooler will have to be replaced.

There is house insurance to renew but he can leave that for another while as he has the car to tax. He totals his income and the outgoings, sits back and sucks a breath in through his teeth. The spring will be lean but he'll be careful and get through it as he always does. One thing the neighbours can't say is that Victor Deegan is a bad provider. There isn't so much as a lazy dream in that man's head. Fifty-nine more payments. He does the arithmetic in his head. Five twelves are sixty. It will take almost five years but won't the years pass anyhow? Deegan looks again at the numbers, and sighs.

The boy, who has all this time been lying inside his hay shed, looks out. 'Is it money, Daddy?'

'What?'

'Mammy says you think of nothing else.'

'Does she now?'

'Aye. And she says you can sew your *own* arse into your trousers. Why would you sew your arse into your trousers?'

'You watch your tongue,' Deegan says but he can't stop himself from laughing. The boy, like much else in life, has been a disappointment. He gets up, opens the curtains. The sky looks clear, the moon changeful. He predicts a bad year and draws them closed again. On the sideboard lie the girl's new copybooks, her name written neatly on their covers: Victoria Deegan. The child's name gives him pride; it is so much like his own. A cold feeling crawls up his back. He tries to think of nothing but instead he thinks of Martha saying she won't leave him.

With bills, school uniforms and a wife's unspoken desire to leave, another year begins. Martha's desire to leave wanes when a flu clouds up her head and returns just as soon as she gets well again. Judge follows the girl everywhere. One night she runs a bath without bolting the door. The retriever gets up on his hind legs, pushes the handle down and walks calmly in. He looks over the edge of the tub and sniffs the water. It smells strange as fruit but it is warm. Before the girl knows what he's doing, he's in beside her.

In January, Dublin shops advertise their sales. Martha takes the bus to O'Connell Street but she does not go near the shops. She walks past Clery's, on down across a Liffey bridge and winds up in a D'Olier Street cinema eating sweets, crying while a tragedy concerning an Irish girl who left for America flashes across the screen. She comes back with her eldest boy and sticks of rock, disillusioned with her thoughts of leaving. Where would she go? How would she earn money? She remembers the phrase, 'Better the devil you know,' and becomes humoursome. Deegan puts it down to the fact that she is going through the change of life, and says nothing. He has become more than a little afraid of his wife and, to feel some kind of tenderness, often sits his daughter on his knee.

'Tutners,' he calls her. 'My little Tutners.'

And his daughter, in turn, begins to tell him that she loves him.

One Friday evening when he is low, feeling the pinch, Deegan drives down to the neighbour's house to play forty-five. He thinks it might cheer him up to see the neighbours and play but when he gets there he cannot concentrate on cards. After five games he's lost what he normally doubles in the night, and so he gets up to leave. The neighbours do their best to make him stay but Deegan insists on going, and bids them all goodnight.

When he is getting into his car, a stranger who holds his cards close to his chest comes up.

'I understand you have a dog you'd sell.'

'A dog?' says Deegan.

'Aye,' he says, 'a gun dog. Do you still have him?'

'Well, I do.' Deegan is set back on his heel but he recovers quickly. 'I bought him last September but I've little time for hunting and it's a shame to see him wasted.'

Deegan goes on to describe a retriever. He is a good salesman and begins to talk easily about pheasants and how his dog can rise them, how the soup off a pheasant tastes finer than anything you can find in a hotel. He talks about the turf basket and how it is never empty since the dog came to the house. As soon as he mentions turf, the man smiles but Deegan does not notice for he is remembering the girl on her birthday and how she and the retriever now bathe in the same water. But it is too late to back down.

'How much would you be asking?'

'Fifty pound,' says Deegan. It is a crazy price – he will be lucky to get the half of it – but the man doesn't flinch.

'If he is what you say, I'd be interested. When can I see him?'

Deegan hesitates. 'Now would suit me.'

'Now? Right. I'll follow you, so.'

That night Judge recognises O'Donnell before he comes through the door. He always leads with his left foot and the foot always hesitates before crossing the door. If there is any speck of doubt in Judge's mind, it vanishes when he gets the hunter's scent. It is a mixture of silage and some kind of oil he uses to keep his hair in place. Deegan comes in first and then O'Donnell. Judge leaps up and rips his velvet jacket on the corner of the armchair.

'Well look at you in your finery,' O'Donnell says, and begins to laugh.

Deegan, feeling slightly embarrassed, joins in the laughter.

' 'Tis only a thing the child put on him.'

Judge does his best to escape but every door off the kitchen is closed and it is only a matter of time before the two men catch him and place him, whimpering, in the boot of O'Donnell's car.

'There now,' says Deegan. It is all he can do not to hold out his hand. 'You won't be sorry you bought him.'

'Bought him?' says O'Donnell. 'When did you ever hear of a man buying his own dog?'

As Deegan watches the tail-lights sailing down the lane he tries not to think of the girl in her yellow dress, thanking him. He tries not to think of her sitting on his lap, telling him how she loves him now. He tells himself it doesn't matter, that there is nothing he could have done. When he turns to go inside, something above him moves. He looks up. Martha is standing at their bedroom window in her nightdress, watching. She raises her hand and Deegan, feeling surprised, raises his. Maybe some part of her is glad the dog is gone. While he stands there watching, his wife's hand closes into a fist and her fist shakes. So, it is all out in the open.

Needless to say, the girl wonders why Judge doesn't wake her the next morning.

'Where's Judge?' she says when she comes down. She looks at her parents. Deegan is sitting at the head of the table forcing hard butter into a slice of white bread. Her mother is holding a cup of black tea to her lips, staring at her husband through the steam.

'Ask your father,' Martha says.

'Daddy, where is he?' Her voice is breaking.

Deegan coughs. 'A man came looking for him.'

'What man?'

'His owner. His owner came looking for him.'

'What do you mean, his owner? I own him. You gave him to me.'

'In truth,' Deegan says. 'I didn't. I found him in the wood and brought him home, that was all.'

'But Judge is mine,' the girl says. 'You gave him to me.'

She runs outside and calls his name. She searches the land and all their hiding places: 'The Spaw' where he buried his bones, the tunnel in the hay shed, the grove beyond the hazels where the pheasants sleep. She searches until the knowledge that he is gone sinks in and changes her state of mind. Her father never loved her, after all. She can know that now. For days Victoria isn't able to go to school, refuses to cry and eats little more than a robin. By the time a week has passed she has stopped talking to anyone in the house. For her, only one word remains. Every evening she goes out on the boy's bicycle calling his name:

'Judge! Judge!' is heard all around that parish. 'Judge!'

Deegan knows the girl has gone a bit mad but the girl will get over it. It is only a matter of time. Everything else in Aghowle stays much the same: the cows come down to the gate to be milked, the milk is put in creamery cans and collected. Martha's hens peck at the seed, roost for the night and lay their eggs. The pan is taken down early in the mornings, put back on its hook and taken down again. And the boys fight as always over what is and isn't theirs.

Sometimes, sitting in the wood with his flask and sandwiches, Deegan regrets what happened with the dog but most of the time it doesn't cross his mind. The consequences, not their origin, strain him most for his wife no longer speaks to him, no longer sleeps at his side. One half of the girl's bed has become hers.

Martha doesn't care about the money any more. Money, she concludes, is useless. A millionaire could not bring her daughter back to the way she was. Sometimes she sees herself throwing stones at Judge in the wood. His tail is between his legs and he is running away. So much of her life has revolved around the things that did not happen. The girl is lighter than a bale of straw. Martha tries to convince her that she should get another dog, a little pup who can be the girl's own, a dog that she can love. But the girl will have none of it. Martha keeps insisting until the girl turns on her:

'What would you know about love?'

'Maybe I know more than you think I do.'

One evening when Deegan is crossing the hill, more smoke than usual is rising from Aghowle. Deegan sees it. Somehow he had almost suspected it. In the yard, eleven cars are parked. He recognises every one. He has never known so many neighbours to come in the one evening – nor any to come so early. Davis is here, and Redmond. And Mrs Duffy, the *Evening Herald*. The maroon hatchback is the priest's.

When Deegan steps over the threshold, every light in the house is burning; inside a massive fire is throwing waves of heat across the kitchen floor. Deegan, in his old clothes, bids them all good evening and takes his hat off.

'Ah, there's the man himself!'

'No man like the working man!'

'Have you enough space to get in there for your bit of dinner, Victor?'

'We're intruding on ya.'

'Not at all, sure weren't ye asked?' says Martha. She puts a warm plate down in front of him. A rare sirloin, roast potatoes, mushrooms. There's a bowl of stewed apples brimming with custard for later on. Deegan sits in to his dinner, blesses himself, picks up the knife and fork. He finds it difficult to eat and be hospitable at the same time but he does his best. There is no sign of the children. His wife is handing round the stout, the Powers.

'Drink up!' she says. 'There's plenty. Wasn't it awful about that young Morrissey chap?' Her voice is strange. Her voice is not the one she uses.

The neighbours sit there chatting, talking about the budget, the swallows and the petrol strike. They are warming up, getting ripe for an evening's entertainment. A little gossip begins to leak into the conversation. Redmond starts it, says he went up to the Whelan sisters for the lend of a billhook after he broke the handle on his own and caught them eating off the one plate. 'Dip to your own side, Betty!' he mimics. There is a little laughter and, in the laughter, a little menace.

The shopkeeper tells them how Dan Farrell came down and ate five choc-ices, standing up. 'Five choc-ices! Wouldn't he have a nice stool? And then, when he'd slathered the last, he tells me to put them on the slate!'

Martha smiles. She seems genuinely amused. She reaches for a cloth, takes tarts and queen cakes out of the oven. The tarts' crusts are golden, the buns have risen.

'Would ya look at this?' Mrs Duffy says. 'They'd win prizes at any show. And there was me thinking you didn't bake.'

Martha stacks them high on Deegan's best serving plates and hands them round. She's acting, Deegan realises. She's acting well. Nobody couldn't believe this didn't happen every day. The cows stand bawling at the gate to be let in but Deegan cannot move. He can't bear to hear his cows roaring but if he leaves, he'll miss it. Everything in his body tells him to get up but his curiosity is stronger than his common sense.

He crosses his legs and accidentally kicks the simpleton who is sitting, attentive, in Judge's old bed.

'Sorry,' he says.

At the sound of his voice the neighbours turn, remembering he is there.

Davis says he walked all the way to Shillelagh but by the time he got there one of his feet got terrible sore. He took his boot off and there, inside, was a big spoon. Not a small spoon but a big spoon.

'You're joking!' Sheila Roche says. It's what she always says after hearing something she doesn't believe.

Tom Kelly says he's going to do away with the milking parlour, that there is no money in milking any more. 'The farmer's days are numbered,' he says. 'Sure isn't milk the same price now as it was ten year ago?'

That subject keeps them going for a while but sometime later the subject of farming dwindles and comes to a halt. A few balls of speech are kicked out into the darkening conversation but nothing catches; they roll off into silence. The neighbours get more drink and begin to look at Martha. They turn quiet. Someone coughs. Davis crosses his legs. Because the priest is there, the request is left to him:

'I've heard you're a great woman for a story, Mrs Deegan,' he says. 'I've never had the pleasure.'

'Ah now, Father, I'm not at all,' says Martha.

'Aye. Spin us a yarn there, Martha!'

'God be good, nobody can tell them like her.'

'All she needs is a bit of coaxing.'

'Ah, I'll not.' Martha swallows what's left in her glass. She likes this taste. A dull thought crosses her mind. Her mother always said that her father's people had tinker's blood and that this tinker's blood would take them to the road. More than once she has been mistaken for a tinker. She settles down, knowing the story she'll tell. It is only a matter of deciding where, exactly, she should start.

'Haven't you heard them all before,' she says.

'If you don't tell us a yarn, we'll all go home!' Breslin shouts.

'That's no way to persuade the woman,' says Redmond.

Martha concentrates on the room. She has a way about her that is sometimes frightening. She looks at her feet and concentrates. Before she can begin she must find the scent; every story has its own, particular scent. She settles on the roses.

'Well, maybe I could tell ye this one.' Deegan's wife pushes hair back off her forehead and wets her lips.

Davis rubs his hands. 'Now we're in for it.'

'There was this woman one time who got a live-in job in a guest house by the sea,' Martha says. 'She wasn't from there. She was a Bray woman who had gone down south to look for work. The house she worked in was a bright, new bungalow – much like the ones you see down in Courtown. Nothing fancy but a clean and tidy place. Mona was a big, fair-skinned woman. She was tall and pale, freckled. People sometimes mistook her for a tinker but, despite what people thought, she hadn't a drop of tinker's blood. She was a postman's only daughter and one of the things she could do well was dance. That woman could swing on a thrupenny bit and not step on the hare's ear.'

'That's a lovely type of woman,' Breslin says quietly, remembering something of his own.

'In any case, she went off this one night to a dance. It being the summertime, there was a great big crowd in the ballroom. She wasn't really looking for a man but this night the same farmer kept asking her out to dance. He was a wiry fellow with a big red beard but he was light on his feet. That man moved over them floorboards same as a cat's tongue moves along a saucer of cream. With the easy way they moved, they had to talk, but the farmer could talk about nothing only the place he owned. All the acres, the trees along the lane, how fine the house was. He talked about the new milking parlour and the orchard and the big high ceilings. For the want of a better name, I'll call him Nowlan.

'Now Nowlan asked the woman if she'd meet him again and she said no but Nowlan wasn't the type of man to take no for an answer. Being the eldest boy he was used to getting his own way. He followed the woman here, there and yon. One time she looked up from eating her bit of dinner and there he was, looking in through the window. He hounded the woman and the woman gave in. In the end it was easier to court him than to not court him, if you know what I mean. But he was good in his own way, would buy her cups of tea and scones, would never let her put her own hand in her pocket. And, always, they danced.

'They danced the foxtrots and the half-sets and the waltzes same as they were reared on the same floor but in her heart Mona didn't really take to him. He smelled strange like pears that are near rotten. His scent was too sweet. Really, he was past his prime. Everything was all right when they were dancing but as soon as the band stopped and he went to put his lips on hers, the woman felt disappointed. But like every woman who is no spring chicken, she got lonely. The woman wanted something of her own. She thought about living in the place Nowlan had described. She could see herself out under the trees sitting on a bench in the shade, reading the Sunday newspaper.

'One night Nowlan asked her if she'd marry him. "Would you think of marrying me?" He said it with his back to the light so she couldn't see him properly. They were close to the sea. Mona could hear the waves hitting the strand and the children screaming. It was the end of summer. The woman didn't really want to marry him but she wasn't getting any younger and knew, if she refused, that his offer might be the last.'

'Now we're getting down to it,' says Redmond.

'Well, to make a long story short—'

'Ah, what hurry is on us?' says the priest. 'If it's long don't make it short.'

'Isn't that the very opposite of what we say about your sermons?' Davis is getting full. He has taken over the whiskey bottle, giving out the measures while it lasts.

The priest lifts a shoulder, lets it fall.

'My stories aren't a patch on your sermons, Father,' Martha says and looks across at Deegan. Her husband's arms are frozen across his chest. She sees the boy beneath the table, and hesitates but it's too late to back down now. She remembers her intentions and goes on:

'Well, this woman, Mona, accepted his proposal. She married this man and went off to live on the nice farm. She thought by all his talk that the place would be a mansion so she got a terrible shock when she walked in through the door. The only thing you could say about that auld house was it wasn't damp. Nowlan had a herd of cows, all right, and a milking parlour but the furniture was riddled with woodworm and there was crows nesting in the chimneys. She made half-hearted attempts to clean the place but when she found two pairs of dentures in with the spoons, she stopped. On her wedding night she felt springs coming up like mortal sins through the mattress. It was all she could do some days not to cry.

'Nowlan spent his every day and half the nights in the fields. You see, as soon as he'd won her, he paid her little or no attention. Most of the time he was gone. Where he went, Mona didn't always know. It wasn't that she thought he'd be gone with another woman. She'd seen him look at other women during the sermons at mass, when he was bored. But he'd never lay his hand on any. If he laid his hand on another woman, the neighbours would find out and Nowlan, above all things, feared the neighbours.

'He'd come in complaining, looking for a hot dinner. Mona didn't care much for food or the niceties of it but always she had a few spuds with a steak or a stew. A few years passed in that place and still there was no sign of a child. The neighbours began to wonder. A few comments were passed, a few dirty remarks. One man, a shopkeeper, asked her where they met and when she told him, he said, "Didn't he go far enough for you?" Some began to feel sorry for Nowlan. And Nowlan, knowing what people were saying, began to feel sorry for himself because – saving your presence, Father – he thought, like many a man who hasn't a babby, that his seed was falling on dry ground. Naturally, he blamed his wife for, no matter how many times they laid down together in that bed, she never once showed any signs of bearing a child '

'I think there must be nothing worse then being married and not being able to have a child,' Mrs Duffy says. 'I've often thought, since I had me own, that I am blessed.'

'And aren't you?' says Sheila. 'Sure haven't you the finest childer that ever walked through the chapel gates?'

'Ah, now, I wasn't saying that.'

' 'Tis the truth all the same.'

'Shut up, will yez?' says Davis. 'Why won't yez all shut up and let the woman tell it? I've been waiting for this one.'

'Sure wasn't I only chipping in?' says Mrs Duffy.

'Isn't that what it's all about?' says Martha.

Martha looks again at Deegan. His eyes are asking her to stop. So, it's working. She smiles, puts her head down and waits for silence to rise again. Now she is determined. Nothing will stop her now. No matter how long this takes, she'll bear it out, she'll tell it. She thought she'd tell it in disguise and make the disguise as thick as possible. Now she isn't sure. She rests her nose against her fist, breathes in. She thinks of her daughter. She can now carry her daughter all the way to the bathroom and back.

'Where was I?'

'I wouldn't blame you for not knowing where you were,' says the priest. The priest is on her side.

'Oh, aye,' says Martha, who knows exactly where she is. 'They were married. They were married six years and then this man called to the house. A stranger he was. Mona didn't know his name, had never before laid eyes on him. Nowlan was away that day buying seed in the co-op and whenever he went to the co-op he never came back in a hurry. Anyway, Mona answered the door. She had grown a little thinner by now. She was older. She was worrying, and failed. There, at the front door, stood this salesman—'

'Oh, what was he selling?' Davis whispers.

'Shut up, Davis will ya?' Redmond says.

Martha pauses and lets her anger rise. They all sense it. Mrs Duffy gives her a look of sympathy but Martha isn't interested in sympathy any more.

'Roses. He was selling roses. "Would you be interested in roses?" he asked her. He was a good-looking fellow, tall and clean-shaven. He didn't have that dirty beard Nowlan had and Mona was able to get a good look at his chin. Her hand wanted to reach up and touch his throat but he was a good many years younger than herself.'

'A mere child!'

'She was robbing the cradle!'

Martha likes to think it is too soon but maybe they're already understanding. Mrs Duffy thinks she knows.

'In the back of his van this stranger had all kinds of lovely things – rose bushes and fruit trees, everything under the sun. She bought every last one of his rose bushes and took him inside for the tea. As she was scalding the pot he asked if she was married.

' "I am but my husband is gone off to get seed."

' "Has he no seed of his own?" the salesman asked. He was talking about potatoes but realised, when the woman looked at him, that she thought he meant something else.

' "No," she said honestly. "He has no seed of his own."

'The way she said it made the salesman nervous. He got up and went over to the window. He said her rhododendrons were the loveliest he had ever seen. He went out and touched the blooms. It was the sun shining on the man touching the rhododendron that attracted the woman. She'd never meant to touch the salesman but when she touched him, his thumb came up and stroked her lips. His hands were soft compared to Nowlan's. He told her her eyes were the colour of wet sand.'

Under the table the boy is concentrating on his mother's words. This is a different kind of story. This story has something to do with what really happened for he remembers the man, and the rhododendrons. And then there are those things his sister taught him at Christmas, the things in the biology book. He wants his mother to go on, to finish it. He likes the people in the kitchen. He wishes they could be this happy all the time.

'The woman planted the rose bushes outside the hall door,' Martha continues. 'Late that night when Nowlan came home he called her a fool for spending all his good money. "What kind of a woman spends all the money on flowers?" Not only that, but he accused her of never making him a decent bit of dinner. "Spuds and cabbage is no dinner for a working man."'

Deegan cannot stand it any more. There are some things he doesn't need to hear. She will bring in the dog, the girl. God only knows where she will stop. The neighbours are listening in a way they have never listened, as though it is the only story Martha has ever told. He stands up. As soon as he stands, the neighbours turn to look at him.

'I can't listen to them poor cows bawling any longer,' he says. 'You'll have to excuse me.'

The neighbours push their chairs out of his way. The wooden legs screech on the floor as they let him pass. When he reaches the door he doesn't know where he gets the strength to open the latch. Outside, he feels close to tears. He leans against the wall doing his best not to listen. In his heart he has always known the girl was not his own. She was too strange, too lovely to be his. Isn't that the reason why he sold the retriever? He listens for a while to Martha's voice, trying not to hear the words. But he cannot help listening; he too, wants to hear the end. Finally he hears his son, the boy, shout, 'Mammy had a boyfriend!'

Deegan's feet carry him down the yard, his hand rises up to switch on lights and somehow, one by one, he gets the cows into their stalls, finds the clusters and milks them. He takes his time. He is thorough. As he is finishing his work, the neighbours come out. They are leaving, coming out through the front door. He had other ambitions for his front door but they don't seem to matter now. He waves to a few and they wave back but not one of them asks if he will walk them down the lane.

Deegan stays for a long time in the milking parlour. He scrubs the aisles with the yard brush, rinses off whatever dirt is left on the stalls.

He has always been particular, he believes. He takes his time, puts fresh hay into the troughs and replaces a loose link on a chain.

Finally, he goes in. It is his house, after all. He thinks this then thinks of the bank. Martha hasn't gone to bed. She is still there, sitting at the fire. He looks under the table but the boy is no longer there.

'Are you happy now?' he says.

'After twenty years of marriage, you're finally asking.'

'Was that all you wanted?'

Martha raises a glass of whiskey which is no longer hot and stares at her husband. 'Happy birthday, Victor.'

A lid of silence comes down on the Deegan household. Now that so much has been said there is nothing left to follow. The neighbours stay away these times. Deegan gives up going to mass. Not being a hypocrite, he doesn't see the point in going any more. He works later than ever, eats, milks the cows and throws money on the table every Thursday.

Martha buys food and lets the house go but Deegan doesn't care. She looks older. White hairs like threads off a spool grow out through her scalp. The girl goes back to school and although she gets on well, she isn't the same. There's no more talk of being the captain of a ship, of marrying the Taoiseach.

By this time the simpleton has turned the whole parlour into a farm. His sheds are bedded, his combine parked against the skirting board. The fields have taken up the parlour floor and Martha's curtains come down like sheets of rain at the edges of his land.

One night when everyone else is asleep he hears a noise in the kitchen. Thinking it's a mouse, he gets up and goes in for the kill. He has twice seen his father break a rat's back with a shovel. He stands holding the poker, keeping as quiet as he can, and listens. He can hear claws. Maybe it's just the roses pawing the windows.

When he opens the door, a dog is standing there, a stray. Something about him suggests something else. The boy strokes him, feels the bones under the dirty coat. The dog is shivering and the boy has sense enough to realise he's cold.

'Come in to the fire,' he says. That's what his mother said to the stranger and the stranger had followed her. Now the stray follows him, down the steps and on into his home. The boy is the man of the house now. He tries to remember how to light a fire, convinces himself it isn't hard. Hasn't he built a whole farm by himself? He takes newspapers out of the scuttle and twists them. His sister taught him how to do this. He places the papers on the hearth of his house, where the carpet meets the plywood. It takes a long time but finally he manages to strike one of the matches.

'Damp,' he says. 'They're damp.'

The paper oaks catch fire and the boy piles high the hedges. Only last week he'd had them cut.

'It's all right,' he says to the dog. 'Come up to the fire and warm yourself.'

Intrigued, the boy watches the flames. They turn the paper black and cross into the hay barn, set fire to his roof and spread on up through the nylon sheets of rain. The heat is lovely, unlike any fire Aghowle had ever known. Some small part of the boy is upset yet he stands back, and laughs.

He looks around to share the moment with his visitor but Judge is already on the stairs, heading for the girl's room. When he jumps on the bed he lands on Martha. Martha isn't really wake. She is cross and it takes a while for her to recognise him.

'Judge,' the girl says. 'Where were you?'

A smell is coming through her sleepy head. Martha gets it too. They shout for Deegan in the far room. He is such a heavy sleeper.

'Daddy!' the girl shouts.

Smoke is crawling through the rooms, filling up the house. The boy is standing with the doors open watching the blue flames cross the ceiling boards. Martha, in her nightdress, drags him out. Deegan doesn't want to get up. Through sleep he looks at the dog. For some reason he is glad to see him back. He turns over and tries to sleep again but the dog bites him. An age, it seems, passes before he will admit that the house is on fire and summons the courage to get down the stairs.

When they are all out they can do nothing more than stand staring at the house. Aghowle is in flames. Deegan breaks the parlour window to throw water on the fire but when the glass is broken, the flames leap out and lick the eaves. Deegan's legs don't work. This is a new feeling. He looks at the children. The boy is all right. The girl has her arms around the dog. There is a minute during which Deegan still believes he can save his home. The minute passes. The word 'insurance' goes through his head. He sees himself standing out on the road but that, too, passes. Deegan, in his bare feet, goes over to his wife. There are no tears in his eyes.

'Are you sorry now?' he says.

'Sorry for what?'

'Are you sorry now you strayed?'

He looks at her and it dawns on him that she isn't the slightest bit sorry. She shakes her head.

'I'm sorry you took it out on the girl,' she says. 'That's all.'

'I didn't know what I was doing.' It's the first admission he's ever made. If he starts down that road there might be no end to it. Even in his surest moments Deegan never really believed there would be an end to anything. They stand there until the heat becomes too strong and they have to back away.

They must now turn their backs on Aghowle. To some the lane has never seemed so short. To others it is otherwise. But the lane has never been so bright: sparks and ash are flying through the air. It looks as though the oaks, too, could catch fire. The cows have come down to the fence to watch, to warm themselves. They are ghastly figures and yet they seem half comic.

Martha holds on to her daughter's hand. She thinks of her money, the salesman and all those obsolete red roses. The girl has never known such happiness; Judge is back, that's all she cares, for now. It hasn't yet occurred to her that she's the one who taught her brother how to light a fire. The guilt of that will surface later. Deegan is numb and yet he feels lighter than before. The drudgery of the past is gone and the new work has not yet started. In the lane, the puddles are reflecting fire, shining bright as silver. Deegan grasps at thoughts: of having work, that it's just a house, that they are alive.

It is hardest for the boy whose farm is gone. All his work, through his own fault, is wasted. Nonetheless he is intrigued. He looks back at his creation. It is the biggest fire anyone has ever built. At the foot of the lane the neighbours are gathering, coming on slowly towards them. Before the Deegans can reach them and their offers of beds for the night, the boy finds words.

'Who cares?' he keeps whispering as he goes along. 'Who cares?'

What is it Called, your Country, behind the Mountain?

Colum McCann

From every final amount of fact another fact is missing: it's Tuesday but it feels like Sunday because I didn't go to school today and they've dressed me up in a pale-green suit that's tight in some places, a blue tie that pinches on the side of the neck, and Mammy is staring ahead, and my older brother is silent, and I see myself in the back window glass of the moving car and I think that's me on the day my Daddy dies. The car goes down the road towards the church. This morning his shoes were set far apart beneath his bed like the corners of gates. It's a bad winter and all the boats have been taken in and the few seaside trees are bent into the wind and the curled leaves are jumping the stone walls, catching in the tangled fishing nets laid under bricks in the gardens. There's the bang of unpainted doorways far away and the seagulls are swooping down on whatever they can find, small pickings. All the curtains in the houses are drawn. Nobody has gone fishing for a week or more now. That he drank. That he sang. That he had a foul temper. That he wore a blue teal feather in his hat. That he fell over the side of the boat just eight days ago. That he never normally went out on boats. That he was found tangled up in the seaweed and two seals stood curious over his body. That now I'm nobody's favourite and his life is beginning to sound in my ears. That the car goes far past the church towards the mountain which will only later, in another language, become a hill. That he made up stories about the dark times in a dark tongue. That he rescued a boy from an orphanage in Dresden, me. That nobody believed him or the story. That there is no forgetting. That he was gone for long times, that he brought things back for Mammy, that she smashed them, that he went walking up and down outside the phone box, waiting for it to ring, that it didn't. That he wore patent

257

leather shoes with a single scuff. That the sea came up to his feet like the opening of hands. That they took him to a mental hospital. That he loved the weather radio. That he listened for curlews. That they would never let him stand at the window unless there was a fog. That I will search for his story, years later, in the National Library, in the British Museum, in Saint Petersburg where the Russian records are, and later in the library on Fifth Avenue, about an Irish soldier who strays to Dresden to adopt a child for a man he has shot in France, or a man he has found shot, a man whose wife later gets killed in the carpet-bombing, but the child survives, and is carted off in this, the least and most human of centuries. That he steps onto a tram. That the city is destroyed. That the orphanage is by a lake. That there are no cribs. That the ceilings are tall. That the bandages are washed in buckets grown brown. That my father buys a boy from the nurses, and brings him back home to what is still the mountain, to his wife who has another boy, waiting. That she stares at him coming down the street, carrying a bag from Rineanna airport. That she pulls a handkerchief from beneath the sleeve of her dress. That one boy in her hand is dark and the boy at his side is fair. That all of us are, for the first time, in one place. That there must be something beyond this silence. That she will turn. That he will touch me on the small of the back and push me along. That I will find that it is true, this story, since the best stories are the ones we are most ashamed of, the ones we hate, that the struggle of memory is the struggle against forgetting, that there is always something absent, that life is unfinished, that the car is still going along the sea road, today, that my Mammy is staring straight ahead, my brother is silent, the hearse is ahead of us, there is mud on the hubcaps, and I hear the crunch of gravel as the car turns into what I was about to say was a parking lot but is, of course, not.

Gaeltacht 1953 – New York 2004

Love's Lesson

Edna O'Brien

Midsummer night or thereabouts. The heat belching up from the pavement, trumpet or was it trombone, the ghost hands of the homeless outstretched like suppliant twigs, a gasp of unspent semen and on your cummerbund a ruby scar, the signifying kiss.

Cities in many ways are better repositories for a love affair. You are in a forest, a cornfield, or walking by the sea shore, footprint after footprint of trodden sand, pebbles, bits of driftwood mottled and hewn by water, the kiss or the handshake gets lost in the vastness of things, in the enormity of sea or forest or cornfield. In the city there are places to remind us of what has been. There is the stone bench, for instance, where we sat to quench our thirst, but really to call it into existence, the little copse of young trees shivering not from cold but from heat, a wall with two water nozzles cemented together, tubers, bearing the trade name Siamese, yes a bit of wall against which you threw me cruciform-wise to press your ebullient suit.

Will you give me one night in one city, was what you said. Yes. Yes, was the answer. We walked up and down not knowing what to do with ourselves, not knowing whether to part or to prolong it, and within the gusts of heat, a little shiver, portent of dread. I asked what you thought of the tall, brown building that seemed to sway like a lake above us, a brown lake of offices, deserted, and poised as if to come heaving down into the street. You admired it but would have varied the cladding. I found the words so quaint and teased you for it.

Only fools think that men and women love differently. Fools and pedagogues. I tell you, the love of men is just as heart-breaking, just as copious, just as bewildered, just as disseminating and in the end as barbaric as the love of women. Men have talked to me of their dalliances. A man I met at a conference described to me how he, who had been unfaithful for twenty-odd years, upon learning of his wife's first infidelity, went berserk, made a car ride, beat up an opponent, came home, broke down, sat up with her all night thrashing out the million moments and non-moments of their marriage, the expectations, the dullnesses, the small treacheries, the large ones, the gifts they gave or meant to give, and then, weary and somehow purged, they had made love at dawn and she had said to him, this unslept, no-longer-young but marvellous wife – If you must have an affair do but try not to, and he swore not to but feared that somewhere along the way he would succumb, yield to the smarms of the Sirens, be sucked in.

Of all the things that can be said about love, the strangest is when it strikes. I chose the verb advisedly. For instance, I saw you once in a theatre and you struck me as a rather conventional man. I thought, there is a man with a wife and possibly two motor cars, a cottage in the country to which you repair at the weekends, one car stacked with commodities, cereals, virgin olive oil, things like that. Maybe like my friend you have sat up with her one entire night atoning, and maybe it seemed as if everything was forgiven, but something always remains and lodges.

Of course I knew you by reputation, and read about your buildings, those wings and temples and rotundas that have made you famous and bear the granite melancholy that is your trademark. Between that austerity and your wine-red cheek, where the blood flowed in a velvety gurgle, I saw your two natures at odds, your caution and your appetite.

We walked and walked. The truffle-hound and his Moll pacing the teeming street, wishing that the pavement might open and draw us in to the soil and the succulence within. We stood outside my hotel and looked at the display, pictures of master bedrooms done in golden chintz. You did not come up. But it was a near thing. Words and tongues pleached together. The allegorical mesh.

Your gift arrived the next day after you had left. It stood in a cake-box, the pot filled with pebbles, friendless, grey-white pebbles that recall wintery seashores. The orchid itself resembles a pleached butterfly, white, eager to escape its spindly stalk, but it stays, a captive, its face milk-white in the dark. I imagine giving it hands, black spidery hands that will tell me the time. I think that if I know the time where you are, in your country, that it will draw us nearer, hasten things.

You had put me in such a flowing state of mind and body that I determined to befriend those I met. A tall black wraith of a man with one missing eye put his hand out for alms and on getting it launched into a spiel of how he fought to defend the right of God in the Civil War, and seeing the fawn flap free of the eggy pupil I touched your foreskin and wished that you had come up to the chintz room. I became a little expansive about it, a little excited, dwelt on it after all those shriven and lampless years.

Strange how suited we were. The right height, the right gravity, the right crouch and oh, idiocy of idiocies, the right wall. Does something of us remain there, shadows, like the frescoes in caves, sometimes seen, sometimes not. Will you give me one night in one city, was what you said. Yes. Yes, was the answer. Yet a friend who saw us leave a room together said that I looked back at him, disconcerted, like Lot's wife.

An affair. It is a word we all know. A state of unequilibrium. So many dire things happen, plus so many ridiculous things. Letters getting opened by the wrong source or the gift of a little trinket going to the wrong address. Wrongs come galloping in. A woman I know read the list that her husband's young mistress had jotted down for her Christmas stocking – wine, victuals, a bracelet and last, but by no means least, a baby. Yes, in capitals – A BABY. The wife went into action. She took him to the Far East on a cruise, around islands, all very rustic, wooden boats with wooden chairs, huts, dancing girls; garlands of gardenias put around the necks of the estranged mistrustful pair. Before she left the wife had done something rather clever and rather vicious. She had sent the brazen young woman copies of other letters written by other women allowing her to see the idiocy, the cupidity and the similarity of those missives, reminding her that unfortunately she was one of many. A touch of the Strindberg. Another woman, a friend, told me that she first got a whiff of her husband's affair not from his neckline or his handkerchief but from the simple fact that when his mistress came for cocktails she brought her rival a bunch of dead flowers, carnations. Later that evening, when they all repaired to a restaurant, she saw husband and mistress cooing, she remembered the dead flowers, stood up and made her first somewhat pathetic scene – I am going to the bathroom now and then I am going home, was what she said. He did not follow immediately but soon he followed, found her eating the flowers like coconut shreds and he simply said that he hated scenes, women's scenes, then went out onto the verandah and walked up and down, but stayed, as she said.

A woman calls from the coast most days. I met her after my lecture and sensed that we had something in common. A little thing happened to unite us. The contents of her handbag fell out and I said, What's wrong, Clarissa, what's wrong, at which she turned and asked if I thought she was having a breakdown. She is seeing a trauma specialist. Her mother, whom she scarcely knew, had recently died and in the wake of this death a mountain of troubles have come galloping in. Her mother's death has opened the lid. Her mother, who was beautiful and I believe rich, never really discussed things, and is causing her now to drop handbags, oversalt the food and have a sherry in the morning, she who does not like drink. She wants to ask her dead mother a key question about a naked man in the room. Her mother shouted at her to get out. Was he father, grandfather or lover? At camp, when she was young, she saw a photo of a woman who resembled her mother which she went and kissed when others were out of sight. She kissed it and smelt a nightdress, hanging by itself in a wardrobe. It smelt of mother. She has something to tell me but she does not know what. She trusts me because of the debacle of the handbag.

Graffiti, graffiti. graffiti. They seem to be done by the same unseen phantom hand. Defecations of hate. There was even one on the torn leatherette of the back seat of the taxi. The driver kept hurtling against his cape of beads, his photo staring out of a hanging tag showed a sour, bearded, clumpy face. Suddenly he was shouting to another driver who cut in on us – Mohammeds, Mohammeds. I asked why he said that, to which he replied that they were all dirty, unwashed Mohammeds and looking at the bearded photograph, I thought this man has forgotten everything, and I wanted to tell him something human, how for instance, when you decided not to come up you picked up your rucksack and said you would walk home to your hotel. The rucksack was a dead weight. Had you stones in it. What did you think as you walked home.

Earlier at that function, at the long table, you were flushed from nerves and the hot flame off scores of candles. We were not together, but in the same archipelago as you said. There was also a hint of shyness to you. You were talking to a woman and I knew by your hesitance that you knew she desired you but you could not return her ardour. Her skirt was glaringly short. She spilt red wine on her thigh. She asked for advice, sundry advice. Someone suggested white wine to counteract the red, for good measure someone else suggested salt and she handed you two dainty little cruets filled with salt and pepper with which to minister to her. It was then you looked across at me, it was then you caught my eye through one of the cubed spaces between the twisting trellis of iron sconces, indifferent to the red and white wine in an estuary on her thighs. A great glorious surge of pride took hold of me then on account of both of us being so smitten and in that firmament of hectic candle flame we fell. Chambering. Chambering. Later, when we had all stood up, you saw me link a man both to be friendly and marginally to nettle you and quite openly you said, am I taking you home or have you better fish to fry.

I wish you were only torso, only cock. No penetrant eyes to welcome me or send me packing. No mind to conjure up those little qualms that nascent lovers indulge in. No hold-all of memory with its entourage – mother, father, wife, child, calling you back, calling you home. I wish I were only torso, to meet you with my wares. I recall a postcard of the seventh century, a headless woman, a queen, her body pale apricot, leaning a fraction to one side, her girdle gossamer, breasts like persimmons, one arm missing, the second lopped at the elbow, pregnant with her own musks.

I have been to our wall, to pay my respects. You would think it was the Wailing Wall in Jerusalem where I once was and stuck a petition written on a piece of paper, hid it between the cracks. People see me standing there but make nothing of it for they too loiter for no reason. It is a city of nomads. You see a man or a woman with carrier bags or without carrier bags, walk up to a corner, cogitate and walk back again. Everyone eats on the street, you see hollows of bread, stumps of pickled dill, noodles with the elongation of maggots, phosphorescent in the sunlight, titbits for the pigeons. People sit on steps, or sit at empty tables and stare. They are homeless or they are lonely or both. One such woman I have been told was a bridesmaid at Grace Kelly's wedding but came down in the world, went 'cuckoo'. Cuckoo is a word they use all the time. Why is she thought of as she. Treachery perhaps. Woman's treachery, different to man's. A mutual woman friend said your name, said it several times in my hearing, to unnerve me. Her eyes glittered like paste jewellery, that pale unchanging glitter which palls. But men and women are alike in this ferment of jealousy. I don't want to see you get hurt, darling – a male friend said noticing my shudder. Actually it was peas falling off a fork. Are you leaving *it* here or are you going home to *it*, he asked. Neither I said. That flummoxed him.

A tall, red-bearded figure, a 'Finn McCumhal' of the pavement with green eyes and a tartan rug which he wears as a toga. He sells things.

He had prints, cheap prints – spots of red and green, like swarms of undroning bees and the wounded orchids of Georgia O'Keeffe looking both spent and fertile. I wondered if he ever felt down in the dumps. He looked surprised. Said never. He was a mountain man and a Green Beret man. Plus I have God. Yes, that was his reply. Plus I have God!

Hot food.

Home-made pizza.

Warm brisket.

I could not think what to eat. I had gone downtown to do some chanting, to chant the taste, the touch, the smell, the half-taste, the permeability of you, out of my mind. I thought I knew the place from a previous pilgrimage but found myself in wrong hallways, talking to janitors, who were surprisingly talkative, the old homestead and so forth. I went to telephone, to find out from Information. The kiosk looked to have been someone's ongoing abode – a dirty baseball cap, punched cans, orange rinds and a cassette tape in such a tangle that it looked animate. On the wall a neatly printed card – 'Word Perfect in ten hours: – Lotus'. Word Perfect in what. The Lotus was a riot. Up the street two of the most pugilistic women I have ever seen, denouncing pornography. They had photographs of breasts being sliced, then hanging off, skewered with arrows. In the café a newly married woman gave a dissertation on marriage, said, Yes . . . It's good to be married . . . He's a great anchor, Frank . . . I wouldn't have said that six months ago . . . Not overnight do you trust a husband, but it comes . . . It comes. Then she described their getting a dog. Her husband wanted a large dog, a labrador. She wanted no dog. Eventually they settled on a small pedigree poodle as being a compromise between no dog at all and a large dog. They have named her Gloria, after Gloria Swanson.

Clarissa called very early. There was something she needed to tell me. She has had female lovers as well as men. It is not that she is promiscuous, her needs change. I asked her what it was like. She said it was a hunger for a ghost, a hunger not altered by man or woman and not altered by marriage. Then she said something so poignant that I wanted to go to her immediately. She said the reason love is so painful is that it always amounts to two people wanting more than two people can give.

My room is a washed pink with gilded mirrors and a chaste white bureau which looks like a theatre prop. The centre drawer does not open, the side ones do. On the lining paper of one, I wrote with your pen, I wrote Remember. Another occupant will come in due course and think there were high jinks. They are bound to think that. Even though you didn't come up I stood in the doorway, watching each time the lift door was opened and people disgorged. Some were quite drunk, one couple gallingly amorous.

One poor creature yesterday, on her throne of rubbish, wept. I said, Why are you weeping. A man had played a dirty trick on her. He had put a hundred dollars in her plastic mug and taken it back again after some altercation. In the window behind her a ruby necklace on a dainty velvet cushion which simply said 'circa 1800'. Riches untold. Yes he played a dirty trick on her. It was the word dirty that set me thinking. Had there been a proposition of some kind. Further down a tall black man held his cap and said the same thing again and again – I'm broke. I'm homeless. I'm broke. He scratched his head when he thought of Georgia. A third one was more vociferous, said it was a city of abuse, a shit-hole, abuse. His trolley was lined with covers of Rambo, Rambo's chest and torso and bearing staring out at me and on the wall above someone had written 'You're dead'. I have never felt so alive, so raven-ously alive. Out there on the street, after I had done the rounds, the sky darkened and thunder began to rumble as if marching in from the backwoods, from Georgia itself, marching in on the city, and on the elect in limousines stately as hearses, marching in to hearten the homeless. Many of them look like country people because of their torn boots and their torn fillets of clothing. Late at night I saw the Rambo fiend pee on Rambo's roped muscles and laugh. The trolley was a swamp. Further up a man was bent over a refuse basket. What struck me was his hair. A short bouclé crop of it, Titian-coloured. He had the stealth of a hunter. What he hauled out was a loin bone with shreds of meat, half-cooked, dripping. Without ado he began to gnaw it. His eyes were incomparably placid. I thought to approach him to give him money but didn't dare. The pupils of his eyes were too proud and full of distance, that unfathomed distance of the Savannah, his sacrament with the bone too complete.

I went to a hen party – women in short skirts and slashed hairdos. What hat de clock? one woman said, remarking how the English language had originated in her part of Saxony. Her husband had recently left her for a younger woman. She travels. Her theme was funds. Stella, the acquaintance who invited me, had a stricken look. She stood in the doorway with a child clinging to her, holding a handful of cutlery and trying by her expression to tell me that much had happened, too much since we last met. In a moment, darling, she kept saying to her daughter who had a little paper crown that she wanted clipped to her hair. Stella's sister was an altogether more assertive type and, looking through the French windows into the garden, she complained about the unlaid table.

I ironed the cloth, Stella said. It was only half-ironed. The creases on it were like the mimicry of waves upon water. It had begun to drizzle. The glasses in which the drinks were going to be served had encrustations of fruit on them, pineapple and melon in sugar-coated ungainly wodges. Each woman, as she arrived, brought the ultimatum of her sex with her. It might have been the short skirts. They seemed not like garments but like weaponry. Each bore a gift. It was a birthday but I did not know that. One woman brought white roses to an aunt which she held to her chest as she might an infant. She wanted Bourbon and inveighed against iced tea which was being offered. Another woman, very thin with darting pupils, insisted she had the perfect cure for jet lag. Wherever you are, or happen to be, you simply alter the time on your clock and go to sleep at whatever is your usual time and wake up, likewise. What hat de clock. I ground a biscuit, out of nerves, Stella got down on her knees to wipe it up and by mistake overturned a glass. I'll keep you to that, she said, it was something I had described from a book. Some wretched moment. The rain by now was coming down in buckets and sadness seeping into me. I thought I would have to think of you and to think of you I would have to be alone. The capable sister was making a raspberry dressing, said I could not possibly leave, but I did. I was given a present on the way out and in the street I opened it. It was a ladle onto which the rain fell in fat spatters and standing there in that leafy suburban limbo I thought of you with every pore of my being, drew you into me as if you were sun, moon and rain and prayed that nothing will come between us and that one night, and senselessly led on by longings I untied a knot in you.

On the way back I asked the taxi driver to go by the river. My mother had come here by boat over eighty years ago and in some way I was trying to imagine a voyage that took flesh before I was born. You see I have always thought that in some way my mother has come between me and the man I hold dear. I was trying to imagine myself there ahead of her, as if she had never been, I was trying the impossible which was to shed her. In the little walkway by the railings were the invalids and their nurses. In starched uniforms they stood emotionless behind the wheelchairs. It was the invalids that frightened me. The spleen in their expressions was quite shocking, quite pitiless. It was like a sick-room although we were out of doors and the patina of their skins recalled those sad, studious, elderly misfits in Rembrandt's haunted interiors. Their eyes frightened me most. Eyes onto which the pennies would soon be pressed. The cruelty in the eyes could be quenched only by these compresses of metal. Their lives, their youth, even their wealth was already dead to them and I thought I am alive, you are alive, and remembered the night of our simmer, your throwing me against the wall quite cursorily as if you wanted to smash my bones.

On Saturday there was a group by our bench, under an arc of trees, young black men with shiny plaited hair. They did headstands, arm-stands, they became trees, the trunks and limbs of trees, then bodies crawling over each other like larvae, then upright with the prowess of panthers. 'Breakdance' it is called. They were wearing white cotton T-shirts with black lettering and in the sunlight the black seemed like pitch. Die or Dance. Dance or Die. I never know which is which.

Mercedes does the room. She had a skill at crying. Her tears are plenitude itself. A few of them would fill a coffee cup. Some months ago her man failed to come home, he who had shared her bed for a year. Only next day at work did she learn why and then merely overheard it. He had had a massive heart attack while holding the car door open for his boss and had died in an ambulance on the way to hospital. Neither the boss, nor any of the people in the apartment building, knew of his relationship with her because of their not being properly married. His funeral, which she arranged, was a lonesome affair, her lawyer, herself and one wreath. Chrysanthemums, she thinks. His wife is making her claims. First it was artefacts, then his watch, then his cufflinks, then the one valuable water-colour that he owned. She dreads that his wife will come and occupy the apartment. She has had to bring her brother from Columbia to stay indoors all day. He plays the guitar and eats. She eats too. Every day she says the same thing – Oh Lord, learn me how to bear it, and embraces me as if I had some influence with the Lord. She says he was the kindest man alive, washed her feet, pared her corns. She also says if I can get a photograph of you or handwriting she can have a friend do spells. It involves the blood of cockerels but she assures me it is not sinister.

Clarissa has read my thoughts. I am invited there. She has a cottage in her grounds. We make no secret of our muddle. She says to have a woman carnally opens up as many minefields as to have a man. She thinks it might help me. She is not sure about you. She has misgivings. She thinks you might be a philanderer. I tell her that just is not so.

I bought an English newspaper to catch up with you. Reading it I could picture those hamlets, steep country roads, faded coats of arms on manor gates, old people's homes and the convolvulus so profuse one expects it to be the shelter of birds. Then the picture slid into night, that hushed de-peopled time of night when the cottages that Shakespeare wrote of are sunk in dew, poplars like sentinels along a hillside, fairy lights still twinkling outside the shut public houses and I thought of you as being part and parcel of these things and prayed that you would admit me to that land of yours, to those cold and mocking sensibilities, sprung from the loins of admirals – give me my innings. I wonder why you chose me. A death perhaps. A close one's death. Often it is a parent. Departures make us deep, they cut, so that we run here there and everywhere, like lunatics, knowing that we cannot replace that which is gone. I detest those cozy hush-hush affairs which your race excels at. I sniff them all the time. Women in their upstairs drawing rooms, done up to the nines, at lunch hour, standing by the folds of their ruched curtains, besmirched. Sherry and gulls' eggs in wait, the marital chamber stripped of all traces of a spouse. Lamb cutlets and frozen peas for the entrée and lots of darling, darling.

When one is smitten, what does one want known, unknown. If for instance you say I am hell to live with it has a certain bravura to it, and does not simply mean that you are lazy and sullen indoors and expect someone else, a wife, certainly a woman, to pour the coffee or put a log on the fire and that you show yourself to best advantage when visitors are coming up the path and soon you are making jokes and pouring wine, flirting even for courtesy's sake. Oh how I hate the façades of ordinary social life. Sunday lunches, Sunday dinners, Sunday teas, the gibberish that gets trotted out. A woman telling the assembled guests how clever her Charlie is, while notching up grievances inside. It's everywhere. I was with a couple one Sunday and the wife pronounced on some book, a spy book, whereupon her husband said have you read it and oh the look, the withering look she gave back to him with a have *you* read it and in the icy aftermath a hundred thousand spermatozoa congealed.

The tenderest moment I recall was when you saw me come up from the Ladies in that dark catacomb of a place, saw me look around, a bit taken aback at how jarring it all was and then make my way by a long route back to my place setting, a detour so that I would have to pass close to you but of course not touch you, simply pass, and what happened was, you guessed, you stood up and said my name with such urgency and such pity, like two people destined not to see each other again. You kissed me. They saw you kiss me and they nudged, our friends twigged. I don't know how I got back to my chair.

Sometimes I think you might have returned and be standing in front of the wall, gazing. I went on a little gallop before dark. It was quite beautiful, warm and pregnant with that kind of excitement which evening heralds. Musicians had gathered and taken up their posts at several corners. Skeins of sound sweetening the air. At one corner a young African held up his wares, ropes of pearls, scarfs that fluttered like veiling. They looked quite magic, ritualistic. The whites of his eyes were orbs, full of the wonder of evening, the wonder of Africa, the sense of a day done, even though he was possibly going home to a hovel. It mattered not to him that I didn't buy. The violet hour when Lilith, guardian of night-women, sets forth. The homeless had already decamped for the night, in doorways, in recesses, on church steps, lying there, heaps, filled potato sacks. I watched one man turn over on his stomach and I am certain that he was dreaming. I thought perhaps food, the maggoty noodles, and then I thought no, some great feast, baskets and platters and cornucopias.

Thunder shook the foundation of my room but I was shaking anyhow. I had had this dream that I had telephoned you in a hotel in Zurich. You were out. I telephoned again and again. A man – I believed he was Moroccan – was getting impatient but I persisted. At one minute to midnight I called again but you had not returned. Then, five minutes later, I was put through and you were sound asleep. You must have come in tired, or maybe a little drunk and flopped down under a big duvet. You recognised my voice immediately and said how did you know I was here. I put the phone down because I sensed the naked terror of a man who believes he has just been trapped. Yes, thunder shook my room and lightning lit up the showroom across the way. Without any deliberation I rang the airline. There were spare seats. Probably because it was midweek. What made me do it so suddenly. As far as I can honestly say, it was the simple action of looking out the window to the room across, the rather shabby showroom where they exhibit dress material and costume jewellery, put them on dummies for customers to view. The lightning had illuminated the fawn torso and just as quickly all was quenched, devoid of jewellery or raiment. It gave me a chilling thought, which is that darkness is our last abode. It brought whisperings of death, my father's death (even though I had wished him gone), my own and yours.

And now in the sodden rain with the East River veritably swollen, tall buildings and warehouses draped in rain as if in their own sackcloth, I set out for home but not for you my friend. Oh no. Sooner or later one has to give up the habit of slavery. In singling out only the lame and the halt, watching every move and muscle of the starving, I felt myself to be at one with them, to be an outcast, and I realised that meeting you had magnified my hungers a hundredfold. That cannot be love. Or can it.

Now we will never know for sure.

When God Was a Comedian

NIALL WILLIAMS

This is the story the Bolivian Samuel Vargas told me in the Café Presidente in the city of La Paz when I asked him what he meant when he said that my God was a comedian.

'You are Irish,' he said to me, 'you should understand this.'

There is in Peru, not far from the shores of Lake Titicaca, a town I had visited by the name of Pomata. The town itself is poor, the buildings low and thin-roofed, some of adobe brick that seem to be falling in upon themselves or slowly returning to the earth. But here, just a little bit down from the broken road that winds from the small Andean villages into Bolivia, is a famous church dedicated to the Madonna. From outside this church looks unremarkable, a plain building of old stone blocks that turn pink in the sunshine and red in the rain. In the early mornings the Peruvian women gather and spread out colourful wares before the gates for the tourists that will stop on the way to the border. But inside, in the cool dimness of the church, is a strange atmosphere of religious intensity such as you will rarely find these days. When you pass in through the heavy door, your eyes lose their sight. At that height, over three thousand metres, the nearness of the Andean sun in the blue sky has been of such ferocity that when you step out of it you think you step out of the brilliance of life into the murk of dream. Soon you see there is a man inside the door. He has a bucket of water and a mop. When the door opens he lowers his eyes and stands still. He makes no sound, he holds on to the mop, and with an air of deep humility he waits while you visit his church.

The floor of black and white marble shines in the places where diffused sunlight falls through the high windows and strikes it. There are wax candles burning or burnt and the air is tinged with smoke and aftersmoke. Along the side are statues of the saints. Like all the statues in the churches of that country, they are fully dressed, and from the startling combination of light and craftsmanship they form a strange company of witnesses watching from the wall.

On the main altar is a large statue of the Madonna with a blue surround. She is dressed in white lace and pale-blue velvet cloak. You look at her and you feel how lifelike she appears and notice the expression in her features is not compassionate but fierce. As if she has unfinished business with you. You look away and go around the church but you come back to her. There is something happening there but it just escapes you. Some message being broadcast, but it is just beyond the fringes of hearing, and you cannot translate its meaning.

But I will tell you.

Once, some years before, there came through that town of Pomata a man called Francisco. It was night. He was on foot. He was walking to escape a crisis in his life and did not know how far he would have to go. He lived in a village on the shores of Titicaca where he was the new husband to a woman called Maria. They lived in the small cramped house of Maria's parents, made smaller still by her father's disapproval of her choice in marriage. The old man was a mechanic. When he asked Maria what her Francisco did for a living she told him he played music on the guitar. That evening the mechanic could be heard telling his wife in the bedroom and blaming her loudly for the stupidity of her daughter. When Maria married Francisco he promised he would support her well and soon would build a new house for them at the edge of the village. In the small space of their bedroom he sat and recounted their wonderful life in the future as if he had already visited it and had only just returned to tell her how it would be. When he finished the telling, he played the guitar. Soft romantic songs made pink the air and infuriated the old man next door.

The following day, on the prompting of his wife, he drew Francisco aside and told him he would begin to teach him about machines. He took Francisco into the small lean-to garage at the end of the house where an old truck was dismantled.

'This is how you make a living,' he said.

But in truth Francisco was ill-suited to the work. He did not like the oil and the grease on his guitar fingers, and within a week had driven the old man to the edge of despair.

'What will you do?' his father-in-law cried at him; 'my daughter will starve.'

'She will not,' Francisco shouted back, and with the screwdriver still in his hand walked outside.

That evening when he played the guitar in the bedroom Maria was not listening. She asked him to explain again why he had left the garage. He strummed the strings with stained fingers and sang more loudly. In the bed next door the old man beat his hands against his head and decided that the only lessons in life are hard ones. Just so then he rose and went into the bedroom and in a raging voice told Francisco and Maria they were to leave the house in the morning.

'We will leave now!' Francisco shouted back at him.

'Very well, leave now,' the old man said, 'and take your cursed guitar.' And he picked it up and threw it across the room and its head hit against the wall and broke off with a strangled twang. Francisco looked at it and, as if it were his old life, he left it there and pulled Maria up by the arm.

In a moment they were in the street. The cold of the night came about them. The light in the house went out. They had no money and nowhere to go. Ahead of them the broad moonfaced waters of the lake slapped. With their small bundle they went along the road. Maria was fearful of the mood her husband was in and said nothing for a time. Francisco too did not speak. He did not seem to her now the handsome easy fellow for whom the world was a pastime. At last they found a shed without a door and though the floor was damp and the place cold, it was where they stopped. Francisco opened their bundle and spread the clothes as a bed. In the dark there Maria wept. He held her in his arms, but she wept all the more. At last, in a measure desperate and yet familiar, he told her to listen and he would tell her of what their life would be like.

He told her the fantasy of their future selves until she slept. Then he rose and went out in the night and walked.

He walked fifteen miles until he came to the town of Pomata. He came in along the empty streets and for reasons unknown to himself stopped when he saw the church of San Cristobel.

Later, he would ask himself if there were a light shining from the window, if there were a sign that bade him enter.

A side door was unlocked. He came inside the church by the small altar to San Martin and made his way to the centre aisle and there knelt down to pray.

But he could not keep his head lowered, for from above on the main altar came a bright glimmering. Francisco looked up and saw the statue of the Madonna and the beautiful surrounds inlaid with silver. And from whatever prompted him then he stood in that empty church and went up along the aisle and genuflected and crossed himself and walked up the three steps to the statue herself.

He reached out a hand and touched her and asked her to help him.

Then he let his fingers move around to the silver behind her. As the history books tell us, it was crafted in the sixteenth century in Madrid by the celebrated silversmith Corza and was of such a fineness that it felt to the hand like silk. Into the silver were delicately wrought images of the life of Christ.

Francisco let his hand move over it in the dimness of the empty church. Then he took from his belt the screwdriver and began to prise the silver away.

When he walked back along the road the sun was just then beginning to rise, streaking the sky with pink and purple over the lake. He had taken off his jacket and wrapped the silver inside it. Maria was sleeping and he shook her gently awake. There were two hours before the Irish priest Father Sullivan would come to say the first mass and discover the crime.

'Wake up, we have to hurry,' he told her.

'Are we going home?' she said.

'No. We are crossing the border into Bolivia.'

They hurried down through the town and out the other side of it and met with an alpaca farmer who was grateful of their company on the road as he herded five thin animals towards the border town of Quoqui. There they found a room in the house of a widow, who took one look at Maria and asked her when the baby was due.

'A baby?' Francisco said, and wondered if this blessing was not a sign that the theft was already forgiven.

He took the silver wrapped in his jacket up into the hills and there in the company of five curious sheep he worked hard to break off a piece of it, which he later sold in La Paz, returning to his wife with food enough for a week.

In the meantime, in the town of Pomata, the priest Father Sullivan had arrived in the church for morning mass and discovered the silver gone. But in the twist of these things, rather than raise the alarm, he was stricken with guilt.

('He was Irish, after all?' Samuel grinned at me.)

He swallowed thorns of blame when he realised he must have forgotten to lock the side door. He hurried quickly to the front door of the church and as three slow bundles of women were coming in the front gates he told them go home, the morning mass was cancelled and the church closed. He went back inside then and was almost sick to his stomach on the diet of guilt. He could not bear to look up at the Madonna, but neither could he look away. It was his fault, he was certain of it. He had come there from a town in Tipperary thinking to bring the light of faith into the lives of these Andean Indians. But the more he looked at the ravaged altar the more he saw a judgement on himself and on his vanity. His whole life came to this moment.

Father Sullivan kept the church locked and covered the altar with a cloth. He knelt and prayed. He prayed to God to make things right, to reach out into the heart of the thief and to make him realise what he had done.

'So now,' Samuel said. 'Now you think some terrible thing began to happen to Francisco. You think the priest on his knees inside the locked church was able to reach God and He in turn to send misfortune into the life of the thief. You think Francisco's wife lost the child, or fell into a sickness, or that the selling of the silver brought him ill luck and grief?

'It was not so. Your God is a comedian.'

The priest stayed on his knees and prayed all the prayers he knew. He kept the church doors locked behind him, even on the third day when the women came knocking on the doors and shouting in to see if he was there. He prayed for something to happen to relieve him of this terrible thing. At last, with weakness in his body, he walked up and took away the cover as if without his looking a miracle might have happened.

And then one did.

But not the one he was expecting.

The statue of the Madonna rose in the air. The statue, that had been cast in the foundry in Catalonia and brought to Peru on the ship *Santa Isabella* and weighed over two hundred kilos, lifted itself above the altar. Father Sullivan cried out. He reached for the statue as if he could save her. But of course he could not.

She fell to the floor and the open arms broke off.

Samuel Vargas paused. He tapped a fresh cigarette on the box and lit it.

'She was repaired later,' he said, casually; 'there are some marks beneath the arms, that is all. But they say there is something strange about her ever since. Still, that is the same one you saw when you visited that church in Pomata.'

'I see.'

'And you saw a man there with a mop and a bucket?'

'Yes.'

'And because you believe in justice you think now maybe he is Francisco, come back to redeem himself at last, to offer penance? It is not. Francisco is the owner of a well-known hotel here in La Paz. I can bring you there. I told you, kind of strange comic, your God. And the man with the bucket? He is the priest who was, and who is no longer so, Francis Sullivan, who stays there waiting until the silver is returned.'

The Other Silence

Tom Mac Intyre

I spend lots of time on the shore these days. It pulls me, gently. Not that I'm inclined to resist, no, no. With white hair, oyster-white of the eye, comes (sometimes) a scrap of knowledge. Touching? Direction. Roads. Want to know about roads? They end. On the shore. Tarred road, by-road, highway, autobahn, all end on the shore. Where other roads begin? Oh, yes.

I am on the shore. Excitement in the wanton air. I'm, no surprise, alone. Find myself increasingly alone on that margin, and, spiced conundrum, more and more in company. Today, on the sand beside me, body of a hare, emptied body, looks like. Imagine a garment thrown away, jacket that's served its turn. Perched hard by, the hare's head. Ears on full alert, eyes strobe-lit. It's – what is it? Space-capsule. Ready for anything. Take-off. Orbit!

And I'm aware of a silence that surrounds. We've met. A long time ago, I was unwell, often been unwell, one of my healthier habits. It's winter, night, and I'm alone in the living room, standing by the window. There's rime on the pane. I'm wiping – spittle-and-thumb – the rime away. Now I can see out. Snow on the lawn, silhouette of the trees, evergreen mostly. All quiet. No longer. The quiet shifts to a silence that imbrues. I can hear, fugal and murmurous, the Unknown.

Which brings me to the dove-grey horse. I met Dove-Grey first on the grandmother's farm. A brown horse there too but nobody passed any remarks. Dove-Grey took the eye, never gave it back. Why so? I didn't know but blood knew. Old expert blood, special kind of juice! When, as Dove-Grey cantered past, a fir-tree whispered, 'Pale horse, pale rider,' my veins raced understanding. Dove-Grey was here, powerfully, but, just as powerfully, somewhere else. Dove-Grey was. Is. Will be. Scattered your wits. Captive, you daren't caress this beauty. Your hand would come out the other side. So. You watched from an acolyte remove. Others partook of the cult. Nothing was said. Just – guard your candle, its shy flame.

We're born to forget. Seems. I forgot until I was reminded, this fine day in dark of the night. It was on an island. Do you like islands? I find them floaty, ductile, schooling. Midnight, yes, I was, fortunately, taking a ramble on heights of the eastward dunes. An old man approached. I knew him, had, indeed, recently bought his currach. Here was a boatsman born, fast friend of the tides. 'Listen,' he said, 'the brown horse is a daylight job, any *gom* could tell you that. Dove-Grey's story is other . . .' And my beauty was beside us. I looked, and through Dove-Grey – transparency allowed – I could see the currach moored in the cove below. Freshly tarred, her shiny black rose and dipped against green of the wave.

A 'useful meeting'! But. Habit is your only deafener. Again I disremember – meeting, offered counsel, bright transparency. I am, after all, a busy man, pelf preoccupies, cunt, cock, sultry scrotum. Let's not get into *mea culpa*. Facts, please. Right. The lambent calendar, no warning, wheels to ache and pain, falling teeth, the rheum and the rheumatics. On cue, ushers – dulcet, undemanding – arrive from the shades. It's their season! Don't ask them for identification, you know – all you need to know. It is they who introduce you – for, odds on, the last time – to an old friend, Dove-Grey. In feisty fettle. Hasn't changed since the first sighting. While back. Hello.

Dove-Grey is bridled, saddled, game for the road. Thinking – 'Strange how patterned the briary world can be,' I climb aboard. No creak, *nota bene*, of joint, that infirmity dissolved. And we're off. Release. Morning. Journey. I feel light, could be feather-grass, pensive shadow of feather-grass. And I hear a silence I know. Dove-Grey's hooves are soundless. Likewise bit, bridle, saddle, stirrups. No sounds now except sound of this mother silence, inviolate, beckoning . . .

Finally. A word on daffodils, breath of daffodils. When, regal, she came with the bouquet (this was only last week), I was in bed. Alone. Waiting for her? Could be. I should never forget this meeting. Green of the stalks, gold of the blossoms. Her reach of gentleness. Was I up to the moment? Not at all. Being on the horizontal as recipient wasn't a help.

But I've no excuse, really, I've never been prepared for anything. Birth. Coupling. Separations. Next time round I may do better. Is there a next time? I don't know. Talk of it now and again.

Tell you about her? That she was a Queen, I knew, you know a Queen when you meet one. Such *puissance*. Style. Chic – I'd go so far as. She delivers the daffodils, and she's gone. I'm musing (it was December, as I write still is) – 'Daffodils – harbingers of Spring – come before the swallows' – and so on. But, as you may have noticed, I'm not content, best thing to be said for me, it's been remarked, an appetite for unease. Daffodils – I'm not easy. Have they a *sotto voce* tocsin? Look it up. The father comes into this, his presbyter thumb working the pages of dictionary or reference book, that's how I recall him. I find the book, flip pages – Daffodils: *Prosperina's flower, they grace the meadows of The Underworld. Word comes from the Greek 'asphodelus'. Etymology unknown* . . . Shook, I put the book aside. Now, ye boy ye. So it was She. Dear Goddess down below. Take pause, son. Listen for a silence. That silence. And it arrives, brimming embrace. Comes a moment you begin to long for it. Court it. Head bowed, name it home.

Water

COLM TÓIBÍN

On the Monday, when the others had gone to the hotel for soup and sandwiches, Fergus stayed alone with his mother's body in the funeral parlour. She would, he knew, have so far enjoyed her own funeral. The hush of conversation with old friends, the conjuring up of memories, the surprising arrival of people she would not have seen for years, all of this would have put a gleam into her eyes. But she would not, he thought, have enjoyed being alone now in the shadowy candlelight with her son, all the life gone out of her. She was not enjoying herself now, he thought.

He was tempted to whisper to her some words of comfort, to say that she would be all right, that she was at peace. He stood up and looked at her. Her dead face had none of her live face's softness. He hoped some day he would be able to forget what she looked like as she lay inert in her coffin, with faint traces of an old distress behind the mask of stillness and peace and immobility. The undertakers or the nurses who laid her out had made her chin seem firmer and more settled, almost pointed at the end with strange creases. If she spoke now, he knew, her old chin would come back, her old voice, her old smile. But that was all gone now; anyone seeing her for the first time would never know her. She was beyond knowing, he thought, and suddenly realised that he was going to cry.

When he heard the noise of feet outside, a man's heavy shoes against the concrete, he felt almost surprised that someone should come now to break his vigil with her. He had been sitting there as though the door were closed and he could not be disturbed.

The man who appeared was middle-aged and tall; he walked with a slight stoop. He had a mild, modest look; Fergus was sure that he had never seen him before. He paid no attention to Fergus as he moved towards the coffin, staring intently down into it, blessing himself, and then reaching down gently to touch the dead woman's forehead. He had the look of someone from the town, not a neighbour, Fergus felt, but someone she must have known years earlier. Being on display like this, being touched by anyone who came, would, he knew, have horrified his mother, but she had merely a few more hours of it before the coffin would be closed and taken to the cathedral.

The man sat down beside him, still watching his mother's face, gazing at it as though waiting for it to do something in the flickering candlelight. Fergus almost smiled to himself at the idea of telling the man that there was no point in looking at her so intensely, she was dead. Suddenly, the man turned to him as he blessed himself again and offered his large hand and his open-faced sympathy.

'I'm very sorry for your trouble,' he said.

'Thank you,' Fergus replied. 'It was very good of you to come.'

'She's very peaceful,' the man said.

'She is,' Fergus replied.

'She was a great lady,' the man said.

Fergus nodded. He knew that the man would now have to wait for at least ten minutes before he could decently go. He wished that he would introduce himself or give some clue about his identity. They sat in silence looking at the coffin.

As the time elapsed, it seemed odd to Fergus that no one else came. The others surely would have finished at the hotel; his mother's friends had come all morning, and some relatives. It made no sense that all of them had left this gap for Fergus and a stranger to sit so uneasily beside each other in a stretch of time that appeared to Fergus to belong to a dark dream which took them out of all familiar elements into a place of dim, shimmering lights, uncomfortable silence, the unending, dull and neutral realm of the dead. As the man cleared his throat, Fergus glanced at him and saw in his dry skin and his pale face further evidence that these minutes did not belong to ordinary time, that they both had been dragged away by his mother's spirit into a place of shadows.

'You were never a great hurler,' the man said quietly. His tone was friendly.

'That's right,' Fergus said.

'Conor was the hurler of the family,' the man said.

'He was good in his day all right,' Fergus said.

'Are you the brainy one?' the man asked.

'No,' Fergus smiled. 'That's Fiach. He's the youngest.'

'Your father,' the man began and hesitated. Fergus looked at him sharply.

'Your father taught me in school,' he continued.

'Is that right?'

'I was in the same class as George Mahon,' the man said. 'Do you see that dove on the wall there? George drew that.'

He pointed to the back wall of the funeral parlour.

'He was to make a big painting,' the man continued, 'when the place opened. That was just the drawing for it, a kind of preparation. He had to fill in the colours still.'

Fergus looked at the faint outlines in pencil on the wall behind the coffin, marks which seemed faded but clear enough to make out a dove, a few figures and perhaps a hill or a mountain in the distance.

'Why did he not finish it?' Fergus asked.

'Matt the undertaker's wife,' the man said, 'died suddenly a few weeks before he was ready to open this place and he had to decide whether to coffin her himself or give it to the other man, the main competition. So he did it himself, even though this place wasn't finished. It was fine, there was no problem with it, but the painting hadn't been done. And once Matt's wife had been laid out here, George Mahon said he wouldn't come back. He'd be too frightened, he said. The space was all ruined. Or so he said. He couldn't work. You'd never know what'd come up behind you, he said, when you'd be painting here.'

The man spoke in a monotone, staring at the coffin all the time. When Fergus looked away from him, he tried to picture his face, but he could not; his features seemed to fade as soon as Fergus turned. He would, Fergus realised, be hard to describe: tall, but not especially so; thin, but not very thin; his hair brown or sandy-coloured; the face was unremarkable and the voice disembodied. In the silence of the funeral parlour when the man had stopped talking, if someone were to whisper that this man had come to take away his mother's spirit, it would not have seemed strange. It was, for a few seconds, the most likely possibility that this visitor had suspended time to utter banalities and tell stories while all the time he was working to take Fergus's mother away so that all that was left of her to be buried was her spent and useless body.

Soon, however, when the man had left and the others come back, and some neighbours called, the spell was broken and the man's visit seemed ordinary, what was to be expected in a small town, not worth describing to the others, even though it had left its mark.

The next day, as they followed the coffin down the centre aisle of the cathedral towards the waiting hearse, Fergus kept his head down. He listened to the music, the last hymn to be sung for his mother, and tried not to think of the people, congregated on either side of the aisle, standing now, studying him and his sisters and brothers and his aunt as they walked slowly towards the main door. When he came to the last few rows, however, he looked around him and was surprised to see three friends from Dublin, from his life at the weekend and from a recent trip to Amsterdam, standing sombre-faced, as though they were ashamed of something, catching his eye now, but not smiling or even nodding at him in recognition. He had never seen them serious before; this must be how they had looked in school when they were in trouble, or during job interviews or when questioned at airports or stopped by the cops. He was tempted to whisper to them, ask laughingly if they had any drugs, but by the time he thought of this he was out in the open.

In the graveyard, his father's gravestone looked like history now, the carved dates already fading. The priest had set up a microphone and a stand at the other side of it. The early September sunshine made the day warm. There was no wind, but nonetheless, the whole scene seemed oddly windswept. He wondered why they did not grow trees in this graveyard, even evergreens. As the priest began to intone the prayers, Fergus noticed George Mahon the painter and decorator standing close to a gravestone in the distance. He was the only figure in the graveyard who did not come close to huddle in the crowd standing close to the grave. He was over six feet tall and was resting one of his elbows on the headstone. Fergus could feel, despite the distance, the power of his gaze, and could sense that George Mahon had drawn an invisible line in the graveyard which he would not cross. He was, as the man who had come to the funeral parlour explained, afraid of the dead. He had known Fergus's mother all of his life so he could not have easily stayed away, but his fear of coming close to the grave, his keen, distant study of the scene around the priest and the hearse and the coffin, the fierce independence of his stance, made Fergus shiver as the coffin was moved towards the open grave.

Afterwards, Fergus stood and shook hands with anyone who came, thanking them and trying to smile. He noticed that one of his sisters was crying. At the end of the line, shyly, stood Mick, Alan and Conal.

'The three musketeers,' he said.

'I'm sorry for your trouble, Fergus,' Mick said and shook his hand. He was wearing a jacket and tie. The other two approached and embraced him softly.

'I'm really sorry,' Alan said.

Conal held his hand and shook his head sadly.

'Will you come to the hotel for a bite?' Fergus asked.

'We'd love to, but we have to get back,' Mick smiled. 'When are you heading back to Dublin?' Mick asked.

'Thursday, I think,' Fergus said.

'Will you come around Thursday night, or give us a ring on my mobile?' Mick asked.

'OK, thanks, I'll do that,' Fergus replied.

On the night after the funeral, he and his siblings and his brother-in-law drank until four in the morning. Most of them stayed over the next night, promising each other that they would go to bed early, but over dinner they began to drink wine and then went on to beer and whiskey until there was nothing left but more wine, which Fergus and his sister and brother drank until the dawn had long appeared. He did not wake until the early afternoon. It was Thursday now and time to go back. He had planned all along to stop at the graveyard on the way out of the town and stand by his mother's grave and offer to her, or receive from her, some comfort, but he was tired and drained. All night they had laughed until there were no more funny stories left. He felt a strange guilt at her death as he drove past the graveyard, as though he were implicated in its cause. Rather than move closer to her, he needed to get away from her house, her grave, the days of her funeral. He drove directly to his house in Stoneybatter, dreaming that he would never go out again, but sleep once darkness was down and do this night after night.

As he was preparing for bed, the phone rang. It was Mick.

'It doesn't matter about tonight,' he said. 'It matters about tomorrow night. We have something special for you. The lads are coming. It's a beach rave.'

'No,' Fergus said. 'I'm not coming.'

'You have to come,' Mick said.

'I'm too old for techno,' Fergus said. 'Actually, I take that back. Techno is too boring for me. And I hate beaches.'

'This is special. I said it was special. Bring two warm pullovers and a big towel.'

'No.'

'Nine o'clock at my place. I'm driving. If it's boring I'll leave with you. But please come.'

'Nine?' Fergus asked and laughed for a moment.

'Nine sharp,' Mick replied.

'And we can stay for half an hour?'

'It'll be nine in the morning and you won't want to leave,' Mick said.

They set out from the city when night had fallen. It was warm as they drove north; they kept the windows open until Alan lit a joint and then they closed them so they could enjoy wallowing in the smoke. Already, in Mick's flat, they had each snorted a line of cocaine, which had made Fergus feel sharp and nervous, and strangely lucid. He pulled on the joint suddenly with all his energy, taking too much smoke in, and then concentrating on holding it, relishing the taste and the power as he closed his eyes; he felt almost faint. He put his head back as a thrill of weakness coursed through him. He was ready to sleep, but it was a readiness which came with darting thoughts which led nowhere. He tried to relax in the back of the car, enjoying the battle going on between the golden lethargy which the dope brought with the sweet electric shock of the cocaine.

'You know something?' Alan said. 'I felt so bad after your old lady's funeral that I decided I was neglecting mine. So I bought her flowers and went out to see her.'

'A small step for mankind,' Conal said.

'I should have phoned her first,' Alan said, 'but she's no good on the phone; she treats it like it was a poisonous snake.'

'How long was it since you'd seen her?' Mick asked.

'June,' Alan continued. 'And the time before that was February and she kept nagging at me about it and I said: "Well, I'm here now," as though that would make up for everything. And she nearly bit me. She kept saying: "That's all very well." She gets very bitter.'

'Is that why you are so sweet?' Mick asked.

'So I turn up with the flowers and there's no one there and Miss Bitch next door appears in her apron and shouts at me that I am not getting the key. "And your mother's in Italy," she adds. "And on a beach, if you don't mind, one of the trendy places, with oul' Mrs Kingston, buying up property the two of them, or new earrings." '

'What did you do with the flowers?' Mick asked.

'I fucked them into the bin beside the bus stop.'

'Jesus,' Conal said. 'Maybe we shouldn't be talking like this in front of Fergus. Are you all right, Fergus?'

'I'm fine,' Fergus said. He had his head back and his eyes closed.

'There'll be more white powder when we get there,' Mick said. 'Don't worry.'

'I'm ready for bed,' Fergus said. 'When I was a kid I used to love staying in the car while the rest of them went down to the strand.'

'Well, you've grown up now,' Mick said.

Mick drove slowly, once he was off the main road. Fergus guessed that they were somewhere between Drogheda and Dundalk but heading directly towards the coast, or driving parallel to it. He noticed that Mick had difficulty seeing in front of him because of patches of thick fog which appeared at intervals. He stopped several times and switched on the dim overhead light so he could consult a page of elaborate directions.

'We're very near now, but I have instructions not to ask for directions from anyone or behave suspiciously,' Mick said. 'I'm looking for a second bungalow on the right and then I have to turn down a narrow, sandy lane.'

'Are you sure someone is not making a complete eejit out of you?' Alan asked.

'Yeah, I am. It's the same crowd who did the last one. They're sound.'

He stopped at the second bungalow and got out of the car to check in the fog that there was a lane to the right.

'We're here,' he said. 'One mile down this and we park.'

Briars and brambles hit against the body of the car as they moved slowly along the narrow lane, so rutted that a few times something sharp seemed to cut through the underbelly of the car and Mick was almost forced to stop. They were silent as though frightened as the car rocked from side to side more than it seemed to move forward. When the lane ended, Mick opened the window and they could hear the roar of the sea. He parked the car close to a number of others. Once they opened the doors and stood out in the foggy night the sound of electronic music came clearly towards them from the distance.

'We should have a snort here in the car so the wind won't blow it away,' Mick said.

He sat back into the car, closing the doors and the windows, and laid out the lines neatly on the surface of a CD cover. Fergus noticed that there was a mild, warm wind coming in from the sea, like a summer wind, even though the summer just ended had offered nothing but low cloudy skies and constant rain. Having waited his turn to snort the cocaine, using a fifty-euro note which Mick recommended, he relished the sour taste of the powder as it made its way towards the back of his throat. He swallowed hard so that he could taste it better and then, since he was the last, he put his finger on the CD cover to absorb any stray grains of white powder; he rubbed them into his gums.

In a hold-all, they carried pullovers and towels, bottles of water and cans of beer, and a bottle of tequila. They stood watching as a set of headlights appeared and a car approached and parked and six or seven dazed figures emerged from it. Mick lit a joint and passed it around.

'We're not too early and we're not too late,' he said.

Mick, with the help of a torch, guided them along a headland towards the music, which came from a sheltered cove, down a set of steep stone steps from a field which they had crossed.

'The music is boring,' Fergus whispered to Mick.

Mick handed him the joint again. He pulled on it twice and then handed it back.

'I want you to close your eyes and open your mouth,' Mick said when they had reached the cove. He shone the torch into Fergus's face as Alan and Conal stood by laughing. Fergus saw Mick biting a tablet in two; as he closed his eyes, Mick put one half on his tongue.

'Swallow that,' he said. 'It's what doctors recommend for boredom.'

The organisers must have been working all day, Fergus thought, as soon as he saw the lights and the generators and the powerful speakers and decks. They had set up an elaborate, instant disco in the cove, with throbbing lights and loud techno, but far away enough from the nearest house or road, that if they were lucky they would remain undisturbed all through the night. It was still early, he knew, and even though the Ecstasy tablet had not begun to affect him, the cocaine, the dope and the fresh sea air made him suddenly exhilarated, ready for a night which would not end, as nights in the city invariably ended, with bouncers shouting and places closing too early and no taxis in the city centre and nowhere to go save home.

As they joined the crowd, leaving their belongings in a safe place in the darkness, about thirty people were dancing. Some of them looked like friends who had travelled together, or maybe they had just become friends, Fergus thought, as they co-ordinated their movements while also remaining tightly apart from each other.

He stood at the edge of the dancers sipping from a can of beer which Mick had handed him, aware that he was being watched by a tall, skinny, black-haired guy who was dancing to a beat of his own invention, pointing at the sky with the index finger of his right hand and then pointing at Fergus and smiling. He was glad that he had spent so much time among straight people to know that the dancer had taken Ecstasy; he was happy and was smiling to display this. It was not a come-on, even though it could seem like one; there was no sexual content in what he was doing. He was like a child. Fergus pointed his finger at him to the stark dull rhythm of the music and smiled back.

He noticed that his nose and chin were tingling with pins and needles as the Ecstasy coursed through his body with its message of support. He began to dance, noticing Mick and Alan and Conal dancing close by. He was pleased that they were beside him, but he felt no need to look at them or speak to them, or even smile at them. Whatever was happening now with the drugs and the night and the tinny piercing sounds as the tempo rose and the volume was turned up meant that he was wholly connected to them, a part of the group they had formed. He would need only to feel that and a golden rush of warmth went through him and he hoped that he might stay like that until the dawn and maybe after the dawn into the next day.

When he and Mick had shared another tablet and drunk some water and smoked a joint together, the music, in all its monotony and strange, almost imperceptible variation in register, began to interest Fergus, pull him towards it with a greater force than the faces or the bodies around him. He listened out for changes in tone and beat, following the track of the music with the cool energy which the night, as it wore on, offered him. Nonetheless, he kept close to the others and they to him, pushing against each other sometimes in mock aggression, dancing in strange and suddenly invented harmonies, smiling at each other, or touching each other in reassurance, before moving easily away, dancing alone in the surging crowd.

Mick was in control, deciding when joints would be lit, more pills taken, beer sipped, water swigged, or when all four of them should retreat from the crowd, lie on their towels on the sand smoking, laughing, barely talking, knowing that there would be much more time to dance, and that this was a small respite which Mick thought they would need from the shifting beauty of the music and the dancers.

All night they moved around each other, as though they were guarding something deeply playful and wonderful that would fade if they ceased to remain close to each other. Fergus could feel the sand in his hair and embedded in the sweat down his back, and in his trainers. Sometimes, he felt tired, and then it seemed that the tiredness itself was impelling him, allowing him to move with the music, and smile and close his eyes and hope that time was passing slowly, that this cocoon of energy had been left alone for the moment, and could enclose him and keep him safe against the night.

It seemed hours later when Mick took him aside and made him move away from the lights and showed him the first stirrings of the dawn in the horizon over the sea. It resembled grey and white smoke in the distance, no redness or real sign of the sun. It looked more like fading light than the break of day. As they moved back among the dancers, they knew that it would be an hour or more before the frantically flickering lights which made the music more exciting would mean nothing against the light of day.

As the first rays of sun hit the strand, the light remained grey and uneasy as though it were building up for a day of low clouds and rain. Suddenly, they were shivering; they moved over to where they had left the pullovers and towels and began to swig from the tequila bottle. At first it tasted like poison.

'This is rich in toxic energy,' Fergus said. Alan fell down on the soft sand in laughter.

'You sound like God the Father, or Einstein,' Conal added.

Mick was folding the towels in the hold-all, and checking to make sure that they had left no litter.

'I've got bad news,' he said. 'We're going for a swim.'

'Ah Jesus!' Alan said.

'I'm on for it,' Conal said, standing up and stretching. 'Come on, Alan, it'll make a man of you.'

He helped Alan to his feet.

'I've no togs,' Alan said.

'And no clean underpants either, I bet.'

Mick handed Fergus the bottle of tequila, which they drank from as they walked away from the last ravers to a point at the far end of the cove, where there was nobody. Mick left down the hold-all, took out a towel and began to undress. He handed an Ecstasy tablet to Alan and Conal.

'This will warm you up,' he said.

He bit on another and handed half of it to Fergus, who was suddenly aware of Mick's saliva on the jagged edge of the pill he put into his mouth and sharply alert to the afterglow of the long hours when they had been sharing the touching and staying close. He stood on the strand watching Mick until he was naked, realising with a gasp that Mick was going naked into the water.

'Last in is Charlie Haughey,' he shouted as he moved towards the edge of the sea.

In the strange, inhospitable half-light, his body seemed oddly and powerfully awkward, his skin blotchy and white. Soon, Alan followed him, also naked, skinnier, shivering, dancing up and down to keep the cold at bay. Conal wore his underpants as he moved gingerly towards the water. Fergus slowly undressed, shivering too, watching uneasily as the others shrieked at the cold water, jumping to avoid each wave until the look of them there began to interest him. Mick and Conal chose the same moment to dive under an incoming wave.

As soon as his feet touched the water, Fergus stepped back. He watched the other three cavorting further out, swimming with energy and abandon, letting themselves be pulled inwards by the waves, and then diving under as though the water itself were a refuge from the cold. This, he thought, as he wrapped his arms around his body to keep warm, and allowed his teeth to chatter, was going to be an ordeal, but he could not return to the strand and dress himself now; he would have to be brave and join the others, who showed no sign of coming back to dry land as they beckoned him not to be a baby.

He made himself think for a moment that he was nobody and nothing, that he had no feelings, that nothing could hurt him as he waded into the water. He crashed into a wave as it came towards him and then dived under it and did a breaststroke out towards his friends. His mother, he remembered, had always been so brave in the water, never hesitating at the edge for a single second, always marching determinedly into the cold sea. She would not have been proud of him now, he thought, as he battled with the idea that he had wet himself enough and could run back quickly to the strand and dry himself. He dismissed the idea, tried to stay under the water and move blindly, thrashing about as much as he could to keep warm. When he reached his friends, they laughed and put their arms around him and then began an elaborate horseplay in the water which made him forget about the cold.

When Alan and Conal waded in towards the shore, Mick stayed behind with Fergus, who was oblivious enough now to the cold that he could spread his arms out and float, staring up at the sky growing lighter. Mick did not move far from him, but after a while urged him to swim out further to a sandbank where the waves made no difference and it was easy to float and stand and float again. As they swam out they kept close and hit against each other casually a few times, but when they found the bank Fergus felt Mick touching him deliberately, putting his hand on his arse and keeping it there. Fergus felt his own cock stiffen. When Mick moved away he floated on his back, too happy in the water to care if Mick saw his erection, being certain that Mick would swim back towards him before long.

He did not move or even open his eyes when Mick swam in between his legs and held his cock, putting the other hand under him. When he tried to stand, he realised that Mick was holding him, trying to enter him with the index finger of his right hand, pushing and probing until he was deep inside. Fergus winced and put his arms around Mick's neck, moving his mouth towards Mick's until Mick began to kiss him fiercely, biting his tongue and lips as he stood on the sandbank. When Fergus reached down, he could feel Mick's cock, hard and rubbery in the water. He smiled, almost laughed, at the thought of how difficult it would be to suck a cock under water.

'I have sort of wanted to do this,' Mick said, 'but just once. Is that all right?'

Fergus laughed and kissed him again. As Mick worked on his cock with his hand, he tried to ease a second finger into him and Fergus cried out but did not pull away. He spread his legs as wide as he could, letting the second finger into him slowly, breathing deeply so that he could open himself more. He held his two arms around Mick's neck and put his head back, closing his eyes against the pain and the thrill it gave. In the half-light of morning he began to touch Mick's face, feeling the bones, sensing the skull behind the skin and the flesh, the elemental thing which made him different to no one, the eye sockets, the cheekbones, the jaw bone, the forehead, the inert solidity of teeth, the tongue that would dry up and rot so easily, the dead hair.

Mick was not masturbating him now, but putting all his energy into his two fingers, moving them in and out roughly. He touched Mick's cock, his hips, his back, his balls; he put his energy, all of it, all of his drug-lined grief and pure excitement, into taking Mick's tongue in his mouth, holding it there, offering his tongue in return, tasting his friend's saliva, his breath, his feral self. He realised that neither of them wanted to ejaculate; it would, somehow, be a defeat, the end of something, but neither could they decide to stop, even though both of them were shivering with the cold. Fergus became slowly aware that Alan and Conal were standing on the strand watching their every move. When they began to wade in towards the shore, Alan and Conal turned away nonchalantly.

By the time they were all dressed and ready to walk back towards the car, the day had dawned. They passed the organisers taking the machinery of the previous night asunder, working with speed and efficiency.

'How do they make their money?' Alan asked.

'They make it on other nights,' Mick said, 'but they do this out of love.'

Mick had to reverse the car without any passengers so that the wheels would not get stuck in the sand. When he had the car turned, Fergus sat in the front passenger seat and the two others in the back. They rocked silently along the lane, the brambles on either side laden with blackberries. Fergus remembered some road out of his town, empty of traffic, with tall trees in the distance, and each of them, his brother and sisters and his mother, with colanders or an old saucepan gathering blackberries from the bushes in the ditches, his mother the most assiduous, the busiest, filling colander after colander into the red bucket in the back seat of the old Morris Minor.

As they made their way from a side road towards the main Dublin road, Fergus realised that he could not face the day alone. He was not sleepy, although he was tired, but he was, more than anything, restless and excited. The taste from Mick's mouth, the weight of him in the water, the feel of his skin, the sense of his excitement, had allied themselves now with the remnants of the drugs and the tequila to make him want Mick again, want him alone in a bedroom, with clean sheets and a closed door. He regretted that he had not come off in the sea, and was sorry too that he had not made Mick come off with him. Their sperm mingling with the salt water and the slime and the sand would have put an end to his yearnings, for a time at least. He knew that his house was the first stop as they entered the city; he wished he could turn to Mick, without the two in the back overhearing, and ask him to stay in his house for a while.

When Alan asked Mick to stop the car, announcing that he was going to be sick, and Mick pulled in on the hard shoulder of the dual carriageway, they watched him without comment as he heaved and vomited, listening calmly to the retching sounds. Fergus thought then that it might be a good moment to mention to Mick that he could not go home alone.

'Conal, why don't you go and help him?' he asked.

'He always pukes,' Conal said. 'It's genetic, he says. There's nothing I can do for him. He's a wimp. His father and mother were wimps too. Or so he says, anyway.'

'Did they go to raves?' Mick asked.

'Whatever it was in their day,' Conal replied. 'Dances, I suppose, or hops.'

Alan, much chastened and very pale, got back into the car. Since there was no traffic, Fergus knew that he would be home in half an hour. He would have no chance now to tell Mick what he wanted. He could try later on the phone, but this would be a day when Mick might not answer the phone. His own fierce need might have abated by then in any case, become dull sadness and disappointment.

His small house, when he came in the door, seemed to have been hollowed out from something, the air inside it felt trapped, specially filtered to a sort of thinness. The sun was shining through the front window so he went immediately to close the curtains, creating the pretence that it was still the early morning. He thought of putting music on the CD player, but no music would please him now, just as alcohol would not help and sleep would not come. He felt then that he could walk a hundred miles if he had somewhere to go, some clear destination. He was afraid of nothing now save that this feeling would never fade. His heart was beating in immense dissatisfaction at how life was; the echo of the music in his ears and the aftershine of the flashing lights in his eyes were still with him. He felt as though he had been ready to grasp something about energy and time, make some great calculation, but the formula evaded him. He had been brushed by the wings of some sudden and sharp knowledge, some fierce and mysterious emotion equal to events that had occurred over the past week. He lay on the sofa, dazed and beaten by his failure to grasp what had been offered to him, and fell into a stupor rather than a sleep.

He did not know how much time had passed when someone banged the knocker on the front door. His bones ached as he stood up to answer it. He had forgotten what he had wanted so badly in the car, but as soon as he saw Mick, who looked as though he had gone home and showered and changed his clothes, he remembered. Mick had a bag of groceries in his hand.

'I'm not coming in unless you promise that you'll wash all that sand out of every orifice,' Mick said.

'I promise,' Fergus said.

'Immediately,' Mick insisted.

'OK.'

'I'll make breakfast,' Mick said.

Fergus deliberately turned the hot-water tap on too high to see if this could restore him to the state of excitement he had been in. He washed and shaved carefully and found fresh clothes. Quickly, he changed the sheets and the duvet on his bed. When he came downstairs the table was set; there was steaming tea and scrambled eggs and toast and orange juice. They ate and drank ravenously, without speaking.

'I would have bought the morning papers,' Mick said, 'except I can barely see.'

Fergus wondered how quickly he could move Mick to the bedroom once breakfast was finished. He smiled at him and nodded in the direction of upstairs.

'Are you ready so?' he asked.

'I am, I suppose, but I haven't been converted or anything. Just once, OK?'

'You said that before.'

'I was drugged. I mean it this time.'

Mick took out a small plastic bag from his pocket and pushed back the tablecloth to the bare wood of the table. With his credit card he began to make two long orderly lines of cocaine. He took a fifty-euro note from his pocket.

'Which of us goes first?' he asked and grinned.

A Way of Making Sure

DERMOT SOMERS

'You shouldn't be here,' she whispered. 'I asked you not to come.'

Valerie sank back into the pillows, black hair loose about her face. When John stooped to kiss her, he saw unconcealed grey for the first time. There were shadows all around her eyes; her skin seemed lined and terribly pale.

He would remember this parting. The hot surge turned to ice in his blood and he knew the occasion was spent before it occurred. Time did not pretend; it guttered in the open like a flame.

Their relationship had been brief. Two years. Something had ignited in them whenever they came together. More than static or the spark of friction, it was a private lightning that shocked and incited them. It would not have existed without her marriage. Burrowing into each other in secret, they illuminated the moment with a flash that scorched the nerves. Afterwards, reality was lit by the memory, and also paled by it, the way addiction sears and blurs at the same time. Neither had known extremes before; neither was a likely lover.

Everything in the hospital room blanched as she turned her head away. The autumn blossoms in a vase were no longer flowers; they were a pale fanfare against the slatted blinds that broke the light into black and white stripes.

'I'm not going.' John shook his head.

'Yes, you are. Don't make it harder than it has to be . . .'

'It can't be any harder. I love you.'

'It's a bit late for all that now.' Sentiment scraped away.

'I don't exist anywhere else, Val.'

'But I do, John. I have to.'

He was numbed with loss, every word a blow. 'I can't leave. It's not possible . . .'

'You have to. He'd know. It's written all over you.'

'All I want is to be here. In the background. At the end of a phone. You don't have to call – but you'll know you can.'

She smiled, stretching dry lips. 'That's what has us where we are . . .' As if he had left, she drifted away.

'John . . .' She reached for his hand a little later, smoothed the sheet instead with agitated strokes. 'I don't want them to know. That means more than anything you can imagine. If you don't go – if you stay around – it'll be obvious. You couldn't hide it. Look at you now!' She was almost contemptuous.

When the worst came to the worst, levity flickered in him. 'I could wear dark glasses . . .'

'You will! Where you're going you'll need them!'

One foot in front of the other. Breath harsh. Lungs strangled. He halted, slumped, boot propped on a stone, both hands braced on one knee. He heard his heart strain like a piledriver toiling to root his legs in the ground before they sprinted again.

If I opened my eyes here, after a coma, would I know where I was? – he played the familiar game. The rugged track, the porter in flip-flops, the river in the ravine, the smell of scorched dust, could be nowhere but Nepal. A bead of sweat formed on his upper lip. If he smeared it away with his slick hand, brushed it with his sleeve, the salt-rub would burn his mouth, invite a cold sore; he blew it off at intervals with a jet of breath he could ill afford. When she broke into his thoughts, prompted by flowers, a tree, water trickling, he speeded up until the pressure in his chest crushed the intrusion. He would keep that up for as long as it took.

Measured steps behind him; steady plod, tap and rattle, stick on stone. 'Take it easy, John. We've all day.' Richard stopped on a lower rock. Tactful. He wouldn't pass just to make a point about fitness. Alan, however, skipped ahead of them both. 'All day?' he barked in cheery tones, '– we've the rest of our lives!'

'That's the trouble.' John whispered. The raw panting had eased. He unlocked his limbs, prepared to shunt upwards. Richard drew alongside.

'I remember you saying,' he remarked, 'that the best thing about being away was the pleasure of living in the present.'

Richard was the most earnestly British of John's friends; yet he was the one most immediately at home abroad. His skin darkened quickly. The endless walking – the pilgrim rhythm – suited him. If he were stripped of the khaki shorts, the tartan shirts, dressed instead in saffron and maroon, with his wire-rimmed glasses he would pass for a monk.

'That wasn't me. You said it. No one else talks like that.'

'Did I really?' Richard wondered. 'Well, you agreed.'

'No I didn't. We were starving.'

'Nothing a boiled egg wouldn't cure. We were in great shape otherwise.' Regret in Richard's voice. 'That was the best trip ever.' Four days out on the present journey, he was disappointed already.

A nauseous belch in John's throat threatened Giardia: but he knew it was the dried-up omelette for breakfast, the gassy Coke on top of it.

'Don't mention eggs,' he grumbled.

Breath rasping again, he felt rather than heard the quiet steps continuing behind. Richard was the one who kept them together, over fifteen or twenty years. Ambitious treks, small expeditions. People had come and gone. John was on every trip but one. Greg and Alan, both from Sheffield, were regulars, since the hungry journey Richard mentioned.

John went with them out of habit, he thought now. Perhaps he lacked the imagination to invent something new for himself. He was the only professional climber among them, working at a modest level in the outdoor-pursuits world. Even while he was married, he had gone away twice with Richard, flying from Dublin to join the trip at Heathrow. The marriage had been difficult; as if in deference to it, Richard had organised their travels at longer intervals.

John recalled, at every view, how they had once hurtled around the trail they were trudging now – the Annapurna Circuit, the loop of valleys around one of the great Himalayan massifs. They'd been single, fit, young enough to care about nothing else; the trail was uncrowded then. They had left it at intervals for side-valleys and ridges, with remote base camps. They climbed two peaks in the Chulus and were not content to stroll over the Thorong Pass at 17,000 feet, while the trekkers slowed and sickened, but they ascended the mountain above the pass, reaching 20,000 feet again and were hungry for further height, as if Annapurna itself, at 25,500 feet, huge in the near distance, could have been their destiny if they chose.

Alan had caught up with Greg ahead. They surged along together, battered rucksacks on broad shoulders carried with accustomed ease. They would make the best of this trip, though their patience with John was running out. Rugged shorts, thermal tops for T-shirts, sturdy thighs and calves, they were skidding towards middle age in every opinion but their own. Anyone with an eye for an expedition could see how things were shaping up after a few uneasy days out. Instead of a close group of four, with patterns shifting according to fitness, there would be two distinct pairs on Singu Chuli, the mountain they had booked on the rim of the Annapurna cirque. Richard was being supportive; he would stick with his partner, despite John's silence and his lack of enthusiasm.

They halted to greet three girls they knew, who were seated at a sunny table by a stone-built tea house. There was a picket fence and an elaborate lunch menu. Stone-walled fields of barley curved down to a calm bend on the river. The sun lay on the yellow corn, time swayed and settled in polished coils; motion seemed irrational, ripening was the only course.

Alan and Greg both worked in Social Services; they had the affability of older brothers on holiday, content with themselves. They slumped cheerfully into chairs, unfazed by their own practical flesh and sweat.

'We saw your porters,' the New Zealand girls teased. 'Why don't you guys carry your own stuff? Call yourselves mountaineers!'

'We thought of that –' Alan flexed a powerful thigh. 'We thought of it, but those guys need the practice.'

'That's right,' Greg assured; 'we're carrying enough weight already.' He pinched his comfortable midriff.

John leaned quietly on the fence by Richard's side, recovering.

'You're Irish, aren't you?' one of the girls scolded. 'You couldn't support this system . . .'

'He's worse than we are,' Richard said. 'He's trying to beat their rates down.'

'No,' John interrupted. 'I'm trying to undercut them. Take the work myself.' He was elated, a sudden mood-swing. The grin stuck to his face like a silly mask. He turned away, gazed down at the river. A single laugh and he felt giddy, tipsy, like the first time he drank alcohol.

There was no shortage of distraction on the trail. They overtook trekkers at every turn, shared lodges with them at night. There was a constant surge of people coming down, trail-hardened, burned and lined with twenty days' exposure to sun and wind on the broad trails of the Annapurna Circuit. Soon, the climbers would leave the main route and head into the Sanctuary, an inner ring of peaks and ridges.

The New Zealanders had discovered that Richard's wife didn't like mountains; she found trekking boring. 'Good for her,' they enthused, '– she knows her own mind.'

According to Richard she went to Spain instead and lay on beaches with her friends. 'I went once,' he admitted, through a mouthful of fried rice, 'but I haven't got the right attitude.'

'Oh! What is the right attitude?'

'Horizontal, I suppose.' His round face was serene. Looking at him, John envied his independence. He excused himself from the company in case the attention turned to him. The parting was still raw as an amputation.

He still hadn't told the others; not even Richard. Secrecy had conditioned him to silence. He felt strangely ashamed. She had two young children, and a husband who loved her.

He had known Valerie for ten or twelve years – long before she had married. She was a friend of friends. She came walking sometimes over the New Year when a group took a house in Kerry. Tall, elegant rather than pretty, she was serious, slightly aloof. He had always found intelligence attractive. It even had a sexual charge.

The custom was to walk the mountains every day in various groups, regardless of the weather. He fell into her company on the Faha Ridge on Brandon, on a windy New Year's Eve, in a group of four. The other pair were fast. He intended it to happen, although the attraction he felt was little more than curiosity. Ann, his wife, was on a different mountain. At the foot of the ridge, there was a shower and they sheltered in the Grotto with Saint Brendan, Saint Patrick, and the Blessed Virgin. There was cloud on the shoulder of the ridge but the forecast was for a clearance.

'Are you sure this is OK?' she said. 'Tell me now if it isn't.' She was keen on the ridge, but she wouldn't overestimate herself.

'You'll be fine. Today is the day.'

'I don't want to hold anybody back.'

'You won't. We're not out to break records. I mean – we couldn't anyway.' He floundered. 'That's not what it's about –' Her face took on a watchful repose when he spoke, a sense of warmth withheld, as if she were unconvinced. When she smiled, he scrambled for the correct response. There was an instant to get it right, the instant passed – she chatted, glanced away. It was a feeling he remembered, picking up four promising cards, staring at the back of the fifth, face down on the table.

She'd been involved in sport: basketball, hockey. There was a man in Germany; whether he was Irish or German, or even a boyfriend, John wasn't sure. Ann, his wife, didn't know much either, though she approved of what she knew. Valerie taught Gender Studies. Equality issues. John's friends kept their heads down in the evenings; there was a kind of combative fellowship among the women. Valerie did nothing to heighten it, but she seemed to provide a quiet focus. There was no gossip about her. That was a sign of status.

On the Faha Ridge the other two had moved ahead. Part way up, before the broad slope narrowed, John steered her to a huge stone rampart that lay in ruins. He was tempted to expound but he held his tongue, brought her to the entrance, pointed out the second wall above. Massive blocks of purple sandstone were built in concentric arcs high on this ridge of Brandon, a southwesterly mountain, surrounded by sea. Among the many outcrops and the tumbled rocks on the shoulder, it was possible to pass without noticing. He stood gazing back the way they had come. Ann was with friends behind Beenbo to the north. They were probably in the valley, tracing the old settlements all the way up to the ridge behind.

'This must be the *Lughnasa* site?'

The information startled him. People were usually surprised at the scale of construction, but the purpose went over their heads. 'Yes it is. How did you know?'

'I've seen it from below. It looks extraordinary from a distance.'

'When you know what to look for. A lot of people see nothing at all.'

'You make it sound like the man in the moon. I'm trying to imagine the ridge with bonfires and processions and Druids celebrating the harvest.'

'Do you want me to dance around a bit and howl?'

'Not really. Save it for the party tonight.'

'It's the perfect place to worship light, isn't it?' he enthused. 'Especially now, we're so close to the solstice. This was the last place in Europe to see the setting sun. The rim of the other world . . .' The way he would talk to Ann.

Valerie scanned the narrowing ridge, prepared to move on. 'I don't know about the other world,' she said briskly, 'but it's certainly the rim of this one.'

Of course she was terrific on the Faha Ridge, surefooted on steep rock and wet vegetation. A trained mountaineer, John hovered discreetly, but he was so determined not to patronise that he would have been useless if she slipped. Shafts of sunlight struck through the clouds, turning dark slabs in the corrie to sudden silver, then the light was lost again and the mountain smouldered in sullen mist. At any moment, John knew, the cloud might melt into a rainbow – or a Brocken Spectre, a halo of colour cast on the seething mist below. But it didn't. The fifth card, this time, was dull.

That evening, when he talked to Ann about the walk he felt no need to hide how impressed he was. He wouldn't be teased or suspected. It was OK to admire Valerie; it reflected well on everybody.

She attended climbing lectures, usually alone. Once, she made a self-deprecating comment that stayed in his mind. 'My friends think I'm really odd to be so interested in mountaineering . . .' followed by a little laugh.

Oh, he thought, so *we're* not your friends. And then he thought: you're not really interested in mountains, are you? It's just occasional . . . The odd thing was that he remembered things like that so clearly, and yet – when he scanned a crowd – he had no image in his head; he could not have described her till he saw her black hair and tall figure with a flash of recognition, as if she had appeared from somewhere that wasn't quite memory.

He gave a talk himself on a climbing trip one winter. He put a lot of effort into it. She had to leave early. He was disappointed, snubbed, but he couldn't hint at such a possessive feeling.

Next Christmas she appeared in Kerry. He made no attempt to spend time with her. Things were not going well between himself and Ann. They tried to conceal it in public, though it was obvious by then. People were tactful and pleasant and made them feel easier in each other's company, but it was too late.

He was six months separated when Valerie married. A private wedding, held in Rome. John was still too numb to be shocked by things that didn't involve him. He met her with her husband, shopping on Grafton Street. Only the Brown Thomas bags connected them. He was a doctor – plump, self-important, older than his wife and shorter by several inches. She seemed inclined to stoop to disguise the difference. There was no time for a cup of coffee, they were late for an appointment. She walked away, her husband strutting beside her, and John turned to look. He realised her reserve had nothing at all to do with high standards and he sensed how lonely she must have been.

John recognised mountain-mode as soon as he stepped into it again. When the torch beam tightened, settled on the snow, life focused to a single act of attention. Physical presence only; feet numb, boots stiff and heavy, handfuls of cold, lungs gagging on black air. The old exhilaration was gone.

Night hadn't changed with the years; dark hadn't turned from iron to silk, the rock hadn't mellowed, snow still scumbled on stone, ice creaked like ancient wheels.

But the feeling had muted, tempered; there was no panic these days – neither fear nor exaltation. He had learned to wait, to pace the approach, find the rhythm that shuffled the parts together. He was hooded, cowled like an old monk working a ritual that would reach the dawn by endurance, and the next night as the night before he would do the same whether the ground steepened, broke into waves, or fell away . . .

But a half an hour of movement set the blood flowing, the misery abated and it was no worse than work. Snowy rock gave way to ice. Alan and Greg worked at the edge, torches probing, merging, glancing off rucksacks and frosted jackets. The banality of the norm; 'Looks like crampons, gentlemen.'

'Change is as good as a rest . . .'

'This is as far as I came yesterday,' Richard called. 'It's glacier from here on.'

'Didn't see your footprints on the snow.'

'I levitated.'

Crampons clamped and strapped. The balance changed. Feet gripped the surface, clawed the slow ice.

John pushed back a sleeve, pawed the glove forward.

Three-thirty a.m. The display blinked in the dark with manic certainty.

'Would you like to rope up?' Richard, cautious as always. John was carrying the rope. Ahead, Greg and Alan had another. One rope would do all four on the straightforward snow ridge ahead – Tent Peak, a warm-up climb on the fringe of the Sanctuary. They would climb and descend together. A steepish step low down to gain the ridge, a few hundred feet in the guidebook. No problem going up on frozen snow, but that would be slush on the way down, mid-morning. They would leave the second rope above the step now, and abseil double-quick in descent. There was a sense of co-ordination, experience, satisfaction.

They had outgrown ambition over the years. Tent Peak was about 18,500 feet; Singu Chuli, their real objective further to the left, was a couple of thousand feet higher. Both peaks were dwarfed by the bulk of Annapurna. Tied in quickly, his fingers warm, John waited. He was the quickest with ropes, tools, techniques – only because it was his job as a mountain instructor. When it came to ability he had no particular edge. They were all competent, no one exceptional. The capacity to work together often outclassed talent and they had built up together a solid record of minor ascents.

John switched off his headtorch, tilted his head. His neck muscles creaked. The night sparked with electric stars. He followed them down the sky till they went out along the black intrusion of the mountain, Tent Peak. The shape seemed to glow dully in the dark, like remembered ivory. Everywhere in the night ice shifted and settled in the grip of frost and gravity. Thin air splintered against his teeth, his eyes bore the weight of the darkness and the streaming stars. The alertness of broken sleep buzzed in his head . . . Once again he felt the rustle of the planet moving through space . . .

Voices murmured behind him, and a shaft of loneliness, unbearably pure, pierced his soul. She was gone. He rocked in sudden dizziness, his bearings lost, groped for the brightest star, locked his eyes upon it and made a wish. It was the closest he would come to prayer.

They were back at the High Camp in the afternoon. One large dome-tent and Nima's cocoon, set on snowy moraine. The humped ridge of Tent Peak, now that they had climbed it, looked tame and low. Away in the distance, Singu Chuli – also known as Fluted Peak – was a finely pointed arrowhead approached by a complex ridge. That approach, they now knew, was out: bulging with soft, impassable snow. They were in the wrong place for an ascent.

Nima was cooking. His job as *sirdar* was to organise porters, loads, camp sites; he didn't climb. This morning, he had scouted low around the shoulder they were camped on, searching out another approach to Fluted Peak. According to the map and guidebook, a hidden valley led up to the rear of the mountain – the South Face. If they could traverse from their present position they might gain the glacier at the head of the valley, a major short cut. Otherwise, they would have to take the long way down and round to the bottom of that hidden valley, losing several days they could not afford.

'Yes, you can go round,' he told them. 'Porters, no. Not possible.' He gave further vague information in his defensive style and returned to the hissing stoves. There were so many expeditions now that Sherpas of little or no experience were setting up as guides. It was obvious that Nima didn't know; he was keeping his options open.

Richard weighed up the position. 'It's a gamble. I'm sure it's possible to reach the South Face that way.' Richard's smooth-skinned, sallow face, his rounded cheeks, persuasive manner, seemed more Sherpa-like than Nima. The others, burnt and stubbled, were classic Westerners.

'Don't forget the altitude,' John warned. 'It's a lot higher than we've been today.'

'We know!' Alan snorted, 'Tell us something new. We'll save at least two days. We've lost too much time already.'

'If we traverse, we'll be dropping down a bit anyway,' Greg reasoned. 'That'll help with the acclimatisation.'

'No, it won't.' John was stubborn. 'The only way to acclimatise is to drop right down, go round below, and come back up. Or else forget it.' They groaned.

'You're right,' Richard placated, 'but we won't get up it that way. We haven't come this far just to shrug our shoulders. You've lost your sense of urgency, John, I don't know why. That face might be steep enough for the snow to have cleared. It's our only chance.'

'Maybe it'll clear while you're on it.' John attacked. 'There'll be serious avalanche risk.'

'We'll judge that up there,' Alan argued. 'If it's bad we'll give it a miss. It won't be the first time. At least give it a go. What's eatin' you this time, man?' Exasperation twisted his face to a scowl.

'This is supposed to be a holiday,' Greg groaned. 'Look at the state of us! We've hardly left the ground yet.' Cracked lips, eyes bloodshot, grizzled stubble, wild tufts of hair, muscle run to fat . . .

John was still arguing. 'It's not just weather that cost us time; Nima's out of his depth. We all know he's the wrong man – he can't even handle porters. I'll bet he didn't go far on the traverse today either. He seems too well rested to me. If we go with your plan, he'd have to get a load into the bottom of that valley and up to meet us. The entrance might be blocked. It could be dangerous for a porter . . .' It was a moral issue now.

Richard glanced with customary tact to see was Nima listening. Hard to tell. He wasn't the cheerful, communicative kind they were used to.

'You're not being helpful, John!' Reproach from Richard was unheard of. 'Those porters make up their own minds,' he continued. 'We've seen that already. If it comes to it, Nima could carry enough in on his own to see us through.'

'Exactly,' Greg agreed, 'and we'll carry his tent and the cooking gear around tomorrow. All he'd have to do is find us.'

'You can carry it!' John argued hotly. 'We've huge loads already. At altitude. There's a lot of things to go wrong here you know! We haven't a scrap of food beyond tonight.'

Richard spread his hands, palms down, damping the anger. 'Nima will have the radio, John. We can direct him to where we are tomorrow evening. If he can't make it, he'll call us and we'll go down. Simple as that. We've enough rubbish to feed us for a day – more, if we save some of these spuds.'

'OK, OK, have it your way! I had to look after him on easy ground yesterday, just getting up here – never mind a glacier. The rest of you shagged off!'

Even Richard was rattled by the accusation. 'The description says it's safe round there. If it's dodgy at all he's not to come. We'll make that clear.'

'We don't *know*. We've no way of knowing.' John's voice rose again. 'There could be crevasses covered in fresh snow. He has no experience –'

Nima stood beside them with a pot of boiled potatoes. 'Tomorrow you go round,' he said with chilly dignity. 'I go down, bring porter up behind. No problem.' He walked away.

In the silence that followed, tension held them back from the potatoes.

John muttered, 'If he gets in, someone will have to go down to meet him. We can't risk the man's life.'

'You're right,' Richard said quietly. 'I'll go.'

'What I saw of that snow –' Greg grinned. 'I'll go too. And be glad of the excuse.'

'Me, me – I want to go down!' Alan hollered.

Suddenly they were grabbing hot potatoes, banging each others' knuckles, laughing like boys.

Noon, the following day, John hurried down the hidden valley. It was a sprawl of glacier, moraine, rock-ribs, funnelling down into vegetated slopes, bounded on one side by sheer buttresses, on the other by a river gorge veering headlong below into a line of cliffs. Several thousand feet lower, the canyon where the valley squeezed shut was still lit by morning sun, as if a bright liquid were flowing in a funnel, soon to be followed by the sediment of shadow. Somehow, the gorge carved its way through those overlapping buttresses . . . either that, or he'd be coming all the way up again.

But of course he'd have to do that anyway. He groaned aloud, contemplated a howl in the desolate waste. Ice-fringed moraine under a clear sky. His ragged voice would flap into the air, harsh as a vulture overhead. There were talons in his chest, a rank taste of feathers in his throat. If he screamed as loud as he needed, they'd hear him back up on the glacier. They'd think he was in a crevasse. He released a hoarse bark of a laugh just to hear himself. It rang hollow as a raven. He could easily produce a vulture. It was straining in his chest. He increased his speed.

Running – a grim pride in the motion – boots skidding on stone-encrusted ice, thudding on ribs of soil. He was going down, as he had done so often; this time without elation or relief. There was nothing down there. The sunny blue and green world of everyday life had frozen over, as if the ice had spread to sea level.

He trembled on the edge of a sudden drop. In the stillness between gasps, he heard the scratch of a radio call and pulled it out. 'Nima! Do you read me? Come in. Over . . .'

'Yes, sir – I hear. Over.' The voice held no warmth or welcome. Nima didn't want to enter the valley. Most Sherpas would have been in already; storming up the moraine nearly as fast as he had come down.

'I will arrive in one more hour. OK, Nima? Over.'

'Yes, sir. Difficult ground, sir. No good for porter.' He sounded strained, uncertain.

'Be careful. I am nearly there, Nima. Over.'

Indeed it was. Over. From what he had seen of the snow, it would take a miracle to climb Singu Chuli in its present condition. It was repulsive, pointless. The others were still intent. He might have been the same in previous years.

The ground grew easier, safer. He ran with abandon. Vegetated slopes, thin grass flattened by the weight of recent snow, plunging towards the gorge. He veered through a thicket of thorny scrub, kicking at the roots to brake.

Cliffs ahead; an unbroken barrier, rising from the depths, shelving skywards. Buttresses on his right. He forced himself to stop, to check the radio.

'Above you, sir. Above! Look up.' The voice was frightened, angry. He scraped sweat from his eye-sockets, cursing. Had he gone down too far? Scanned the impossible buttresses in disbelief. A flare of red, a jacket waving. A faint terrace slanted out of darker shadow. Two figures had reached the end of the shelf, were perched on a thin tongue of vegetation adhering to the rock as if an entire slope had sheared away at their feet.

John cleared his voice of urgency; 'Nima. Can you go back? Back the way you came? Over.'

'No sir. Not can do. Dangerous . . .' He would accept no less than rescue. He had taken a high path, probably a goat-track, to avoid dropping to the gorge below. Ended in a blind alley.

'Who is with you? Which porter? Over.'

'Gurung porter, sir. No good.'

He's better than you, John thought; except he's got a basket on his back and flip-flops on his feet. He considered his options: continue down the canyon, out of the valley, find the path Nima had taken, and lead them out to safety. That was logical; but it would rule out any hope of supplying Richard and the others. They would expect him to contrive some kind of failure; they wouldn't believe the excuse.

Eyes adjusting to shadow, he examined the wall below the trapped Nepalis. Hemmed in by a rock-rib, fringes of vegetation zigzagged steeply down along it like the edges of a shawl, a single rock-step breaking the tenuous line.

Toiling back uphill, he reached the foot of the buttress in half an hour. He cursed everyone involved: Richard, Greg and Alan, Nima and himself. He cursed the porter too, though he was the only one not to blame.

He climbed slowly, marking the best route with stones, kicking steps in the steep soil of the terraces, noting stances and firmly rooted shrubs. It would be much trickier on the way down.

Step by step, one by one, he lowered them down the wall, climbed after them from stance to stance. From here, he saw the proper path, hundreds of feet below, snaking faintly along the rim of the gorge. Nima dislodged a rock and they watched it bound down the cliffs and continue to hurtle down the slope below in ever-increasing arcs till it disappeared over the edge of the ravine.

Once on the rope, the porter trusted it completely, regained his stoic humour and insisted on carrying his basket down, strapped round his forehead with its bandolier of baling-twine. John wanted to lower it separately, but the porter wouldn't have it, as if that would be dereliction of duty, or identity. Nima wouldn't have it either. He saw no reason why the porter wouldn't do his job. The man scrambled dexterously down, found all the sidesteps and traverses, delighting in the rope around his waist, hardly needing it at all – except when he took both hands off the rock and tested the line for the sheer pleasure of it, grinning up at John in gap-toothed satisfaction.

Nima was a different matter. He tried John's patience sorely, depending entirely on the rope, ignoring all the footholds, hacking at the rock with his ice-axe. More than once John thought what a pleasure it would be to watch him sever the rope with the tool. Swinging wildly onto a narrow ledge, he almost knocked the porter off. The man continued to treat him with cheerful deference. They communicated in rushes of Nepali, though it was the Gurung's second or third language. He seemed to discuss direction and technique with Nima, without a hint of derision in his tone. Whenever he caught John's eye, his wide and wordless smile contained no satire, as if he accepted that there were different approaches to descent, and Nima's ice-axe might dictate a completely different style.

Descending slowly, stage by stage, John's instincts flexed like a set of professional muscles, disused but still instinctive. He thought of nothing but the job in hand: precautions, stances, anchors for the rope. The steep rock-step was the crux. His attention could not falter until his companions stood on a narrow shelf below it, the ground still steep, but the angle easier. After lowering them both, he down-climbed the friable rock himself while Nima swished at the vegetation below, impatient at the delay. John was tempted to order the young Sherpa to scramble on down, but he bit back the impulse. There was still a long, bouncing drop to rocky slopes in the shadows below. No chance now of making it back to Richard's camp site. They would have to bivouac.

Again, for the last time, he protected Nima till he reached a lower ledge. He pulled the rope back up, the porter stepped into the loop, adjusted it to his waist, lowered himself over the rim. John braced himself firmly, leaned back against the tugging rope to take any strain. Below the porter, in the line of fire, Nima stood stolidly, as if he had never seen a stone dislodged. They were out of danger now . . .

Yawning, paying out the rope, John craned sideways to see how far the sun had retreated up the valley. The rope jerked viciously in his hand, bit into his back like wire. His body lurched forward. The view below whipped past like a shred of broken film. In that split second, he knew the rope was embedded in the palm of his hand, his boots had skidded under him . . . and yet the world stood still. His belay-anchor had plucked him from behind; held him, held the rope, the porter, held gravity at bay. Already, the man was on his feet, looking up. He stared into John's eyes, his mouth open on a bite of darkness. His eyes were huge – white and glistening against the brown skin. They were riddled with thin red lines, as if the shock had cracked open the illusion of his face and squeezed the rawest tissue to the surface. He tore his gaze away and continued the descent. His basket had swung sideways and betrayed him. All three would have tumbled beyond control into the shadows below.

Entirely unaware, Nima stamped out his impatience on the lower ledge. John turned to inspect the flake of rock behind him; he had draped a loop of rope about it, tied it back around his waist . . . It was loosely embedded in the soil, he hadn't trusted it, almost hadn't bothered. He'd dug in his heels, braced his feet against the ground for purchase . . .

. . . Early evening when they finished. They found a shallow cave, a water runnel, dry brushwood for a fire. They had two sleeping-bags. Nima's was in the basket, while the porter had a thin blanket. John gave him his jacket; Nima didn't offer his. John thought of hitting him with the ice-axe, but it would hardly help the porter. Anyway, he suspected his own feelings were a sham: emotional drama whipped up to take his mind off everything else. The cave-mouth was packed with flat, sandy soil; there were traces of older fires, an underlying smell of goat.

The following night he was there again. Richard and the boys had explored above the glacier. A futile exercise: they were driven back by avalanche conditions. Nima and the porter, after climbing up with John to relieve them, had left along the lower path in the last of the daylight. They would dismantle Base Camp and be ready to depart tomorrow. Richard wanted one last night in the Hidden Valley before rejoining the crowded trail.

Flames crackled among the twigs, light danced on weary faces and bodies, as if the bones were branches, the skin dry bark. Behind John's back, the cave was a familiar pocket in the harsh rock. There was a hollow for his hip scooped in the sand, the rope placed for a pillow. In the mountains, two nights in succession could make a place feel permanent.

'She'd been having tests,' he told them. 'They were getting worse. I knew nothing about it. Apparently her mother was the same.'

He had never been easy with men, despite the time they spent together. There were always stories, all kinds of stories, but he'd never told one before without irony or defence, with no return. They had asked him.

'She must have decided to do something she'd never done – as if she hadn't lived maybe. Not that I could change anything.'

Alan nodded, 'And you were the innocent bystander. Christ! It happens . . .' As if he too would have a tale.

'No, I wasn't. Far from it. I was in love with her for years. If anything –' he laughed abruptly – 'she was doing me a favour.'

Greg shifted in the shadows. You could never gauge his response. 'Maybe she's got better. It doesn't need a miracle. Things happen.'

'No. I've missed the end,' John told him. 'When I was coming down I felt something change. Nothing dramatic, but I knew. A friend e-mailed Kathmandu and the agency sent a message with another group. Nima had it yesterday. He forgot to give it to me until last night.'

'Why did you come with us?' Richard asked the question; almost an accusation. 'Why didn't you stay at home?'

'She wanted me to go. Her family had no idea. I'd have cracked up and he'd have seen through it. She couldn't allow that.'

Greg nodded. He knew about men. 'She was right. He'd never be sure he was their father.'

'Well, why –' Alan wondered – 'why did she start it in the first place then?'

'She thought I was different. Temporary, I suppose. She thought I'd walk away when it was over. She got me wrong . . .'

In the back of his mind a perception glinted; a spark in the cave. Had she really got him wrong?

'So she loved her husband.' Richard had to get that right.

'No. She loved her children. She didn't want them to know anything else but that. This was her way of making sure.'

The Cocktail Hour

Sophia Hillan

In Virginia she was a princess, a Southern belle by a magnolia tree. Even the waiter ignored the others and made her feel she was a girl again, Daisy Fay before Gatsby. Mostly, she was Scarlett O'Hara: certainly the night they dined in the hotel whose staircase had been used as a model for that in *Gone with the Wind*. After a day and a half of this, he said it was high time they were going, as he was not travelling with Scarlett O'Hara another minute. He said he didn't care how many staircases had been used as the model for *Gone with the Wind*. He said in case she had forgotten there was work to be done. She said: 'Why, how you do run on, Captain Butler'; he said nothing, and they got on the train for Boston, where her newly clipped tones gave rise to terse comment from him.

'Well,' she said, 'you didn't want to travel with a Southern belle. Right now, I'm as played by Katherine Hepburn.'

'It's something of a relief,' he replied to Harvard Square, 'but, just for me, don't be her all the time.'

In the peaceful space of JFK's glass mausoleum, she did not speak until he said: 'Please don't do the Kennedy inaugural at me,' after which she felt compelled to recite it from start to finish, while he ignored her, looking out beyond the glass pyramid at Kennedy's sailing boat and the sea beyond.

Now, increasingly tired, they were on a train to New York. They registered, one to the other, silent recognition when they heard the guard call 'all aboard', just as in films. Past them sped magic names – Mystic, New Haven. They were in a Scott Fitzgerald story, silent, imaginary, through a glass. They said nothing for a long time.

Then, quietly, without turning, still looking through the window, he said: 'Do you know where I belong?'

She shook her head. It was not clear that he was speaking to her; it was not clear that speech was required.

'I belong in the cocktail hour,' he continued, barely audibly, almost to himself. 'In the thirties.'

'You're the Thin Man,' she said. 'You're Nick Charles.'

He gazed a long moment at her, as if he had just remembered her. He nodded, looking down at his folded hands. Then, she said that Nick Charles wasn't really the Thin Man, that the Thin Man was the villain whom Nick and Nora caught, after which the name stuck to the series. The words fell into silence: one moment, two.

'Could you,' he said, looking up, 'just leave it there?'

It happened that she had already left it, because she had begun to hear her own music, Gershwin, *Rhapsody in Blue*, soaring and triumphant inside her head. They were pulling into Penn Station.

'We won't hang round this place,' he said. 'I believe it's dangerous.' They could hear the klaxons of taxicabs: dangerous was exciting too. And now a yellow cab drew up, and from it emerged a jovial, homely black taxi driver who told them his name was Arthur. Arthur and he sat in front, after she was handed into the back, by Arthur, who addressed her as 'ma'am'.

'Don't you folks worry none,' said Arthur. 'I'll get you and your wife just anywhere you want to go in this town.'

To this he replied, 'That's not my wife,' and Arthur cast a reproachful look back at her.

'I'm sorry, miss,' said Arthur, and begged her pardon. She thought, Arthur thinks I'm no better than I should be, and the thought made a smile begin. She looked to see if her companion noted this in the mirror, but his eyes gave no answer. Like a dreamer, he gazed at the buildings soaring above them, meeting in the horizon of the sky. He seemed to have forgotten the presence of anyone else in the world. Arthur meanwhile, downcast, kept his eyes on the road in silent dismay. When they pulled up at the hotel Arthur handed her her luggage with his eyes averted. 'Don't forget your mittens, miss,' said his sad old voice, as he gave her her gloves from the back of the seat.

And somewhere between amusement and embarrassment, she was still thinking about Arthur as they passed through the opaque glass door of the hotel. When they were in the lobby, they stopped together. They almost collided. Everything looked wrong, and smelled wrong. They said nothing, but they exchanged glances as, unusually, he took her elbow, lightly, as if they were crossing a busy road. The lobby was cramped and gloomy, its light garish. Apprehension flowed between them as they walked to the reception desk, where a lazy, unwashed clerk looked them up and down. His badge said: 'Hi. I'm Enrico. How may I help you?' She thought, Can this be where they booked us? Yet, even she knew that the Saturday before St Patrick's they would get nowhere else.

'You're lucky we kept these rooms,' said the clerk. 'You're not early, and it's Saturday night.'

'Enrico,' he said. His voice was level, but his hands on the edge of the desk were whitening. 'We've been on a train for six hours. We can't help the time of our arrival.'

The clerk shrugged and said, 'I don't make the rules.'

There was a long silence. She looked up at her companion, and noted, irrelevantly, that he was a surprisingly tall man. He is not heavy, she thought, but he is tall. Nor, at that moment, could she read the expression on his face. All she felt was the edge of fear.

'We'll take a look at the rooms,' he said, spreading his hands wide on the desk, 'before we decide whether we stay or not.'

He leaned slightly forward, and she noticed the hands beginning to form themselves into fists. The fear edged further in.

'Suit yourself,' said the clerk, with a shrug, 'but you're booked in advance, and I'll have to charge you anyway.'

The two men, one small and lithe, the other long and poised, looked hard at one another. The clerk's face was insolent, amused; her companion's, as he turned away suddenly, a shuttered mask.

Enrico did not make a move to help them with their bags. Nor did the heavy, silent porter, slumped in a swivel chair, watching him so far with detachment, watching her with something else. She saw this and, picking up her bags with as defiant a gesture as their weight would permit, moved to the lift, which clanked slowly, endlessly, to the ground. She thought fleetingly of Mary Astor, her face shadowed by the crossed bars of the lift, led down to her execution, while Humphrey Bogart watched her, his face impassive but for the haunted eyes and the mobile, noble, sardonic mouth.

This lift reeked of alcohol and other, worse things. Hospital, she thought. Urine and vomit and sickness. They were silent. She could hear her heart, and thought she could hear his. His upper lip was slightly lifted, as if in distaste. The lift was slow and creakingly noisy, the odour foul. He was white, almost blue round the mouth. For a moment she was sure he would pass out in the rancid, cramped space. Then, as it seemed they could endure not one second longer, they thudded to a lurching stop. Beyond the bars they could see and smell dank walls and mouldy carpets. He took in a long breath and, holding the lift doors open with one foot as he hefted the luggage out, said: 'Let's get you to yours first. Then I'll look at mine.'

He left her bags just inside her room. This was hard, because the heavy door was narrow and geared to automatic, immediate closure. He was breathing hard.

'I'll be back in a minute,' he said. 'I want you to bar this door, and not open it to anyone but me. Do you hear?'

She nodded and, turning in some trepidation, switched on the light. It flickered, clicked, flicked, wavered and finally flashed into white, pitiless light and she saw grimy net curtains above a corroded, flaking radiator, a lopsided, nylon-covered bed with greying sheets. Looking in the bathroom, carefully touching nothing, she sensed before seeing that the lavatory had not been flushed. On the dark-ringed bath, a small square of scum-covered soap half-lay in a paper wrapper. A used condom, torn, was placed upon the still-dripping shower head. She thought, They rent by the hour.

The door was knocked. Three sharp raps. She let him in, almost taking him by the hand. His face was terrible, a Mount Rushmore profile. He was deathly white and the thought occurred to her that he had been sick in the interim. He looked at the room and, shaking his head, like a swimmer shaking water, moved slowly past her. He leaned against the lintel of the dirty bathroom. His back was bent, his shoulders stooped. Even though the room was chilly, even cold, she saw him wipe perspiration from his face with a handkerchief. He tapped his teeth with the forefinger of a clenched fist.

'Mine smells even worse,' he said, and sat down on the filthy bed as if his legs had suddenly given way. He looked so ill that she stopped herself from telling him that she thought the sheets might be alive. He lifted the phone.

'Whatever about me,' he said, as though to himself, 'I can't have you stay in a place like this.'

In that second her astonished heart took flight, not to Virginia, not to the magnolia tree, but to a place immeasurably beyond, a soaring sky that was now and for ever, while the filthy, sordid room fell away like the sea below the eagle. From that light and dizzy place she watched as he replaced the receiver, and put his head in his hands.

'We're not connected,' he said. She thought, What does he mean? How can we not be connected? His voice was low, despairing. 'He won't connect us until he knows we're staying.'

Now giddy with understanding, she waved her hand. 'Oh, he's charging us anyway. Tell him we're staying. Tell him anything.'

He lifted his hands from his head, and something that was almost a smile began about his mouth. He said: 'Is that Miss Hepburn talking, or Miss Scarlett?'

'It's just me,' she said, 'just me.'

Still looking at her, he put his hand on the telephone. And, sitting in the suddenly magical room, she wondered without anything more than mild surprise how it was that she had never noticed he had the face of an angel. Quite unable to look, she turned away and, as from a great distance, heard him speak into the phone, but did not hear any of what he said. Her heart was too much filled. There was no more fear. The room was music; it was light.

Then gradually, slowly, she floated down from the place where she had been and remembered that they were in a fearful situation, that the room was filthy and foul. She noticed, as one who wakes from a dream, that he had stopped speaking. She heard rather than saw him writing, scratching something with a stubby pencil on a dirty piece of paper beside the bed. He handed this to her.

The tension broke. She laughed. 'Your writing,' she said. 'It's appalling. This looks like Death Club to me. You've booked us into a place called the Death Club?'

He reached across and, taking it from her, gently, silently, put it in his pocket. He said: 'We are going to a place called the Downtown Athletic Club.'

'Which is?'

He said: 'An athletic club, I think.'

He reached out his hand and raised her to her feet. 'I understand it's downtown.' And, without any further words, they pushed open together the unyielding door.

She did not notice the smells in the lift going down. She did not care that they were charged for rooms they did not use. She scarcely paused to notice the language of the boys in the gauntlet they ran from the door to the kerb to dive into the yellow cab. She felt slightly drunk.

Safely in the cab, he gave the address, and leaned back beside her on the leather seat. She could feel him breathing. Their heads were almost touching. She could smell his aftershave, expensive, subtle and mixed with it fresh perspiration, not unpleasant, quite the reverse, like that from an athlete. The Downtown Athletic Club. Now she heard her own breathing. Just in that moment, they were completely relaxed, entirely at ease.

And then, without warning, he leaned closer, and very quietly, almost like a lover, began to speak.

'Here's a story for you,' he said. 'You write it. Maybe it's a movie. Two people get off a train. They've been travelling for many days in a strange and wonderful country. They're tired. They're dizzy and dazzled, and they don't even know what period they're in. They hardly know who they are. They have quite a bit of luggage. One of them has many books. The other one is carrying them. He has a red mark on his shoulder from carrying them, but he carries them willingly. They are in a taxi, going to an address. They have been very badly frightened, and the address sounds good to them. It sounds like heaven, like home. But they don't really know where it is, because they've never been to New York before.'

They were parked at lights. Stop. Go. Don't walk. Don't even think about parking here. His voice dropping almost to a whisper he continued:

'And where did they get this address? From an anonymous voice on a phone in a sleazy room. Why should they trust this voice? Maybe they're being set up. Maybe not. Maybe this happens all the time – maybe there is a ring, a group, who send unsuspecting tourists to lonely places and murder them. How do they know?

'Then, suppose they arrive, and to their relief feel the taxi stop in, let's say, the financial area of town. That's solid, isn't it? The financial area? Wall Street? The air is cold. They can smell the sea. They are right down at the tip of the island, at the Battery.'

She interrupted: 'The Park is up and the Battery's down,' but he continued, quite as though she had not uttered. His voice was dreamy, mesmeric:

'There is a large building, covered in scaffolding and plastic. They get out of the taxi, so relieved to have arrived, and wait for the driver to help them with their luggage from the boot. But he doesn't. No sooner are they outside than he drives away. Nothing but tail-lights and the screech of brakes. Then nothing. Silence. They are alone in the darkness of the New York night with no luggage. It is deathly quiet. Nothing much happens in the financial area at night. Nothing at all, in fact. And then in the silence, the eerie nothing silence, they see a door opening, a slow door, a widening square of light in the scaffolding. Out come one, two, five, seven big guys. All young. Big. Young guys. Black maybe. Maybe Hispanic. Like those guys who taunted us outside the hotel. You remember?'

She nodded. She remembered.

'Maybe they're even the same ones. Maybe they took their own taxi. They are holding – no, brandishing – bits of hosepipe, and rubber piping and chains. One of them, bigger than the rest, very good-looking, very threatening, with even white teeth, smiles at the two people on the kerb, wrapping a heavy chain round his big, powerful hand. And he says: "Welcome to the Downtown Athletic Club." '

Lights again. Stop. Go. Red flashing; green. She thought, Could we get out? Could we run? She looked across at him. He had leaned away from her again, head slumped upon his chest. His bones were very sharp. In that second, he looked like the prisoners who survived, or did not survive, Auschwitz. She thought, He means it: this will happen.

And sure enough, the air grew colder. They were down by the sea, and she thought, We are going down to the end of the island; we are at the edge of the world, and no one knows.

Then, with a lurch, the taxi swerved across the road.

'Here you are, folks,' said the taxi driver, in a voice surprisingly normal. They looked at each other. Out of the window they could see scaffolding, and green plastic. Her heart began to pound again, but in a low, feeble fashion, like a heart that has died twice and cannot make the effort another time. He inclined once more towards her, as if to speak. She thought of the Kennedy assassination, Jackie's memory of her fatally wounded husband turning, slumping toward her with his hand to his throat. Jackie said later she had only one thought: 'His mouth is so neat.' It was like that moment, but he was not shot. He was not slumping. It was just a moment, and history could here be changed, if they could do the right thing. She felt between them a final, despairing resolve to rise to the occasion, and to do what had to be done, together, now. His mouth was so neat.

And then, as suddenly as it had come, the moment passed. They stepped out of the cab and, standing on the kerb, in the quiet street they had so vividly foreseen, the dark dream somehow dissipated. The quiet street was only quiet. And the driver, sweet and normal as Arthur, did not speed off, but helped them in quiet courtesy with their bags, and accepted their modest tip with some graciousness. They turned, in near-astonishment, to the door. And they saw It open, slowly, felt themselves bathed in light, and saw a tall, elegantly uniformed doorman come easily down the steps, reaching for the bags which were frozen in their hands. He said: 'Welcome to the Downtown Athletic Club.'

Through a door of glass, they stepped into the thirties, to the home of the Heisman trophy, to an entrance hall as big as a ballroom, to heavy gleaming furniture and soft lights, to a place which was waiting for them. Momentarily, she closed her eyes, in case. When she opened them, it was all still there. Suddenly weak, she leaned against the edge of one of the deep sofas and said: 'Have we arrived?' He said: 'We have. And just in time for cocktails.'

And looking at him she saw, not a tired colleague in crumpled travelling clothes, but a handsome, austere man in a dinner jacket, a man with style and flair and panache, with just a little, a delicious hint of the reckless. She saw Nick Charles. And in that instant, she was his haughty, sophisticated Nora, somewhere in the thirties, one pencilled eyebrow quizzically raised, a slender cigarette holder in her fingers, a single witty bracelet on her wrist.

For the second time that evening, he took her arm. And finally, utterly themselves, they drifted into their club, an elegant pair, looking for the cocktail lounge.

Biographical Notes

MARY BURKE Born in Galway, she graduated from Trinity College, Dublin, in 1995. She has lived and worked in Asia, N. Ireland and the US, and is currently writing her first novel.

PAULA CUNNINGHAM Born in Omagh in 1963, she lives in Belfast, where she works part-time as a dentist. She published her first collection of poems in 1999 and has now started on a novel.

GERARD DONOVAN Born in Wexford in 1959, he is a graduate of Galway University. His first story was a finalist in the Chicago Tribune's Nelson Algren Story Award, and his debut novel, *Schopenhauer's Telescope*, published by Scribner's, was the only Irish novel to be long-listed in the 2003 Booker. Last year it won the Kerry Group Irish Fiction Award at Listowel's Writers' Week.

RODDY DOYLE He was born in Dublin in 1958. His widely admired Barrytown trilogy of novels were all successfully filmed, and his *Paddy Clark Ha Ha Ha* novel won the Booker Prize in 1993.

HUGO HAMILTON Born in Dublin in 1953, of a German mother and Irish father. He published five novels and a collection of short stories, and also won the prestigious Irish Rooney Award. In 2003 his memoir *The Speckled People* was one of the most widely praised books of the year.

SOPHIA HILLAN A graduate of Queen's University, Belfast, in English and French Language and Literature. In 1999 her story *The Cocktail Hour* was runner-up in the Royal Society of Literature's first V. S. Pritchett Memorial Prize.

NEIL JORDAN Born in Sligo in 1951, he grew up in Dublin. His first book, a collection of short stories, *Night in Tunisia*, was greatly praised by Sean O'Faolain, and he has followed with four novels, the most recent being last year's *Shade*. His world reputation as a film scriptwriter and director has already won him an Oscar.

CLAIRE KEEGAN Born in 1968 and raised on a small farm in Wexford, she studied English Literature and Political Science in New Orleans. One of

Ireland's most widely acclaimed new writers, she has won many story awards, including the 2000 Rooney Award for her debut story collection, *Antarctica*, published in 1999 in Britain by Faber and in the US by *Atlantic Monthly Press*.

COLUM MCCANN Born in Dublin in 1965, his first story collection, *Fishing the Sloe-Black River*, was published in 1994 and won the Rooney Award. He has written four novels, the latest being drawn from documented facts created into an extraordinary work of fiction about the great dancer Rudolf Nureyev.

MOLLY MCCLOSKEY Born in Philadelphia in 1964, she moved to Co. Sligo in 1989 and won the George A. Birmingham Short Story Award in 1991 and in 1994, and the RTE Francis MacManus Award in 1995. Her first story collection, *Solomon's Seal*, was published by Phoenix House in 1997, and her novella *The Beautiful Changes*, with four other stories, was published by the Lilliput Press in 2002.

TOM MAC INTYRE Born in 1931 in Cavan, his first book was a short story collection, *Dance the Dance*, published in 1970 by Faber, which was followed by his first novel, *The Charollais*.

BLÁNAID MCKINNEY Born in Enniskillen, Co. Fermanagh, in 1961. A Political Science graduate of Queen's University, Belfast, she was a leading executive officer of a number of British Government Departments. Her first story collection, *Big Mouth*, was followed by her first novel, *The Ledge*, published by Weidenfeld and Nicolson.

BERNARD MACLAVERTY Born in Belfast in 1942, he later moved to Scotland. He published four collections of short stories and three novels. *Lamb* (1980) and *Cal* (1983) were adapted by him for the screen and became successful movies, while his third novel, *Grace Notes* (1997) was shortlisted for the Booker.

MARY MORRISSY Born in Dublin in 1957, her first story was published in 1984 and won her a Hennessy Literary Award. Her debut story collection, *A Lazy Eye*, was published in 1993 by Cape, and her debut novel, *Mother of Pearl*, was followed by *The Pretender* in 2000.

GILLMAN NOONAN Born in Kanturk, Co. Cork, in 1937, and educated at University College, Cork. He published two short story collections, *A Sexual Relationship* (1976) and *Friends and Occasional Lovers* (1982), which many critics said stood comparison with John McGahern or William Trevor. He now lives in Scotland.

EDNA O'BRIEN Born in 1930 in Tuamgraney, Co. Clare, her many novels and story collections have made her reputation as one of Ireland's outstanding world writers.

GEORGE O'BRIEN Born in Enniscorthy in 1945, he was reared in Lismore, Co. Waterford. He was awarded a Hennessy New Irish Writing Award in 1973 for his short stories. *The Village of Longing* (1987), the first volume of his autobiographical trilogy, won the 1988 Irish Book Awards Silver Medal for Literature. The second volume, *Dancehall Days*, was published the same year, and the third, *Out of Our Minds*, appeared in 1994. For many years he has been Professor of English in Georgetown University, Washington, D. C.

JULIA O'FAOLAIN Daughter of Sean and Eileen O'Faolain, she was born in Dublin in 1932. A graduate of University College, Dublin, she continued her education in Rome and Paris. She wrote a number of short story collections and a novel, *Godded and Codded*, all of which were published by Faber.

CÓILÍN Ó HAODHA Born in Galway in 1975, he studied at University of Dublin, graduating in 1998 with a degree in English and Philosophy. In the same year his story *Her Blood Dripped into Grass* won the RTE Francis MacManus Award. He lives in Galway.

DERMOT SOMERS Born in Roscommon in 1947, he moved to Dublin when he was thirteen. His career has included building, broadcasting and writing, and his two published collections of short stories have won awards in Britain and Canada. A climber for twenty-five years with world-wide experience, including Everest, he has written and presented, in Irish, many series for RTE and TG4 on mountain landscape, adventure and tradition.

COLM TÓIBÍN Born in Enniscorthy, Co. Wexford, in 1955, he was educated at University College, Dublin. His prize-winning first novel, *The South*, was published in 1990, followed in 1993 by *The Heather Blazing*, and in 1996 by *The Story of the Night*. His latest novel, *The Master*, based on the life and work of Henry James, was published last year.

WILLIAM WALL Born in Whitegate, Co. Cork, in 1955, he became a teacher in Presentation Brothers College. In three successive years from 2000, Sceptre published his first three novels, *Alice Falling*, *Minding Children* and *The Map of Tenderness*. He has also written many outstanding short stories.

NIALL WILLIAMS Born in 1958, he lives in Co. Clare. A playwright, he has also published two novels, *Four Letters of Love* and *As it is in Heaven*.